Backcast
—— a novel ——

Ann McMan

Bywater
BOOKS

Ann Arbor

Bywater Books

Bywater Books First Edition: December 2015

Map of Lake Champlain from
Lake George and Lake Champlain: A Book of Today
(S.R. Stoddard, Glen Falls, NY, 1915),
Library of Congress collection

Printed in the United States of America
on acid-free paper.

Cover designer: TreeHouse Studio

Bywater Books
PO Box 3671
Ann Arbor MI 48106-3671
www.bywaterbooks.com

ISBN: 978-1-61294-063-2

For Anne McMullan Tullar—
who saved my life.

Table of Contents

Backcast

Cast thy bread upon the waters:
for thou shalt find it after many days.

—Ecclesiastes 11:1

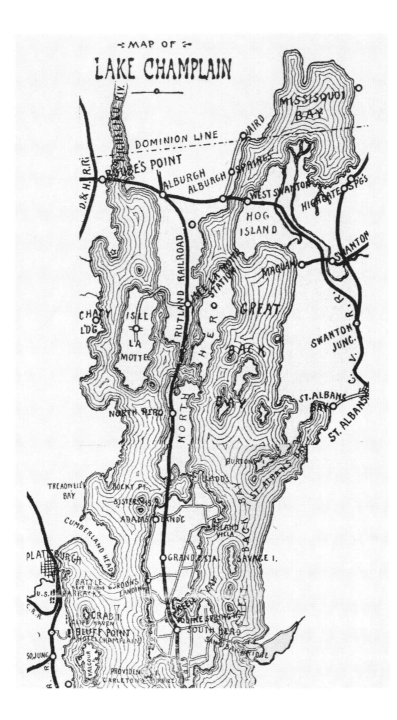

Prologue

Mornings were the best times. And that was especially true of mornings on the east side of the island, where the lake was like polished glass. When you got up early like this, you could watch the sun creep up over Mt. Mansfield. And if you were lucky and it wasn't raining, lake and sky would sometimes collide in a spectacular display of purple and orange. It didn't look real, but it was. The first time she saw it, it reminded her of the skies that dominated the backgrounds of those old religious paintings that were stuck together in the back of her mother's Bible—"The Road to Emmaus," or that other one of Jesus walking on the water.

She never believed that skies like that existed in real life. Not until she came here.

Nobody was out on the lake this early—nobody but the occasional kayaker, enjoying an easy paddle along the shoreline. She could hear some Canada geese making a fuss as they buzzed the water looking for breakfast. And off in the distance, there was the faint purr of a boat motor. More than likely, that belonged to a bass fisherman—out to hit some favorite spots before the recreational boaters churned things up and pushed the nervous fish into hiding.

She took another sip of her hot coffee. It was her current favorite—Red Eye Roast. She liked to think that this blend was a lot like her: robust, full-bodied, and black.

She pulled a pack of Camels from her shirt pocket and tapped one out. The first smoke of the day was always the best one, and she liked to savor it.

It still seemed incredible to her that she'd ended up here. Her gramma always said that you never could predict how things would work out, so it was pointless to worry about what might or might not happen.

That was certainly true. But she had to wonder what her gramma would say about this.

Something startled the geese. They took off together and roared back over her head like an angry cloud, honking and complaining.

Then she heard it—faint but distinct. Sirens.

Sirens? At five-thirty in the morning?

Yep. Sirens. *Lots of them.* Headed straight for her.

She swiveled around and looked up the path toward Route 2 in time to see five sheriff's cars roar by. They were heading south—going so fast that the daylilies lining the road in front of the café laid flat in their wake.

What the hell?

Less than a minute later, the sirens stopped.

Great.

Mavis stood up and ground out her cigarette. She took a last, wistful glance at the lake before tossing the rest of her coffee and heading up the path toward her truck.

"Goddamn rug munchers. What've they done now?"

Three months earlier . . .

Barb Davis looked at her plasma cutter with disgust. The damn thing had been on the fritz for the last couple of days, and now its gas-powered motor was refusing to turn over at all. Of course it would quit working now, on Sunday night when there was no place open to fix it.

She ought to just take a helve hammer to it.

She looked around her studio. She could try the oxy torch? Nah. It was too high-powered for the contours she needed to make along the serpentine edge of the giant Calla lily she was slowly freeing from its iron prison. When this sculpture was finished, it would be the grand centerpiece of a cluster of fountains in the vestibule of a new hotel on Mission Bay.

Assuming, of course, she could get her damn torch to work. Right now, the lily looked like it was retreating back inside the hunk of iron. She didn't really blame it. She wouldn't want to spend eternity in the lobby of an overpriced hotel, either.

It was past time for a smoke. She'd been in here for a couple of hours already. Trying to quit was a bitch. She'd cut back to just six cigarettes a day—not too shabby considering she started out as a two-pack-a-day gal.

She was on her way to retrieve her pack of Camels when the wall phone rang.

"Hello?"

"Hello? Barb?" the anxious voice belonged to Brian Devere, curator of the prestigious Rolston-Devere Gallery in Los Angeles—the place that represented Barb.

"Yeah. What's up?"

"Everything's up . . . including my commission."

Barb was fishing a Camel out of her pack. *Damn. Only two left.*

"Hello? Are you there?" Brian asked with impatience.

"Yes, I'm here." Barb stifled a cough. "Hold your damn horses—I'm trying to light a smoke."

"I thought you quit?"

"I'm *trying* to quit. It's not the same thing."

"Oh, come on, Barb. People who say they're 'trying to quit' are pussies who cannot commit."

Barb sighed. Brian loved to quote lines from Kenneth Branagh movies. He said it made him quirky and esoteric, and it was a great way to pick up hot men at cocktail parties.

"*Dead Again*?" she asked.

He sighed. "How do you always do that?"

"I'm twenty-five years older than you, and I watch a lot of TV."

"Could've fooled me," he said. "If that's the case, then why aren't you sprawled out in your La-Z-Boy watching *Downton Abbey*, like the rest of the planet?"

Barb took a drag off her cigarette. The smoke filled up her lungs and burned like a stray tongue of fire. It felt glorious. She blew it out with reluctance. "How do you know I'm not?" she asked.

"Duh," he said. "I called the studio phone."

"Okay. Busted."

"What are you working on?"

"The Mission Bay hotel gig."

"Well, forget about those small potatoes—I've got something *huge.*"

Barb sighed. "You're not going to email me more pictures of your new *inamorata* in a Speedo, are you?"

"Very funny. *No.* As it happens, I just got off the phone with Emily Gascoigne."

"Who the hell is Emily Gascoigne?"

"She works with Sybil Fenwick at the NEA. I ran into her tonight at the Keating."

Barb was all ears now. "And?"

"And, it looks like our proposal got funded."

"No shit?"

"No shit. All phases. A hundred and ten thousand bucks."

Barb dropped down onto a metal stool. "Fuck me."

"Sorry, girlfriend. You're on your own for the kinky stuff."

"I'm stunned."

"You shouldn't be. I told you it was a great proposal. I mean—a touring exhibit of thirteen sculptures that chronicle the female metamorphosis? The NEA eats that shit for breakfast. Especially now, while the Tea Party continues its campaign to turn women in this country back into clones of Harriet Nelson."

"I'm stunned."

"You already said that."

"I know. I don't know how else to respond."

"Well fortunately for you, I do." Brian cleared his throat. "You need to wrap up that water-lily creation and get cracking on pulling your contributing authors together."

Barb's grant proposal involved inviting thirteen leading lesbian/feminist authors to write first-person essays about formative, transitional experiences in their lives. She would pair those narratives with original sculptures, and the whole shooting match would get boxed up and shipped out for a six-city tour next year during women's history month. Rolston-Devere would get serious props for being the sponsoring gallery, and they would host the debut show.

"All right. I hear you," Barb said. "I can't do any more work tonight anyway—my plasma cutter is refusing to cooperate." She didn't mention that her hands and feet were aching from being in the studio for so long.

"Well, why don't you just fire up that beard blaster thing?" Brian asked.

"*Bead* blaster," Barb corrected.

"Well, with you butch types, it's hard to know the difference."

Barb rolled her eyes. "I'm hanging up now, Brian."

"Ciao, baby. Call me when you have your list of authors nailed down, and I'll get started on the press releases."

"Roger."

Brian disconnected.

Barb hung up and took a last drag on her cigarette.

Getting the grant had been the easy part. The grant money would fund the production of the sculptures and the costs associated with promoting, insuring, and shipping a travelling exhibition.

Now the hard part began. Now she had to find twelve authors who would agree to work on the project with her for free.

She looked into her nearly empty pack of Camels. One cigarette would never be enough to see her through solving this puzzle. It was time to haul out the big guns.

—◉◉◉—

Barb poured herself a big glass of Wild Turkey, light on the ice. She was fond of telling people that it was the only kind of poultry she really liked.

Where to do the work was no problem. Her cousin, Page, ran a gorgeous inn on Lake Champlain in Clifstock, Vermont. It was the perfect venue for an intensive, two-week workshop. And if she could get everyone together in early to mid-June, they wouldn't overlap with the busiest part of the tourist season, so it would be easier to grab a bunch of rooms.

Her coffee table was covered with a couple dozen books pulled from the sagging shelves in her living room. Writers of every shape, size, and genre were represented. She grabbed a tablet and a pencil that had more teeth marks than paint on its yellow barrel, and started jotting down pros and cons for likely candidates.

After about twenty minutes, she had a pretty expansive list of prospects. Her roster of ideal contributors ran the gamut. After ten more minutes of looking the list over, she'd crossed off two-thirds of the names. Some of them lived in other countries. Others had literary agents who made Cerberus look like Adam's house cat. A few more were famous for their eccentricities. Another two or three were better known for their epic rages.

Barb pushed her notepad aside and picked up her drink. This was getting her nowhere.

Her cell phone rang. She recognized the caller ID.

"Hi there."

"Why are you still awake?" the voice on the line asked.

"I could ask you the same question."

"I'm always awake."

"True." Barb glanced at her watch. It was nearly ten-thirty. "So why are you calling me?"

"I thought it would roll to voice mail. I was going to leave you a message."

"What about?"

There was a pause. "I wanted to see if you were feeling better."

Barb smiled. "Better than what?"

"Better than you were yesterday at lunch."

"Mavis? You need a new hobby."

"White woman, I got plenty of hobbies. Checking on your ass ain't one of them."

"All evidence to the contrary."

"Whatever. You wanna answer my question?"

Barb sighed. It was pointless to lie to Mavis. She always saw through it. "I'm tired. My joints are aching. Too much time on my feet today."

"Maybe you should go to bed and get off them?"

"Nice try. I'm not *on* them."

"Then what are you doing?"

Barb picked up her notepad. It had enough scribbles and cross-outs on it to double as a Jackson Pollock sketch. "Remember that big NEA grant I applied for?"

"You mean that feminist navel-gazing project?"

Barb rolled her eyes. "Yeah. That one."

"What about it?"

"I found out tonight that I got it."

"No shit?" Mavis sounded impressed. "That's a chunk of change."

"It is. But I'm having trouble coming up with a good list of writers to work on the essay components."

"What kind of writers?"

"Any kind of writers."

"Why is that so hard?"

"For starters," Barb bounced the notepad against her knee, "most of the ones I can think of are either too busy or too big to work for free—and I can't wait around for a dozen of them to become available at the same time."

"Hell." Mavis laughed. "Why don't you just ring up that list of wackos you bailed outta the can last year? Those crazy bitches that started that riot?"

Barb's mouth fell open. Mavis was talking about the CLIT-Con 13.

It was a stroke of genius.

"You're a fucking genius," she said to Mavis.

"What the hell are you talking about? I wasn't serious."

"Too bad. I am."

"Barb?"

"Lemme call you back, okay? The sooner I get this finished, the sooner I can knock off."

Mavis sighed. "Okay. Call me later."

"Count on it."

Barb hung up and tossed her cell phone aside.

Mavis was right.

Nothing brought women together like spending a night in the

slammer. Those "Free the CLIT-Con 13" t-shirts they printed up after the riot that ended last year's literary conference were still selling like hotcakes. Hell. Barbara Walters just got photographed wearing hers on a beach in Montenegro.

It was perfect. This crew already had a functional, group dynamic. Barb propped her sore feet up and started making another list.

Me.
My essay is a cakewalk.

Vivien K. O'Reilly
She's a solid choice with a good-sized following. But can I deal with having her hands all over my ass for two weeks?

Quinn Glatfelter
Oh, god. She could do it—but I'll go blind if I have to see her in those chaps again.

V. Jay-Jay Singh
Maybe if we hide all the flashlights and metal utensils? On the other hand, it would be useful to always have a bottle opener handy.

Towanda (a.k.a. Wanda Faderman)
Might work out if I can catch her between kale cleanses—and her husband agrees to keep their five kids. No way we're adding that to the equation.

Darien Black
Definitely want her. Know she has some great, totally bleak childhood angst to work out. I think her grandmother was pretty eccentric.

Cricket MacBean
Those "Naughty Nurse" tales she writes are esoteric reads—but she's a very disciplined writer, and she has some rich background from her years in a M.A.S.H. unit.

Montana Jackson
She's the lesfic equivalent of Scarlett O'Hara—*and* Rhett Butler. Still, she has a pretty broad following in the Southwest—and the show will be travelling to Santa Fe.

Kate Winston
Now that she's such a hot commodity on *GMA*, she might not be available. But if I can get Shawn, I can probably get her, too.

Shawn Harris
Simon & Schuster will be releasing her second novel soon—so this timing could be perfect as an interlude before she starts her next project.

Gwen Carlisle
Shawn's agent. But she cut her teeth as a comedy writer for Second City.

Linda Evans
Doesn't do much writing these days, but that early work she did for *Mother Jones* was terrific. Heard her arthritis was pretty bad now. She may not want to travel.

Of course, the last member of the motley crew was no longer available. She had given up writing to pursue a lucrative career as a ventriloquist. But Barb already had a bead on the perfect person to replace her. She'd have a little fun revealing that solution later on.

Barb tapped her pencil on the pad and reviewed her list. This was quite a team.

God, she thought. *If I threw in a stunt driver and a munitions expert, I'd have the cast of a* Mission: Impossible *episode.*

She tossed back the rest of her Wild Turkey and reached for her cell phone.

Once more unto the breach.

1

Rabbits

Fifty-four degrees. That's what the thermometer on the dashboard read.

Fifty-four? In June? *Seriously?*

She'd never vacationed in Vermont before. Not unless you counted that one freebie ski weekend she spent in Stowe about ten years ago.

Kate won the all-expense-paid trip for garnering first place in a *Mademoiselle* magazine essay contest. Her ski instructor, "Brandi" Alexander, was more interested in teaching her how to navigate the bed linens in her hotel room than she was in showing her how to master the slopes. What a nightmare that experience turned out to be. Kate ended up clocking Brandi with one of her own ski poles, and checking out of the hotel. She spent the rest of her prize weekend cooling her heels at a Hampton Inn near the airport in Burlington, waiting on her flight back to Atlanta. She'd never had the interest or the inclination to return to Vermont—until now.

Barb Davis's venture appealed to her on several levels.

For one thing, it was a great excuse to get out of New York for two weeks. Her job as a pop culture and social media reviewer for *Good Morning America* was exhausting. On air days, she had to be at the studio by 4:00 a.m. She only got back to Atlanta about one weekend a month, and that was getting old fast.

She wasn't cut out for life in Manhattan. Her temperament was too cranky, and she didn't really like people. Especially when those people were about eight million Yankees—most of them rude and equally cranky. Her third-floor walkup "apartment" in Midtown was about the size of a Frigidaire—and nearly as cold. It was a terrible situation for her dog, but she refused to leave him in Georgia.

Behind her on the bench seat, Patrick sat up and yawned.

Kate reached back and rubbed him behind his floppy, black ears. "Isn't that right, buddy? Mama couldn't leave you all alone."

Patrick licked her hand a few times before shifting his weight toward the partially open back window. All manner of smells were chasing each other on the early summer air. And mercifully, some of them were less like cow manure and more like something— interesting.

Kate smiled at him and lowered his window a few more inches.

No. She could never be without Patrick. She'd miss him too much. And, as hard as it was for her to admit, she was finding that she missed Shawn too much, too.

That was the thing that surprised, and irritated, her the most. They had only been able to see each other about five times in the last year, and that wasn't working well for either of them. She knew Shawn was growing frustrated by her constant lack of availability, and no matter how hard Kate tried to explain that it was a function of her job and not her romantic inclination, the results were the same. Kate knew that it was only a matter of time before Shawn grew tired of carrying out a relationship by phone.

Shawn was coming to Clifstock, too—and was scheduled to arrive later that afternoon. The two-week, intensive writing work-shop Barb had organized would provide them both with the biggest block of time they'd ever spent together. And it was an opportunity to do some serious writing. She missed that. Her reviews for *Gilded Lily* were now few and far between, and she felt the need to recon-nect with her first love.

And maybe, with her second.

She turned off U.S. Route 2 at the Hero's Landing sign, and drove her rental car down a long gravel road that led toward a cluster of white buildings. A wide swath of water was visible in the distance. The driveway curved around in front of a barn with a blue metal roof. Kate did a double take as she drove past it. A couple rows of terra cotta rabbits lined the deep sills inside the windows. Their black eyes stared back at her with suspicion.

"What the hell is up with those?"

Patrick woofed in agreement.

On the backside of the barn, she noticed a big Harley parked in one of the open bays. It was nicely rigged out with studded saddlebags and a flip-up windshield. Its tiny license plate read *BDSM 69.*

Quinn, she thought. *Great.*

She drove on toward the main entrance and parked in the visitor lot. There was a simple elegance to the place with its snow-white buildings and lush, green lawn. There were rocks everyplace. They lined the walkways and surrounded flowerbeds that were filled to bursting with early-blooming tickseed, iris and bright yellow day-lilies. Through a narrow breezeway, she could see the dark blue water of Lake Champlain, moving beneath the June sky.

It didn't look calm. It looked irritated.

She took a deep breath. Something smelled like roasted turkey. It reminded her of Sundays in her grandmother's kitchen, back in St. Louis. At least the food here would be a welcome change. Twelve months of wandering among Manhattan's hyperforaged Scandinavian eateries, ramen and kale pizzerias, and liquid nitro, colon-cleanse smoothie stands made her long for the simple things—like a burger. Or an egg salad sandwich that didn't descend from free range, flexitarian chickens that wintered in Boca, and never ingested oxidized omega-3 fats.

Kate's stomach growled. She was always hungry.

She began to understand why Barb chose her cousin's inn as the place to host their retreat. Staying here for two weeks wouldn't be a punishment at all.

And it was dog friendly, too.

Patrick's head was bobbing up and down like a bandleader's baton. She gave him a pat.

"You stay and be a good boy. Mama will be right back."

He looked at her and sighed. He knew the drill.

She climbed out and walked toward an entryway covered by a

blue canvas awning. She heard the voices as soon as she opened the door.

"It's an insane idea."

"It's *not* insane. It could totally work."

"It *is* insane, and you're crazy."

"I'm not crazy. Unlike you, I have creative vision."

"You have creative delusions."

"Why do you always have to be this way?"

"What way?"

"*This* way. Negative."

"I fail to see how you can equate reason with negativity."

"Reason? How are your objections reasonable? You don't know anything about watercraft."

"Neither do you. And that would be where the 'reason' part comes in."

The big woman dressed in black huffed and sagged back against her chair. "I've been on a boat before," she muttered.

Her companion refused to concede the point. "Olivia cruises don't count."

"Fuck you, Viv." The big woman got to her feet, and headed toward the lobby.

"Wimp," Viv called after her.

Kate watched the woman in black approach, and raised a hand in greeting. "Hello, Quinn."

"Kate!" Quinn gave her a big, toothy grin and stepped forward to wrap her up in a bear hug. "When did you get here, sugar plum?"

Kate's face was smashed into Quinn's massive shoulder. "About two minutes ago." It was hard to talk with a mouthful of fabric. Quinn loosened her hold.

"What'd you say?"

"I said I just got here." Kate worked her jaw from side to side to test whether it was still properly aligned.

Quinn jerked a thumb toward the dining room where she had been seated. "Viv and I both got here yesterday."

Kate leaned around Quinn and waved a hand at best-selling

18

mystery author, Vivien K. O'Reilly. The small redhead smiled back at her and got to her feet.

Quinn was still talking. "Barb and Mavis got here the day before us. Everybody else is supposed to show up later today."

"Mavis?" Kate asked Quinn. "Who's Mavis?"

"The bailiff."

Kate was still confused, and her expression must have shown it.

"From the jail," Quinn explained. "In San Diego, when we all got busted after the Con riot? You know. *Mavis*. Black. About my height. Bad attitude. Wields a mean nightstick."

Oh. *Mavis*. The cranky matron who was in charge of their holding cell.

"I remember, now. What's she doing here?"

Quinn shrugged. "Beats the hell outta me. Barb needed a driver, and she hired Mavis."

"Barb *drove* to Vermont from San Diego?"

Quinn nodded.

"Why?" Kate was incredulous.

"She hates flying. Always has. And I think there were some issues about transporting her bead blaster."

"I'm not even going to ask what that means."

"Wise woman." Viv had joined them. "How are you, Kate?"

Kate smiled at her. "Tired."

"I hear you." Viv was giving her a good-once over. "Boy, it's really true what they say. TV does add ten pounds."

"Jesus, Viv." Quinn was shaking her head.

"What?" Viv held out both hands. "Am I lying? Look at her. She's a wraith."

"The food options in New York are a bit too eclectic for my tastes," Kate explained. "I'm really looking forward to some home cooking."

"Well, you came to the right place for that." Quinn leaned closer to her and lowered her voice. "But avoid the tomato aspic—it's pretty shitty."

Viv was nodding. "I'll second that. They serve it at every meal, too—even breakfast. They must buy it in bulk."

19

"I've never cared much for aspics," Kate added.

"Then you'll certainly want to avoid this. I think you could use it to stucco a house."

"Get checked in." Quinn pointed toward the front desk. "We're all gonna reconnect in here later today for cocktails. Barb's gonna give us an intro and talk about process."

Kate nodded. "Sounds good."

Quinn was still staring at her.

"What?" Kate asked.

"You ever done any fishing?"

"Not since I broke my Playskool rod in the second grade."

Viv laughed. "That makes you more qualified than Quinn."

Kate looked back and forth between the two of them. "Am I missing something?"

Quinn pulled a folded sheet of paper out of her back pocket and handed it to Kate. "Take a gander at this."

"What is it?" Kate took it from her.

"It's a flier advertising a bass tournament that starts up here next week."

"A bass tournament?"

Viv rolled her eyes. "Quinn is persuaded that we can enter and win."

Quinn was nodding energetically. "The purse is twenty-five thousand bucks."

Kate looked at Quinn. "Don't you need a boat for that?"

"A boat is the least of what we'd need," Viv explained. "This would require about seventy-five thousand dollars worth of bodily injury and property damage, coverage for uninsured boaters, comprehensive and collision options, fuel spill liability, provisions for on-water towing and wreckage removal."

Quinn cut her off. "Wreckage removal?"

Viv glared at her. "Will you be at the helm?"

"Of course."

Viv looked at Kate. "I reiterate: wreckage removal—and a hefty provision for personal effects replacement. Besides," Viv pointed at a line of type on the flier. "It's a Pro-Am Tournament."

Kate was confused. "What does that mean?"

"It means that the competitors will all have corporate sponsors and seriously tricked-out rigs."

"Not all of them," Quinn protested. "That's what the 'Am' part of Pro-Am means. Amateur."

"Well, that's the one aspect of this you can cover with confidence."

Quinn threw up her meaty hands. "Do you have to be a goddamn actuary all the time?"

"I take my day job very seriously. And so should you. It's likely to save you from certain disaster."

"I still think it could work." Quinn kicked at a chair leg.

Viv rolled her eyes at Kate. "She doesn't even have a boat."

"I do, too." Quinn jerked a thumb toward the road that ran past the inn. "Big Boy and Junior might have a boat I can borrow."

"Who the hell are Big Boy and Junior?"

"The guys who run the marine salvage place just north of here. Page Archer told me about them. Big Boy is a tall, skinny dude—and his little brother, Junior, is a champion angler."

Viv squinted at her. "And you asked about them—because?"

"I saw one of their cards tacked up on the bulletin board in the men's room."

"Do I even want to know what you were doing in the men's room?"

Quinn gave her a smile that was more like a leer. "Probably not."

Viv looked at Kate. "Erotic authors. It's like they all got stalled in puberty."

Kate didn't bother to disagree with her. It was widely known that she held pretty much the same view of everyone now writing in the entire lesfic genre.

Including herself. And lately, she hadn't been doing much writing at all.

"What time is Shawn getting here?" Viv was giving her the once-over again. It made Kate feel uncomfortable—itchy beneath her clothing.

"I'm not sure. Sometime later today."

Viv kept shifting her weight from one foot to the other. The odd, rocking motion made her resemble a metronome—an uncommonly short metronome, with hair the color of spring carrots.

"What?" Kate knew better than to ask, but she couldn't stop herself.

"It's nothing."

"It doesn't look like nothing."

Quinn waved a hand. "Don't burn any more rubber trying to keep up with what *she's* thinking. You'll just end up wrapped around your own axle."

Viv cut her eyes at Quinn. "Nice image, Quinn. Still reading *Popular Mechanics*, I see."

Quinn sighed and looked up at the tiled ceiling.

Kate had had about enough of this interview.

"If you two will excuse me, I'm going to go get checked in. I left Patrick in the car."

"Patrick?" Viv was all ears. "Color me intrigued. Who's Patrick?"

Kate didn't reply.

"Jesus, Viv." Quinn managed to stretch her three syllables into a whine that sounded like ten. It seemed clear that she got a lot of practice. "Will you dial back the fucking drama machine? Patrick is her *dog*."

Viv looked disappointed.

"What time did you say we were meeting in here later?" Kate asked.

"Two. Barb wants to do some orientation and put us all together in teams." Quinn was plucking at a striped lily that drooped from a blue vase on a nearby table.

Teams? That didn't sound good. Kate wasn't much for teamwork. To her, words like "teamwork" brought back unhappy memories of smelly gym shoes and always being the favorite target in dodge ball.

"I'm not very comfortable working in groups," she said.

"You're preaching to the choir, honey." Viv sounded sympathetic. "But Barb's the head honcho on this little production, so she gets to call the shots."

"Wonderful."

The door to the parking lot flew open and two big dogs came bounding in. One was Patrick.

Kate was mortified. "How did you get out of the car?"

He came dancing over to greet Quinn and Viv, with his tail swinging around in lopsided circles.

The second dog had peeled off. It was now frozen in place, barking at a couple of clay rabbits that were huddled together on the floor near the lobby desk. Something about the golden retriever looked familiar.

Allie.

"Those clay things really creep me out," Quinn muttered.

But Kate wasn't listening to her. She was too busy watching the door. Seeing Allie could only mean one thing: Shawn had arrived.

"Why'd you bring so many clothes?"

Shawn had all the dresser drawers pulled out. She was trying to find space to stash her stack of shorts and t-shirts. Kate had already finished putting her clothes away, and remaining space was next to nonexistent.

Kate shrugged. "Why'd you bring so few?"

"Maybe because it's summertime and we're supposed to be on vacation?"

"It's fifty-four degrees."

"So?"

"This is Vermont. It'll probably be snowing by dinnertime."

"Oh, come on." Shawn checked the closet. It was full, too. "You're exaggerating."

Kate sat down on the end of the bed. "Don't say I didn't warn you."

Shawn pulled out a wooden hanger that held a skimpy-looking black garment.

"A cocktail dress? Seriously?"

Kate shrugged.

"Did I miss something? Are we auditioning for *Dancing with the Stars*?"

"If so, I'll have to look for another partner."

Shawn lowered the hanger. "Why?"

Kate pointed at her feet.

Shawn looked down. "What's wrong with my shoes?"

"Nothing, if you're planning to muck out a stable."

"These Chucks cost forty bucks."

"Wow. Forty whole dollars? You're really living high on those *Bottle Rocket* royalties, aren't you?"

"Are you being sarcastic?"

"Do you have to ask?"

"Apparently." Shawn returned the dress to the closet. "I'm out of practice."

"Well," Kate crossed her arms. "That would be the point of this trip."

Shawn smiled. "That and contributing to Barb's little project."

"I don't think I'd refer to a one hundred and ten-thousand dollar project as 'little.'"

"I don't think I'd refer to our experiment as 'little,' either."

"Experiment?"

"Sure. You. Me." Shawn hefted her stack of t-shirts. "Cohabitation."

"We've spent time together before."

"True. But not this much time."

Kate nodded in agreement.

Shawn walked over and sat down next to her. "So I guess that means we're working on our own performance art project?"

"So it would seem."

Shawn smiled at her. "I wonder if that means we can deduct the expense of this trip twice?"

"You'll have to ask Gwen about that."

Shawn looked toward the window. "Is she here yet?"

"I have no idea. I only arrived about ten minutes before you did."

Shawn bumped shoulders with her. "So. Whattaya wanna do until two o'clock?"

24

Kate started to answer but before she could get the words out, Patrick unleashed a barrage of flatulence that strafed across the room like machine gun fire. Allie, who had been dozing beside him on the doormat, lifted her head and sniffed at his behind.

Shawn's face contorted. "Good god. What the hell have you been feeding that dog?"

Kate shrugged. "We stopped at an Arby's in Albany."

"Arby's?"

"He loves their roast beef."

"Kate."

"Hey. It was five sandwiches for five bucks, and we were in a hurry."

That last part got Shawn's attention. "You were in a hurry?"

Kate nodded.

Shawn leaned closer to her. "Care to elaborate?"

Another staccato burst of enemy fire rang out from the carpet near the door.

Shawn dropped her chin to her chest.

Kate patted her on the leg. "I guess we need to take him for a walk."

"You think?"

"I suppose we could just light a match and see if it burns off."

"Are you kidding?" Shawn fanned a hand in front of her face. "This joint would go up like a Roman candle."

"Okay." Kate stood up and extended a hand to Shawn. "Walk first. Get reacquainted later."

Shawn didn't quit her position on the bed. "That could take some time."

Kate smiled at her. "For once, time is something we have."

Shawn did not disagree.

After all, the sun was shining. And out along a rocky coast where the sloping lawn met lake and sky, purple martins soared on warm drafts of air.

They had all the time in the world, too.

Quinn thought Big Boy looked like he'd weigh about ninety pounds dripping wet.

His "little" brother, Junior, on the other hand, looked like he rarely missed a meal.

The Ladd family had been a mainstay in the Champlain Islands ever since the twenties, when Lars "Laddie" Ladd piloted his wooden boat up the Saranac River in search of rock bass. His first sight of lush wetlands and a great lake fat with fish of nearly every variety drew him in like a siren's song. It wasn't long before Laddie moved his growing family down from the Adirondack region to Plattsburgh, New York, and opened his first salvage shop on a bleak scrap of land near Cumberland Head.

Many years later, he'd earned enough money to move his wife and sons across the lake to the greener pastures of Vermont's Hero Islands. There, he devoted himself to running his burgeoning salvage business and indulging the true passion of his life: bass fishing. Laddie's superb knowledge of the geography of the lake and its inlets, bays and tributaries—known by the locals as the Inland Sea—soon made him one of the most lauded and sought-after anglers of the region. "Daddy Laddie," as he came to be known, passed his love of the sport on to his sons, and the old man's legacy was solidified when his grandson, Junior Ladd, took top honors in the region's very first Pro-Am Bass Open. Since then, an angler named Ladd usually occupied one of the top spots in the winners' circles of each of the six or seven high-dollar tournaments that were held on Lake Champlain every summer.

When Big Boy and his co-angler, Junior, weren't out on the lake hustling to haul up the biggest bags of fish, they were content to run Ladd's Marine Salvage, where they bought, sold, and rebuilt boats of every shape and size.

It was here that best-selling BDSM author Quinn Glatfelter came, hoping to cut a sweet deal on a used bass boat. She had the flier that detailed specifics about the upcoming tournament folded up and tucked into the back pocket of her tight jeans. She'd read it over enough times to know that she needed some very specific equipment to qualify for the competition. That was problem number one. Coming up with the hefty entrance fee was problem number two.

But if Quinn had learned anything from being pounded by the endless objections of Vivien K. O'Reilly, noted mystery author and professional actuary, it was how to break bigger problems down into their manageable, component parts.

Boat first. Equipment second. Fee third. And she had most of a week to pull it all together.

It really was that simple.

Learning how to fish could come later. After all, she'd seen some of those Sunday afternoon shows on TV. It wasn't rocket science. It seemed to her that the superstars of the sport were mostly a bunch of low-talking bubbas who wore camouflage and had bad haircuts.

Not that different from the clientele at most lesbian bars.

They were her people.

Quinn looked around the interior of the big, dark space. Big Boy and Junior had a pretty impressive inventory. Most of the larger boats were stacked up outside on dry storage racks. Inside, smaller boats and motors in various stages of repair or refurbishment were scattered around on worktables. On a low table near a side wall, Quinn saw a jumble of freshly Parkerized engine parts that looked like they belonged to a Panhead motor.

If there was one thing she knew how to recognize, it was pieces of a Harley.

In a corner of the room beneath a grime-covered window, the Ladd brothers reposed in two natty-looking La-Z-Boy recliners. They were watching something on an old console TV. It sounded like a game show. The regular bursts of cheering and applause that roared up from the big mahogany box made it clear that it wasn't a show about fishing. The top of the set was littered with empty grape Fanta bottles.

"I'll give you forty-five dollars if you've got a bobby pin in that bag."

Quinn smiled. Monty Hall. *Let's Make a Deal* was one of her favorites, too. Even in syndication, Carol Merrill looked pretty damn fine.

Success in retail was all about making connections. Quinn now had two solid leads on her side. She walked toward the makeshift living room. There were gaudy trophies topped with gilded fish and faded photographs of old men in waders spread out along a shelf behind their recliners.

"You boys rebuilding a Harley?" She tipped her head toward the shiny pieces of metal.

Big Boy stared up at her with dark, owlish eyes. They looked like holes in a blanket.

"Mebbe." He didn't add anything else.

Junior wasn't saying anything, either. He was finishing off a party-sized bag of Doritos. Cool Ranch style. Those were Quinn's favorite, too.

Make that *three* solid leads.

"Those Panheads are pretty hard to come by," Quinn observed. "Where'd you boys get the bike?"

Junior wiped his fingers across the arm of his chair. The trails of orange dust they created blended nicely with the plaid fabric.

"It was our granddad's," Junior explained. "Course, he never did ride it any. He was too old when he got it."

It was clear to Quinn that Junior was the talker in the family. Big Boy wasn't doing much besides staring at her and blinking a lot.

"You rebuilding it, then?" Quinn asked.

"Yeah. Been workin' on it now for some time."

"Really? How long?"

Junior shrugged and looked over at his brother. Big Boy blinked at him.

"'Bout twenty years," Junior replied.

Twenty years?

"That's a long time," Quinn observed.

"Parts is hard to come by. They didn't make many of them bikes."

Quinn nodded. "Those Panheads are pretty rare."

Junior looked surprised. "You know somethin' 'bout motorcycles?"

"Oh, yeah. You might say that."

Big Boy made a puffing sound and slowly shook his head.

Junior translated. "Ain't that kinda unusual for a—" he took a closer look to be sure, "girl?"

"Not where I come from."

"Where's that?"

Bingo. Quinn knew she had them now.

"Have you boys ever heard of Hog Heaven in Batavia?"

Big Boy and Junior exchanged glances.

"I reckon everybody's heard of that," Junior said. "At least, everybody that knows anything about rebuilding motorcycles."

Quinn reached into her back pocket and pulled out her wallet.

"Here's one of my cards." She held one out to Junior. He gave his fingers another swipe across the chair arm before he took it from her and looked it over.

"Well, shit," he said. He passed the card over to Big Boy. "This here woman owns the damn place."

It didn't seem physically possible for the holes in Big Boy's face to get any wider, but somehow, he managed. Quinn wondered how he kept his eyeballs from falling out.

"Umm. Ummm. Ummmmm." Big Boy was looking at the card and shaking his head.

"So what kind of bike did your granddad get?" Quinn asked.

"It's a '65 Electra Glide." Junior took the card back from his brother so he could return it to Quinn, but she held up a hand, indicating he should keep it. "Nice one, too. Rare, I'm thinkin.'"

Shit. A '65 Electra Glide Panhead wasn't rare—it was extinct.

Quinn knew collectors who wouldn't bat an eyelash at shelling out sixty thousand for a vintage Panhead in working condition.

"You got that right," she agreed. "It's probably one of the last ones."

"That's what we think, too. Can't get parts no ways."

"I might could help you out there," she said. "I've got good sources all over the place."

"Well." Junior scratched between the folds of his expansive belly. "Parts is one thing. Findin' somebody that knows how to put 'em back together right is somethin' else."

"That's true." Quinn went in for the kill. "What you boys need is a crackerjack Harley mechanic with lots of experience rebuilding vintage bikes."

"Ain't likely to find that 'round here."

"Not 'til now." Quinn smiled at them.

"You a mechanic?" Junior sounded dubious.

"Yes sir, I am—one of the best, too."

"I'll be."

"I'm staying up here for a couple of weeks. Maybe we can work out some kind of a deal."

"Deal?" That got Big Boy's attention. His eyes shrunk to an almost normal circumference. He glared at Quinn like she had suggested something lewd.

Junior wasn't far behind him. "We don't have money for that right now."

"Well, lucky for you, I'm not talking about money." Quinn pulled the fishing tournament flier out of her pocket and held it out to Junior. "You boys familiar with this contest?"

Junior nodded, but didn't say anything. Big Boy was silent, too.

"I was thinking about entering," Quinn explained. "But I don't have a boat or any gear."

Junior raised an eyebrow. "Kinda hard to enter without a boat."

"Yes sir, it is." Quinn waved a hand toward the warehouse full of salvage. "That's why I thought maybe you boys could fix me up with everything I need to compete."

"You ever done any tournament fishing?" Junior handed the flier back to her.

"Nope."

"You ever done any other kind of fishing?"

Quinn shook her head. "Only for compliments."

Junior looked confused.

"That would be a 'no,'" Quinn explained.

"How come you want to start out this way? Why not just get a rod and see if you like it?"

Quinn knew she'd really never to be able to explain it to him. She barely understood it herself. Viv's dire predictions of catastrophe and mayhem were still careening around inside her head like bumper cars—slamming into her impressive collection of all the other "girls can't do that" pronouncements people had been hurling her way since childhood.

Another round of applause roared up from the TV. Monty Hall was trying to tempt someone to trade what lay behind door number two for a big box on the stage.

"Good things can come in small packages," he said. The crowd seemed to agree with him.

"Trade! Trade! Trade!" they bellowed.

Door number two could be concealing the Big Deal of the Day. Or it could be hiding a Holstein and a milking stool. It was a crapshoot. You just never knew.

Junior was still staring at Quinn, waiting for her explanation.

She pointed at the TV. "I'm like that woman right there," she explained. "All my life, I've wanted to be brave enough to go for the Big Deal, and not settle for what everybody told me was good enough."

Junior looked at the TV, then back at Quinn.

"You think bass fishing is the Big Deal?" he asked.

They all knew that no woman had ever won one of these high-profile tournaments.

Quinn shrugged. "Maybe. I don't know."

He huffed. "Well if that ain't the damnedest thing I ever heard."

His brother nodded his agreement.

"We can't pay you to fix the bike." Junior wanted to be sure to drive this point home.

"I understand that. I'm offering to rebuild it for free, at my own expense—including parts—if you'll agree to lend me everything I'll need for this tournament."

The brothers looked at each other. Big Boy scratched his ear.

Junior shook his head.

"What?" Quinn asked.

"Who's gonna teach you how to fish or where to go or how to drive the damn boat?"

"I'm assuming that you will."

"Me?"

Quinn nodded.

"I don't know as that would be fair."

"Why not? It's a Pro-Am tournament. You'd be the Pro and I'd be the Am."

"I wasn't thinkin' about entering this year. My back's givin' me a fit."

"You wouldn't have to do anything but supervise."

"Supervise?"

She nodded. "Just be there and tell me what to do."

He thought about that. "Who gets the purse if we win?"

Gotcha.

Quinn smiled. "You think we might win?"

He held up a puffy hand. "I ain't sayin' that. I'm just asking. Hypothetic-like."

Quinn glanced down at the flier. It had been folded and refolded so many times it was starting to feel like a piece of flannel. She reread the awards section. Top prize was twenty-five thousand dollars—and a fully loaded, twenty-one foot Ranger bass boat equipped with a gas-guzzling, two-hundred-and-fifty horsepower Evinrude ETech motor.

"I won't have much need for a bass boat in Batavia," she offered.

Big Boy cleared his throat.

Junior took the cue. "We already got a bass boat."

"True. But you could sell this one."

"You'd give it to us free and clear?"

Quinn nodded. "Yes sir, I would."

"And you'd fix the bike for free?" Junior asked. "No charge to us for parts or labor?"

"That's right. And if I can't get it done here, I'll even pay to trailer it out to my shop and back."

Even to a crusty old New Englander, that had the ring of a pretty sweet deal.

Junior folded.

"How tall are you?" he asked.

Quinn didn't really understand his question. "Excuse me?"

"You appear to be about six foot, maybe more. I'm six-three. And don't neither of us look like we ever say no to a plate of seconds."

She got where he was headed. "You mean we wouldn't both fit into the same boat?"

"Not likely," he said.

"Well, I'm glad you brought that up, because I have a couple of associates who will want to ride along, too."

"Associates?"

"Yep."

"Fishing ain't a group sport."

Quinn shrugged. "Is it against the rules?"

He took his time answering. "Nope. But it don't work that way."

"Why not?"

Junior thought about it. "Are these 'associates' women?" He paused. "Like you?"

"Mostly. But not as big."

"You can't have a bunch of women squawking on a boat. All that yammering would drive the fish into hiding."

"Can't we use a bigger boat?"

"Bigger? Bigger'n what?"

"I don't know." Quinn waved a hand. "Bigger than the usual." She gestured toward the yard, where all manner of boats were trailered or stacked up on blocks. "What about one of those float boats you have out there?"

"You mean them pontoons?" He shook his head. "They don't go fast enough."

"Can't you put a bigger motor on one?"

"Maybe. But it's gotta have a cutoff switch on it."

"I can rig that."

"They don't have no live well on 'em."

"What's that?"

"It's where you keep the fish until they can be weighed up and measured."

"You mean like a big fish tank?"

"Kinda. But it has to have fresh water moving inside it."

Quinn looked around the interior of the warehouse. "I thought

I saw an aerator back there on one of those shelves near the door. Couldn't we connect that to a big cooler with some water line and run it off a twelve-volt battery? All we'd need is some marine glue and a couple of alligator clips."

Junior looked surprised. "It has to stay cold."

"The water?"

He nodded.

Quinn sighed. He was really making her work for it.

"I suppose we could fill a couple of those grape Fanta bottles with water and freeze them—deep-six them in the cooler with the fish?"

Junior was silent for a few moments. Quinn hoped that meant he'd run out of obstacles.

"It costs fifteen hundred bucks to enter."

"I can cover that. I have a lead on a sponsor that'll kick in the whole fee in exchange for us putting their name on the boat."

Big Boy cleared his throat. Junior looked at him. Big Boy shrugged. Junior blew out a breath and slowly shook his head before turning back to face Quinn.

"So all I gotta do is show up and ride along? And if we win—which ain't gonna happen—I get the rig and you get the cash?"

"Yes, sir."

"And you fix granddad's bike—for free?"

"Yes, sir."

He sighed again. "Okay, then. I guess I done stupider stuff in my time."

Quinn gave the brothers her biggest, toothy grin. "You won't regret it."

"Hold on a minute." Junior had one more question. "Who is this sponsor you got in mind?"

She smiled. "You boys ever heard of Astroglide?"

―᷍᷍―

"I've been kicking some ideas around, and I'm leaning toward sculpting this whole thing as a latticework of stylized webs—

separate, but interconnected." Barb laced her fingers together. "Made from found objects—things I've been collecting and stockpiling for years, waiting for a project like this. I envision a structure the viewer will walk through to experience—much like each of us walked through the experiences depicted by our stories."

Viv chuckled. "That sounds vaguely like the funhouse at Coney Island."

"Yeah," Darien Black agreed. "But in my experience, funhouses were rarely fun."

"Precisely." Barb pointed her web of fingers at Darien. "That's just what I'm getting at."

Barb and her coterie of authors were scattered around the lobby area of the inn on comfy chairs. The bar wasn't officially open yet, but Barb made arrangements with her innkeeper cousin, Page, to use the space in the afternoons for their bull sessions. Part of that deal included opening the bar early for afternoon cocktails.

When the weather warmed up, they'd move their meetings outside to the big white Adirondack chairs that dotted the lawn.

"I still don't get it." Montana Jackson was confused. "What possible relationship do spiderwebs have with writing? And what the hell is a 'found object'?"

"A found object," Viv explained, "is something you *find*. Right, Barb?"

"You mean like your lost virtue?" Quinn asked.

"Ha." Towanda slapped Quinn on the arm. "She never had any virtue to lose, you nimrod."

"Fuck you, Wanda." Viv shot her the bird. "You're just still jealous that I beat your ass out for that Lammy shortlist last year."

Towanda glared at Viv. "It's no accident that your name shows up on any list with the word 'short' in it. Besides, that wasn't even my category. My publisher made a mistake on the submission forms."

"Right." Viv rolled her eyes. "I get it. Because your book should have been entered in—what was it? *Genderqueer Scatological Anthologies?*"

Quinn looked at her. "They have that category now? I never hear about this stuff."

Kate rolled her eyes. "Can we please return to the original topic, ladies?" Her exasperation was starting to show. Shawn patted her on the knee.

Barb sighed. "As I was saying—Virginia Woolf wrote about this very thing in *A Room of One's Own*." She held up a paperback and opened it to a bookmarked page.

> ... *fiction is like a spider's web, attached ever so lightly perhaps, but still attached to life at all four corners ... these webs are not spun in mid-air by incorporeal creatures, but are the work of suffering human beings, and are attached to grossly material things, like health and money and the houses we live in.*

"What's so material about the houses we live in?" Towanda asked.

"Nothing in your case," Viv replied. "I don't think double-wides count."

Towanda narrowed her eyes. "Nice one. Too bad the only double-wide around here is your *ass*."

Gwen Carlisle chuckled and drained her tumbler of Scotch. "I'm empty. Anybody else ready for a refill?"

Quinn held up her pilsner glass. "I'll take another one of those Backcast ales."

Darien looked at her. "Was it any good?"

Quinn nodded enthusiastically.

Darien held up a finger. "I'll take one, too." She looked at the white-haired woman, slumped on the sofa beside her. "How about you, Linda?"

Linda Evans shook her head. "I don't much care for microbrews—and I'm fighting a migraine. I'll stick with my Pellegrino."

Gwen was on her feet. "Anybody else?"

Cricket MacBean held up her glass. "Oban. Two fingers."

"Got it. Back in a jiff." Gwen wandered off toward the bar.

"What I'm still unclear about," V. Jay-Jay Singh asked, "is how we decide what to write about, and how those narratives will relate to each other?"

"That's the beauty of this approach," Barb explained. "What you write about is what you write about. Because we're all women—and we're all lesbians." she glanced at Towanda. "Or women *connected* to lesbians—it's ninety-five percent likely that our stories will overlap organically. We shouldn't have to script anything."

V. Jay-Jay didn't look convinced. "I don't really subscribe to the view that anything about writing is organic. I've never been a 'panster.' I don't think things just magically come together without an outline. We need a plan—something to write to. A grand design for how all of these narratives will fit together and compliment each other."

"Well, I've never been called a panster before. But I guess I agree with Barb on this." Darien turned in her chair to face V. Jay-Jay. "I don't know about you, but my story could pretty much write itself."

V. Jay-Jay wasn't buying it. "Frankly, I don't relish the idea of revisiting my 'story.' Some sleeping dogs should be left to lie in peace."

"If that's how you feel, then why did you agree to come?"

V. Jay-Jay looked at Quinn. "I didn't say that I didn't want to participate—just that I was uncomfortable with an open-ended process."

"Well. I, for one, work better without any confinement." Cricket glanced toward the bar area.

Gwen was returning with the drinks.

"Okay, then—how about we do a combined approach?" It was clear that Barb was ready to move on. "How many of you would feel more comfortable working in teams, or writing to some kind of master plan?"

A few hands went up. Barb counted.

"Four. Okay." Barb waited until Gwen finished distributing the refills. "How many of you feel comfortable developing your essays more organically?"

Quinn looked perplexed. Barb noticed her expression.

"On your own," she clarified.

Four more hands shot up.

"That's eight." Barb considered the remaining three authors who had not indicated a preference for either approach. "So, you three who indicated no preference? What does that mean?"

"We can't commit?" Towanda offered.

"She wasn't talking about relationships," Viv quipped.

Shawn smiled.

"Okay." Barb made some notes on a pad. "That was easy. You three are now lodge sisters."

"Do we get a flag and a song?" Viv asked.

Barb looked at her. "Do you need them?"

"No. But I've always wanted them."

Barb rolled her eyes. "I'll see what I can do."

"How about the rest of us?" Quinn asked.

"Gimme a second." Barb made two more lists on her pad. "Okay." She took off her glasses. "Here's what we'll do. I've divided you up into three teams based on your preferred work styles. I want team members to get together with each other at least once a day. I'll call us all back together a couple of times each week so the teams can share progress and talk about where we are. That will help me begin to get a handle on the direction of the physical aspects of the project." She looked around the room. "Any questions?"

There were none.

"Okay." Barb held up her notepad. "Here are the teams. Pansters: Darien, Quinn, Gwen, and Cricket. Outliners: V. Jay-Jay, Kate, Montana, and Linda. Pantyliners: Viv, Shawn, and Towanda."

Kate snickered.

"Pantyliners?" Shawn asked.

Barb looked at her. "You got a better term?"

Shawn thought about it. "I guess not."

"Great." Barb smiled at the group. "Ladies, start your engines."

Essay 1

Hunters are not holy men.

That's what the Bible says. I guess this saying is kind of like the *CliffsNotes* version of the Jacob and Esau story. Do you remember that one? The great hunter, Esau, surrenders his birthright for a bowl of lentil stew. And Esau's brother, Jacob, later tricks their blind father into blessing him instead of Esau by covering his neck and hands with skin from a freshly killed goat.

I guess Esau was kind of a hairy guy.

Lord knows, we heard enough about Bible stories like this one every day. But as much as people in my family loved to talk about the Bible, not very many of them paid attention to the lessons it taught.

I lived my life trying to find ways to steer clear of being hurt. One thing my childhood gave me were lots of opportunities to practice my art. I got pretty good at it. I learned that if I distracted myself enough, I could get through just about anything without being scarred—at least on the outside. It was really a creative way to make the bad stuff happen to somebody else. After a while, it worked so well that I stopped feeling anything. I didn't really mind that, either. But, sometimes, I'd find ways to try and test that out—just to see where the boundaries were between numbness and pain.

One of the things I'd do was subject myself to things I was sure would scare me or creep me out. That's why

I agreed to go along when my uncle, another hunter, asked me if I wanted to watch him skin some rabbits he'd just shot. He'd been hunting with my grandfather that day. It was wintertime, and I guess rabbits were in season. Or not. It didn't really matter. They had a lot of their own land to tromp around on whenever they wanted to. And it wasn't like anyone would try to stop them.

He said it would only take a few minutes, so I pulled on my coat and followed him outside. I didn't bother putting my mittens on, since he said we weren't going to be out there for very long. But once I joined him on the wooden porch behind the house, I wished I had. It was still snowing, but not very hard. The air was frigid, and my breath swirled around in front of my face like a dense fog. I shoved my hands into the pockets of my cloth coat to try and keep them warm. The lining inside the coat was torn, but I twisted my hands up inside the wool fabric as best I could.

The rabbits were all bunched together in a big bucket that sat on the ground next to the steps. It was nearly dark, but I could see them all clearly. They were cottontails, and there were probably six or eight of them. They were stuffed into the bucket, headfirst. Their floppy legs drooped over the sides like wilted flower stalks. Splotchy bits of wet snow stuck to their dense, dark gray fur.

They looked like they were sleeping—all except for that part about being facedown in a tin bucket, pockmarked with tiny red holes from the .410 shells.

I tried to be tough and not show my uncle how scared and sick I suddenly felt. I really thought I was strong enough to watch this. After all, I knew where most of the meat my family ate came from. I'd just never gone hunting—I wasn't old enough yet. But both of my brothers had, and my sister had, too. In my family, it was what you did.

My uncle pulled the first rabbit up out of the bucket and held it aloft. Before I had time to prepare myself for what was about to happen, he took hold of one of its legs and twisted the skin beneath its foot until it tore and separated from the bone. Then he grabbed hold of the loose flap and yanked it free in one quick motion. The skin made a hissing sound as it peeled away from the tiny frame. There was no blood, but the warm, pink flesh he exposed glowed in the fading light. Steam rose off the small body as it hung there in the early night air, swaying in his grasp like the censer our priest waved over the altar during Mass.

I felt my insides begin to churn. I knew I was going to throw up. Why was this bothering me so much? My uncle wasn't paying any attention to me. He was working quickly now. He had his skinning knife out, and he was gutting the rabbit. When he laid the small, naked body down on the porch floor and took up a bigger knife to separate its head, I felt myself starting to sway. Suddenly, I was the rabbit—and it was my own naked body that lay there exposed to him—small and afraid. It was my warmth and innocence that were being torn away and discarded with the same, swift precision.

Rows of lifeless eyes stared up at me from the backdrop of cold, white snow. They were like the eyes that looked back at me from the dark windows of my upstairs bedroom, where I'd sit, hunched-up and vigilant through the long winter nights, waiting. Waiting to hear the faint creak of floorboard that would signify my own unveiling.

Inside the pockets of my coat, I clenched my hands into fists so tight I could feel my fingernails cutting into my palms. The blood felt warm and sticky as it filled up my palms. That helped. That worked. I could concentrate on that and not on the small heaps of fresh death that steamed on the cold ground at my feet.

I wanted to take up the discarded wads of fur and skin and wrap myself in them. Maybe then, like Jacob, I would be mistaken for someone else, too—someone bigger, wiser—without weakness or fear.

Instead, I stood and watched without speaking. And soon, the pain in my palms replaced my sickness and terror.

I had passed another test.

Hunters were not holy men.

But neither were the brothers who stole their birthrights.

2

Found Objects

"What the hell are those two crazy-ass white women doing?" Mavis blew out a chest full of smoke. It snaked out across the lawn in a meandering, white stream, headed toward the spot where Quinn and Montana stood together at the end of the dock. They appeared to be engaged in some kind of erratic activity that involved snapping long, whip-like poles back and forth at the sky.

Barb followed her gaze.

"Casting," she explained. "Can I have one of those? I left mine in the room."

Mavis handed Barb her pack of Camels. "Casting? What the hell is that?"

"It's a fishing thing."

Mavis huffed. "They look ridiculous."

"They *are* ridiculous." Barb laughed. "But that's unrelated to casting."

Mavis took another long drag off her cigarette. She slowly wagged her head from side to side. "She's really serious about this tournament thing, isn't she?"

"It appears so. She said she got a lead on a boat to borrow. Montana is helping her learn how to use some of the equipment."

"Hell. Those look like the normal tools of her trade. I don't know why she'd need any help learning how to swing a damn whip around."

"Those aren't whips. They're fly rods."

"Say what?"

"Fly rods. Special kinds of fishing poles."

"I don't know why you all can't just go bowling like normal people."

"We *are* normal people."

"Not where I'm from, you ain't."

Barb raised an eyebrow. "Really? Maybe we should ask Marvin about that?"

"Maybe not."

Barb laughed. It turned into a cough.

"You need to start tapering off on those things."

"Why?" Barb cleared her throat. "It won't make any difference. I've been at it too long."

"You don't know that."

Barb looked at her. "Yes, I do."

Mavis held up a hand. "Hey? Don't shoot the messenger, okay?"

"Forget about that. I've been wanting to talk with you about something else."

"What?" Mavis already knew Barb pretty well, and spending a week with her in the cramped confines of a pickup truck during their cross-county drive bred even more familiarity. It was enough to make her suspicious.

Then again, suspicion was pretty much Mavis's first response to any kind of request. It made her day job as a bailiff in the San Diego jail a lot less eventful.

Barb was giving her that look. "Don't automatically say no."

Mavis rolled her eyes.

"I'm serious. I know how you are."

"Woman, you don't know jack shit about how I am."

"I know enough to know that I want you to write one of the essays for my exhibit."

Mavis was incredulous. "Are you crazy?"

"Not usually."

"I'm not a writer."

Barb shrugged.

"And we both know that I'm not like the rest of these bimbos, either."

"I wouldn't call them bimbos."

"You know what I mean."

"I do." Barb nodded. "But that doesn't matter. You have as much right to talk about your experience as they have to talk about theirs."

"Suppose I don't *want* to talk about my experience?"

"Just do me a favor, and consider it. Okay? I think you have an important story that other people should hear—and I need a thirteenth essay for the show."

Mavis didn't reply. She finished her cigarette, and ground out the butt against the sole of her shoe.

"Think about it," Barb said. "That's all."

Mavis ignored her comment. She was watching Quinn and Montana again. They really did look ridiculous—like a lesbian Abbott and Costello.

"Somebody's going to end up getting killed on that damn boat."

"Why?" Barb asked.

"Cause piloting a boat ain't like riding a Harley."

"And you know this because?"

Mavis looked at her. "I live in San Diego."

"You know something about boats?"

Mavis shrugged. "I used to. Before I signed on with the PD, I worked on the Coronado ferry."

Barb's eyes widened. "You drove a ferry?"

"Hell fuck no. You have to have about a zillion hours of time to be a ferry pilot. I was just a deckhand. But I know enough to know that you don't go roaring out, half-cocked, when you can't tell goddamned bow from stern."

"Maybe you can help her out?"

Mavis looked at her like she was a creature from another planet. "Are you crazy?"

"I thought we'd already covered that?"

"No fucking way."

"Why not?"

"Look at them!" Mavis waved a hand toward the dock. "They look like a preview of tomorrow's headlines."

Barb laughed. "And you said you can't write."

Mavis gave up. "There's no arguing with you."

45

"I'm glad you agree."

"I didn't say that."

"I know. But it's a starting point for negotiation."

"Crazy white woman."

"Maybe. But I always get my way."

Mavis shook her head and tapped out another smoke.

Barb held out her hand. "Give me another one?"

Mavis extended the pack. "These things will put us in an early grave."

Barb gave her an ironic look.

"Don't say I didn't warn you." Mavis handed her the lighter.

"I promise."

"I have a feeling those words are gonna come back to bite me on the ass."

Barb laughed and lit up another cigarette.

They didn't talk anymore. There wasn't any need to. They stood, and smoked, and watched as endless arcs of white light flashed across the sky behind a pair of swinging fly rods.

"Ten o'clock. Two o'clock. Cast."

Montana kept repeating the same phrase over and over.

Quinn was pretty sure she had that much down.

"It's all about rhythm and syncopation," Montana explained. "A lot like writing."

"And sex?" Quinn leered at her. She was glad that Montana was the one who offered to help her out. Montana was pretty hot. She was tall, but had a compact frame. She reminded Quinn of one of those QVC garment bags that could fold up small enough to fit inside your wallet.

Quinn always did go for the boyish types. Lipsticks never did much for her. Especially lipsticks like Viv. Viv was just too sharp. She was all points and angles. Plus she had a voice like a cheese grater.

Montana gave a tired-sounding sigh. "Yeah. Like *sex*. Now concentrate. Ten. Two. *Cast*."

"Aren't these poles too skimpy for bass?"

"You won't use these poles in the tournament. They're just for practice." Montana shook her own pole so its tip danced back and forth. "You know? So you can learn how to cast?"

Quinn took the hint and tried it again. It seemed to go pretty well. The line sailed out and the fly skipped across the water a nice distance from the dock. A lone kayaker, out for a midday paddle, shot them a concerned look when he heard the soft splash near the side of his boat.

Quinn was pleased. Maybe she was starting to get the hang of this? Just like she was starting to get the rhythm of how the dock kept bobbing up and down beneath their feet.

"How was that?" she asked.

Montana shook her head. "More like nine, six, hurl."

Quinn lowered the pole and looked at her. "Hurl?"

"Yeah. You tossed that line about halfway to Mt. Mansfield."

"Where's Mt. Mansfield?" Quinn looked toward the small island that was about two miles away from where they stood.

"No." Montana touched her on the elbow before pointing off toward the blue-green horizon. "Over there."

Quinn could see several ranges of mountains. They didn't look as big or imposing as the Adirondacks that framed the view on the other side of the island. These looked—softer. More like they'd been worn down to a size that fit the landscape better.

She squinted her eyes. "Which one is Mt. Mansfield?"

"That big one in the middle. The one that looks like a man's profile."

Quinn was pleased. If she really managed to cast her line halfway to that, she had to be doing it right.

She turned to face Montana. "Isn't that the point?" The sun was glinting off Montana's short, blonde hair. It looked like the top of her head was glowing.

"No." Montana shook her head. "The *point* is to exercise control, not power."

"I don't get it."

"Clearly."

47

It was Quinn's turn to sigh. "You said you'd help me out with this."

"I *am* trying to help you out. Fishing is about patience and finesse—not speed and force."

"How come you know so much about this?"

"Because I grew up in Missoula and spent my summers on the Blackfoot."

Quinn blinked. "Am I supposed to know what that means?"

Montana narrowed her eyes. "Ever seen the movie *A River Runs Through It?*"

Quinn shook her head.

Montana took a deep breath and let the air out slowly. "Tell me again why you want to do this?"

"Fish?"

Montana nodded.

"I don't care anything about fishing. I just want to win this tournament."

"But you can't separate the two."

"Sure you can."

Montana was staring at her like she was the blue light special at K-Mart. Quinn didn't mind. She got that a lot. "I guess that doesn't make much sense to you?"

"Not really, no." Montana stared out across the water for a few moments, then looked back at Quinn. "In one week, this lake is going to be choked with professional anglers from all over the country. And they'll have every single advantage—the fastest boats, the best tracking equipment, the most expensive tackle, and hundreds of hours of tournament experience. And every one of them will have the same objective: to bag the biggest, fattest fish they can flush out of hiding, and take home that prize money."

"That's my goal, too."

"Yeah, but, see? That's the *point*, Quinn. To do this, you have to know how to *fish*."

"Junior knows how to fish."

"I thought you said that Junior was just going to ride along on the boat?"

48

"Well." Quinn smiled at her. "You know how to fish."

"Me?" Montana pointed a finger at her own chest.

Quinn nodded.

"Nuh uh. *Forget it.* I am not getting on that damn boat with you."

"Why not? It'll be fun."

"It'll be suicide."

"Oh, come on. Quit listening to Viv."

"While I do agree with you that Viv is pretty much a pompous windbag—when it comes to this, I happen to agree with her."

Quinn huffed. "This is a goddamn conspiracy."

"I'm just trying to get you to see reason."

"The only reason I see right now is *no* reason. As in, there's *no reason* why I don't have as good a shot at winning this thing as the next person. So what if the other people in the tournament have better or faster boats—or more 'experience' whipping these stupid rods around at exactly ten and two o'clock?" Quinn paused in her tirade. "I really want this. I don't understand it, and I'm not sure I have to. I just know that this—thing—feels different to me. Not like anything else." She sighed. "Haven't you ever felt that way about something that nobody else understood?"

Montana didn't reply right away.

"Well?" Quinn asked again.

"Sure. Of course I have."

"Does that mean you'll keep helping me?"

"Quinn. This is a lost cause. I couldn't teach you even half of what you'd need to know to compete in this tournament. And it's less than a week away. Besides," she made an oblique gesture toward the lawn behind them, where a team of authors sat on white chairs that had been arranged in a semicircle, "we're supposed to be here to write—not to fish."

"Why can't we do both? The tournament only lasts three days. And it ends each day at one-thirty."

"Yeah, but you have to get out there and practice. Learn the lake. Learn the equipment." Something unreadable flickered across her face. Quinn was pretty sure that meant she'd thought of something new. "Please tell me you know how to swim."

Quinn shrugged.

"Jesus."

"Hey, I don't plan to fall off the boat."

"Nobody ever *plans* to fall off a boat, Quinn."

"Well, what if I wear some of those floatie things?"

"Floatie things?"

"Yeah, you know. Like kids wear at the pool?" She extended her arm and displayed her wrist. It was nicely wrapped with a faded blue tattoo of concertina wire. It was also the size of a coffee can. "Floaties."

"On your wrists?"

"Yeah."

Montana looked her over. "I don't think those would get the job done, Quinn."

"Well, I bet we can figure something out that would."

Montana sighed. "What about your essay?"

"What about it?"

"Don't you need time to work on it with your team?"

"I can meet with my team, but I already wrote my essay."

Montana's jaw dropped. "You already wrote it?"

Quinn nodded.

"We're only in our second day."

"I'm a panster, remember? It's how we roll."

"Have you shown it to Barb?"

Quinn nodded again.

"And she's okay with it?"

"I think so. She wants me to share it with my group later today."

"Holy shit."

"She said they all had their drafts done, too."

"Good god. Why didn't she just book us at a Days Inn near the airport?"

"Nah." Quinn jerked her head toward the group on the lawn. "Look at that crew. They'll be lucky to finish up by winter."

Montana followed her gaze and studied the trio of authors. It was obvious that they were arguing. Viv was pointing at something scrawled in a notebook, and Towanda was energetically shaking her head from side to side. Shawn Harris looked like she wasn't paying attention to either of them—probably because Kate Winston was out meandering along the rocky coastline with both dogs in tow.

Montana looked back at Quinn. "Maybe you're right."

"Does that mean you'll help me?"

"*Cast*," Montana clarified. "I'll help you learn how to cast."

Quinn gave her a lopsided smile. "That'll do for now."

"Whatever." Montana gestured toward the churning lake. The dock was pitching more dramatically now. "Aim for that yellow swim dock. Try to drop your line halfway between here and there, okay?"

"Okay." Quinn started swinging her rod.

"Ready?" Montana asked. "Ten. Two. *Cast*."

"That's absurd." Towanda crossed her arms and sat back against her chair.

"It's only 'absurd' because you didn't think of it."

Shawn snickered at Viv's comment.

"What are you laughing at?" Viv shot the words at her like they'd been fired from a slingshot.

Shawn looked at her apologetically. "Sorry. I was watching the dogs." She pointed toward the cliff. "Patrick is eating goose poop."

Towanda snorted. "That's an appropriate metaphor for Viv's idea."

Shawn discreetly checked her watch. They'd been out here for nearly an hour, and they weren't making any progress at all.

Viv glared at Towanda. "Maybe if you ever had an original idea, I wouldn't have to do all the heavy lifting."

"The only heavy lifting you do happens when you try to stand up."

"Fuck you, Wanda."

"Fuck you, Viv."

"Ladies. Really?" Shawn held up a hand. "You two make Samuel L. Jackson sound like the Singing Nun."

They both glowered at her. An implied "fuck you" hung in the air.

51

Shawn tried again. "How about we take a break?"

Viv tapped her pen against the notepad. "Fifteen minutes?"

Shawn glanced toward Kate and the dogs again. "How about thirty?"

Towanda laughed. "A half-hour for a nooner? You two must work fast."

Shawn blushed.

Viv rolled her eyes. "Fine. We meet back here in half an hour."

"Who made you the fucking cruise director, O'Reilly?"

"Somebody has to be in charge." Viv waved a dismissive hand. "You're plainly incompetent, and Shawn is only able to concentrate on her—nether bits."

"Nether bits?" Towanda stole a glance at Shawn's lap.

Shawn noticed and crossed her legs.

Towanda looked back at Viv. "It's good to see that you're still a master wordsmith."

"Sorry." Viv smiled sweetly at her. "I'd have said 'cunt,' but I didn't want you to accuse me of plagiarism."

"Okay." Shawn stood up. "I'm outta here. See you all in half an hour."

⁓

"Wait up."

Kate slowed down so Shawn could catch up with her.

Patrick and Allie danced around Shawn's feet for a minute or two before taking off to chase some geese that had the temerity to risk landing on a wide field adjacent to the inn's lawn.

"They look really happy," Shawn commented.

Kate agreed. "I know Patrick is. He doesn't get many opportunities to be off leash like this."

"We were lucky that Barb picked a place that's dog friendly."

"I think we'd have gotten a dispensation, anyway. Her cousin is the innkeeper."

Shawn was surprised. "Page Archer is Barb's cousin?"

"Yep."

"Small world. I wondered why she didn't pick a place that was more centrally located."

"I'm glad she didn't." Kate took hold of Shawn's arm. "This place is like heaven."

Shawn smiled at her. "It is pretty nice."

"You're hardly objective. I think you'd say that even if we were shacked up at a hot-sheet hotel in Poughkeepsie."

"That does sound rather charming."

Kate rolled her eyes.

"So sue me. I like spending time with you."

"Goofball."

"Don't you?"

"Don't I what?"

"Don't you like spending time with me?"

Kate gave her an ironic look. "You have to ask me that after last night?"

"Well."

"I could hardly walk straight this morning."

"Hey, that part wasn't my fault. You were the one who got into the acrobatics."

"Only because I accidentally kicked Allie in the nose, and she flew off the bed like she was being chased by aliens."

"Can you blame her? I'm sure that scared the crap outta her."

"It scared the crap outta *me*. Why do you let her up on the bed, anyway?"

Shawn shrugged. "I don't. She just kinda sneaks up there."

"Sneaks?"

"Yeah."

"A seventy-five pound dog cannot 'sneak' onto a bed."

"She can if it's one of those very good plush tops, with pocketed coils and edge protection."

Kate looked at her.

"One of the characters in my new book sells mattresses."

"How do you come up with these ideas?"

"I like to write about real people."

"Right. Like chicken sexers."

"They're real people."

"In what universe?"

"In *any* universe." Shawn was starting to feel offended. "Why are you always such an elitist?"

"I am not an elitist."

Shawn stopped walking. "Kate. You work for *Good Morning America.*"

Kate looked at her impassively. "So?"

"So? And you tell me that *my* subjects are unreal?"

"Not your subjects—your characters. They strain credibility."

"Oh. I get it. And your features about deeply important topics like Fake Miami Clubbing don't?"

"That was a perfectly respectable story about a new fitness craze."

"Right. Because people who work out at six in the morning, under strobe lights with Shakira tunes blasting overhead, are more 'real' than people who plod off to dull day jobs selling mattresses."

"I fail to see your point."

"No. You fail to concede my point."

"Fake Miami Clubbing is a legitimate form of aerobic workout."

Shawn squinted at her.

"What?" Kate asked.

"Are you drinking the Kool-Aid at that place?"

"What place?"

"New York."

"Oh, come on. It's not that weird."

"No." Shawn pointed at their dogs, now sniffing around a colony of fake bunnies that were artfully arranged at the base of a tree. It was a plum maple, and its shiny, dark red leaves were shimmering. The wind was picking up. "*That's* weird."

"What is?"

"Those clay rabbit things that are all over the place."

"I thought so, too, at first. But now I think they're kinda—sweet."

Shawn looked at her. "Do I know you?"

Kate rolled her eyes. "Think about it. They're quirky little emblems of hope and innocence, inveighing against the harshness of the elements up here. They create a perfect, metaphorical point-counterpoint."

"Wow."

"What?"

"You really should think about quitting your day job and writing lesbian fiction full time."

"Oh, come on."

"No. I mean it." Shawn indicated the tree where Allie was still cautiously nosing around the clay bunnies. "If those things could animate during the full moon, sprout king-sized incisors, and embark on an apocalyptic, twilight rampage, feasting on the flesh of all the well-fed Canadians that seem to inhabit this place, you'd have one hell of a paranormal best-seller on your hands."

"What about the whole lesbian angle?"

"Oh, that part is easy."

They'd reached the tree and the dogs. Kate stopped and crossed her arms. "Enlighten me."

"One of the zombie bunnies could really be the reanimated daughter of the Canadian Prime Minister. She could have been killed and cursed because of her love for the exiled Minorcan Princess Anastasia."

"Anastasia?"

"Just go with me here."

"She was exiled from Florida?"

"It could happen."

Kate sighed.

"As I was saying, Princess Anastasia was the hapless victim of her guardian, Vorlich—an evil, white-haired Scottish woman with a dark and sinister past. Insert all kinds of eerie, druid-like, occultish undertones here."

"Druids?"

"Why not?"

"In Canada?"

Shawn shrugged. "It's lesfic."

"Okay. I'll give you that one."

"Vorlich uncovers the love affair between Anastasia and Felix— and flies into a jealous rage."

"Felix?"

"Her name is really Felicia—but she goes by Felix."

"Right." Kate nodded. "Androgynous names. A very important story convention . . . Shawn."

"Hey." Shawn feigned umbrage. "I did *not* create this name to be cool or androgynous. It was just easier to spell—and it kept me from getting beat up every day at school."

Kate studied her for a moment. "What *is* your real first name, anyway?"

"You know what it is."

"No, I don't."

Shawn sighed. "Shoshana."

"Like Rosh Hashanah?"

"No." Shawn corrected her. "Like Sho-sha-na. It's Hebrew for Rose."

"Your name is Rose?" Kate smiled.

"Yeah, yeah. My name is Rose. Go ahead. Yuck it up."

Kate touched her on the arm. "I think it's sweet."

"Oh, thanks. Sweet. Just like these zombie bunnies."

"Stop it. Tell me more about the love affair between Felix and Anastasia."

"Well, it pretty much follows the plot of every lesbian zombie love story."

"Which is?"

"Girl gets girl. Girl loses girl. Girl eats other girls—literally and metaphorically. Girl gets girl back. Girls live happily ever after in some exotic location, free from the curse of reanimation."

"The familiarity of the story does elicit a certain margin of comfort."

"Right. It's no different from any book by Laura Ingalls Wilder."

"Only with flesh-eating bunnies?"

"Right."

"And hot, girl-on-girl sex?"

"If you're lucky."

"I feel so foolish. I never noticed the similarities."

"Pantyliners." Shawn tapped her chest with an index finger. "We know some things."

56

Kate smiled at her. "I have missed this, you know."

"Missed what?"

"These dialogues."

"What do you mean? We talk all the time."

Kate shook her head. "Not like this."

They resumed walking. Allie and Patrick were now racing along a split-rail fence, flanked by beds of bright orange daylilies.

"You, know, I've been thinking about quitting."

Shawn was surprised. "Your job?" She tired not to sound as hopeful as she felt.

Kate nodded.

"Why?"

"I could give you a dozen reasons, but they all end up in the same place. I'm just not happy."

Shawn started to say something, but didn't. Kate noticed.

"What?"

"It's nothing."

"I doubt that."

Shawn bumped her shoulder. "I wanna hear what you have to say before I express any opinions."

"Does it occur to you that maybe I want to hear your opinion?"

Shawn looked at her. "Do you?"

Kate's nod was so slight it was barely perceptible.

"I don't want to be selfish." Shawn had a healthy appreciation for the value of caution, especially where Kate was concerned.

"Maybe I want you to be selfish."

"For real?"

"I think so. At least, for now."

Shawn sighed. "This is always a lose-lose proposition for me. You coerce me into telling you what I think, then you hand my ass back to me on a platter."

"I don't do that." Kate looked out across the lake, then back at her. Intently. "Do I do that?"

"Sometimes."

"I'm sorry. I don't mean to be so fractious."

"I know."

Kate waved a hand around in frustration. "I've never been very good at listening to feedback."

"So I've noticed."

"I'd like to change that."

"I hear that twelve-step programs can be great little ways to jump-start the process."

"Be serious."

"I *am* being serious."

"Are you going to tell me what you think, or not?"

"What I think, or what I want?"

"Aren't they the same thing?"

Shawn shook her head. "Not in every case."

Kate sighed. "Okay. Let's start with what you *want*."

Shawn still felt a little wary about saying too much. She decided to wade in slowly—just like the rotund, wannabe swimmer down on the beach below them, who kept dipping his big toe into the water every five seconds to see if the lake was warming up.

It wasn't.

After five or six tries, the big man in the blousy, blue trunks gave up. He collected his striped towel and his flip-flops and headed back toward the inn.

Shawn doubted that she'd have any better luck, but decided to take the plunge anyway. After all, Kate was asking for her opinion. No. Kate was asking what she *wanted*—that wasn't the same thing. She decided to go for it.

"I want you to come back."

Kate raised an eyebrow. "Back? Back to where? Atlanta?"

"No. Back to me."

"You want me to move to Charlotte?"

"It doesn't have to be Charlotte. We could live anyplace. I could live anyplace."

Kate didn't reply.

"Was that the wrong thing to say?"

"Is it what you want?"

Shawn nodded.

"Then it wasn't the wrong thing to say."

"What do you think?"

"Nuh uh." Kate held up a palm. "This is your inquisition, not mine."

Shawn sighed.

"Now." Kate wasn't finished yet. "Tell me what you *think*."

"What I think?"

Kate nodded. "You said that what you want and what you think are not necessarily the same thing. You told me what you want. Now I'd like to hear what you think."

This was going no place. Apparently, the round man in the baggy blue trunks had been right. The water was still too cold.

Shawn tried to buy some time. "I'm not even sure I understand what we're talking about."

"New York. Me." Kate glared at her. "*Us*. Ring any bells?"

"A few." Shawn didn't bother mentioning that the bells she was now hearing sounded more like the ones that tolled in advance of a funeral procession.

She tried a different approach.

"So that word 'inquisition' bothers me."

"Why?"

"Because I feel like I'm being cross-examined."

"Oh, come on."

"I mean it."

"So now we're arguing about semantics?"

"See?" Shawn held out both hands in appeal. "That's exactly my point. We're *arguing*. Which, I might add, is always what happens whenever you ask me to tell you what I think."

"It does not."

"Does, too."

"Why do you always use words like 'always'?"

Shawn didn't respond.

"You know absolute statements like that piss me off."

Shawn was tempted to point out that the list of things that pissed Kate off could fill several volumes. But she didn't. She kept silent.

"Well? Are you going to say anything?"

It was worth noting that keeping silent usually pissed Kate off, too.

"Wanna hand me that platter?"

"What are you talking about?" Kate looked around. "What platter?"

"The one that has my ass on it."

For a moment, Shawn was afraid that Kate might slug her. But she was wrong. Kate smiled. Then she started to laugh. Loudly. Loudly enough that Patrick and Allie heard her and raised their heads from the rich swath of fresh goose poop they'd just discovered.

"How much more time do you have left on your break?" Kate asked. She was still smiling.

Shawn looked at her watch. "About ten minutes."

Kate grabbed her by the hand and started walking toward the inn.

"Where are we going?" Shawn was more confused than ever.

"Back to our room."

"Our room?" Shawn practically had to trot to keep up with her. The dogs were racing along behind them. "Why?"

"Because I just thought of something *I* want," Kate explained." And if we hurry, we'll have just enough time to take care of it."

Shawn was still confused, but not crazy. She tightened her hold on Kate's hand and followed her back to the room.

Essay 2

I'll never forget the day my parents sat me down and explained to me that I had been born with "ambiguous" genitalia. Really? I've never felt ambiguous a day in my life. Well, maybe just that one time at Christmas when my Aunt Tootie took me to Toys R Us to redeem a gift card and asked me to choose between Western Barbie (who kinda looked like Jennifer Aniston, but came with a really cool, prancing Palomino), or the remote controlled Special Ops Spy Car with Rockets and a Rear-Firing Cannon.

I stood there staring down into the depths of that bright red shopping cart for so long that Aunt Tootie, who really had the patience of Job, finally started cracking her wad of Dentyne to let me know she was *thinking* about getting annoyed.

In the end, I went with the Barbie—but only because I liked the fringe on her shiny white outfit and, like I said, the plastic yellow horse was pretty awesome. It looked a lot like Mr. Ed. My aunt never found out that, later, when I got Barbie alone in my room, I cut off most of her hair and re-named her Wilbur.

Even then, my tastes were pretty eclectic. At least, that's how my mother described them to her guests when I showed up at one of her Tupperware parties wearing a pair of mukluks, and a camouflage jacket over a pink tutu. I've never been afraid to take a fashion risk.

Growing up, it didn't much bother me that I had a

penis. (In fact, it's really just a super-sized nub, but I'll talk more about that later.) I mean, I knew I was a girl. Mostly. I didn't even know there was anything unusual about me until I was ten, and I saw Melissa Boatwright in the shower at the Y. I learned some other useful things about myself that day, too—like it suddenly became clear to me why I wasn't really interested in boys the same way most of my friends were starting to be. You see, Melissa was three years older than me, and she looked pretty great stark naked and dripping wet. And unlike my Western Barbie, I had no desire to cut off any of her hair to make her look like a guy. I thought she was just fine the way she was.

That's when I went home and asked my mom to explain just what was up with my body—and why didn't I look like other girls "down there."

She gave me one of "those" looks—the ones that always meant we were in for a long conversation—and said we'd talk about it later, when my dad got home.

Okay. That meant it was a bigger deal than I thought. For the very first time in my life, I felt afraid. Why was I different? Why hadn't anyone ever said anything to me about it? What was this going to mean? And why did my nub get bigger whenever I thought about Melissa in the shower?

That night, after we ate our pot roast and creamed spinach, my parents pushed their plates back and faced me with identical pairs of folded hands.

"Pumpkin," my father began, "there are some things that mom and I never told you about the day you were born."

I glanced over at my mother. Her face had that pinched-up look it got whenever Sally Struthers was on TV talking about sick babies in Africa.

I looked back at my father. "What is it? And why does Mom look so scared?"

He shot a nervous glance at my mother and cleared his throat.

I knew it was bad now. I was sure he was going to tell me that I was adopted. That had to be it. My whole life was a sham. How would I ever hold my head up in school? And how would I ever break the news to Wilbur and Mr. Ed?

We were orphans now.

My eyes started to fill up with tears. "I'm adopted, aren't I?"

My father looked surprised. "No, honey, that's not it."

"It isn't?" I wasn't sure I was ready to believe him. I mean, he'd waited all this time to tell me whatever it was.

"No." He looked over at my mom again.

She took up the explanation. "Sweetie, when you were born, the doctors weren't sure about whether you were a little girl, or a little boy."

Okay. That one stopped my surge of panic.

"Why not?" I asked.

My mother leaned across the table and reached out to push my bangs away from my eyes. "Well, honey. You know how little boys have penises, and little girls have vaginas?"

I had a pretty good idea where this was headed now. I nodded.

"It seemed that you were born with both," she said.

"And," my father chimed in, "the doctors wanted us to make a choice about which sex we wanted you to be."

"But," it was my mom's turn to talk again. I felt like I was watching a tennis match on TV. "We didn't think that was our decision to make—so we decided to wait."

Wait? Wait for what? Wait for my nub to drop off, or for me to have to start shaving?

"You gave me a girl's name," I said. "And you bought me *dolls*." I said it like I was Matlock, cross-examining a witness.

"We also bought you trucks and guns," my father corrected. It seemed like he'd had time to prepare for this conversation.

"And your name is a family name, that could work for either a girl or a boy," my mother added.

That was true. At least they hadn't named me after Aunt Tootie. Then I might have had a reason to use one of my toy guns.

I looked down at my lap. "Is this why I have a big nub?" I asked.

My father chewed his bottom lip. Nobody said anything for a moment. I could hear our dog, Rex, getting a drink of water in the kitchen.

"Yes, honey," my mom finally replied.

I sighed. It was true that my big nub was—unusual. I knew that now. But it was a part of me, and I was used to it. Plus, it was feeling pretty good these days. I didn't think I wanted to have it go away. My panic started to creep back. Is that what this conversation was about? Were they going to make me lose my nub?

I knew that right then, I probably looked a lot like Rex, whenever Mom got the vacuum cleaner out.

"Can I keep it?" I asked.

"Oh, honey," my mom was starting to cry. "Of *course* you can keep it."

Dad was now staring at something fascinating in his own lap. Maybe all this talk about losing nubs was making him think about his own?

Gross.

"Okay," I said.

"Is there anything else you'd like to ask us about?" My mom was still leaning toward me.

I shrugged. It occurred to me to ask if they ever thought that Joey Heinz, who lived in the apartment upstairs, looked just like the Unabomber—but I knew this probably wasn't the kind of question she meant.

"Not right now," I said, instead.

My father had apparently finished contemplating the crease in his trouser leg.

"Just know you can always talk with us about this," he said, "or anything else that worries you."

My mother nodded in agreement. "Don't ever let anyone make you feel like you're odd or strange. You are a perfectly wonderful and normal person."

Right then, I realized how lucky I was that she didn't know about Western Barbie's new hairstyle. I'd grown tired of the buzz cut, and colored her head with a black Marks-a-Lot. She had a beard and sideburns now, too.

"Can I go outside and play until dark?"

"Did you finish your math homework?" she asked.

We were doing long division at school—and I hated that stuff worse than creamed spinach. I looked down at my plate. I'd done a pretty good job hiding most of it beneath what was left of my Parker House roll. I knew it didn't really fool my mother, but she usually let me get away with it.

"I did most of it," I said. "I need help with some of the harder ones."

Mom started to protest, but Dad interrupted her. "You can go out and play—but when you come back inside, we'll sit down and solve the rest of your problems."

I pushed back my chair, and raced for the front door, not wanting to waste any more of the soft, warm night.

It was only later, as I fell asleep wrapped in the snug awareness that my parents would always do exactly what they promised, that I realized how lucky I was to be born me.

3

An Obscure Object of Desire

Junior wasn't talking. He pretty much just sat back on his plaid throne and let Quinn figure things out.

They'd moved one of his big, Dorito-stained recliners out of the warehouse and set it up on the pontoon. It reposed there proudly, dead center on the carpeted area beneath the red canvas awning, like a makeshift captain's bridge. It looked sort of good, too—almost like it came with the boat as part of some luxury package.

The way Quinn saw it, these damn boats were just like double-wide trailers on floats—so why not trick one out with real furniture?

When she suggested the idea to Junior, he didn't say much. He just stared at her and plucked at a stray chin hair.

She took that as a "yes." Montana helped her haul the big chair outside and drag it down to the dock so they could move it onto the boat. They also took along a full-sized Weber grill that had seen better days.

Quinn loved hot dogs, and so did Junior. It was another thing they had in common.

Now they were out for their first motorized tour of the islands.

While Quinn got the hang of driving the boat—which was really more like aiming it in the general direction you wanted it to go— Montana sat on the bow, cleaning the grill racks with steel wool. Quinn didn't bother to suggest to her that it might make more sense to do her scraping at the back of the boat. Ancient flecks of carbonized meat kept billowing across the deck in rust-colored swarms.

Montana sat with her long legs spread-eagled, riding the swells like a pro. She was wearing cutoff jeans and a loose-fitting tank top. Her short blonde hair glowed like a second sun.

Nope. Quinn didn't mind the chunks of rust and burnt grease that kept hitting her in the face. It was worth it to enjoy the view.

She caught Junior watching her watch Montana. She smiled at him and shrugged. He stared at her for another moment before nodding and returning his gaze to the front of the boat. It was pretty clear that he was enjoying the view, too.

They were making their second trip around Knight Island. It was shadier on the backside, and there were some outcroppings of rocks and places where old trees had fallen and were partially submerged in the water.

"Stop!"

Junior's command surprised Quinn. She cut the motor without hesitation. The water wasn't very deep through here, so they hadn't been going all that fast. It didn't take the boat long to wind down to a gentle drift. The pontoons rocked up and down on the waves that rolled in toward the shore.

"Why are we stopping?" She asked Junior.

He pointed a fat finger toward one of the felled trees. "I just saw her."

Her? Quinn looked toward the tree and the bank beyond. There were no people in sight. There wasn't anything in sight but what was left of a cracked concrete slab and a beat-up picnic table. Knight Island was part of a state park, and people could still camp on it.

"I don't see anyone."

Junior shook his head. "Not a person. A fish."

A fish?

"What fish?" Quinn looked again toward the tree. She could feel a twinge of excitement. Even Montana dropped her steel wool pad and climbed to her feet.

Something splashed in the water ahead.

"Right there!" Montana cried. "I saw her. My god. She's *huge!*"

Junior nodded. "That's her all right."

Quinn still didn't see it. "What the hell are you two looking at? Who is 'she,' and why are you so damn excited?"

"It's Phoebe."

Quinn looked at Junior. His face had taken on an odd expression. It was almost reverential.

"Who?"

"Phoebe," he said again. "The biggest damn bass in this lake."

"Her name is *Phoebe?*"

Junior nodded. "Been called that for nigh on a hundred years now. She ain't never been caught. Hooked a time or two, but never brung up." His voice dropped an octave. "I had her once. She fought me like a tiger. I damn near bested her, too—but my line got tangled up when I was tryin' to pull her into the boat." He held up his hand to show Quinn where part of his pinkie finger was missing. "She done this to me when I tried to get a net under her."

"Jesus Christ."

Junior was watching the water again. "They don't come bigger or meaner'n Phoebe."

Montana was shaking her head. "She has to be at least a twenty-pounder."

Junior agreed. "Some of them Japanese anglers come over here a year or two back, just hopin' to get a hook into her. But she's too smart for 'em. Ain't nobody ever gonna catch Phoebe."

Quinn was still watching the water. She was mesmerized by Junior's tale about the great fish.

"You said she's a hundred years old?"

He nodded. "Mebbe two hundred. Nobody knows for sure. Only thing I can tell you is that she's been swishin' her fat tail around these islands ever since my granddad was runnin' hooch down from Montréal."

Quinn's eyes grew wide. "Your granddad saw her?"

"Yep. Lots a times. He said she always knew where to find the sacks of whiskey they'd deep-six when they were bein' chased by the boat patrol." He chuckled. "Granddad said that ole Phoebe liked to nip on more than just night crawlers."

"Look!" Montana was pointing at the water on the port side of the boat. "I think she's coming by again."

Quinn could see her this time—heading straight for them in bold flashes of brown, green, and silver. She was liquid and solid all at the same time. And she was moving fast—uncommonly fast—as she twisted and shimmied just beneath the surface of the water. She skimmed along the side of the pontoon and at the last second, dipped her head and dove deep, flipping her wide tail up and out of the water in a hail of spray.

"My god." Quinn wiped the drops of water from her face.

But Phoebe wasn't finished yet. She made another pass. And this time, Quinn saw her eyes, deep, dark eyes that were empty and full all at the same time. Fish eyes. Just like the camera lenses that distorted reality by twisting everything into macabre circles of burlesque shapes. The eyes looked at her and through her, seeing everything and seeing nothing. "I know you," they said. "You're just like me—and no one will ever catch you, either."

"She's beautiful." Quinn was staring at the water like she was in a trance.

Montana didn't share her assessment. "That thing is a freak of nature."

Junior agreed. "You take my advice and leave that'n alone. Ain't no good gonna come from chasin' this piece of tail."

Quinn stared at him. Junior was still reared back in his recliner, but his expression looked serious enough to suggest that he was *thinking* about sitting up.

"You said nobody's ever caught her?"

"Didn't say that," he corrected. "Said that nobody'd ever brung her up. She's been hooked 'bout a dozen times. Just always gets away."

Quinn watched Phoebe's wake slowly dissolve into the rolling water. The lake had closed back up over her.

"Why do you call her Phoebe?" Montana asked. "That seems like an odd name for a fish." Before Junior could answer, she added, "Not to say that there are other names that make more sense." She picked up her steel wool pad and prepared to go back to work cleaning the grill racks.

"Nobody knows for sure." Junior was watching Quinn watch the lake. "Most people think she was named for that Phoebe Campbell woman—the Canadian who chopped up her husband with an axe."

That got Quinn's attention. "When did that happen?"

Junior shrugged. "Don't know for sure. Some time after the war."

"World War II?"

"Nope. Civil War."

"Canada had a civil war?" Quinn asked.

Montana rolled her eyes. "He means *our* Civil War." She looked at Junior. "Isn't that what you meant?"

Junior nodded.

"Great." Montana sniggered. "A fish named after the Canadian Lizzie Borden."

"Why'd she do it?" Quinn was fascinated by Junior's tale.

"Why does any woman do anything?"

Quinn sighed. She was getting pretty used to Junior's economy of words. "Why'd she kill him? Come on, Junior. Even you have to admit that most women don't end up hacking their husbands apart with axes. Even if they fantasize about it."

He shook his head. "I think she was gettin' some on the side from a farm hand, and they done him in together. But nobody knows for sure. She hanged for it, though, and he got off." Junior chuckled. "More'n once, I'll wager."

"So why'd they name this fish after her?"

"Probably because she's mean as a snake and craftier than a politician."

Quinn didn't say anything. She continued to stand near the side of the boat, studying the water. There were no other boats out on this part of the lake. It was quiet here. The only sounds came from the slosh of the water rocking the pontoons and the scrape of Montana's steel wool against the rusty iron grate.

"She ain't gonna come 'round again."

Quinn looked up at Junior. He really did make a ridiculous picture, bobbing up and down on that absurd chair. He had his feet hooked beneath the footrest so he could ride out the swells like a champion broncobuster. He was the stuff of legend, too.

71

"Why do you say that?"

"I know her," he explained. "She saw what she came for. By now, she's likely halfway to St. Albans."

"Can we go over there?"

"No."

"Why not?"

"Because that ain't why we're out here." He gestured toward their drink cooler. "Give me one of them grape Fantas."

Quinn sighed and walked over to retrieve the soft drink for him.

Junior was still scrutinizing her. "Don't go gettin' no half-cocked ideas about tryin' to catch her. That ain't what this whole circus here is about." He took the frosty bottle from her and cracked its seal. The slow hiss it made underscored his warning. "Better men'n you have wasted their lives thinkin' they was gonna be the ones to catch her. All they got for their trouble was a lot of mangled hopes and beat-up body parts to match."

"He's right." Montana spoke up from her seat on the deck. "You've got one shot at this tournament, Quinn. Don't waste your time trying to nail Jell-O to a tree."

Quinn was unconvinced. "I think you're both wrong."

"Whatever." Montana went back to her scraping.

"Just keep your priorities straight," Junior cautioned, "and give up on them bass-ackward notions."

Montana chuckled.

"What's so funny?" Quinn asked her.

"I think Junior just gave us the perfect name for this stupid boat."

"What?"

"Bass-ackwards." Montana was still smiling. "You gotta admit, it's catchier than *The Raft of the Medusa*." She got to her feet and displayed the mostly clean grill rack. "Who wants a hotdog?"

———

"I am so not eating that."

V. Jay-Jay looked at the congealed mass of red goo. "Why did you order it?"

72

"I didn't." Darien pushed her plate away. "This stuff looks like the aftermath of a miscarriage."

V. Jay-Jay did not look amused. "It's aspic."

"I know what it is. I think it's disgusting."

"Maybe you should mention your disdain for it to the wait staff?"

Darien glared at her. "How come you never get this crap on your plate?"

"I explained my special dietary needs on the first day."

"Really? Is that some religious thing?"

"Religious?" V. Jay-Jay looked confused.

"Yeah. Like a Hindu thing?"

"I'm Presbyterian."

"I thought you were from India?"

"I am. But being Indian and Presbyterian are not mutually exclusive."

"So, why don't you eat this crap?" Darien poked at the aspic with a fork.

"I'm a vegan."

"Aren't tomatoes vegetables?"

"Normally. But aspics are always made with some kind of meat stock."

Darien stared at her plate. "Gross."

"I agree."

They were sitting at a window table. It gave them a great view of the lawn and the lake beyond it. There were several clusters of people outside, standing around in tight little groups or sitting in the big white chairs. They laughed and sipped on cocktails while they waited for their tables to be ready. There were several impressive-looking boats tied up at the long dock. Some of them were clearly built for speed. Others looked more like aquatic SUVs, with loud paint schemes and built-in stereo speakers that probably pushed enough amps to fill Yankee Stadium with top-40 tunes. Darien knew all about people who blasted around in these high-dollar rides. Sooner or later, a lot of them ended up on her list of "assignments." But there were a couple of vintage Chris Craft launches tied up out there, too. The wooden boats looked downright regal with their polished decks and dark green upholstery. They bobbed up and down, sandwiched between the modern monstrosities, with all the understated elegance of old money. They were like stray orchids in a vase full of dyed carnations.

This restaurant was apparently a popular destination for Lake People.

That's what Darien called them. *Lake People.*

They appeared to be a savvy and refined lot. The men had thinning hair and spreading middles. Their impossibly thin wives all had tight features, perfect tans, and summer wardrobes that contained enough organic cotton to revitalize the nation's flagging textile industry.

They were like refugees from a Flax catalog.

"What are you scowling at?"

Darien looked at V. Jay-Jay with surprise. "Was I scowling?"

"I thought so."

"It's the Lake People."

V. Jay-Jay glanced out the window at the lawn. "What about them?"

"They bug me."

"Why? They look pretty ordinary."

"Not where I come from."

"Which is?"

Darien shrugged. "Virginia. Mostly."

V. Jay-Jay looked out the window again. "I haven't spent a lot of time in Virginia, but I'm pretty sure that places like Richmond and Charlottesville have their share of pampered elite."

"Yeah. Well. I'm not from Richmond or Charlottesville. 'Pampered elite' where I grew up meant you didn't have to punch out the catalytic converter on your pickup."

V. Jay-Jay laughed.

"I'm not kidding."

"I know. That's what I think is funny."

Darien regarded her with curiosity. "You think *that's* funny?"

"Sure." V. Jay-Jay quirked her head toward her shoulder. "You should think about putting more elements like that into your writing."

"What elements?"

"Those kinds of colloquialisms. They'd really lend authenticity to your stories."

"I don't write about Virginia."

"Really?" V. Jay-Jay sat back and folded her tanned arms. "So those macabre little vampire yarns you spin aren't masquerading as searing social commentaries on your humble origins?"

"I didn't say that."

"I thought so."

"There's nothing wrong with writing about vampires."

"I agree."

"Besides," Darien was trying hard not to let her annoyance show. "Vampires aren't any weirder than all that Gyno stuff you obsess about."

V. Jay-Jay was the author of a very eclectic and popular series of books that all fell under the rubric *Gyno Galaxy*. At last count, there were four volumes, and V. Jay-Jay was hard at work writing the fifth book in the series, *Gyno Galaxy: Black Holes and Anterior Spaces*.

It was clear that she did not share Darien's assessment of her work. "I write hard-hitting, edge fiction."

"And you can open beer bottles with your hooha."

"*Hooha?*" V. Jay-Jay made air quotes around the word.

"Oh, come on. A woman with this ability can't pretend to be insulted by my use of a common term."

"It's common, all right."

"And your special skill isn't?"

"My 'special' skill is part of a carefully crafted public persona."

"Like your 'edge' fiction?"

"Precisely."

Darien rolled her eyes.

"You disagree?"

"Um. Let me think. Yes."

"I don't see why."

"Oh, come on. It's thinly veiled soft porn."

"And your moonlight vampire romps aren't?"

Darien noticed that V. Jay-Jay did not bother to disagree with her categorization of the Gyno books. "Soft porn sells copy. Especially in this galaxy."

V. Jay-Jay smiled at the analogy. "Sad, but true."

"So why do we do it?"

"Why do we do what?"

Darien waved an inclusive hand around. "*This*. The writing. And all the concessions we have to make to popular culture and bad taste."

"Speak for yourself."

"Oh, come on. Are you trying to have me believe that you *choose* to fill your books with spread-eagled women and vaginal swabs?"

V. Jay-Jay looked amused. "As a matter of fact, I do."

"You are so full of shit."

V. Jay-Jay didn't reply. But Darien noticed that she was absently tapping an index finger against the top of her folded napkin. Was it irritation or intrigue? She really had no idea, but she decided to go for it. "What's your story, anyway?"

V. Jay-Jay raised an eyebrow. "My *story?*"

"Yeah. You have one, right?"

V. Jay-Jay shrugged.

"Come on. Nobody knows anything about you. Your 'official' bio gives nothing away. Why all the secrecy?"

"I'm no more or less secretive about my private life than anyone else in this business."

"I find that hard to believe."

"I told you I was Presbyterian."

Darien gave her a confused look. "Is that supposed to be some kind of index to your character?"

"Maybe."

"Let's try another approach. What's your day job?"

"My *day* job?"

"Sure. You have one, right? Or do you make enough money in royalties that you no longer have to pack a lunch and trudge off to the sweatshop every day like the rest of us?"

V. Jay-Jay looked amused. "I never pack my lunch."

Darien sighed. "Of course you don't. I guess there are charming little vegan restaurants about every ten feet in LA."

"There may be. But I don't live in LA."

Darien lifted her chin. Now they were getting someplace. "Okay. Where do you live?"

"Boston."

"Massachusetts?"

V. Jay-Jay gave her a deprecating look. "No. *Idaho.*"

"So sue me. I was just surprised."

V. Jay-Jay folded her arms. Darien thought her skin looked like polished olive wood.

"Why?"

Darien shrugged. "I don't know. You seem like a left-coaster to me."

"Well. I did live there for a while, many years ago. But I've been in Boston for nearly a decade now."

"And what do you do there?"

"What's with the twenty questions?"

"I'm just trying to make conversation."

V. Jay-Jay stared at her for a moment without replying. She could've been thinking about unreeling her entire life story, or she could've been getting ready to tell Darien to fuck off. It was pretty even money.

"I'll make you a deal," she finally said. "I'll tell you one thing about my private life if you, in turn, share one detail about yours."

"Mine?" Darien was confused. "My life is not a secret."

"I said your 'private' life. Not your public persona."

"What? You mean like kinky stuff?"

V. Jay-Jay let out a slow breath. "No. Not like kinky stuff. However enthralling those details are certain to be, I don't possess any real curiosity about them."

"Too bad. I could probably teach you a few things."

"I somehow doubt that."

"Okay. Fine. I go first." She leaned forward over her abandoned dinner plate. "What kind of work do you do in Boston?"

"When I do work, which isn't often, I do product development consulting for a medical implement company."

"Of *course* you do."

"You asked. I never pretended it was exotic."

"So, what does that mean, exactly? You make fur-lined speculums?"

"Something like that."

"I bet the people at Hobby Lobby just love paying for those benefits."

V. Jay-Jay ignored her comment. "My turn. What do you do during daylight hours?"

"Daylight hours? Sleep."

"Sleep? You don't work?"

"Oh, no. I work all right. Just not during daylight hours."

"Oh. I get it. You're a night watchman? A security guard?"

"Do I look like a security guard?"

V. Jay-Jay gave her a once-over. "You appear to be in pretty good shape."

"Why thank you."

"So. Am I right? Are you a security guard?"

"Not even close. I work in asset recovery."

"Asset recovery? What on earth is that? Some kind of financial service?"

"You might say that."

"And you do this at night?"

"It's generally safer that way."

V. Jay-Jay sat back against her chair. "I don't get it."

"For someone who makes a career out of writing 'edge' fiction, you sure aren't very quick on the uptake."

"Am I supposed to know what that means?"

Darien sighed. "I recover monster RVs from people who are behind on their payments."

V. Jay-Jay's brown eyes grew wide. "You're a repo man?"

"Man?" Darien pointed both index fingers at her shirtfront. "Seriously?"

V. Jay-Jay gaped at Darien's chest before realizing what she was doing. Her cheeks took on a rosy tinge. "Oh, god. I'm sorry."

"It's okay. Most people call us that—regardless of gender."

"But this is fascinating." V. Jay-Jay leaned toward her and lowered her voice. "Is it dangerous?"

"Sometimes." Darien shrugged. "I've been shot at a couple of times."

"My god. What did you do?"

"Fired back."

V. Jay-Jay was mesmerized. "Really?"

"No. Not really. Jesus." Darien snapped her fingers in front of V. Jay-Jay's face. "Earth to Singh? It ain't like the movies. Those things are built like Fort Knox on a bus chassis. You pretty much hook 'em up to a tow bar and haul 'em off. And most of this happens in the dead of night, while the owners are snored off in their McMansions."

"I had no idea."

"You don't think things like this happen in Beacon Hill?"

"I never really thought about it."

"Trust me. Your Brahmin buddies are among the worst offenders."

"I don't know many people with—what did you call them? RVs?"

"Sure you do. It's just that their excesses are likelier to be stick-built time shares in Cape Cod—not Freightliners parked on the back lot of the local mini-storage."

"Incredible."

"It's a job."

"How long have you been doing it?"

Darien held up a finger. "Tit for tat."

"What's that supposed to mean?"

"You said 'one detail.' So if I have to answer another question, so do you."

V. Jay-Jay sighed.

"Well?" Darien asked.

"Fine. Ask me another question."

Darien smiled. This was like blood in the water. "What's your real name?"

V. Jay-Jay blinked, but didn't reply.

"You have one, right?"

"Of course I do."

"Well?" Darien asked again. "What is it?"

"Why do you want to know?"

"I don't know. Maybe because your nom de plume is so unique."

"I told you. My public persona is carefully crafted to enhance my writing."

"You got that part right."

V. Jay-Jay didn't say anything.

"So?"

"So what?"

"Your name. What's your name?"

V. Jay-Jay sighed. "It's Vani. Vani Jaya."

"Vani Jaya Singh?"

V. Jay-Jay nodded.

Darien shook her head. "Is *everyone* in India named V.J. Singh?

"Pretty much."

"It must really simplify having your luggage monogrammed."

"It's a Presbyterian thing."

Darien blinked.

"That's a joke."

Darien was studying her. "You're an odd fish."

"I'm an odd fish?" V. Jay-Jay pointed out the window toward the dock. "*That's* an odd fish."

Darien followed her gaze. Some kind of commotion was brewing on the lawn outside the restaurant. People were getting up from their chars and shading their eyes to study the lake.

"What is it?" she asked V. Jay-Jay.

"It looks like Santiago is coming in from her first foray at sea."

"Oh, Jesus."

Darien saw the pontoon, roaring in toward the dock at full throttle. Quinn was at the helm. Montana was clinging to a railing on the bow, wildly waving her free arm and yelling. The big La-Z-Boy was empty—which meant they'd either dropped Junior off at his place on their way back to the inn, or he'd had the wisdom to jump ship.

People out on the lawn were shouting now, too. Heads at every table in the restaurant were turning toward the big windows that faced the spectacle.

She had a feeling this was going to end badly.

Apparently, Page Archer did, too. She left her post at the bar and roared toward the exit door so fast that tablecloths fluttered in her wake. She was moving like a Valkyrie in full battle mode. But Darien was beginning to learn that this was pretty much how the innkeeper approached everything.

At the last minute, Quinn reversed the engines on the pontoon and the boat lurched backwards, slamming into its own monster wake. Waves crashed over its stern and surged across its deck, racing toward the flotilla of small fortunes tied up at the dock.

Darien closed her eyes.

"I *told* you all this would happen." A voice rang out from a nearby table. Darien turned toward the sound. Vivien K. O'Reilly was on her feet, wagging a finger at the impending disaster. The feisty romance author stamped her foot. "That woman is an actuarial nightmare."

Quinn apparently overcorrected by jerking the wheel hard to starboard, causing the back end of the pontoon to swing wide toward the shore. The whole shootin' match was now coming in sideways, heading straight toward a floating yellow swim dock that, mercifully, was unoccupied. At the last minute, Montana gave up trying to salvage the landing. She tossed the tube rail fenders over the side, and jumped off the pontoon into the rolling waves. Her dive was spectacular. For a few perfect seconds, her long frame hung silhouetted against the orange and purple evening sky like a startling, Technicolor homage to Esther Williams. Even though they were caught up in the throes of certain disaster, a few of the onlookers were impressed enough to offer up a smattering of applause. But Quinn's boat just kept right on sliding sideways toward the bright yellow dock, missing the stern of a twenty-five foot Hunter sailboat by inches.

Page Archer was now out on the end of the dock, standing with her arms akimbo. The wooden platform beneath her feet rocked up and down, smacking the water with increasing volatility, but the innkeeper stood bolted in place. Darien thought she resembled one of the galvanized iron dock cleats—with a temperament to match.

Inside the restaurant, all eyes were glued to the spectacle. Diners at every table were spewing dire warnings about how this comedy of errors was certain to end.

"It's comin' in *hot*."

"They're toast."

"That guy driving must be drunk—or stupid."

"Did you see how close they were to that Hunter? I don't know how the hell they missed it."

"What the fuck's the matter with that asshole?"

"I hope he's got insurance."

"Page Archer will have his ass on a cracker."

"It'll have to be a big goddamn cracker."

"Could I have another double Oban, please?"

That last comment got Darien's attention. She looked around. Cricket MacBean was still seated at her table near the fireplace. She was attempting to flag down a server by rattling the ice in her water glass.

Darien rolled her eyes. *To each his own.*

There was a collective gasp, and the room fell silent. The only sound came from a dozen overhead speakers playing soft music. It sounded like Enya. *Sail Away.*

Darien turned back toward the window. V. Jay-Jay was shaking her head.

"What happened?"

V. Jay-Jay gestured toward the water. "It looks like she stuck the landing."

Sure enough, the pontoon was perfectly snugged up against the side of the swim dock, just like it belonged there. Quinn was standing on the side of the boat holding her bright blue dock line, looking for a place to tie up. It was clear that the stationary ladder would have to do. She bent over and began tying her clumsy knots.

People out on the lawn were shaking their heads. A couple of them bumped fists and raised their pint glasses toward the miracle of maritime maneuvering they'd just witnessed.

Page Archer, however, did not appear to share in the combined relief that a near disaster had been averted. She stormed back up the length of the dock like a thundercloud. Darien was pretty sure this didn't bode well for Quinn, who now stood on the stern of the pontoon waiting for Montana to return with a rowboat to fetch her.

Other diners appeared to agree with her assessment of the situation.

"Page is gonna open a can of whoop-ass on that guy."

"He deserves it. What an idiot, coming in hot like that."

"How come Doug didn't go out there with her?"

"He's too busy pouring drinks for that mouthy redhead by the fireplace."

"It looks like that woman who dove off is going out with the rowboat to get her."

"Why doesn't she just swim in?"

Vivien K. O'Reilly stepped into the void on that one. "Because that idiot can't swim any better than she can drive a damn boat."

Darien turned to face Viv. "That might be true. But you have to admit she's got a lot of heart."

"Heart?" Vivien threw an arm out to encompass the scene on the lawn. "You call that *heart?* I call that a spinal cord that doesn't touch her *brain.*"

There was a titter of laughter. People reclaimed their seats and returned to their unfinished meals.

"I had no idea that coming up here would be so dramatic."

Darien looked back at V. Jay-Jay with amusement. "It didn't occur to you that you were going to be stuck on an island for two weeks with your cellmates from the CLIT-Con fiasco?"

"The thought did cross my mind."

"But you came anyway."

V. Jay-Jay shrugged.

"Admit it. The riot that ended that conference made great fodder for a lot of books."

"It certainly put the 'creative' into last year's Creative Literary Insights and Trends Conference."

"I didn't hear a lot of complaints coming from the organizers. They made a fortune on all that post-riot tchotchke."

V. Jay-Jay didn't reply. Darien continued to study her.

"What?"

Darien shook her head. "It's nothing."

"It didn't look like nothing."

Darien gave a little head toss. "I was just wondering."

"About?"

"About you and that special skill of yours."

"My special skill?" V. Jay-Jay raised an eyebrow.

"Well. Yeah. You have to admit that it's pretty uncommon."

"Not really."

"Oh. So now you're going to tell me it's another Presbyterian thing?"

"Hardly. It's an ability that many women acquire after successful treatment for SUI."

"What the hell is SUI?"

"Stress Urinary Incontinence."

Darien's eyes grew wide.

"Don't look at me like that. I don't *have* it—I just understand the prevalence of the condition, and am familiar with some of its less conventional treatments."

"And you know this because?"

"Let's just say I've had some firsthand experience."

Darien sat back against her chair. "I'm totally confused. What does treatment for incontinence have to do with being able to open beer bottles with your hooha?"

V. Jay-Jay sighed. "It's not rocket science. You *are* familiar with your Kegel muscles, aren't you?"

"Well. Yeah."

"After pregnancy, or as a natural part of the ageing process, many women lose elasticity in these muscles. Often, specific exercise regimens are enough to strengthen them. In other cases, workouts with vaginal weights prove efficacious."

"Vaginal weights?"

V. Jay-Jay nodded.

"You're kidding me, right?"

"Not so much."

"So, you work out with—what did you call them? Vaginal weights?"

"Occasionally. But only to maintain my stamina."

Darien shook her head. "Kettle bells for the hooha." She looked at V. Jay-Jay. "Are there classes for this at the local Y?"

"Doubtful."

"Pity."

V. Jay-Jay was looking at her strangely.

Darien held up her pint glass of Backcast ale. "I'm just thinking about how useful that particular skill can be when you find yourself in a jam."

"Why? Are you planning on getting arrested?"

"You never know."

"Save yourself the trouble and get a good attorney."

Darien gave her a shy smile. "Or I could just make sure that you're on hand any time I plan to get into a bind."

V. Jay-Jay didn't say anything right away. Darien thought her expression was hard to read. She worried that maybe she'd gone too far. Then she saw the corner of her mouth twitch.

"That could work, too," V. Jay-Jay said.

—◆—

Across the room, from her seat by the fireplace, Shawn was studying a group of people standing next to the bar. She'd been watching them for some time.

"Earth to Shawn? Hello?"

Shawn gave Kate a guilty look. She had no idea what they'd been talking about.

"Excuse me?" she asked.

Kate rolled her eyes. "What in the hell has you so fascinated over there?"

Shawn shrugged. "I don't know."

Gwen chuckled. "Well, I know what *I* find fascinating. That woman in the red sundress has about the nicest ass I've ever seen in captivity."

"Really?" Cricket followed her gaze. "Where?"

Gwen tipped her head toward the bar. "Over there, standing beside the gangly man who looks like Mr. Green Jeans."

85

"Who is Mr. Green Jeans?" Shawn asked.

"Oh, come on." Kate nudged her. "You never watched *Captain Kangaroo?*"

"It was a little before my time. Yours, too, come to think of it. So how come you know who he is?"

"I guess I have more esoteric tastes than you do."

"Or a better cable package," Cricket quipped.

Shawn didn't disagree. "She gets, like, nine million channels in New York City."

"An enviable situation, to be sure." Gwen took a healthy swig from her beer glass. "So, apart from the awesome display of assets, what *do* you find so intriguing about the group at the bar?"

"I don't know. They all kind of remind me of something."

"What?" Cricket asked. "A remake of *The Stepford Wives?*" Gwen snorted.

"Maybe." Shawn decided to change the subject. "Anyone notice how chummy Darien and V. Jay-Jay are looking over there?" All three of her companions' heads swung toward the tables that lined the windows of the restaurants. "Don't look *now*," Shawn hissed. "Jeez, you all."

Kate elbowed her. "Will you lighten up? This place is like an IHOP on a Sunday morning after church. No one is paying any attention to us."

"Ain't that the truth?" Cricket rattled the ice cubes in her empty tumbler. Again. "What does it take to get that damn server's attention? Flares?"

"They might be doing you a favor, Crix."

"Favor?" Cricket gave Gwen a dubious look. "What kind of favor?"

"Think about it." Gwen held her nearly empty pint glass aloft. "They could all be participating in the annual 'Save the Liver' campaign."

"*Save the Liver?*" Cricket slammed her tumbler back to the table. "You are so full of shit. I've never heard of that."

"Sure you have," Kate added. "Wasn't Julia Child a big proponent of that one?"

Gwen was nodding enthusiastically. "It's right up there with the Walk to Cure Nail Fungus."

Shawn snickered.

"Why did I ever consent to sit with you three?" Cricket was staring across the room again. "You know, those two do look kind of chummy."

"Told you."

Cricket looked back at Shawn. "Don't act so smug."

"Come on." Shawn waved a hand. "I told you this morning there was some kind of something going on there."

Kate looked at her. "Some kind of something? Wow. With an ability to turn a phrase like that, you should think about becoming a writer."

"Hey, hey." Shawn tapped her chest. "Let's not forget about my Simon & Schuster contract, okay?"

"How can we? You won't let us."

"Oh, like you're suffering." Shawn glowered at Gwen. "Feel free to shovel that fifteen percent right back my way if it ever gets to be too much of a burden for you."

"Ooh. Catfight. *Great.*" Cricket turned in her seat. "I really need another drink for this."

Gwen was chuckling, but Shawn was still offended.

"Really, baby cakes." Kate patted her hand. "You need to lighten up."

Shawn sighed and pushed her plate away.

"Are you on the rag?"

Shawn rolled her eyes at Cricket.

"Well?" Cricket suggested. "It seems like a reasonable explanation."

"And they say our memories are the first things to go."

"Fuck you, Gwen." Cricket finally succeeded in flagging down a busser, who was hurrying by with a tray full of dirty dishes. "Could you please ask our server to activate her GPS and find her way back to our table?"

The busser looked at her with confusion.

"We need another round of drinks," Gwen explained.

The busser nodded politely and continued on toward the kitchen.

"I'm sorry for being a bitch."

All eyes at the table shifted toward Shawn.

"I have been on edge today." She looked across the table at Cricket. "And, no, I'm not having my period."

"I gave that shit up for Lent."

Cricket looked at Gwen. "I know I haven't been a practicing nurse for more than a decade, but I'm pretty confident that it doesn't work that way."

"It does when you tell your doctor that you want all that apparatus left behind in a surgical dish when they wheel you out of the OR."

"What-*ever*." Cricket appeared to notice something over Gwen's shoulder. "Red light! Our bogie is on the move."

"Where?" Gwen swiveled around on her chair.

"Over there." Cricket pointed a stubby finger at the magnificent, red-draped ass winding its way between the crowded tables. "My god. That woman is *hot*."

"Really girls?" Kate looked back and forth between the two older women. "Do we need to behave like dogs in heat?"

Gwen nodded enthusiastically. "You cannot refuse to dance when so much beauty is before you."

"Dance?" Cricket looked confused. "What the hell are you talking about?"

"She's quoting *Pride and Prejudice*," Kate clarified.

Gwen looked at her with surprise.

Kate shrugged. "I have nine million cable channels, remember?"

"You should be an agent." Gwen looked back to admire the view. The owner of the world's-most-remarkable ass had reached her table, and the red-robed object of desire was now hidden from view. "Shit. She sat down."

"Nothing gold can stay," Cricket opined in a singsong voice.

Gwen looked at her. "Really?"

"It's Robert Frost," Cricket explained. "You're not the only person here who's read a book, you know."

Gwen rolled her eyes and regarded Shawn. "Apropos of books, how is yours coming along?"

Shawn shrugged and didn't reply.

"She's stuck," Kate explained.

"I am *not* stuck." Shawn glowered at her.

"What do you call it, then? You haven't written anything in a month."

"I'm not up here to work on my book. I'm up here to work on Barb's essay."

Kate shook her head.

"What?" Shawn asked.

Kate looked at Gwen. "She's stuck."

Gwen sighed. "Are you still worried about writing something 'good enough' for your new editor?"

Shawn shrugged.

"Sweet pea, you gotta let that shit go. Just write the damn book and forget about who's going to be reading it with a red pen."

Shawn's eyes grew wide.

"Oh, great." Kate pointed at Shawn's expression. "You just had to invoke the dreaded *red pen*. Now she'll be up all night, munching on Tums."

"Any port in a storm," Cricket quipped. "But if she's going to be up all night munching, I'd offer her something better to gnaw on."

"Could you get your head out of your ass for two seconds?" Gwen asked.

"I might if I had something else to occupy myself with—like another goddamn drink."

"Well take heart." Kate smiled at their approaching server. "Here come our reinforcements."

The server arrived to pick up their empty glasses and deposit a fresh round of cold drinks. When she departed, the women all hoisted their glasses and clinked rims. Gwen led the toast.

"Here's to successful new ventures for all of us."

"Here, here." Cricket sipped her Scotch and smiled. "Hell hath retreated to its box."

"Is that another quote?" Gwen asked.

"Beats me. I just thought it sounded good."

Across the table from Cricket, Shawn was still sulking. She didn't care for that "stuck" comment of Kate's. It irked her. A lot. Mostly because she knew it was true.

She felt something skate across her thigh. Kate's hand settled on her knee and gave it a warm squeeze. Shawn looked over at her.

"I'll help you get unstuck," she whispered.

Shawn didn't reply, but she smiled. Kate could be very creative when it came to finding ways to get unstuck.

She glanced at her watch and wondered how quickly they could finish their drinks.

Essay 3

When it comes to questions about my tenure in psycho-therapy, I like to tell people that I was on the five-year plan. Don't laugh—I'm not really kidding.

I didn't think my "issues" were all that complicated. Not at first, anyway. I thought I was breezing in there with some pretty textbook stuff. You know—castrating mother, alcoholic father, upper-middle class angst and umbrage, yadda, yadda, yadda. The usual. I figured I'd be good for about six months of group therapy—then I'd get my parking validated, and sally forth into high-functioning relationships and marriage to someone solidly enmeshed in a thirty-three percent tax bracket.

That would make me an unqualified success in my mother's eyes. At least until I could convince her that I wasn't spitting out kids because of early onset meno-pause. This would be a bold-faced lie, of course, but if it kept her out of my sex life, it would be worth the expres-sions of pity and disappointment I'd be sure to get from the women in her bridge club—all of whom, I might add, catapulted from their sister college sororities equipped with pelvises that would make Chinese peasants green with envy.

I know this probably sounds like I spent a lot of time strategizing about my future, but in my family, that was generally a safer way to proceed. It was a skill I acquired while learning how to off-load double twelves in cut-throat games of Mexican Train.

Games were like leitmotifs in our lives. My mother had a compulsive addiction to order, and that played out on an endless succession of game boards that, laid end to end, could have circled the globe twice. Even at a young age, I found this to be an ironic passion for someone who really could control next to nothing in her own life—or anyone else's, for that matter. As small children, we played so many successive games of *Sorry!* that my brothers would salivate whenever they heard the sound of a bell ringing. (In case you were wondering, we were partial to the version of the game popularized on *Mama's Family* because the bell drove our mother nuts.)

Playing games was a passion my father learned to love, too. In his case, it offered a perfect excuse to be out of the house between the hours of dinner and breakfast. It was amazing how he managed to find so many "all night" golf courses. I was well into my teens before I figured out that my mother's snide references to "night putting" had little to do with golf, and everything to do with our father's secretary, Frau Hertzog—a former stewardess for Lufthansa. I didn't blame my father for this indiscretion—Frau Hertzog wasn't that much of a prize, either. I never really understood why he'd cheat on our domineering mother with a leviathan who could toss him around like a shot put. I guess it's true that water seeks its own level.

My brothers (we'll call them Biff and Scooter) proved the truth of this hypothesis in pretty rapid succession. Sadly, Biff's longest-term relationship ended up being with his parole officer. After four bouts of rehab, he finally succumbed to his cocaine addiction and collapsed in his college dorm room at age twenty-one. He died before the EMTs could revive him.

Scooter didn't fare much better. He married so many clones of the Stepford wives that he eventually just kept his divorce attorney on speed dial. He was in Cancún on his fifth or sixth Club Med honeymoon when a freak scuba diving accident rendered him brain dead. Fortunately or unfortunately for him, the majority of his ex-wives were unable to discern the difference. He died in relative penury less than a week later.

If I sound callous, it's not because I didn't care about my brothers. I did. But we were more like polite strangers than siblings. I suppose that, for me, the real impact of these tragedies showed up later on—like a bruise that finally surfaces days later, when you've already forgotten about whatever it was you banged into. In my case, it might be more accurate to say that the cumulative weight of all of these losses came crashing down on me like a piano dropped from the sky. But unlike Wylie E. Coyote, I was unable to shake it off and walk away.

Although, in retrospect, I did often wonder how Road Runner got his paws on a Steinway in the middle of the desert. It must've had something to do with "the willing suspension of disbelief"—a philosophical concept that has never really had much resonance for me.

My hardcore realism has always been the bane of my existence. It's a paradox. The same personality trait that probably allowed me to escape my childhood mostly unscathed later became my relational undoing. I reached a point where I couldn't make anything work— even a two-minute conversation with the guy behind the counter at Jiffy Lube turned into a slugfest. I was a mess, and I knew it. I was like an obscene parody of Robert Browning's "Last Duchess." I despised whate'er I looked on, and my looks went *everywhere*.

After years of sinking deeper into anger and depression, or repression, or a mixed bag of all those words with the "-ession" suffix, a cadre of the few remaining friends I had descended upon me en masse and told me I needed a shrink. Immediately. Tess, one of my best friends, even shoved a folded-up piece of paper into the palm of my hand and muttered, "Use it—you two are perfect for each other," as she headed for the door of my small apartment.

I sat down on my couch for about two hours, holding nothing but my pent-up rage and that small wad of paper. I sat there for so long that my cat, Shadow, strolled into the room to see what was going on. Understand that my cat didn't like me much, either. He generally only made forays out under the cover of darkness.

Finally, in a last gasp of hope—or resignation—I unfolded the torn slip of notepaper. It took a minute to decipher Tess's illegible scrawl.

½ doz. eggs
Diet Coke
trash bags
tampons
Dr. Anne McCall 583-3127

I stared at the list. Was good mental health generally found on the same aisle as feminine hygiene products? It made a kind of quirky sense, so I decided to give it a try, and make the call.

Anne McCall, a.k.a. "Mickey," was a big woman—larger than life, really. And Tess was right: she *was* perfect for me—especially in all those "don't come in here and blow smoke up my ass" ways that made it impossible for me to run my numbers on her. She was smart and tough. A refugee from Scranton, Pennsylvania. That fact alone was enough to garner my respect. My father was from Scranton, too. And, believe me, you had to have titanium cojones to walk away from that place and be able to drink without drooling.

It took me most of the first year in therapy to figure out that Mickey wouldn't put up with any of my shit. So we spent many of our forty-five minute "hours" in silence, staring at each other from our respective chairs (I quickly claimed a seat on the couch, but staunchly vowed never to lie down upon it). I thought the silent treatment would crack her. Why not? It always worked with everyone else. When it eventually became clear to me that Mickey was quite content to endure my silence and still bill me one hundred and twenty-five dollars per session, I realized that it might be prudent to give voice to at least some of the behavioral issues that led me to spend most of an hour every week admiring the postmodern artwork and hand-thrown pottery that ornamented her truly tasteful office.

We started out with my mother, of course. Then moved on to my father and my "issues" with his alcoholism and philandering. The deaths of my two brothers came next. It soon became clear to me that this process was the psychological equivalent of moving through the hot bar at Golden Corral—without the yeast rolls. It was a good thing I had no idea about the tasty confection that was lying in wait for me at the end of the dessert line.

Our conversations pretty much followed a typical pattern.

"How was your week," Mickey would ask.

Silence.

Eventually, I'd shrug. "It sucked."

"Why?"

"Who knows? People are assholes."

"What people?"

"My mother."

Mickey would re-cross her legs. "This is hardly a breaking news item."

More silence.

"Do you want to tell me what happened?" she'd ask.

"Not really."

More silence.

"Is that a new piece of pottery?" I'd point at something with sleek lines that sat atop her white bookcase.

"No." She'd take a sip from her mug of hot tea.

I'd look at my watch. Six or seven minutes would have passed. Finally I'd quit stalling and cough it up. "So, this guy at work asked me out."

"And?"

"I don't want to go."

"Did you tell him that?"

"No."

"Why not?"

"I don't feel like I can."

"Because?"

I'd shrug.

More silence.

"I feel like I have to go, and it pisses me off," I'd confess.

"Which part pisses you off? Going, or feeling like you have to go?"

"Yes."

"Say more about that."

It drove me nuts when she said, "Say more about that."

"It drives me nuts when you say that," I'd say.

She'd raise an eyebrow. "Say more about that, too."

I never really noticed that the not-wanting-to-date thing was becoming my own leitmotif. I don't know why I thought that projectile vomiting was a normal response to being asked out for dinner by a good-looking guy. Of course, Mickey seemed to figure this one out right away—the way they *all* do. I remember that I even tried to take her to task for that once—suggesting that she already knew all the outcomes and was just waiting for me to catch up. She looked at me like I had two heads (which, in retrospect, would have provided a unique opportunity for double billing).

"Why would you think that I'm sitting here with all the answers?" she asked.

"I don't know. Maybe because that's what you get paid for?"

"If I knew the answers, don't you think I would share them with you?"

I didn't reply.

"Believe me," Mickey continued. "I'm not clairvoyant. I don't have a magic eight-ball that I consult as soon as you leave the office. When I have insights, I share them with you. My job is not to conceal things from you until you figure them out."

"It isn't?"

"No."

"Not even when it's about my mother?"

"Especially when it's about your mother. In fact, I think your mother should will herself to science."

I found it hard to argue with that one.

"So," she continued. "Do you want to tell me about the rest of your week?"

I nodded. "It was pretty uneventful. Work sucked. But on Tuesday night, I went to a recital with Byron."

Byron was my gay best friend. We pretty much did everything together.

Mickey waved a hand at me. "And?"

"It was a great concert. Cecilia Bartoli in an all-Rossini program. We had excellent seats—right in the center of the second row."

"Sounds wonderful."

"It really was." I thought about the event for a moment. "Something weird happened when she came out on stage."

"What?"

I shrugged. "I don't know. She was wearing this really gorgeous, low-cut red dress—it fit her like a glove."

Mickey nodded, but didn't say anything—so I kept talking.

"I just felt—*strange* when I saw her. I don't know how else to describe it. It was just—weird." I shook my head.

"After the concert, Byron and I went out for a late supper at the oyster bar and ran into some friends of his from graduate school. That was a drag because they sat down with us, and proceeded to talk prevailing issues in library science for the duration of the entire meal. You cannot imagine how interesting a discussion of subject-based information gateways *isn't*. At one point, I seriously thought about impaling myself on a seafood fork. Trust me, there weren't enough glasses of Rioja on the planet to keep my interest up during that meal. Fortunately for me, Byron was driving that night, so I didn't have to monitor my intake. The rest of the week was just pretty ho-hum. I got a reprieve of sorts because my mother is still down with bronchitis—it's hard for her to be as castrating as usual when she can't breathe. My obnoxious neighbor stepped right up to fill the void, however. He's still blasting *The Best of Prince* at three a.m. Last night was the second time this week. I called my landlord about this...again. But he plainly doesn't give a shit. What do you think I should do about this? It's really driving me crazy."

Mickey stared at me in silence. Then she raised an index finger. "Let's go back to that red dress thing."

I was surprised. "What about it?"

She was giving me an odd look. "Say more about it."

I rolled my eyes. "It was just a red dress. No big deal. I didn't attach any particular significance to it."

"Say more about your reaction to the woman *wearing* the red dress."

I narrowed my eyes. "Just what are you getting at, here?"

She looked at me over the top of her glasses.

"Oh, come on, you cannot be *serious*." I thought about it. Was she serious? What *had* I felt? Whatever it was, it wasn't—sisterly. No. It was far from sisterly. In fact, it was downright predatory. I raised a hand to my face. This was *not* happening. Not to me. And not this fucking *easily*.

I peered at Mickey between my spread fingers. "Are you kidding me with this?"

It was her turn to shrug. "What do you think?"

"What do I *think?* How the hell should I know? If I knew what to think, I wouldn't be sitting here on this couch in an office that looks like it got ripped from the pages of *Metropolitan Life*."

She said nothing. That was probably my biggest clue that an epiphany was at hand. She was always silent during the big ones. I sank further into the cushions on the sofa. Yep. This one had all the earmarks of being a big one.

"Oh, good god." I looked at her. "Is this it? Is this all there is to it?" I shook my head. "I'm gay? That's what this lifetime of puking has been about?" I held out my palm to stop her before she could ask me what I thought. Again. "You mean there's *nothing* wrong with me? I just don't want to date men because I like women *better?* Is that it? Is that all there is?"

Suddenly, I felt like Peggy Lee. All the mysteries of life had finally been laid bare before me, and they were— unremarkable.

"Oh, sweet Jesus. *I'm gay.*"

Mickey leaned forward in her chair. "How do you feel?"

I noted that she wasn't asking, "Are you sure?"

I sighed. "The truth?"

She nodded.

"I feel relieved."

She just nodded again, like that answer made sense. I guess, in a way, it did. It *was* a relief to understand, finally, that I wasn't sick or twisted because the idea of having sex with men always made my insides churn. I wasn't limping through life with some festering wound that turned me into an emotional mutant. I was just gay.

"Holy shit." I sat there shaking my head. Then I looked at her. "So I guess this means our work here is finished?"

"Yeah." She picked up her inevitable mug of tea. "Not so much."

I sighed.

"Are you okay?" she asked.

I nodded. For the first time in my life, I felt like I was. I smiled at her.

She knew me well enough to be suspicious. "What is it?"

"I can't wait to tell my mother."

Throughout all the years I continued to work with Mickey, I never again heard her laugh quite that hard.

4

Bologna Sandwiches

"I can appreciate that you all prefer a more delineated process. But, please? Can we acknowledge the reality that we've only got ten more days together to work on this project?"

Barb was beginning to lose patience with The Outliners.

They'd met every day now, and were making next to no progress on their essays. Linda Evans had even unearthed an old white board that had been stashed upstairs in the attic over the restaurant, and they were using it to create flow charts for their various narratives.

Barb made an oblique gesture toward some scribbling on the board. "Seriously. This looks like a schematic for the F-18 fighter jet."

"That's V. Jay-Jay's," Linda explained. "So it probably has a lot of similarities."

Kate rolled her eyes.

"Don't even try to scoff, Miss Thing." Linda chided her. "Yours is just about as prolix."

"I know." Kate shook her head. "I'm rethinking the whole stream of consciousness approach."

Barb thought that sounded hopeful. "Because you realize it might enhance the spontaneity of the narratives?"

"No." Kate looked at her. "More because I'd like to get out of here before my womb drops."

V. Jay-Jay choked on her glass of water.

"I hear you." Montana clapped V. Jay-Jay on the back between

101

her shoulder blades. "But if it does drop, I think V. Jay-Jay here can hook you up with a special workout regimen to get everything right as rain."

Linda waved a hand. "Who needs a womb, anyway? I dropped mine someplace between Broadway and 7th Avenue in New York City, and I've never missed it for a second."

"You mean it fell out?"

Linda shrugged. "Mostly."

"Gross." Montana stared at her. "That's gross."

"It was right in front of H&M. 'Gross' is a relative term."

Barb ran a hand over her face. She already had a headache and this exchange wasn't helping.

"What's the matter with you?" Montana asked. "You look kind of—puny."

"I'm fine." Barb noticed that V. Jay-Jay was looking at her curiously, too. "Just didn't sleep well last night."

"You probably ate too much of that aspic."

"Yeah." Linda refilled her glass. The straw-colored sauvignon blanc was one of her favorites. She called it her breakfast wine. "Can't you use your connection to the owners of this joint to get that shit off the menu?"

Barb sighed. Again. "I don't mind it."

"That's gross." Montana looked at Linda. "Isn't that gross?"

Linda shook her head. "Do yourself a favor, kid. Get a thesaurus."

"What's that crack supposed to mean?"

"It means you've used the word 'gross' four times in the last two minutes." Kate stood up and collected her notebooks and pens.

"So?" Montana looked offended.

"So," Linda replied. "I think you're spending too much time with Quinn on that damn boat."

"What does that have to do with anything?"

"My point, precisely."

"You know, it wouldn't hurt you to spend a little more time on the water."

Linda drained her glass with a flourish. "I have all the liquid I need right here."

"Ladies, really?" Barb regarded them all. "I'm beginning to think that putting you four together was a bad idea."

"I've never worked well in groups." V. Jay-Jay stood up. "Are you leaving?" she asked Kate.

Kate nodded.

"I'll walk out with you."

"Wait a minute." Barb held up a hand to stop them. "We need to make some progress here."

Linda looked at her watch. "It's time for a break, anyway. We've been at this for nearly two hours now."

Two hours? Barb sighed and stared at the scribbling on the marker board.

This whole thing was starting to unravel. Mavis was still refusing to participate, and she wasn't making any progress on her own essay, either. And now these damn Outliners were approaching the whole exercise like they were being asked to redraft the Magna Carta.

She wondered if she could get the show to work with eleven sculptures instead of thirteen?

It could work. Eleven and thirteen were both prime numbers.

Barb liked prime numbers. To her, prime numbers made sense. Prime numbers imitated life. A prime number was perfect because it couldn't be divided by anything but one.

Or itself.

This year, she'd turn fifty-nine.

Perfect.

"What are you smiling about?"

Barb looked at Linda with a guilty expression. "It's nothing." She addressed the group. "Linda's right. Let's take a break."

―◆◆◆―

Setting up a split mojo-Carolina rig was a bitch.

Junior was teaching her how to tie her own lures and sinkers, and Quinn found the work to be dull and tedious. It reminded her of vacation Bible school, when old Mrs. Firth made her weave calico-colored hot pads on one of those tiny metal looms. Quinn didn't care much for Bible school and she really didn't give a shit about hot pads. The endless stories about Jesus were too ridiculous to take seriously, and nobody at her house cooked enough to need protection. Not from the stove, anyway.

But these lures were something else. Putting one together wasn't at all like rebuilding an engine. The tools were too small. The pieces were too delicate. And her fingers were too fat and clumsy to handle the tiny steel beads and spinners with any kind of dexterity. In fact, the whole process was sort of like making jewelry.

No. Not sort of like making jewelry—*exactly* like making jewelry. Junior said color was important. So was movement. He explained that the lures needed to float just above the bottom of the lake, which meant the sinkers would drag along beneath them as you slowly pulled in the line. The jerky motions and the flashes of bright color from the day-glow lures were supposed to attract the fish. As smart as these fish were reputed to be, Quinn doubted that they would fall for such an obvious ploy. But she really had no idea what alternative approach would work better. The whole process was like one giant science experiment.

Driving the boat was an experiment, too, but at least she was getting the hang of it. And it was a lot of fun on days like today when the lake was calm. She liked calm. Calm meant she could concentrate on other things and not have to worry so much about the parts of this enterprise that usually landed her in hot water.

Like mooring the boat.

It wasn't her fault that when she came in last night, the dock at the inn was like a Walmart parking lot on the day after Christmas. Page Archer really had no right to speak to her that way. She was a paying guest, after all—and so what if she came in a little hot?

Well. Maybe more than a *little* hot. But hitting the throttle had been an accident. She'd been too preoccupied watching Montana squatting and bending over to ready the deck lines. Quinn didn't realize that she was leaning on the throttle as she strained forward to get a better view.

Montana had great legs.

And great lungs, as it turned out. If Montana hadn't started screaming at her, they'd surely have taken out that big sailboat. Why didn't anybody give her any credit for managing to miss that? It wasn't fair.

But today was different. Today was like a fresh start. Today she was going to practice casting from the boat with her new lures—without an audience. So she was out here alone, slowly drifting along the back of Knight Island. She had another agenda, too. She was hoping for a second look at the great fish.

Phoebe.

Quinn knew she was out here. She could feel it. Even though Junior told her they'd probably never see her again in the same place.

Phoebe liked to move around. Quinn understood that. She didn't much care for staying in the same place either. She'd been in Batavia for five years now, and she was starting to get restless. Her Harley franchise was doing great and she was making tons of money. But it wasn't enough. Something was still missing. She didn't have any roots there, and it wasn't looking like she was going to be putting any down. She guessed that after she got Junior's bike squared away she'd think about selling out to those Chicago guys and heading further west. Maybe Minnesota? Or Montana.

She wondered if Montana would help her scout out a new place to set up shop? All that wide-open space would be like heaven for Harley riders. *Heaven.* That's what she called all her shops. Maybe one day, she'd find it.

Damn. The knot on this thing was still not right. She'd retied it six or seven times now, and the line was so crimped that she was going to have to give up and cut it off.

She looked down at the discarded pieces of fishing line that were piled up around her feet. They looked like broken strands of vermicelli.

That made her hungry. But it was only ten-thirty, and if she ate her lunch now, the rest of the afternoon would drag. Still. She glanced over at the cooler. Those thick bologna sandwiches would taste great. Quinn hadn't had bologna sandwiches since she was a kid—but when she snuck into the kitchen last night to scare up something for her lunch today, Gwen was in there making herself one. Quinn hadn't seen much of her since they'd arrived, and that disappointed her. They'd had some fun together in California.

"Why are you up so late?" Quinn asked her.

She thought about their one-night stand in San Diego last year. Gwen was an early riser. Or it could just have been that Gwen wanted to leave Quinn's hotel room before anyone else would be up to see her make the walk of shame back to her own floor.

"I couldn't sleep because I had the munchies," Gwen explained. "There aren't many options back here, but I found this big ring of sandwich meat in the walk-in cooler."

"What is it?"

Gwen hacked off another big slice. "It's Lebanon Bologna." She handed a piece of it to Quinn. "Oddly, it's Canadian. Really pretty good."

Quinn took it from her and sniffed it. "I don't really like lunch meat."

"This isn't like any Oscar Mayer stuff you've ever had. Try it."

Quinn took a small bite. It was good. Beefy. It tasted like mild salami. She looked it over. "What are all these little white flecks in it?"

"It's best not to ask."

Quinn ate the rest of it. "Why did you say it's 'oddly' Canadian?"

Gwen was now piling several rings of the mystery meat atop a thick slice of bread. "Because it's a Pennsylvania thing. Amish, I think."

"Amish? They live in Canada?"

"Who knows?" Gwen finished making her sandwich. "They keep moving further and further away to find cheaper land, so it wouldn't surprise me."

Quinn didn't have any trouble understanding that one. She pretty much wanted to avoid civilization, too. But only in places where she could still get Harley parts.

Gwen held up the sandwich. "Do you want one?"

Quinn nodded. "I came in here to make something for my lunch tomorrow."

"Are you going fishing again?"

Quinn nodded.

Gwen began making the sandwich.

"Can I have two?" Quinn asked.

"Sure. There's also some liverwurst back there, if you'd rather have that."

Quinn looked over her shoulder at the walk-in cooler. "No. I hate that stuff."

Gwen chuckled. "Bologna, it is. Mustard?"

Quinn nodded.

"Brown or yellow?"

Quinn thought about it. "One of each?"

Gwen smiled. "That can happen."

Quinn watched her assemble the two sandwiches. She noticed that Gwen had a large glass of wine sitting on the cutting board beside her plate. "Where'd you get the drink?"

"My room. I brought some of my own. Do you want some? I can get you a glass."

"No. It's okay. I was hoping I could score a couple of those Backcast ales to take out with me tomorrow."

"You're on your own with that one." Gwen smiled at her. "I could, however, point you in the direction of some aspic."

"No thanks. That stuff tastes like shit."

"You won't get any argument from me."

Quinn got an idea. "Where is it?"

"In a huge vat in the cooler, right next to the salad stuff. Why?"

"I might take a little bit of it with me tomorrow."

"Why? You think it might taste better out on the water?"

"You never know." Quinn looked around for a container. "Anything I can put it in?"

Gwen handed her a Ziploc bag. "How about one of these?"

"Perfect."

Gwen wrapped up the two sandwiches while Quinn retrieved the bowl of aspic. She handed Quinn a spoon so she could scoop some out to fill her plastic bag. "You know, the food at this place is really first rate. I don't understand their fascination with this nasty stuff."

"I guess somebody here really likes it. Maybe it's some kind of local thing?"

"I doubt that." Gwen took a sip of her wine. "What are you going to do with it?"

"I want to try an experiment."

"On the water?"

Quinn nodded.

"What kind of experiment? You want to see if it floats or eats bacteria?"

"Maybe."

"Talk about your red tides."

Quinn grinned at her. She thought Gwen looked pretty good in the soft, low light. It was mostly dark in the big kitchen. Gwen hadn't turned on the overhead fluorescents—probably so she could avoid detection. Nobody wanted to get on the wrong side of Page Archer. Quinn knew that firsthand.

She decided to take a chance.

"Are you going back to bed?"

Gwen studied her for a moment before answering. Quinn thought she was weighing her options.

"No," she finally said. "I think I'll take another swing at my essay."

Quinn tried to hide her disappointment. "I thought you were finished with that?"

"I did, too. But now I think I want to rewrite some parts of it."

"Why? Have you changed your mind?"

Gwen nodded. "About a lot of things."

Quinn wasn't known for being quick on the uptake, but she was smart enough to realize that they were talking about something else.

"Going in another direction, now?" she asked.

"Trying to. I think it works out better for me when I make different choices."

Quinn looked down at her bundle of sandwiches. Gwen had wrapped them up in white butcher paper with tight, sharp creases. The package resembled a freshly made bed, complete with hospital corners. It looked tidy and complete. It looked finished.

And it didn't look like anything associated with Quinn.

"So, I guess we're done here?" She tried not to sound too pathetic.

"With that part, yes. But not with our friendship."

"We have a friendship?"

"I'd like to think so."

Quinn didn't know how to reply to that, so she decided to tell the truth.

"I don't really know what that means."

Gwen gave her a small smile. "I know you don't. But maybe your time up here will help you figure it out."

"You think that can happen?"

"Yes. I do."

"You don't think what I'm doing is crazy?"

"The fishing?"

Quinn nodded.

"No. I think it makes perfect sense."

"I wish it made perfect sense to me."

"Just keep doing what you're doing, Quinn. Just keep trying. That's the best any of us can do. Sooner or later, it will all come together." Gwen picked up her sandwich and her glass of wine. "Now, I've got a date with my laptop."

"Okay. I guess I'd better get going, too." Quinn backed away and headed toward the swinging doors that led to the restaurant.

"Quinn?"

She stopped and looked back at Gwen.

"I meant what I said about us being friends. You be careful out on that boat."

Gwen sounded like she meant it.

Thinking back over their conversation, Quinn thought it should've left her feeling frustrated and empty—like rejection always did. But instead, she felt fine. Better than fine, really. In fact, she felt almost hopeful.

And tired.

She'd been out here for nearly two hours now, and had yet to cast a single line.

She looked out over the swells of gently rolling waves that surrounded the pontoon. Being on the lake today was like floating on

109

a sea of blue cornflowers. Shadows in the water moved and shifted in endless patterns on the soft summer air, just like tall weeds in the meadows of her childhood. It was perfect.

Or *would* be perfect if she could just figure out how to tie these damn knots.

Screw it. I'll just use one of Junior's.

Quinn attached one of the small, perfect lures to her line.

She lifted her rod and repeated Montana's monotonous mantra. "Ten. Two. Cast."

The line sailed out over the water in a perfect, textbook arc. It floated away on a stray current of air and slowly unfurled into one long, glorious, seamless straight line that hovered along the surface of the water before gently touching down without even making a splash.

Quinn gaped at the rod in her hands.

How the hell did that happen?

Then she felt it. An unmistakable tug on the line. She held her breath and waited. Sure enough, there was another tug. More determined this time. Her heart rate accelerated. She took a firmer hold on the rod and tried to remember what Junior told her. Then the reel started spinning and the rod was nearly yanked from her hands.

Jesus Christ! Hang on a minute.

She yanked the rod hard—up and back over her head.

Set the hook. I have to set the hook. Then I let it run to wear it down.

Quinn stumbled forward on the deck as she struggled to hang on.

My god.

The thing was flying now. She needed to stop it. She needed to start reeling it in. She needed to take control.

"God damn it! Just slow the fuck down, will ya?"

She yanked and reeled and yanked and reeled.

How had so much line gone out?

Her pole was bent at an impossible angle. She dropped its tip closer to the surface of the water and kept winding up her line—praying it wouldn't break before she could haul in her catch.

Her catch. Her very *first* catch.

And nobody was here to see it.

Montana would never believe her. Not if she couldn't bring the fish in to show her.

It was closer now. She could see something splashing in the water dead ahead. It looked big. It felt big, too. The line was straining. It was getting harder to wind the reel. She didn't think it would hold. Not much longer. Not when something was fighting this hard to be free.

The net. Where was the net?

She grabbed for it with her right hand and nearly lost the pole. *Jesus fricking Christ!*

Now the fish was at the side of the boat. She could see it just below the surface of the water—writhing and thrashing. It was huge. And it was mad as hell.

It looked up at her with murderous eyes.

Phoebe.

Oh my fucking god. It's Phoebe.

Quinn dropped to her knees and pushed the net into the water, reaching down as far as she could to try and get it beneath the leviathan fish. She closed her eyes and tried not to think about Junior's mangled finger.

But something had changed. The line was suddenly slack. Phoebe had stopped fighting.

Quinn opened her eyes, expecting to see that the line had broken and the great fish had once again bested her would-be captor.

But Phoebe was still there, sitting almost placidly inside the net and staring up at her.

"Well," her gaze seemed to say. "What are you waiting for?"

Quinn dropped the rod and took hold of the net with both hands. *Jesus. She was a monster.*

She pulled her up into the boat and stumbled backward, landing on her ass. The two of them sat there in a pool of sweat and water staring at each other.

Now what?

"Are you going to quit gawking at me and get me into that cooler of water before I prune?"

Quinn blinked. Did Phoebe just speak to her?

111

"Is something wrong with your hearing?" Phoebe twitched and hit Quinn in the face with a splash of water from the puddle she lay in. "Hurry the hell up. Time is money."

Quinn scrambled to her feet and grabbed hold of the five-day cooler that served as her live well. She hauled it over to where Phoebe lay, twitching on the wet carpet.

"How do I get you in here?" she asked the giant fish.

"How do you think, Einstein? Just pick my ass up and drop me in there."

Quinn hesitated.

"That would mean *now*," Phoebe demanded.

Quinn obeyed. Phoebe sank to the bottom of the big cooler and waited. Quinn quickly turned on the makeshift aerator and oxygen began pumping into the cold water. After a minute, Phoebe drifted back up to the surface and faced Quinn again.

"So. What did you want to talk with me about?"

"What?"

Phoebe rolled her dark eyes. "Why are you so hell-bent on catching me?"

Quinn's head was swimming. "How can you be talking to me?"

"I have an I.Q. in the triple digits—which is more than I can say for most of your ilk."

"My what?"

"Your *ilk*. It means . . . never mind what it means." Phoebe tossed her head toward the smaller, red Igloo cooler that contained Quinn's lunch. "Go get us something to eat. That wrestling match wore my ass out."

"You're hungry?"

"You were the smartest one in your class, weren't you?"

"Hey. You don't have to be so nasty."

"Fuck you. I'm two hundred years old. You think I give a shit about your feelings?"

"Jeez. Alright already." Quinn retrieved the cooler. "Do you like Amish bologna?"

Phoebe stared at her. "I don't even know how to reply to a stupid question like that. You got any clam strips in there?"

Quinn looked before answering. After all, she was sitting here having a conversation with a giant bass—so the sudden appearance of clam strips in her lunch box wouldn't be any more incredible.

But, alas, there were no fried anythings.

"Nope. Just the bologna." She remembered the Ziploc bag full of gelatinous muck, and lifted it up. "And some of this stuff."

Phoebe's eyes narrowed. "What the hell is that?"

Quinn jiggled the bag. "Some kind of aspic."

"Aspic? Tomato aspic?"

"Yeah."

"Fork it over."

Quinn looked at her. "Are you serious?"

"Do I not look serious?"

"No. You look like a bigmouth bass."

"That's *largemouth* bass, nimrod. Now, gimme the damn aspic. I haven't eaten since I left Baie Missisquoi this morning."

Quinn blinked.

"It's in Canada. You know? Where they make Amish bologna?"

"You know about Canadian bologna?"

"I know about everything."

Quinn bent over the live well and carefully squeezed some of the aspic out of the plastic bag. It hit the surface of the churning water in a flat, gooey glop. Phoebe ducked her head and sucked it up with greater efficiency than a Shop Vac. When she finished she eyed the bag.

"Any more in there?"

Quinn was surprised. "You like it?"

"Of course. Why wouldn't I?"

"I don't know." Quinn shrugged. "I think it's kinda gross."

"Gross? You ever eat a night crawler?"

"No."

"I rest my case."

Quinn gave her the rest of the aspic. Phoebe dispatched it with ease.

"I can't wait to tell Junior that you like this crap." She looked at her box of fishing tackle. "But I don't know how I'll ever get it to stick to the end of a hook."

"Well look at it this way: you won't have to worry about tying flies any more."

"I guess that's true." She looked at Phoebe. "Do all bass like this stuff?"

"How should I know?"

"I thought you said you knew everything?"

Phoebe twitched her tail. "Don't play twenty questions with me, asshole. You'll lose."

Quinn sat down and pulled a bottle of beer out of her lunch box. "Want some of this?"

"No. That stuff gives me gas."

"Junior said you liked hooch."

"I've been known to indulge in a bit of rye now and then, but beer just makes me stupid."

"Stupid?" Quinn cracked open the bottle.

"Yeah. The last time I drank it I ended up getting hooked by some assholes from Jersey."

"I thought you'd never been caught before?"

"Before what?"

"Before now."

Phoebe tsked. "I've never been caught *period*. Including now."

Quinn took a big swig of the beer. It was fine. Frothy and ice cold. Just the way she liked it. "Well," she said, "I think you might need to rethink that. I mean, I'm here and you're there."

"What's that supposed to mean?"

"It means that you look pretty 'caught' to me."

Phoebe looked up at the sky and shook her head. "Zero to stupid in one swallow."

"Hey."

"Let me explain something to you, Einstein. You didn't *catch* me. I saw you the other day and realized that you'd never give up this ridiculous quest until I explained a few things to you."

Quinn blinked. "You wanted to talk to me about the tournament?"

"No. I wanted to give you fashion advice."

Quinn sighed.

"You need to lighten up, Einstein. And you need to quit wearing those dog collars during sex. You're seriously cutting off the flow of blood to your brain."

"How do you know about that?"

"It's not rocket science. You BDSM authors are all alike. Every one of you is stalled-out someplace in stage two. It's textbook Freud."

"Stage two?"

"Don't ask. Eat your sandwiches."

Quinn unwrapped one and took a big bite. This one had the brown mustard. It tasted sharp and tangy. That made her think about Gwen. She tasted sharp and tangy, too. Quinn was sorry that Gwen didn't want to rekindle their relationship.

"It wasn't a relationship."

Quinn looked at Phoebe with surprise.

"You and Gwen at that hotel in San Diego?" Phoebe explained. "That wasn't a relationship."

"How do you know about that?"

"Please . . ."

Quinn sighed and looked down at the soggy carpet beneath her legs. Her pants were completely soaked. It would take hours for them to dry out. She really needed something else to wear on the boat, but she'd only packed black jeans. That was because she pretty much only wore black jeans. Ever.

"Gwen's a good woman," Phoebe explained. "But she drinks too much, and that clouds her judgment."

"What does that have to do with me?"

"Nothing. That's the point."

"I don't understand."

"I know you don't. And you never will until you figure out that you can't control everything."

"I don't try to control everything."

Phoebe sighed. "Let's try another approach. When was the last time you had sex without tying somebody up?"

"Um."

"Or simulating some other kind of violence or force?"

115

Quinn didn't reply.

"Or making yourself vulnerable?"

"I don't see what this has to do with fishing."

"It has everything to do with fishing because it has everything to do with why you want to catch me."

"I don't get it."

"That's because 'catch' and 'release' are concepts that elude you—in every part of your life."

Quinn didn't say anything. She honestly had no idea where Phoebe was going with all of this.

"You never let go of anything, Quinn. And you don't understand that things don't happen *to* you—they just happen. There is no grand design or plan that dictates the way your life evolves. There's no big reveal waiting for you around the next corner, no matter how fast or far you go on that hopped-up Harley of yours. Life is just what it is. Right now. In this moment. And if you're lucky, you get the next moment after this one. That's it. That's all there is. Things don't have meaning. Things are just things. Shit happens. We get over it and we move on. We don't keep making more of it and smearing it all over everything in our paths because it's the only thing we know. Once you understand that, you can relax and stop equating feeling with pain. And then you can learn how to let go."

Quinn put down her sandwich. She didn't feel hungry anymore.

"So that's it?" she asked Phoebe. "I want to catch you so I can let you go?"

"Pretty much."

"Am I supposed to know what the hell you're talking about?"

"You tell me."

Quinn shook her head.

It was Phoebe's turn to sigh. "Okay. That's all I got. Nobody can say I didn't try." She flipped her tail. "Toss me back in. I've been up here too long and I've got to be in St. Albans by twelve-thirty."

"You're leaving?"

"And they said you weren't trainable."

Quinn got to her knees. "Do I pick you up or use the net?"

116

"Just pick me up—but don't get any ideas and try to cop a feel."

Quinn thought about that. An idea occurred to her. "Are you married?"

"Married? You mean, like to another fish?"

"Yeah."

"Hardly."

"Why not?"

"Have you ever seen a male bass?"

"Only in books."

"Yeah, well, they look a lot worse close up."

Quinn carefully lifted her up and carried her over to the side of the pontoon. "What about the females?" she asked.

"What about them?"

"Do you like them?"

"We're in Vermont. What do you think?"

Before Quinn could reply, Phoebe flipped out of her hands and dove back into the lake.

"Wait!" Quinn called after her, but it was too late. Phoebe was gone.

Quinn strained to see her beneath the surface of the water, but she'd already disappeared from sight. There wasn't even a wake to show where she'd been.

Something hit her in the face.

Then it happened again. Harder this time.

She blinked her eyes open. Rain. It was raining. Hard. She could hear thunder rolling in the distance.

When the hell did that happen?

She looked down at her clothes. They were soaked. So was her partially eaten sandwich. Three empty Backcast bottles were lined up in a tidy row next to her red Igloo.

She slowly sat up and looked over toward the live well. It was empty.

And the aerator wasn't connected.

Jesus. I fell asleep. She rubbed her eyes. *What a crazy-ass dream.*

Thunder rolled again. It sounded closer this time. She needed to get off the water.

It wasn't until she picked up her lunch box and the half-eaten sandwich that she noticed the empty Ziploc bag.

She stared down at it for a moment before looking out over the slate-gray water, which now was rolling like thick soup in a cauldron.

No fucking way . . .

Essay 4

"The question has been asked, 'What is a woman?' A woman is a person who makes choices. A woman is a dreamer. A woman is a planner. A woman is a maker, and a molder. A woman is a person who makes choices. A woman builds bridges. A woman makes children and makes cars. A woman writes poetry and songs. A woman is a person who makes choices." —*Eleanor Holmes Norton*

A woman is a person who makes choices.

I learned that when I was ten. Maybe eleven. Certainly, I was ten or eleven, because we were living in upstate Pennsylvania. Our house was located on the outskirts of a small town on the Allegheny River. It was a sprawling, once-dignified area that had seen vast fortunes made and lost a century earlier during the Western Pennsylvania oil boom. Since those days, life on the river was anything but refined—and most of the town's residents led unremarkable lives. They lived, worked, and died in the long shadows cast by faded reminders of a better time. All around us, wide avenues and empty mansions hinted at how rich and storied life used to be. How elegant and full of promise.

But we knew better. We lived lives without promise.

At least, I did.

My father wasn't a cruel man. Not really. He was

ordinary—at least, he was ordinary in all the ways that passed for ordinary in those days. He quit school at fifteen to get a job. He enlisted in the U.S. Marine Corps and served in the Pacific Theater during the latter years of World War II. He came back to Pennsylvania after his tour of duty and got a job on the railroad. And one day, he gave an orange to a pretty young woman.

A woman is a person who makes choices.

The woman who became my mother wasn't ordinary. Not in the ways other girls were. She was smart and ambitious. She excelled in things like music and Latin. She wasn't ordinary because she dared to imagine a life that was different than what she had been led by experience to expect. She had promise.

But one day, when she was sixteen years old, a good-looking man with a blinding white smile gave her an orange.

A woman is a person who makes choices.

Our house was small, but it seemed huge to me. It had three bedrooms. My two brothers shared one, and I shared another with my older sister. Looking back, it seems strange to me that I never noticed that none of the rooms in that house had doors. I didn't realize then that the absence of doors was a curious metaphor for the absence of boundaries. We moved in and out of each other's physical and emotional spaces with thoughtless ease and frightful intent.

My father worked hard. In the late afternoons, when his shift at the printing plant ended, he cut grass and pruned shrubs around some of the old oil mansions that graced the Market Street historic district. In the winter months when there was no landscaping to do, he worked nights cleaning a bakery. He prided himself on keeping our massive, back-porch freezer stocked to the gills with beef and making sure that we all had new clothes for school every September. Those were the parameters that defined fatherhood for him—food and clothing. When he had met those two obligations, he gave himself permission to indulge his own passions for alcohol and philandering.

My siblings and I were silent witnesses to the brutal excesses of our parent's marriage. We sensed, rather than observed, our mother's desperate unhappiness. She never showed that face to us—but we saw glimmers of it in the fresh bruises that were sometimes visible in the mornings after their late-night shouting matches.

A woman is a person who makes choices.

At age ten—or eleven—I was unaware that choosing was an option. I only knew that I would forever be tasked with accepting whatever set of circumstances ended up befalling me. That was the way we defined "normal." That was the way we understood our lives. At least, that was the way I understood *my* life.

I never told my parents about the repeated incidents of sexual abuse that were slowly making me old before my time. I never told anyone. I silently accepted it as part of who I was—and part of what I could expect my life to contain. In retrospect, it didn't seem different or unique to me at all—it seemed consistent with the rest of my life experience. And without knowing why, I understood the silent compact I kept. I embraced the secrecy, and I didn't look beyond the twisted, achingly familiar landscape of my life. There was no promise of a better life. There was only what *was*—and what *was* promised to extend into a future that was as bleak as a Western Pennsylvania winter.

A woman is a person who makes choices.

The stairway from the second story of our house came down into the kitchen. I remember that the kitchen was the biggest room in our small house. My mother filled it with wonderful sights and smells. At any time, the countertops would be lined with baked goods—all made by her. Breads, rolls, cakes—even doughnuts—would magically emerge from an old, indifferent oven that never maintained a constant temperature. The chrome-legged table would be piled high with craft projects that she had undertaken for my sister's Girl Scout troop, or my brother's Cub Scout pack—or for any of our various Sunday school classes. When we couldn't afford new drapes, my mother bought packs of crayons and we all sat together around the kitchen table and colored in the geometric shapes on the old ones. Then she heat-set the waxy blotches of new color with her ancient iron, and re-hung them. We would spend hours with her at that table, wrestling with multiplication tables, reading works like *Robinson Crusoe* from our prized set of "Illustrated Classics," or pasting page after page of S&H Green Stamps into fat books that could later be redeemed for things like Coleman camping lanterns or electric frying pans. The most prized and least confounding hours of our lives were spent with her, in that big kitchen.

One dark winter morning, I went downstairs before the others. The porch light was on, and through the kitchen door, I could see the piles of snow my father had created when he shoveled his way out of the house to leave for work. Across the room, I could see my mother, quietly standing in front of the far counter. She was packing lunches—four of them. I stood on the bottom step and gazed at her. The chipped linoleum floor tiles stretched out between us like milestones. In that instant, she seemed to be a hundred, even a thousand miles away from me. I watched her as she worked, arranging four thick slices of homemade bread in a row and topping each with fat rounds of bologna. I watched her.

Then I saw her.

I saw her, not as a victim, but as a woman who chose the life she had. I saw her as a woman who surrendered the promise of her youth to a hapless indiscretion, but discovered the courage and the resourcefulness to tap into a depth of character that sustained her throughout the indignities of a brutal and unequal marriage.

And I saw her as a woman who had made choices that would never be *my* choices.

I stood frozen in place, and I knew with certainty that I would never stand at a counter in a dark winter kitchen, packing four lunches for children I had made with a man I no longer loved. I knew that I would never live the life my mother lived, because I would never choose it. And in that moment, I understood for the first time that I was a woman—and that I was a woman who could make *choices*.

Standing on the bottom step that day, separated from my mother by age and experience, but united with her by blood and love—I chose. I chose to stop being a victim. I chose to embrace a life that contained promise. I chose to believe that if I could be true to myself, I would have the strength to survive the worst that life could throw at me. And I chose to accept and understand the reality that I would never share my life with a man.

A woman is a person who makes choices.

My mother chose, and she lived with her choices. I chose, and I live with mine.

5

First Blood

Kate was crying again.

That had been happening a lot since they got up here. But she always managed to wait until Shawn was out of earshot. She knew this hyper-emotionalism wasn't entirely her fault. Part of it was the damn group dynamic that hovered over this retreat like a dense cloud. It was widely known that women acted strange when they all got together like this. They tended to be more excitable and more likely to experience dramatic shifts in mood. Men made snide comments about these phenomena all the time—and that fact never failed to piss her off.

Probably because they were right.

Hell. By now, they probably were all "cycling" together.

Allie, Shawn's retriever, got up from the rug in front of the door and walked over to stand beside her. When Kate didn't respond, Allie nudged her arm.

"Sorry, girl. I'm okay." She patted Allie's broad head and wiped at her eyes with the sleeve of her sweatshirt. The garment was about two sizes too big for her and the rolled cuffs at the ends of the arms flopped over her hands. It was dark green. "North Carolina," two-inch white letters proclaimed. "I love it here."

She knew she was being ridiculous. But part of that was simply because she was a loner who didn't like being around other people all that much.

It was a paradox. When Sophie, Kate's partner of ten years, announced that she was leaving her to move in with a woman half her age, she felt oddly relieved. They argued all the time, too—but their disagreements were nothing like the verbal jousting matches she was now having with Shawn. Kate and Shawn struggled with each other because they wanted to be together and couldn't—not because they were stuck with each other and couldn't find an escape route. It took Kate six months in therapy to realize that Sophie's affair was a gift. They'd both been pretty miserable for some time.

And her time with Shawn was just—different. Shawn made Kate laugh—and that wasn't an easy thing to do. Life was good when they were together. It was full of great smells and wonderful sounds. They both liked to cook. And while they chopped things and banged pots and pans around, they listened to scratchy old recordings by sharp-tongued crooners like Mildred Bailey and Dinah Washington.

Kate sniffed and swabbed at her eyes again. She looked at the door for about the twelfth time. She wanted to go after Shawn, but she knew she wouldn't. She wasn't made that way. It would be too much like admitting she'd made a mistake, and that wasn't something she ever did. When Sophie walked out on her, it broke something inside her. It was like the conduit that connected her head and her heart got severed, and all the little livewires that ran along inside it carrying messages and impulses back and forth just fell silent. She was like a cell phone without a signal—always trying to connect, but never quite succeeding.

Intellectually, she knew she just needed to quit roaming. She was never going to find anyone even remotely as perfect for her as Shawn. Everyone could tell they were right for each other—even the crazy man with the lisp and the bad comb-over who shouted rude things at them when they walked the dogs in Piedmont Park. He knew it. He had a half-bald Schnauzer he kept on a bright pink leash, and he'd snatch her back away from them when they passed by—almost like he thought they might try to steal her for use in some satanic ritual. All the while, he'd sputter and snarl at them about how they were a threat to the American family.

His long-suffering dog would groan at the sudden pressure on her scrawny neck and look at them all with milky eyes that were full of regret.

"He's nuts," her gaze would say. "I'd change places with any of you in a nanosecond."

Well, the crazy man was right about one thing: when they were all together, they *were* a family. Kate understood that part, and the power of it terrified her. And it wasn't too long after the crazy man started yelling his insults at them that she began to draw up inside herself. She could sense it happening. It was like moving through a house at dusk, closing all the shutters ahead of the advancing night. Only in her case, the darkness was all on the inside, and it was the light she was shutting out.

That was when she decided to take the New York job. And even though she cried almost every night, the shutters stayed closed so she wouldn't have to worry about too much light sneaking in and complicating everything. Slowly, she got used to her dark, internal world. She moved through it like a blind mouse in a cage. Everything was safe and familiar, and she didn't have to worry about unseen obstacles.

Shawn and Allie were obstacles. *Big ones.* At least they were to Kate. She tripped over them like they were stealth pieces of furniture that someone had moved in during the middle of the night, just to trick her.

Allie gave up on trying to console Kate and reclaimed her spot on the braided rug beneath the window. Even though the curtains were drawn, the breeze drifting in off the water was pushing them around enough to allow a few bands of moonlight to spread out along the floor. Allie liked the light.

Truth be told, Patrick was beginning to like life in the light as well. Kate was the only holdout.

Patrick got to his feet and ambled over to where the leashes were hanging on a peg behind the door. He gave them a good nudge with his nose, causing them to sway and rattle against the door glass like wind chimes.

Kate looked over at him.

"Oh. Do you need to go outside?"

He woofed and performed the little dance that always telegraphed his need to pee.

Allie was already on her feet.

Kate blew her nose on a soggy-looking tissue.

"Okay. Let's go see if we can find Mommy."

———

Cut bait.

That's what Shawn heard Viv tell Quinn over and over. "Cut bait and give up on this insane idea."

Insanity. Insanity was doing the same thing over and over and expecting a different result. Isn't that what the shrinks all said?

But still, she kept trying. And, not surprisingly, the results stayed the same.

Kate was just going to be Kate. Period. No changes or substitutions. Just like that special she tried to order last night at dinner—a coffee-crusted, rib-eye steak served atop mashed sweet potatoes and finished with caramelized onions.

Shawn didn't much care for sweet potatoes, and she really didn't like onions.

"Could I get this with French fries instead of the mashed potatoes?" she asked their server. "And no onions?"

The server nervously shifted her weight from foot to foot.

"No, ma'am," she said. "We're not allowed to make substitutions."

"Why not?" Shawn thought her request seemed like a simple one.

The server shot a nervous glance at Page Archer, who was stationed like a ramrod at her post near the bar. The innkeeper's eyes swept back and forth across the dining room like a lighthouse beacon searching for trouble.

"We're just not allowed to." The server lowered her voice. "It upsets the chef."

Shawn was incredulous. "French fries upset the chef?"

The server nodded.

"I can understand that something like climate change might upset the chef—but French fries seem pretty harmless."

128

Kate cleared her throat.

"What?" Shawn looked across the table at her. "I'm just trying to understand."

"You don't *need* to understand. You need to make another selection."

"But I want a steak."

"Shawn." Kate gestured toward their antsy server, who was absently tapping her pen against her notepad. "Life is not an unending salad bar. You don't always get to pick and choose. Any chef worth their salt undergoes years of training precisely so they can combine foods and flavors in unique and creative ways that will be pleasing to even the most unrefined palates." She paused. "Or in your case, the nonexistent ones."

"Hey." Shawn bristled at Kate's insinuation.

Kate waved her off and addressed their server. "Bring her the flatiron steak, medium rare, with potato pancakes. And add a side of mustard."

"Right." The server collected their menus and hurried off.

In retrospect, Shawn had to admit that Kate knew her pretty well. Even though this diatribe of hers about substitutions was a complete red herring.

"Explain something to me." Shawn sat back and crossed her arms. "How come when I ask for an accommodation it's an endemic example of my total lack of refinement? But when *you* do it, it's an expression of reasonable expectations?"

Kate shrugged.

"Nuh uh." Shawn wagged an index finger at her. "No fair."

"No fair?"

Shawn nodded.

"What? Are we back in the third grade?"

"Maybe."

"I never was very good at those playground games."

"Yeah. I can imagine that 'play' part of playground caused you some problems."

Kate rolled her eyes.

"You know it's true."

"Shawn. Could we please just enjoy our dinner?"

As it turned out, they didn't really enjoy their dinner. Shawn was mostly silent through the duration of the meal, and by the time they got back to their room, it was clear that Kate had grown weary of trying to ignore her.

"Will you please quit sulking?"

Shawn had flopped down on one of the room's two upholstered chairs and was mindlessly tapping the keycard against her thigh.

"I am *not* sulking."

"Really?" Kate was hanging up her jacket. "What is it, then? Terminal PMS?"

Shawn continued with her tapping.

"Do you want to tell me what's really on your mind? Because I somehow doubt that this epic silent treatment has anything to do with not getting the French fries you wanted for dinner."

Shawn sighed. "I'd just like to understand why it is that you feel like you can change the subject whenever something comes up that you don't want to discuss."

Kate raised an eyebrow. "You mean like right now?"

"Very funny."

"I do try."

"Yeah? Well right now it ain't a-workin."

"Honey." Kate sat down on the edge of the bed. "You can't be too upset if you're quoting *Sordid Lives.*"

"I'm pissed, not comatose."

"Okay." Kate took a deep breath. "What do you want to talk about?"

Shawn was suspicious. "Really?"

Kate rolled her eyes. "No. Not really. This is all an elaborate ruse, artfully designed to conceal my sinister plans for world domination."

"Will you please be serious?"

"I *am* being serious. You're just determined to insist that I'm not."

Shawn kicked at one of Allie's dog toys. This one was "Henrietta," an elongated rubber chicken, tricked out with thick, blue eye shadow and a purple bikini.

It was her current favorite.

Allie was rarely seen without the toy, and had chewed it to the point that it was now sporting several prominent puncture wounds. One of them was located in the general vicinity of the groin area, and a thick wad of white stuffing was usually visible when Allie carried the thing around.

Kate nicknamed the toy "Henrietta Husky Snatch."

It made an obnoxious squeal as it tumbled across the floor, causing Allie to bolt up from her post on the rug near the door. She cast about the room like she was certain that someone had just fired off a volley of gunfire. Then she saw her beloved chicken and lunged for it, clamping it between her jaws and hauling it off to safer territory.

Kate shook her head. "That thing really creeps me out."

"I know. But she loves it."

"There's certainly no accounting for taste."

"True dat."

Kate looked at her. "So what did you want to discuss?"

Shawn glared at her. "I repeat: do you really have to ask?"

"Apparently."

Shawn waved a hand in frustration. "I just don't understand why we can't have a civilized conversation about where our relationship is headed."

"Why does it have to be 'headed' anyplace? What's wrong with where it is?"

"Because right now it's nowhere."

"Nowhere?"

Shawn nodded.

"I think that's a little bit excessive, don't you?"

"Not really."

Shawn knew that Kate was miserable right now. The impermanence of a turnpike existence, shuttling back and forth between her New York apartment, her home in Atlanta, and Shawn's house in Charlotte was loathsome to her. And she wasn't exactly passionate about her high-profile job, either. Yet whenever Shawn broached the topic of finding a more centrally located place for them to live together, Kate bristled and changed the subject.

Tonight wasn't the first time that had happened on this trip, either.

"I want to know why you have an embargo on any conversations about our future?"

"That's ridiculous."

"It's not ridiculous—it's the truth."

"Honey."

"Don't try to placate me. You need to step up and answer the question."

"We've already discussed this."

"When?" Shawn's frustration was starting to boil over. "It must have been in some alternate space-time continuum, because I sure as hell don't recall it."

"Would you please lower your voice?" Kate looked toward the door. "People are trying to sleep."

Shawn stood up. "Well bully for them. At least somebody around here is getting some rest."

"What the hell is the matter with you?"

"I'm tired of having you deflect every damn question you don't want to answer."

Kate didn't reply.

"Not saying anything is almost as bad."

It was Kate's turn to show her vexation. "What do you want from me?"

"Seriously? If you have to ask me that then I've obviously been doing a shitty job expressing myself."

"Shawn."

"No." Shawn cut her off. "I mean it, Kate. I'm tired of feeling like I have to tiptoe around your emotional land mines."

"That's ridiculous."

"The only thing that's ridiculous is that I keep beating my head against the same granite wall."

"I think that's a bit dramatic."

"You think *that's* dramatic?" Shawn walked to the door and yanked it open. "Try *this* on for size."

She meant to slam the door on her way out, but thought better of it at the last second. Kate was right: people were trying to sleep. And slamming things in anger was just too reminiscent of her mother's approach to—well. To just about everything.

Of course, the door bounced off her foot when she tried to catch it, and smacked her on the arm. Hard. She was going to have one hell of a bruise tomorrow.

She rubbed the spot as she walked along the cliffs that towered over the lake.

With my luck, Viv will notice it. She'll think Kate had me tied up in a sex swing all night.

In fact, that wasn't too far from the truth. Kate did have her tied up—in knots. And it was about time to shake loose.

There was only one problem. She loved Kate. And that complicated everything.

But she couldn't stay in this place that was neither hot nor cold. Trying to move forward in this relationship was like running a marathon in lead boots. They were going nowhere, and she was tired of feeling hopeless and morose.

She heard a soft noise off in the distance, and looked out over the water to see if a fishing boat was passing by. It wasn't uncommon for the stalwarts to be out at night. She failed to see the appeal of that. Once the light bled from the sky, the lake became a dark, rolling bastion of the unknown. At least it did for her. It was the last place she'd choose to spend any time—particularly on a boat.

She had issues with water.

She had issues with vulnerability, too. She'd never been any good at it. But all of that changed when she met Kate. Now she donned her vulnerability like a well-loved hair shirt, and seemed content to wear it everyplace.

The drumming noise grew closer. She could almost feel the vibration beneath her feet. Something slowly came into focus. It was oddly shaped. Flat and wide with a taller structure looming at its center. In the murky half-light, it resembled a parade float.

Okay. So much for tonight's Fellini moment.

The floating menagerie drew closer to the dock.

Quinn.

Make that a floating ménage à trois.

She strained her eyes to try and see if Montana and Junior were on board, too. Nope. Just Quinn.

Shawn was amazed. Quinn was really taking this tournament thing seriously. She'd never have guessed that the woman was capable of such focus and determination. It was incredible—especially in light of how slim her chances were to win. But those were the breaks, right? You got an idea, you rolled up your sleeves, you faced the obstacles, and you thumbed your nose at the naysayers. She admired Quinn.

Still. She'd never take a floating death trap out on this lake at night. No matter how big the prize was.

She heard another burst of soft, drumming sounds. But this time, the noise was coming from behind her. Before she could turn around to investigate, Patrick and Allie roared up, did a lazy loop around her, then sped off toward the dock to greet Quinn. Shawn watched them go. Their fuzzy tails flashed in the moonlight like sparklers.

"I thought I'd find you out here."

Shawn turned to see an apparition approaching. She watched Kate materialize with mixed emotions. She didn't want to resume their argument, but knowing that Kate had wandered out to find her made her feel less alone.

"I was just watching Quinn come in." She pointed toward the dock.

Kate joined her and they stood together in silence, observing the spectacle. Tonight, Quinn was taking her time. And she'd even managed to dock the boat without endangering any of the other watercraft moored out there.

"She's getting better."

Shawn looked at Kate. "They say that happens with practice."

"So I'm told."

More silence. Quinn was tying her cleat hitch lines. Patrick and Allie were still nosing around on the dock—probably hoping that Quinn had some leftover bologna sandwiches to share. Quinn's nocturnal trips to the kitchen were common knowledge.

"Do you want to talk about what happened?" Kate's tone was unreadable.

"I do if you do."

"What does that mean?"

Shawn shrugged. "It means I want to talk if you want to talk."

"I came out here to find you." Kate offered the observation like exhibit A in a trial.

Shawn shrugged again.

"Well?" Kate sounded vaguely impatient. "What do you call that?"

"I call that a good start."

Kate sighed. "I'm glad. I was afraid you'd tell me to go fly a kite."

"In the dark? No. I'd be afraid you'd fall off one of these cliffs."

"That wouldn't be good."

"No. That would be very bad."

"You'd miss me?"

"If you fell off a cliff?"

Kate nodded.

"Let me see." Shawn tapped a finger against her chin.

Kate slugged her on the arm.

"Hey!" Shawn rubbed the spot. "Would you quit doing that?"

"Don't be such a baby."

"I'm *not* a baby. You don't know your own strength."

Kate was silent for a moment. When she spoke, her voice was softer.

"I'm not."

Shawn was confused. "You're not what?"

"Strong."

Shawn was still rubbing the spot on her arm. "What are you talking about? You're one of the strongest women I've ever met."

"No, I'm not. Not in any of the ways that matter."

"Kate."

Kate held up a hand to silence her. "Don't interrupt me, please. This admission isn't easy for me."

"Okay."

"I suck at relationships, Shawn. I *suck* at them. I always have. And

135

not just at the truly important ones. I suck at them all—in any form. I don't know how to do them. I don't know how to behave when things get—serious. I don't know how to manage my vulnerability. The fear overwhelms me. It's like having my emotions dropped in the middle of an alien planet with no functioning GPS and no landmarks I recognize. I don't know where to go, and it scares the shit out of me. So I resort to the one thing I'm sure about how to do—duck and cover."

Shawn wasn't sure how to reply. Kate noticed her hesitation.

"Don't you have anything to say?"

"You don't have to hide from me."

"Yes I do. That's the whole point. You're *precisely* the one I have to hide from."

That made no sense to Shawn. "Why?"

"Because you're the one person in my life with the power to hurt me."

"I'd never hurt you, Kate." She remembered her behavior in their room a few minutes ago, and how she'd almost slammed the door on her way out. "Not on purpose, anyway."

"Sophie said the same thing."

They'd had this conversation before.

"I'm *not* Sophie."

"I know you're not Sophie. This isn't about you. It's about me."

"I don't understand."

"I know you don't. And I don't know how to make you understand."

Shawn felt like she was fumbling around in the dark. "Can we just start from scratch here?"

"What do you mean?"

"I mean can't we just agree to begin the relationship now defined as 'us' with a clean slate? No baggage and no lingering fears about all the things that might go wrong?"

Kate smiled. "Isn't it a little late for that?"

"No. Not if we don't want it to be."

"I've never been very good at inventing new realities."

"Trust me. It gets easier with practice."

"That's what you said about Quinn and fishing."

"True," Shawn agreed. "Did I mention that willing suspension of disbelief also plays a role in this practice?"

"No. I think you left that tidbit out."

"It's widely known that I self-edit a lot."

Kate shook her head.

"I really do, you know," Kate said.

"Do?" Shawn was confused. "Do what?"

"Love you."

Kate had never said that to her before. Shawn felt the happy gravitas of the simple declaration flood her senses like a rogue wave.

To whom much is given, much shall be required.

Why did the damn New Testament mantra come to her right now?

She knew she needed to say something, but all she wanted to do was dig the toe of her shoe into the dirt and try not to smile.

Kate was watching her.

"I'm sorry for not telling you sooner. I should have."

"No." Shawn reached out a hand and touched Kate's arm. "No 'should have.' No apologies. It's fine. It's right. It's here in its own time."

"Do you really believe that?"

Shawn nodded.

"Okay."

"I do, too, by the way," Shawn added. "Love you."

"I kinda figured."

"Yeah. I don't tend to hide things in my heart."

Kate smiled. "So I've noticed."

The moon had risen over a bank of clouds and was now glowing round and white above the horizon. The night landscape slowly shifted into a muted kind of focus. It was still murky and gray, but something about it seemed softer and less foreboding. Shawn could see Patrick and Allie, nosing around the flowerbeds at the north end of the inn. She got an idea.

"Do you want to go for a walk before bed?"

Kate reached for her hand.

"You can't deny that she's getting a lot better."

Mavis looked at Barb. They were sitting outside on the lawn, sharing a late-night smoke and watching Quinn dock the boat. "Honey, you don't even want to *see* the list of things I can deny."

Barb laughed. "I wasn't talking about fashion sense."

"Neither was I."

"Well, in this case, I think even you have to agree that Quinn is getting more proficient at piloting the boat."

"In the first place, I wouldn't call that contraption a *boat*." Mavis blew out a long plume of smoke. "In the second place, they say that a monkey could write *War and Peace* if it sat in front of a typewriter for long enough."

Barb chuckled. "Oh, yeah? I wonder if we could enlist a few to replace the Outliners?"

"You never know. I bet they'd nail the sex scenes."

"There aren't any sex scenes. They're writing essays, not fiction."

Mavis scoffed. "Tell that to Viv."

Barb was alarmed. "What do you mean? You read Viv's essay?"

"She showed me a draft of it yesterday."

"And?"

"Let's just say that woman must be quintuple-jointed."

"Oh, Jesus." Barb slumped down in her chair. "I made it clear that these pieces were supposed to recount real life experiences."

"What makes you think hers doesn't?"

Barb thought about it. "Good point."

"She's a freak. Just like the rest of this crew."

Barb ground out her cigarette and reached for the pack that sat on the wide arm of the chair. "I'd argue with you, but it would be a waste of effort. Especially since it would be a classic example of the pot calling the kettle black."

Mavis looked at her. "You think you're a freak?"

"You don't?"

Mavis shrugged. "I'd say misfit is a better term."

"I think the universe must share your assessment."

"What's that supposed to mean?"

"You do the math. I've never really fit. And soon, I won't fit in a big way."

"Why do you keep saying shit like that?"

"Mavis?" Barb lit up her fresh smoke. "One of the things I like about you is that I never have to worry about you driving me across hell's half-acre to try and make me feel better. Do me a favor and don't start now."

Mavis didn't reply. They smoked in silence for a minute.

"Don't you have anything to say?" Barb asked her.

"No, ma'am."

"Why not?"

"Cause it sounds like my job is just to drive the bus."

Barb rolled her eyes. "Great. So now you're Rosa Parks?"

"White woman? Rosa Parks didn't *drive* the bus. What do they teach you people in those fancy colleges?"

"Fancy colleges? I went to Chico. It was hardly a charm school."

"Yeah? Well lucky for you, misinformation ain't tied to tuition."

"You know, you're wasting your time as a bailiff."

"Now *there's* a news flash. Why don't you get your buddy Barbara Walters on the horn?"

Barb was confused. "You think she could help you?"

"*No.*" Mavis shook her head. "It's just what you people do whenever you trip over something you don't like. Alert the media."

Barb sighed. "You are one pissed-off woman."

"Watch it."

"You know what I mean."

Quinn had finished docking the boat and was slowly making her way across the lawn toward the inn. Her long shadow lurched along ahead of her like it was racing her back to her room. From their vantage point, it looked like the shadow was winning. Barb thought that was a sad omen. Quinn would always be one step behind.

"She's a lonely figure."

"What are you talking about?"

Barb pointed at the dark shape, which appeared to have changed direction and was now headed toward the restaurant. "Quinn. She's like our resident Don Quixote."

"If you mean crazy, I agree."

"No." Barb shook her head. "Not crazy. Delusional, maybe? But where would we all be without our dreamers?"

"Dreamers?"

"Sure. Think about it. She's not afraid to take a chance on something that has not the first chance at succeeding—and not because she cares about the prize money or the notoriety that would come with winning. No. It's the opposite of that. She's chasing a dream."

"What the fuck kind of dream has anything to do with catching a smelly fish?"

"It's not about the fish."

Mavis snorted. "You haven't been around when she's been talking about that mean-ass one everyone's creamin' their pants to catch. That Phoebe, or whatever-in-hell her name is."

"Phoebe?"

Mavis nodded.

"The fish has a name?"

"According to your 'dreamer,' it has a zip code, too."

Barb laughed. "To each, his own."

Mavis ground out the butt of her cigarette and reached for the pack.

"You ought to taper off on those."

Mavis paused in mid-reach. "Me?"

"Yeah. You smoke too much."

"*I* smoke too much? Don't you have that backwards?" Mavis snapped up the pack and tapped out another cigarette.

"No. You're young. You could do better."

"Better than what?"

"Better than this."

Mavis flipped her Zippo open and snapped its flint wheel. A tiny flame illuminated the broad planes of her face. "Do me a favor and don't start this shit again."

"What shit?"

"This shit. This same bullshit you launch into whenever we're sitting in the dark."

"No metaphor in that," Barb muttered.

"We've had this conversation. I don't *do* metaphors. That's reserved for your crew of wackos back there." Mavis tossed her head toward the inn.

"At least they're trying to make a difference."

"How? By inventing two hundred new sex positions?"

"I wasn't talking about Viv."

Mavis laughed.

"That's it for me." Barb ground out her half-finished cigarette. "I'm turning in."

"You go on ahead and I'll catch up with you. I gotta take a piss."

"Now?" Barb stood up. "You can't make it back to the room?"

Mavis got up, too. "It don't work that way."

"Ooo-kaay." Barb collected her smokes and tucked them inside her jacket pocket. "See you in a few."

Mavis nodded and began making her way toward the cedar trees that lined the cliffs along this end of the property. Barb watched her go until her shape dissolved into the night and the only thing visible was the red-orange glow of her cigarette.

Quinn was rooting around inside the dark kitchen, trying hard to be quiet so Page Archer wouldn't hear her. Even though the innkeeper lived in a house located on the opposite end of the property, she had ears like a bat. She tended to swoop in like a bat, too—out of *no place*. Quinn had learned that one the hard way. If this damn retreat were a movie, Page Archer's theme song would be just like the one that always played before Darth Vader showed up.

She'd been halfway back across the black water tonight when she decided that another one of those funky Canadian bologna sandwiches would taste pretty good. She was hungry from working so hard. People thought fishing was easy. But it wasn't. Not for her, anyway. Fishing was exhausting. You had to pay attention to everything. And in fishing, *everything* meant nothing.

Quinn had spent more time in the last week paying attention to

141

nothing than she'd ever done in her entire life. That was because fishing was all about what happened in those quick, fleeting moments when nothing became *something*. That's when you knew your luck was going to change.

After she made her sandwich, she was going to try to score some of that aspic to take out with her in the morning. Even if that weird dream was just a result of drinking too many of those pale ales, she had an inkling to try an experiment. Who knew? Maybe those stupid fish really would like that shit?

Stupid. Phoebe wasn't stupid. Quinn knew that now. How else would she have been able to avoid being caught for two hundred years?

That's where the aspic came in. Even if that encounter had just been a beer-induced dream, Quinn knew she wasn't the one who ate that crap. That meant something had happened. It wasn't her style to worry things to death or fracture her brain trying to work out the details. That's what those paranormal types like Darien Black spent their time spinning yarns about—all that woo-woo jazz. *Walking dead.* What a crock of shit. Name one person you passed on any city street at high noon of any day in the week who wasn't walking dead? They *all* were. And they didn't need pancake makeup or fog machines to prove it.

Where did Gwen find those Ziploc bags?

Quinn yanked open a drawer and knocked over a precariously balanced stack of baking pans. She tried to catch them but it was too late. They clattered to the floor like cascading sheets of metal thunder.

Now I'm done for.

The swinging door that led to the service area swung open. She heard the snap of a switch and the overhead lights blazed into life. She stood there blinking stupidly and trying to shield her eyes. It could only be one person.

"What the hell are you doing in here?"

Page Archer. Her dulcet tones were unmistakable.

"I was hungry." Quinn began.

"You're always hungry. There's a deli up the road a mile."

Quinn's eyes were finally adjusting to the light. Her scattered sandwich fixings were strewn across the prep board.

"I know," she explained. "But they close at eight."

Page walked closer and *tsk*ed at the mess. "Maybe you should plan ahead."

"I'm sorry. I'll clean all this up."

Quinn began to reach for the loaf of bread, but Page stopped her.

"What kind of sandwich did you want?"

"Um. Bologna?"

Page strode around the island and nudged Quinn out of the way. The woman was short, but strong. Quinn danced out of her path. She glared at Quinn. The overhead light reflected off the lenses of her glasses, but Quinn could still see her set of piercing blue eyes.

"Pick up those baking sheets."

Quinn complied while Page took charge of making her sandwich.

"Mustard?"

Quinn nodded.

"There are some dill pickles in the reach-in fridge." Page gestured toward the large, stainless steel and glass cooler that ran along the side wall of the kitchen.

Quinn didn't really like dill pickles but she knew better than to look a gift horse in the mouth. She walked over to the massive cooler.

"I don't see them."

"Bottom shelf on the left. Behind the aspic."

That gave her an idea. *In for a penny, in for a pound.* Why not ask Page about why they make so much of that crap?

"Can I ask you a question?"

Page was slicing the spiced meat with a knife that could have doubled as a hacksaw. She looked up at Quinn over the rims of her glasses. "As long as it doesn't have anything to do with those sophomoric bondage stories you write."

"You read some of my books?"

"Against my better judgment. Barb sent me copies of everyone's work."

"You didn't like them?"

"Yours?"

Quinn nodded.

"I won't deny that there are some good—*descriptions*—in there. But they get lost in the weeds of all that other drivel."

"Drivel?"

"That's what I call it."

Quinn started to raise her hands in protest, but thought better of it and let them drop back to her sides. *She really did want that sandwich.*

"My readers don't think I write drivel." She did her best not to sound defensive.

"That's because your 'readers' are probably twelve-year-old boys."

Quinn didn't really feel comfortable trying to refute Page's suggestion. Especially since she had a sneaking suspicion that her assessment was right. She handed Page the jar of pickles.

"Not all of them," she suggested.

"You're probably right. I'd imagine they'd be popular in prison libraries, too."

Prison libraries? Quinn had never considered that. Images of an untapped retail outlet spread out before her.

"You mean like those *Sleeping Beauty* books Anne Rice wrote?"

Page stopped spreading mustard on the bread and stared at her. "I have no idea what you're talking about."

Quinn was shocked by her response. "They're *classics*."

"Classics? Classic what?"

Quinn shrugged. "Erotica."

Page rolled her eyes and went back to spreading mustard. "There's nothing 'classic' about erotica. It's porn."

"It's *not* porn."

"Yes it is."

"Why do you say that?"

"Because any book that is required to begin with a disclaimer attesting that all of the characters depicted are consenting adults over the age of eighteen is porn."

"Erotic writing can be beautiful."

"Graphic depictions of sex acts are smut. No matter how beautifully written they are."

"Do you really believe that?"

"Of course." Page was cutting Quinn's sandwich in half. The knife made an uneasy shushing sound as it slid across the butcher block. "It's pandering. A cheap, base way to sell more copies of books to people who are stalled in adolescence and can't keep their hands out of their pants."

"What's wrong with that?"

"Everything. It's part of the same addiction we have to shock value and graphic content in general. Why do you think those videos that show beheadings are always blasted across the Internet?"

"That's different. That's news."

"It's not *news*. It's merchandizing. And it's an epidemic. The more we see, the more immune we become to the horrors being depicted. So the drive exists to invent new and deeper horrors that will attract even greater viewership—or in your case, readership—all to generate more revenue. What gets lost in the shuffle is any conscious connection or response to the awful realities being depicted. We've created an entire culture that is increasingly desensitized to meaning. And that includes what happens when we share love and intimacy with a partner."

Quinn blinked.

"Have you ever talked with Phoebe?"

"Phoebe?"

"Yeah." Quinn made an oblique gesture toward the lake. "Out there. The fish."

Page narrowed her eyes. "Don't tell me you believe all those ridiculous fairy tales about a two-hundred-year-old bass?"

"Well . . ."

Page sighed. "Is that why you're still doing this whole tournament thing? Because you want to be the one to catch her?"

Quinn didn't reply. Mostly because she didn't know the answer.

Page grabbed a plate off a stainless steel shelf and put a pickle and the two, fat halves of Quinn's sandwich on it.

"Don't get caught up in the hype surrounding this. Don't allow

145

yourself to believe that winning this contest means anything more than getting lucky and tripping over the biggest fish—which, by the way, gets tossed right back into the water. There are no great, hidden meanings in this. There's just a lot of smoke and mirrors that don't add up to anything but big profits for the corporate sponsors."

"So you don't think she's real?"

"Who? Phoebe?"

Quinn nodded.

Page opened her mouth to say something, but seemed to think better of it.

"Do *you* think she's real?"

"I don't know. Probably not." Quinn gave Page a shy smile. "Maybe? I'm not really sure."

"Quinn? When you can describe what it is that drives you to do this—when you can explain why you're so captivated by the idea of this elusive fish, when you can be honest about your motivations and desires—you'll be close to understanding the difference between real and inauthentic kinds of storytelling."

"Did Barb ask you to come in here and talk to me?"

Page handed Quinn the plate. "No one asked me to talk to you."

"I don't get it."

"I know."

Quinn deliberated. She glanced back at the reach-in cooler.

"Can I ask you about something else?"

"What is it?" Page was piling up items to take to the dishwashing station.

"That aspic stuff." Quinn gestured toward the big bowl of the red gelatin. "Nobody really likes it."

Page nodded. "I know."

"So why do you always have it on the menu?"

Page sighed. "When Doug and I bought this place thirty years ago, it was little more than a fleabag motel with a pint-sized kitchen and eight tables. But even then, there were a couple of things they were famous for serving."

"Aspic?"

Page nodded. "That was one of them."

"What were the others?"

"Boston cream pie—and turkey dinner on Sundays."

"Those are both good."

"Some people think the aspic is good, too."

Quinn doubted that, but she knew better than to argue with Page Archer. Besides—Phoebe seemed to like it.

"As long as Doug and I own this place, we'll always serve tomato aspic—right along with Boston cream pie, and turkey on Sundays."

"I guess that makes sense."

Page waved a hand over the scattered food items on the prep board. "I'll clean this up. You go on and do whatever it was you were going to do."

Quinn didn't know what to say, so she didn't say anything.

She took her sandwich and headed back outside to find a welcoming spot beneath the dark and endless sky.

Essay 5

It started out like any other summer day. School was out, so there wasn't really any schedule to keep. We could sleep late, but we rarely did. My brothers and I knew that these long, hot summer days were like gifts, and were not to be squandered. Besides, our mother had a propensity for locking us all out of the house after breakfast. I often wondered why she ever had kids: she didn't really seem to like us all that much.

But we made the best of it, and we understood that we generally needed to have plans for how we intended to fill the hours between breakfast and lunchtime. This wasn't hard for my brothers. They pretty much did everything together, leaving me alone to fend for myself. I didn't really mind. I was just about to turn thirteen, and I was starting to fill out in ways that made me feel uncomfortable around boys. And this was especially true around my brothers and their friends, because they were the ones who pointed out how my tiny breasts made the front of my t-shirt poke out. I hated them for that. And right now, I hated being a girl, too. I didn't like all the ways my body was starting to change and take on an unfamiliar life of its own—just like the alien that grew inside Sigourney Weaver. I didn't understand it, and I was too shy and afraid to ask anyone to help me understand it. Even those "films" they made us watch in health class just filled me with fear and despair. After they were over, we'd all walk out of the gym, single file, and nobody would make eye contact with anybody else. The only thing I was certain of was that I didn't want to have to experience any of the things that were about to befall me.

So most days, I'd ride my bike across town to hang out and play with my best friend, Janis—who lived about half a mile away, off Montgomery Avenue. I wasn't supposed to ride my bike along main roads, so I had to wind my way through a fieldstone maze of neighborhood side streets to get there. It wasn't safe to do otherwise: my mother seemed to have spies on every street corner, and I'd been ratted out more than once for daring to cross any street that had more than two lanes of traffic.

Janis wasn't home on the day that everything fell apart. I rode over there after breakfast, as usual, but when I got to her house, her mother's light blue Oldsmobile wasn't in the driveway—and nobody answered when I knocked on their back door.

That was a colossal drag.

I had more than three hours to kill until lunchtime, and I wasn't feeling very well. My stomach was cramping like I'd eaten something spoiled. I didn't have any choice but to climb back on my bike and head for home. Pedaling seemed a lot harder than usual, even though I was backtracking along the same route I took every day. After a block or two, I noticed that something was different. My shorts felt wet. When I slowed down to check it out, I was shocked to see that the insides of my thighs were stained dark red. My heart sank. Standing there, straddling my bike beneath a canopy of maple trees, I understood that my life had just changed forever. Somehow, I knew everything without knowing anything. Words whispered behind hands in the lunchroom came back to me.

"She *started*. That means she can get pregnant."

Pregnant? I touched my fingertips to the red fabric of my shorts. Is that what this meant? Was I going to get pregnant, too? I started to panic. My hand was now red and sticky. I looked around for someplace to wipe it off. But that meant I'd have to get off my bike, and I didn't want anyone to see me—especially not that cranky old man who lived in the big house on the corner, and who always seemed to be out on his front steps, watching to be sure I didn't ride my bike across his grass. So, instead, I wiped my hand on the inside of my thigh, beneath the hem of my shorts. I had no choice, now, but to ride on home and wait for my mother to let me back inside the house.

I didn't want her to know about this, but I didn't know how I could hide it from her, either.

Like I said, she really didn't seem to like us all that much, and I was pretty sure she would be angry with me for causing problems.

Then I got an idea.

My grandmother lived about a mile away, and she always liked it when I stopped by for a visit. She'd make iced tea in those tall, skinny glasses, and we'd sit on her porch and watch the bright purple grackles pick at the ground beneath the chokeberry bushes that lined the perimeter of her backyard. She was kind, and she never asked me a lot of questions. Sometimes we would sit together for long periods of time without speaking at all.

It was mid-morning, so I knew that Bubbe would be back from Shacarite. Morning prayer services were held every weekday at her synagogue, Lower Merion. Bubbe usually walked there with her neighbor, Mrs. Klein. After services, the two of them would sometimes stop off at the kosher bakery for fresh loaves of raisin challah.

I turned my bike around and headed back up Melrose Avenue. If I hurried, the challah might still be warm.

I was in luck. When I got there, Bubbe was at home, and Mrs. Klein had already gone. When Bubbe opened her big front door and saw me standing there, I burst into tears. I couldn't hold it back. She pushed the door open wider and ushered me inside. Bubbe was still wearing her wig, so I knew that she hadn't been home for very long.

"What's the matter, Almah?" she asked.

I looked at her lined face with its kind, blue eyes. "I started," I blurted out.

She looked confused, so I pointed down at my stained shorts.

She stared at me for a moment, then I saw recognition flicker across her features. "You are Niddah?" she asked.

I had no idea what that meant, but I was pretty sure she was asking the right question, so I nodded.

Then she smiled. I couldn't believe it. My world was coming to an end, but Bubbe was smiling at me like I'd just told her that I made the "A" honor roll at school.

She reached out a bony finger and lifted my chin. "No tears. You are now *Ishah*—a woman. There is much to celebrate."

"I don't want to be a woman, Bubbe," I wailed. I couldn't tell her that I wasn't even sure I wanted to be a girl.

"Nonsense. You are a beautiful young woman. Your life is just beginning."

"But it hurts," I complained.

"I know it does, Almah. But it won't always." She steered me back toward the kitchen. "Take off your pants and I'll wash them for you."

I walked along the long, dark hallway ahead of her. "What will I wear?"

She patted me on the shoulder. "You go into the bathroom and wash." She opened a drawer in the kitchen and pulled out a clean, blue washcloth and towel. "I'll bring you the things you need."

A few minutes later, Bubbe tapped at the bathroom door and handed me a blousy pair of women's underwear and some cotton pajama bottoms that must have belonged to my grandfather. They were tightly folded with sharp-edged creases, and they smelled like cedar. She had something else, too—a thick-looking white pad wrapped in some kind of gauze.

"Wear this inside the panties," she said.

It did occur to me to wonder why she had such an item. Bubbe had to be nearly ninety—or so I thought. I looked from the stack of items up to her face. Her expression gave nothing away.

"They belong to your mother," she said, seeming to sense my unasked question.

I took the items from her and she closed the door. "Come out when you're ready and I'll make you some hot tea."

I did as I was told, and soon I was stretched out on her stiff horsehair sofa, with a rubber hot water bottle pressed up against my tummy, and a steaming mug of hot black currant tea in my hand. I could smell the thick slices of fresh challah toasting under her broiler.

"How long will this last?" I asked her.

Bubbe shrugged. "A week. Maybe less. It will pass before you know it."

A week? I wanted to die. I'd never last a week. I sipped the hot, sweet tea. Something awful poked at the edge of my consciousness. Something I remembered from that movie at school. I looked at her.

"Will it happen again?"

She smiled at me. "Of course it will, Almah. Many, many times—until you are old, like me."

I set the mug of tea down on a low table next to the sofa. I could feel my eyes starting to fill up with tears. My life was over. I would never be the same again. I shifted on the scratchy surface. The pad between my legs felt thick and foreign. I felt raw and exposed. I was sure that all my friends would know without my saying anything—and then I would be the one they whispered about behind their small, white hands.

Another thought occurred to me. It was even worse.

"What will I tell Mama?"

Bubbe patted my hand. "I will tell her. You rest now." She got to her feet. "We will eat some bread and jam, and soon you will feel better."

I closed my eyes and let the warmth from the hot water bottle begin to relax my sore muscles. I could feel myself starting to fade.

In the kitchen, Bubbe was still softly talking.

"When enough time has passed, we will take you to mikveh."

I didn't remember much after that. I think I slept for an hour or two, and by then, Bubbe had washed and dried my clothes. At her front door, she kissed me on the forehead and handed me a paper bag. I was pretty sure about what it contained. "For later," she said.

I rode my bike home, and when I got there, I was shocked to find that the back door was unlocked. When I walked inside, my mother met me halfway across the laundry room. She had an odd expression on her face. I couldn't tell if she was angry or sad, but she did not look happy. I started to hand her the paper bag when she reached out and slapped me across the face. It wasn't a hard slap—more of a tap, really. But it made a loud noise that seemed to echo off the walls of the tiny room.

I was stunned. What had I done? She had to know it wasn't my fault.

"It's tradition," she said without emotion. "It means you're a woman now."

I raised a hand to my face and stared at her.

"Don't be so dramatic. Bubbe did the same thing to me." Her voice sounded strange. It was almost apologetic. "Go up to your room now, and change."

I didn't know what else to do so I hurried past her, holding one hand against my cheek and grasping the rolled-up paper bag with the other.

When I got to my room, I was barely holding back the tears. She hit me because of some tradition? None of it made sense. My mother had never really been warm and fuzzy—but she'd never been cruel, either. And I couldn't imagine Bubbe ever slapping *anyone*. Not even that old Mr. Fishel at the deli, who always tried to over-charge her by piling butcher paper on the scale before he weighed the brisket.

I noticed something on my bed. It was a big, square box with pink writing all over it.

Kotex. Judging by the size of the box, it must've contained enough of the darn things to last until I was as old as Bubbe.

I sank down on my bed and looked around the small room. The photos of Mia Hamm and Ellen DeGeneres that I had cut out of magazines and tacked up on the walls stared back at me. The images I woke up to every day now seemed unfamiliar. Like they belonged to some-body else.

My mother's words still sounded in my ears. "You're a woman now."

Was I? The pain in my groin seemed to suggest I was.

I dropped back onto the bed and shoved the big, pink box off onto the floor. It landed with a thud. I had no idea what any of this was going to end up meaning—but I was pretty sure about one thing: because I had started to bleed, my life, as I knew it, would never again belong to me in quite the same way. Somehow, I had stopped being me, and had morphed into some kind of vessel. And all my innocence and childlike aspirations were now seeping out between my legs, and evaporating like gaso-line on a hot, summer sidewalk.

And who was there to save me from such a fate?

No one.

Yes. *They were right.* I was a woman now.

6

Happy Hour

"Hold up. I want to talk with you about something."

Linda had followed Kate out of the restaurant. The Outliners had just finished their morning session and were now splitting up to work on their draft essays.

They were making slow progress. Montana seemed more preoccupied with preventing Quinn from bringing about the apocalyptic maritime disaster that Viv kept predicting. And V. Jay-Jay didn't do much more than sit in her chair and use her body language to make it clear that she thought the entire group process was a ridiculous waste of time. Kate was finding it increasingly hard to disagree with her.

Barb never missed an opportunity to express her concern when the entire group got together to compare notes. They were at the end of the first week, and it was looking uncomfortably like the group would be unable to complete its contributions to the project before their time together ran out.

Kate stopped and waited for Linda to catch up with her. Linda was breathing heavily. Kate wondered if that meant she had started smoking again. Linda was always trying to give up something—usually without success.

"Have you got a minute?" Linda asked.

"Sure. What's on your mind?"

"Let's go out on the lawn and sit down for a minute."

Okay. That sounded serious.

"Is everything okay?" Kate asked.

Linda nodded. "Better than okay. Come on. Let's grab a couple of chairs."

They walked out across the lush, green grass. It was a cool morning, but warm in the sun. Kate made a beeline toward a couple of chairs that were nicely situated in the open, facing the lake, but Linda stopped her and pointed toward a cluster of other chairs that sat in the shadow of a large maple tree.

"How about over there? I have a headache and don't really want to sit in the sun."

"Okay." Kate pulled her lightweight jacket closed. She followed Linda to the chairs she'd indicated. Linda didn't waste any time after they sat down.

"I'm retiring."

Kate was stunned. Linda was only in her mid-fifties. "From the magazine?"

"From everything. I've been at *Gilded Lily* since it first went live back in 2009. I'm tired and I want to quit."

"Is everything okay?"

Linda looked confused by Kate's question. "With?"

"Well. You."

"You mean am I sick or anything?"

Kate nodded.

"No." Linda sighed. "Not exactly."

Kate opened her mouth to follow up, but Linda held out a palm to silence her. "I'm not sick."

"I don't get it. Why don't you just take a sabbatical?"

"From an online magazine? Kate, if I so much as go out for lunch I practically have to reintroduce myself to the staff when I get back."

That part made sense. Working in television was pretty much the same way.

Linda was shaking her white head. "I probably could've handled this intro a bit better. I think I just successfully undercut my argument."

"What argument?"

Linda smiled. "I want you to take my place."

Kate's eyes grew wide.

"Before you ask," Linda added, "I'm not kidding."

In her gut, Kate was pretty sure about what Linda was suggesting, but her brain wasn't allowing her to admit the possibility.

"What exactly are we talking about?"

"I want you to take over as editor in chief of *Gilded Lily*."

Jesus Christ.

She stared at Linda.

"No," Linda repeated. "I'm not kidding."

"Why me?"

"Why *not* you? You're perfect. And now, with your network media following, you've got the street cred to take the magazine to the next level. You need to know that the board is one hundred percent behind this. They're prepared to offer you a very sweet package."

This wasn't happening. It was like fate had just handed her a gold-plated, Get Out of Jail Free card. That is, once she navigated getting out of her GMA contract.

"I have a contract with ABC."

Linda was unfazed. "Patty's people will take care of it."

Patty was the magazine's publisher. Her father was a cutthroat intellectual property attorney with offices on the Upper East Side.

"God."

"Kate?"

Kate looked at her.

"You can get out of New York."

"And go back to Atlanta?"

"Not necessarily. You can live wherever you want—as long as you have access to an airport and high-speed Internet service."

This was not happening. It was too easy. Too convenient. The timing was too coincidental.

She felt herself starting to panic. The sleeping dogs of fear and suspicion that lived inside her began to rear their heads. What if it didn't work out? What if she got what she thought she wanted and it ended up being another colossal mistake?

She wasn't ready. She needed more time—more time to calm down. More time to be sure.

"I have to think about it."

Linda nodded. "I know you do. I'll email you the details of the offer. You can let me know something in a day or two."

Kate didn't reply.

"Kate?" Linda leaned forward in her chair. "This is a great opportunity for you. You can do work you're good at and really make a difference in ways that matter. Don't walk away from it."

"*You* are." The words were out of Kate's mouth before she could stop them.

"Touché." Linda sat back. "One day I'll tell you why. For now, just accept that I've done my time and need to go in another direction—by choice. If you agree to take this job, I'll know I'm leaving *Lily* in great hands—and that matters to me."

"I don't mean to be a bitch."

"I know you don't. It's second nature."

Kate laughed. "You really do know me, Linda."

"That's right. I do. And that's why you need to trust me. This is right for you, Kate. Just right."

Just right? That remained to be seen.

"I'll think about it."

"Good. I can't ask more than that."

"You promise you're okay?"

"Not quite yet." Linda smiled. "But I will be." She got to her feet. "Come on. Let's go make some progress on those infernal essays. I refuse to sit through another one of Barb's exasperated diatribes."

Kate stood up, too.

Avoiding Barb's exasperation was now the least of her problems.

———

"Seriously? Deli sandwiches do not require this much scrutiny."

Darien was drumming her fingers against her pant leg. V. Jay-Jay had been poring over the sandwich descriptions on the menu board for more than ten minutes. It was nearly eleven-thirty, and the place was starting to get busy.

V. Jay-Jay continued to ignore her.

"Come on, Vee." Darien tried again. "It's *lunch*—not a lifetime commitment."

"Do you mind?" V. Jay-Jay finally acknowledged her. "I'm trying to minimize damage here."

"Damage? Damage to what?"

"My gastrointestinal system."

"Oh, give me a break. You weren't worried about your GI system yesterday when you pounded those two Snickers bars."

"That's different. I have a weakness for confections."

"Well, I'm no connoisseur, but I think some people would argue that Snickers bars don't rise to the level of 'confection.'"

"Regardless, I have to be careful about not ingesting too many nitrites or BHA."

"What the hell is BHA?"

"Butylated hydroxyanisole."

Darien rolled her eyes. "Of course. How could I have forgotten?"

"The more you distract me, the longer this will take."

"Fine. Let's simplify. Just get the veggie wrap."

"It's not that simple."

"Yes it is. Vegetables are uncomplicated. You taught me that."

"Not *all* vegetables are uncomplicated. Some have unfortunate side effects."

Darien sighed. "Why don't you just take a break from the vegan stuff and eat half of mine?" She held up a white bag.

"Yours?" V. Jay-Jay looked dubious. "What did you get?"

"A number six." Darien pointed it out on the board. "The Eutaw Springs Special."

"Eutaw Springs? I'm no expert on the American Revolution, but wasn't that a blood bath?"

"Beats me." Darien shrugged. "I must've cut class that day."

"Right." V. Jay-Jay took the bag from Darien and sniffed at it. "What's on it?"

"Pastrami, corned beef, and Swiss on dark pump with coleslaw and Russian dressing."

V. Jay-Jay handed the bag back to her. "I see this sandwich comes by its name honestly."

Darien sighed. "I think I saw some raw turnips in the cooler back there. Why don't we just score a couple of those and be done with it?" She warmed to her idea. "We could even call it a Scarlett O'Hara."

"You're not really achieving your goal to speed this process along. Why don't you go get us some drinks while I order?"

"Great idea. Do you want your usual?"

"I have a usual?"

"Sure. Those weird-ass, Moxie seltzer things."

"Yes. *Right.* Get me one of my weird-ass usual's."

Darien smiled at her. "I'm all over it."

"I'll meet you up front at checkout."

Darien turned around and began to make her way toward the drink coolers. In the time she'd been standing there deliberating the evils of meat preservatives, the place had filled up with hungry, early-season vacationers. The corridors were narrow at best, and now they were rapidly becoming choked with people who seemed to have little inclination to make way for someone wanting to go in the opposite direction.

"Excuse me. Sorry. Excuse me. Thanks."

Good god. It's not like this joint is gonna run outta ham.

She all but slammed into the back of a tall man who was bent over looking at bags of chips. Something about him seemed familiar. He had a full head of carefully coiffed blonde hair and he smelled like he'd taken a bath in Old Spice.

Oh, Jesus.

Darien nearly dropped her bag. She backed away from him in horror and retraced her steps. This time, she didn't bother to apologize as she shoved her way back through the same crush of people. She just wanted to get out. She didn't bother to find V. Jay-Jay. She just made a beeline for the exit.

Once she was in the parking lot, she sagged against the side of the building and tried to steady her breathing.

What the hell was he doing up here? New England wasn't his usual stomping ground.

And why the fuck did I have to trip over him again?

162

She realized that her hands were shaking. People who were walking toward the store were giving her odd looks. She wiped at her nose. It was running.

I gotta get outta here.

She couldn't just take off and leave V. Jay-Jay behind. She looked around for someplace to go and try to settle down.

There were a couple of picnic tables across the road. They overlooked the lake. That might work. She could walk over there and figure things out. Get her bearings. *Maybe I'll see him leave, and I can go back inside and find Vee.*

Fat chance. Even if he left he'd never be *gone*. Her reaction to seeing him again was proof enough of that.

This was fucking surreal. Two seconds ago, her biggest problem was picking out the right kind of fizzy drink. Now she felt like she'd fallen down a rabbit hole and landed right in the middle of her worst waking nightmare.

Looking at the water helped. So did squeezing her hands against the rough planks on the picnic table. Watching the waves advance and retreat was hypnotic. It reminded her that there were bigger forces than her fears. Things like the tides.

"I've got a credit card and a car." That's what her best friend, Amy, told her. "I never have to be a victim again."

But Amy's advice was always predicated on running away—running farther and faster than whatever was chasing her.

Darien was tired of running. She understood that. But, goddamn it to hell. Why did he have to show up *here?* And why *now?*

Asking questions like that was pointless. It didn't get her anyplace and it wasn't like there were any answers to be had. There weren't. There was only the great unending cycle of sameness. Questions, asked and unanswered, ebbed and flowed just like these waves. They would come and go in their uninterrupted patterns forever. Sometimes softly, sometimes violently, but always pulling away before you could reach out and catch them.

Fifteen minutes passed, but she never saw him leave. That wasn't really surprising. She never saw him coming either. Today was proof of that. She eventually saw V. Jay-Jay, though—standing in the parking lot outside the store, looking around like she'd lost her best friend.

Shit.

She stood up and whistled, then waved when V. Jay-Jay looked toward the sound. Darien waited for her to cross the road and join her at the table.

"What the hell happened to you?" V. Jay-Jay set her bag down on the table and looked around. "Where are the drinks?"

"I didn't get them. Something came up."

"Something came up?" V. Jay-Jay looked confused. "What?"

"Just something, okay?"

"What's the matter with you?"

"*Nothing.*" The word came out sounding sharper than she intended. "Sorry. Just—something. Okay?" She held up a palm. "I don't want to talk about it."

V. Jay-Jay was giving her one of *those* looks. The kind that said there wasn't a snowball's chance in hell she was going to let this drop. She sat down and pulled her sandwich out of the bag.

"You want to eat here?" Darien thought they'd agreed to take their lunches back to the inn.

"Why not? It's a nice view."

"It's the *same* view we have at the hotel."

"No it isn't"

Darien looked out across the water. Same small islands. Same hazy view of St. Albans on the distant shoreline. Same Green Mountains looming behind that. Same everything.

"Vee? We're less than a mile north."

"Precisely. That's why it's not the same view."

"I'm missing something here."

"I think you're missing a whole lot of somethings here."

Darien sighed and got out her own sandwich. "Are you gonna tell me what that means?"

"Not if you don't want to talk about it." V. Jay-Jay took a bite of her sandwich.

This was going no place. Just like all those unanswered questions. Darien gave up.

"Okay. You win."

V. Jay-Jay didn't reply. She sat chewing her bite of vegetable somethings.

"I nearly ran into someone inside the store," Darien explained. "Someone from my past. A not-so-good someone. He didn't see me, so I bolted and came out here. End of story."

"Apparently it's not."

Darien was confused. "Not what?"

"The end of the story."

"It is as far as I'm concerned."

"What if you run into him again?"

"I won't."

"How can you know that?"

"Because I'll be looking for him now."

V. Jay-Jay slowly shook her head. "For someone who writes about demons, you certainly seem to be challenged when it comes to facing them."

Darien bit back her initial response—which was to tell V. Jay-Jay to fuck off. "Some demons are harder to face than others," she said instead.

"You think I don't know that? You think you have the market cornered on things you'd like to forget?"

Darien didn't reply, so V. Jay-Jay kept talking. "Move over, sister. Isn't this exercise precisely why we're up here? To lay out our tormented pasts so Barb Davis can recreate them all in twisted little pieces of metal?"

"Nobody forced you to participate in this project, Vee. If you hate it so much, why are you here?"

"Why are *you* here?"

Darien shrugged. "I thought it would be interesting to collaborate with other authors whose work was so unlike my own."

"And yet, not so unlike, as it turns out."

"What's that supposed to mean?"

"Oh, come on. We're *all* damaged—and in some pretty dramatic ways. You don't see that? You don't get that this is why Barb hand-picked us for her project?"

165

In fact, that possibility had never occurred to Darien. Not until right now.

"Why would she do that?"

"Because it's 'art.' And probably because she has reasons of her own."

"What reasons?"

"You'd have to ask her that question."

"Why are you so goddamn mysterious all the time?"

"It sells copy."

"That isn't what I meant, and you know it."

V. Jay-Jay didn't offer any further explanation. Darien gave up on trying to drag it out of her and began to unwrap her own sandwich. At least their exchange had managed to shift her focus away from what happened inside the store. She stole a glance back at the parking lot. *Still no sign of him.* Maybe he went out the other door? Or maybe he was eating his lunch inside?

A car horn blew out front near the gas pumps. Somebody was taking too long tanking up, and a man in a red Dodge was growing impatient.

Asshole. Why's he in such a damn hurry?

The man behind the wheel glanced her way and she felt her blood run cold.

Oh, god.

Darien turned away from the store and dropped her head into her hands.

"What is it?" V. Jay-Jay touched her on the arm. "You look like you've seen a ghost."

Darien didn't reply.

"Is that the man? The one in that red car?"

Darien nodded.

"Who is he?"

"Nobody. Just someone I used to know a long time ago."

After another few moments, V. Jay-Jay touched her arm again. "Well, try to relax. He just drove off."

Darien raised her head and looked at V. Jay-Jay. "He did?"

"Yes."

166

"Did he see me?"

"I honestly have no idea." She paused. "Would it matter?"

Darien gave a bitter-sounding laugh. "Probably not."

V. Jay-Jay didn't say anything else. After a couple of minutes, she began wrapping up their sandwiches.

"What are you doing?" Darien asked.

"Packing these up."

"Why? Aren't you hungry anymore?"

"No. I'm starving. I thought maybe we could take them down there and find a different place to sit." She pointed toward the boat ramp that led to the water.

"You don't like it up here?"

"I like it fine. But I think if we try, we can find you a spot with a different view."

Darien smiled at her. "Different isn't better, Vee."

"No. It isn't. Different is just different. Better takes more than a change of scenery." She stashed their sandwiches back in the bags and stood up. "And we don't have that much time right now. So, are you coming?"

What did she have to lose? In time, this experience would just be a dull memory—another rock on the grave of her lost innocence.

That pile was growing pretty damn impressive.

She looked up at her companion. Vee was obviously cutting her some slack.

Probably so that I'll quit asking her the same damn questions.

"Why not?" She got to her feet. "Different sounds good."

———

"It's not going to fit there."

Quinn was looking for places to apply the Astroglide decal to the boat. The logo was pretty big and it was hard to find a flat surface that was large enough to accommodate it.

Montana was right. It would never work here. Quinn lowered the decal.

"Where the hell are we gonna put it?"

"Beats me. Why did they send one this big?"

Quinn shrugged. "I guess they wanted to be sure people could read it from a distance."

"Well, they got that part right." Montana smiled. "Maybe we should stick it on Junior? He's the only thing on the boat big enough to hold it."

"Very funny."

"Well, I have no other ideas about where it could go." Montana looked the boat over one more time. "Do we really have to display it?"

"Yeah. It's part of the corporate sponsor agreement that gets the entrance fee paid."

"I still don't see why they had to make this thing so damn huge."

"Probably so you can see it from there." Quinn pointed at the shore.

They'd been out on the water for about half an hour. The wind was really starting to pick up. Quinn knew that was a bad sign. It probably meant rain. Again.

Montana laughed. "And probably because the size suggests something about the efficacy of their product."

"Efficacy?"

"Usefulness."

"Oh." Quinn smiled, too. "I guess." She looked at Montana. "Why do you use such big words?"

"What do you mean?"

"You know. Big words." Quinn shrugged. "Like that one. You don't write that way."

"You've read my books?" Montana seemed surprised.

"Yeah. Well. One of them."

"Which one?"

"That *Ho* one."

"*Ho* one? You mean *Westward Ho*?"

Quinn nodded.

"Not my best work."

"What do you mean? I liked it. It was a good story and it was easy to read."

"Thanks. But it was my first book and I didn't know what the hell I was doing." She smiled. "I see a lot of parallels between that and this fishing tournament."

"You don't think we know what we're doing?"

"Quinn. Take a look at this boat. Does it *look* like we know what we're doing?"

"What's wrong with the boat?"

"For starters, it has a La-Z-Boy recliner, a gas grill, and a full-sized refrigerator."

"So?"

"So? It looks more like a floating rummage sale than a bass boat."

"I like it."

"No kidding." Montana shook her head. "Do you want to tell me where *that* came from?" She pointed a finger at the battered Kelvinator, which was daisy-chained to half a dozen twelve-volt batteries. It was a snappy, two-toned 1950s model—teal and white. It looked like a refugee from *The Donna Reed Show*.

"I found it at Junior's. It still works great. It even has the original metal ice cube trays with the ejector levers."

"And you need it on the boat because?"

"I can't get enough beer and grape Fanta in the cooler."

"Those first-world fishing problems are a real drag, aren't they?" Quinn gave her a blank look. "Never mind. Why don't you just wrap the logo around the fridge?"

Quinn looked at the fridge. "You think it'll fit?"

"Sure."

"How will I open the door?"

Montana reached into her front pocket and pulled out her shiny, red Swiss Army knife. "We'll just cut it along the seams over the door."

"I guess that could work."

Five minutes later, they had the purple and white decal affixed to the Kelvinator. Montana made two neat slices along either side of the door, and the thing worked like a charm.

"Voila," she declared. "Let there be lubricant."

Quinn was looking it over. "I wonder if Phoebe will like it?"

"The fish?"

Quinn nodded.

"Why? You think she has issues with vaginal dryness?"

"Maybe. She is two hundred years old."

"You know what I think?" Montana never got the chance to say because a phone started ringing. The sound startled both of them. They stared at each other in surprise before patting down their pockets to locate their respective phones.

"It's not mine." Montana held hers up.

Quinn found hers. The ring tone got louder when she hauled it out of her pocket. The shrill noise rolled out across the water like a sound beacon. She stared at the display.

"It's Big Boy." She pushed the talk button. "Hello?"

That was really all she said except for the occasional "uh huh" and "okay" and "are you sure?"

Montana watched and waited until Quinn said goodbye and hung up.

"Well?"

Quinn stared at her. "Junior's in the hospital."

"What?" Montana was stunned. "What happened?"

"Big Boy says it was a gall bladder attack. They had to take it out."

"Oh, no. Is he okay?"

"I guess so. Now. But he's going to be laid up for a while."

"Well, shit." Montana slapped the side of the Kelvinator with her palm. "Guess you won't be needing all this extra space for grape Fanta."

"It's worse than that."

"Hey. I know this is a tough break. But you've done great learning all of this. You'll do fine without him. Mostly."

Quinn gave her a morose look. "It's not that simple."

"I know. It never is. But I'll help you out. We'll do okay."

"No. I mean we can't compete without him."

"Of course we can. He showed us most of what we need to know."

"Not that part." Quinn was shaking her head. "I mean the contest rules. We can't compete without a man."

170

"Say what?"

"The rules say that every team has to have a man."

Montana stared at her without speaking.

Waves continued to rock the boat. They were more determined now.

Quinn walked over to the bridge.

"Let's get off the water."

Essay 6

I'm not like you, so sad and solemn,
In this place—this place that's light and dark.
Where time creeps by on stout, amber wings,
And black phones ring, but go unanswered.
Sharp, hot words fall down on ears grown deaf,
Like all vague promises made before.
They burn inside a place that's barren,
Where no one waits or cries. And best hopes
Fade in the company of strangers.

I never thought I'd end up here. This was one of those charming appointments with destiny that I thought I'd be lucky enough to avoid. In fact, I would've put money on it.

But here I was just the same. Sitting on a straight chair in a Sunday school classroom. The bulletin board beside me was covered with little construction paper cutouts. Wise men with brown beards, all decked out in robes of purple and red. They were carrying things. Boxes. Bottles. Gold coins.

Gifts. Offerings. Things they'd leave behind.

That's what I was here to do, too. Leave something behind.

I just wished they'd hurry up with all the announcements and get to the rat killin'. That's what my father always called anything he didn't really want to do—a rat killin'.

I looked around the basement room that smelled like old books and bad coffee.

Yep. Rat killin' just about covered it.

A tube in the overhead fluorescent light was humming. The more I tried to ignore it, the louder it seemed to get. Just like all the other things my life I couldn't manage to ignore anymore. The noise it all made was deafening. And there was no place to hide from it. Not anymore. I needed to find a way to silence the noise before my head exploded. Coming here was a start. Coming here was supposed to work.

At least it was quieter.

Except for that damn light. And all these damn announcements.

I didn't realize that I'd been bouncing my leg until I noticed a guy across the room watching me. I dropped a hand to my knee to try and still it. The jitters were a tell—one of many. I was full of those now. I couldn't outrun them anymore. They always caught up with me, and they always telegraphed everything I'd spent most of my adult life trying to conceal. It was another reason why I was here on a damn Wednesday night, sitting on a folding chair in this cinder-block room of last resort.

The guy smiled at me.

It looked like the announcements were finished. Now people in the room were taking turns at the tabletop podium, reading from a couple of small books. I didn't really hear the words they read with their various, stammering tones. It didn't matter, though. The sounds they made were more like chants or anthems. It seemed to me that any value the words had came from the rote exercise of speaking them aloud. That part worried me. It worried me precisely because I didn't have to understand the words to feel their power. Already they were wrapping around my chest like a vice grip. Like a tether.

174

I knew I needed to be careful. Tethers weren't always good. Tethers could hold you hostage as easily as they could keep you safe. Tethers could tie you up in a dark place, or lead you out into the light.

Tethers could go either way.

The only thing I was sure of was that I didn't want to join a cult. I didn't want to swap one addiction for another.

I just needed to stop the noise.

I watched other people watch the readers. They didn't look like freaks or zealots. They mostly looked like me. Another thing that could go either way.

When the talking started, I began to panic. People were taking turns speaking. It was very orderly. Everything in here was orderly. Everything happened like it was part of some unseen pattern. At least, I couldn't see it. But these people walked on through an invisible maze like they all understood that making wrong turns didn't matter. It didn't matter because there weren't any wrong turns to make—not as long as they kept going forward. Some of them had been going forward for a long time. Years. *Decades.* Some were just getting started. Some were more like me—hanging back by the entrance and straining to see around the first corner.

The baton kept getting passed. Some shared. Some didn't. It was getting closer to me, now. My heart was pounding. I wasn't ready. I didn't want to feel this. I didn't want to be pinned into a cheap folding chair by so much benign scrutiny—by this mother lode of acceptance that felt like the worst kind of judgment. *I just wanted to stop the noise.*

It was my turn. Was it? Was I even ready to have a turn?

"I'm . . ." I couldn't get the words out. I looked at the sea of faces in that new company of strangers. "I don't know what I am."

175

Someone replied. Maybe the whole room replied? I didn't know. It was taking all my concentration to hold my legs still. I could feel my car keys through the fabric of my slacks. *Tethers could go either way.*

The baton passed.

It was someone else's turn to decide.

7

Borrowed Robes

The Pantyliners were hosting today's cocktail hour.

The entire coterie of writers had taken to gathering each afternoon around four to share progress and compare notes. It was Barb's best chance to check in with everyone, and it gave the group a good opportunity to bolster each other and keep the momentum going. They were down to the last week, now.

The Pansters had already completed their essays and were working on final revisions.

The Pantyliners were closing in on submitting their first drafts.

The Outliners were still arguing about what kind of notepads to buy.

Barb shook her tired head and called it "business as usual."

But the tone of the gathering today was different. Not as easy or lighthearted. In fact, Darien thought it was downright somber. Most of that seemed to derive from Quinn, who was pretty devastated about having to withdraw from the fishing tournament. It was clear that Junior's hospitalization was hitting her pretty hard. Even though Montana said that his brother, Big Boy, assured Quinn that she didn't have to follow through with her promise to fix up their Panhead Harley. A deal was a deal, he told her. And since Junior couldn't help her fish, she didn't have to fix the motorcycle.

But Quinn didn't seem to care. She just drifted around the property like a dark cloud and didn't talk much with anyone. She'd show up for the daily meetings, but she wouldn't participate. She'd sit quietly, drinking her bottles of Backcast ale, then wander off toward the water as soon as the meetings wound down.

She still took the boat out, though—always early, and always alone.

Darien wondered if she was going rogue, and was still determined to compete even if she couldn't officially participate.

She wandered over to where Montana and Barb were sitting. They were in the shade, conveniently out of Quinn's earshot. When Barb saw her approaching, she stood up to drag another chair over.

"Come and join us."

"Thanks." Darien dropped into the chair and faced Montana. "Can I ask you a question about Quinn?"

"Sure." Montana shrugged. "I don't know if I can answer any questions about her, but you can ask."

"It's about the tournament. Do you think we should try to help her out?"

"Help her out?" Montana looked confused. "Help her out how?"

"You know. With the fishing."

"What's going on with the fishing?" Barb sounded confused.

"Didn't you hear?" Darien explained. "Junior got sick and had to drop out so Quinn can't compete."

"Really?" Barb looked at Montana. "Why not?"

"It's some stupid tournament rule. Every team has to have a man on it."

Barb rolled her eyes. "What year is this? Nineteen-fifty?"

"I guess so. At least on the water."

"It really doesn't seem fair." Darien folded her arms. "Can't we do anything to help her out?"

Montana seemed to weigh her response. "Not unless one of us can acquire the relevant credentials within the next seventy-two hours."

Darien sighed. "There aren't enough hormones on the planet for that."

"What about finding another man in the islands to participate?" Barb waved a hand toward the lake. "There have to be hundreds of bass fishermen up here who aren't already committed."

Montana raised an eyebrow. "You *have* seen the boat, right?"

Darien laughed.

"I think it's ridiculous." Barb drained her drink. "It pisses me off that we still live in a society where anyone gives a shit about gender. Especially when it relates to something as absurd as winning a prize for catching the ugliest damn fish."

"With all due respect," Montana clarified. "The prize is for catching the *biggest* damn fish—not the ugliest. The ugly part is just a bonus."

"Well as far as I'm concerned, they can shove their bonuses up their narrow-minded asses." Barb got to her feet. She stumbled a bit and Darien reached out a hand to steady her. "Thanks." She held up her empty glass. "I'm getting another one. Either of you two ready?"

They both shook their heads. Barb slowly wandered off toward the bar. Darien watched her unsteady progress across the lawn.

"She might want to rethink having another drink."

"She's not the only one." Montana nodded toward another cluster of chairs located not far from theirs. "It looks like those two are at it again."

"Which two?" Darien followed her gaze. "Oh, shit. Viv and Towanda?"

"Yeah. They should just break down and audition for *Friday Night Fights*."

"I wonder what the hell is going on this time?"

Montana stood up and gave her a conspiratorial smile. "There's only one way to find out."

Darien got up, too. "Right behind you."

They tried to appear nonchalant as they sauntered toward the larger group. They needn't have bothered with discretion. No one paid any attention to the fact that they'd arrived to watch the show. Viv and Towanda were both on their feet in the middle of the circle of chairs. The scene reminded Darien of a garden-variety playground fight—something she knew a lot about.

The rest of the group just looked—indifferent. Cricket MacBean and V. Jay-Jay Singh were calmly sipping on their cocktails like this was an everyday occurrence. Shawn Harris, on the other hand, seemed preoccupied with her cell phone.

The decibel level of the insults flying back and forth between the two antagonists rose in direct proportion to their increasing vitriol.

Viv looked spitting mad. Her face was nearly as red as her hair.

"How dare you suggest that my outline lacks cohesiveness?"

"Hey." Towanda gestured toward a dog-eared stack of notepads on the ground beside Viv's chair. "Is it my fault you could drive a Buick through the holes in that flimsy construction?"

"*Flimsy?* You call my work *flimsy?*"

"Let me see." Towanda made an elaborate parody of thinking about her answer. "*Yes.* Flimsy would definitely be the word."

"You know what, Wanda? The only *hole* around here that's big enough to accommodate a Buick is that one you call a vagina."

"Oh, go fuck yourself, Viv. I stopped caring about your opinion the first time I had the misfortune to read one of your ridiculous whodunits."

Viv spread her arms wide to encompass the group. "This complaint from the author of the immortal classic, *MILF Money?*"

"You're just jealous."

"Excuse me?"

"You heard me. My books sell rings around yours, and you know it."

"The only 'rings' your books generate are the kind that require penicillin."

Cricket MacBean chuckled. Towanda shot her a withering look.

"What?" Cricket pointed at Viv. "That was funny."

Shawn Harris lowered her phone. "She *is* a nurse, Towanda. You have to give her that."

Towanda glowered at Shawn.

"Give it up you two." Viv pointed a finger at Towanda. "Interlopers like her don't give a shit about the integrity of our genre. They just want to cash in and make a fast buck riding our coattails."

Towanda was still fuming. "What the hell is that supposed to mean? I don't ride *anybody's* coattails—especially yours."

"Oh, really? Then why aren't you pedaling your petty porn tales in the mainstream markets? Why do you feel the need to clog our ranks with your flimsy, faux lesbian sex romps?"

"My books are *not* faux lesbian."

"Oh, really? Could've fooled me."

"A stink bug with a lobotomy could fool you."

Cricket laughed again.

This time, it was Viv who was un-amused. "Stuff it, Loretta Swit."

Cricket looked around the group. "Why am I always compared to some forgotten actress who played a nurse on TV?"

"Take the compliment, Crix. She was pretty hot."

Cricket flashed a three-fingered "W" sign at Shawn.

"You know what your problem is?" Towanda had taken a step closer to Viv. The women were about the same height, but something about Towanda's stance made her seem taller.

Viv was unfazed. "No. But I'm sure you're going to enlighten me."

"You just can't accept the fact that some of us have more balanced sexual identities."

"Balanced? That's certainly a creative way to describe sucking dick."

Towanda turned purple. "You just resent that I'm married to a man."

"Wrong." Viv wagged a finger in Towanda's face. "I could give a shit that you're married to a man. What I refuse to accept is how you intentionally toss extraneous girl-on-girl scenes into your books just so they can be classified as 'lesbian.' In my view, that's the sleaziest kind of opportunism. It's disingenuous as hell and you know it."

"Why don't you get off your self-righteous soapbox and be honest about what's really chapping your ass?"

"What the hell are you talking about?"

"You know precisely what I'm talking about. You just can't stand the fact that I'm beating you at your own game."

"Writing isn't a 'game' for me. It's a craft. And I take it very seriously. For you, it's just a way to make a quick buck by feeding the fantasies of big-bellied knuckle-draggers who get off watching women get busy."

Towanda smiled at her. "You shouldn't talk about your Sapphic sisterhood that way, Viv. It isn't very respectful."

Uh oh.

Darien saw the slap coming before the blur of Viv's hand connected with Towanda's face. The resulting *smack* reverberated around them like the crack of a rifle. At first, Towanda stood rooted in place like a statue. Darien could see the hazy, pink outline of Viv's fingers materialize on her cheek. Then all bets were off. Towanda was in motion. She pounced on Viv like a golden retriever on a dropped canapé. But Viv was stronger and feistier than she appeared, and within seconds, the two of them were rolling around on the ground in a hail of arms and legs.

"Not again." V. Jay-Jay shook her head in disgust.

Shawn agreed. "Somebody better call for backup. These two can go at it all night."

"This really is disgraceful behavior." V. Jay-Jay looked around at the circle of onlookers. "Isn't anyone going to do anything?"

Cricket MacBean fished around inside her jacket pocket. Her hand shot into the air and she energetically waved a bill back and forth. "Holding! Double sawbuck on the breeder!"

"I'll take some of that." Shawn passed her a twenty.

"I'm in!" Montana stepped forward and handed Cricket a couple of folded bills. "Red lobster on Viv."

V. Jay-Jay sighed and looked at Darien. "If you can't beat em, join em." She dug her wallet out of her messenger bag and extracted a twenty.

"Oh, shit." Darien pointed toward the inn. "Here comes Page Archer."

"Now they've had it." V. Jay-Jay put her money away. "We'll be lucky if we don't all get bounced."

Viv and Towanda were still going at it. If the circle of chairs hadn't penned them in, they'd likely have rolled off the cliff into the lake. Their slaps and smacks were interspersed with curses.

"Cunt!"

"Bitch."

"Fucking imposter!"

"Lying sack of shit!"

"Cocksucker!"

"Rug muncher!"

"Takes one to know one!"

"Fuck you, Viv! And get your goddamn hand off my ass!"

Darien watched Page Archer storm closer to the melee. She did not look happy.

Montana was watching her approach, too. "How the hell does she always manage to show up just when things get interesting?"

"It must be some kind of innkeeper thing." Shawn shook her head. "They have eyes in the backs of their heads."

Page reached their circle and stood with her hands on her hips, watching the two writhing bodies on the ground with disgust. Then she approached Cricket and handed her a fifty.

"Pineapple on the redhead." She waved a hand at the writhing maze of body parts. "When those two get untangled, tell them the bar is closed."

—

"Those two are certifiable."

Shawn made her way back to the room shortly after Mavis showed up and ended the fracas on the lawn. Kate was already dressed for dinner so Shawn was scrambling to catch up. Kate sat on the edge of the bed and watched Shawn sift through her pile of clothes for a clean shirt.

"Were those gunshots I heard?"

"Yeah." Shawn held a dark blue polo shirt up to her nose and gave it a sniff. "Who knew Mavis was packing?"

"I don't imagine that was welcome news to Page Archer."

"Are you kidding? It was Page Archer who sent her down there."

Shawn returned the blue shirt to the pile and pulled out another candidate. A green one this time.

"Aren't you the same person who chastised me about bringing too many clothes up here?"

"Hey." Shawn waved the rumpled shirt at her. "That was before I knew we were expected to dress up for dinner."

Kate smiled at her. "I hardly think having to wear trousers and closed-toe shoes counts as dressing up."

"Says you. I don't do all that girlie stuff very well."

"Trust me, sweetheart. You do all of the important girlie stuff just fine."

Okay. That one stopped Shawn in her tracks. She lowered the shirt.

"I do?"

Kate nodded. "Oh, yeah."

So maybe it wouldn't be the worst thing in the world to miss dinner?

Shawn took a step toward Kate. "I'm suddenly not very hungry."

Kate stopped her with a well-placed, stocking-clad foot to the thigh. "Hold up, Romeo. I missed lunch and I'm starving."

Shawn sighed.

"Don't look so miserable. You can give your girlie goodness a workout *after* we eat."

"I can?"

Kate nodded. "Now finish getting ready and tell me more about what the hell is going on with Viv and Towanda."

Shawn returned to her sorting. "It would take a team of shrinks to answer that question."

"Why do they hate each other so much?"

"I asked Viv that question after Mavis busted up the fight. I walked her around a little bit to try and calm her down. She was still spitting mad."

"What did she say?"

Shawn shrugged. "Nothing very coherent. Although it seems pretty clear that they have some kind of history that predates this retreat."

"I don't remember them being at such odds with each other during CLIT-Con last year."

"Me either. But to be fair, I was kind of preoccupied with other things."

"I guess I was, too."

They smiled at each other a little shyly. Kate shook her head.

"What?"

"I still can't figure us out."

"Us? I thought it was Viv and Towanda we were trying to figure out?"

"They're not mutually exclusive."

"Okay." Shawn put down her stack of shirts and joined Kate on the foot of the bed. "What about us is hard to figure out?"

"We can talk about that at dinner."

"Nuh uh." Shawn bumped her shoulder. "You can give me the CliffsNotes version now."

Kate raised an eyebrow. "You think there's a CliffsNotes version?"

"Of course."

"What makes you so sure?"

"Kate."

"Okay. Okay. So, Linda approached me earlier today. She's retiring from *Gilded Lily*."

Shawn was stunned. "No way?"

Kate nodded. "She wants me to take over as editor."

"What did you say?" Shawn held her breath.

"I said I'd think about it."

Think about it? What the hell was there to think about?

"Have you?" Shawn asked instead.

"Have I what?"

Shawn counted to five. "Have you thought about it?"

"Of course I have. I haven't thought about much of anything else since she mentioned it."

"And?"

"And I think we should talk about it."

"Okay." Shawn looked at her watch. "Now is good for me."

Kate smiled at her. "It's going to take more than one conversation."

"I get that. But there's no time like the present to start parsing it out."

"I kinda figured that would be your response."

"I hate to be so transparent."

"Don't apologize for that. It's very endearing. And it makes planning a lot easier."

"Planning?" Shawn was confused.

"Um hmm."

Patrick and Allie chose that moment to roar to their feet and unleash a volley of barking.

"What the hell?" Shawn turned around to face the door. "Hey. Knock it off, you two."

"That's probably room service."

Shawn looked at Kate. "Room service? This place doesn't *have* room service."

"It does if you schmooze the handsome bartender."

There was a knock at the door.

"Do you wanna go get that?"

"Okaaayyy . . ." Shawn got to her feet and walked to the door. "You wanna call off the hounds?"

"Kids." Kate snapped her fingers. "Over here. *Now*."

Patrick and Allie grudgingly complied. Shawn opened the door.

"Hi there." A cheerful server handed Shawn a tray loaded with covered plates. "Here you go. Two burgers, medium rare. Fries. A bottle of MacMurray Ranch Pinot Noir. And a side of extra mustard." Shawn took the tray. "You folks need anything else?"

"I think we're covered." Shawn was dumbfounded by the fare. "Let me get you a tip."

The server held up a hand. "No need, ma'am. It's already taken care of."

"Okay. Thanks."

"You bet." The server pulled the door closed and headed back toward the restaurant.

Shawn turned around to face Kate, who was watching her with an amused expression.

"Burgers and fries? Just how nice were you to the handsome barman?"

"Telling him he has a nice ass was my opening salvo. The rest happened organically."

"No doubt." Shawn examined the tray. "Extra mustard, too?"

"You never know." Kate shrugged. "Things might get interesting."

"If memory serves, things always get interesting when we have extra mustard."

"I'm counting on it."

These days, having Kate count on anything was an anomaly. It was a small thing, but Shawn decided that it was a step in the right direction.

She set the tray down on the small table.

"I'll do my best not to disappoint you." She walked toward Kate and the dogs.

Kate got to her feet and met her halfway. "You never do."

—*m*—

"You have to help her out."

"Woman, get off my case."

"I mean it." Barb was watching Mavis clean her service weapon. She'd used it to fire a few rounds of blanks into the air to break up the fight after Page Archer summoned her.

"I stopped your damn brawl, now give me a break."

"I know. And thanks for that."

"If you ask me, you should tie their tails together and toss 'em over a clothesline."

Barb considered that. "Not a bad idea. I don't think Towanda has written about that position yet."

"Perverts. Why do they hate each other so much?"

"Beats me. They say the line that separates love from hate has a razor's edge."

Mavis lowered her gun's barrel. "Who says that?"

Barb smiled. "I just did."

Mavis rolled her eyes. "Hand me that can of oil."

Barb passed it over to her. "Do you really have to clean it like this when you only shoot blanks?"

"Sure. You're still firing gunpowder—just no load. So the cylinder gets fouled just the same."

"How did Page know you had this with you?"

"Because I told her about it when I checked in."

"It figures."

"What figures?"

187

"This." Barb waved a hand toward the gun paraphernalia. "Of course you'd disclose that you had it."

"By law, I had to disclose it. This place has a 'no firearms' policy."

"That's my point. You obey the law."

"I wouldn't have a job very long if I didn't."

"And that brings us back to my original point."

"Forget about it."

"Mavis."

Mavis slammed the gun down on the towel she'd spread across the tabletop. "What the fuck do you want from me?"

"I want you to help her out."

"Why should I?"

"Because you can. And because you're a decent human being."

"You're crazier than that pack of loons you call authors."

Barb didn't reply. She sat and watched Mavis work a tiny brush in and out of the gun barrel. It made a soft, whooshing noise. Barb thought it sounded like the waves. She got to her feet.

"Where are you going?"

"Back to work. I'm feeling pretty good tonight. I think I've got another hour or so left in me. Might as well make hay while the sun shines."

Mavis looked out the window. "It's nearly dark."

"I was being metaphorical."

"Don't you stay down there too late."

Barb had a makeshift studio set up in the barn. Doug Archer had even hauled in a workbench to accommodate her tools.

"I won't."

"You said that last night and I had to come get your ass at twelve-thirty."

"I won't. I promise." Barb walked to the door. "Let me know how it goes."

"How what goes?"

"Your talk with Quinn."

Barb was able to duck out of the room before Mavis's oily rag connected with the back of the door.

"How long have you been sitting down here?"

Darien hadn't been looking for V. Jay-Jay, but when she saw her sitting on the rocks that jutted out into the water alongside the pier, she decided to join her. The sun was setting, and the sky was fantastic, overlaid with dramatic swirls of indigo, tangerine, and coral. Darien thought it looked like one of those black velvet roadside paintings that were so omnipresent in the Southwest. V. Jay-Jay was perched atop an outcropping of big rocks that had been pushed in by the winter ice floes. Her stark silhouette was plainly visible against the explosive backdrop. She could've been Elvis. Well. A younger, more svelte Elvis, without the pompadour or sequins.

"I came down to admire the view." V. Jay-Jay nodded toward the horizon. "I can only imagine how electric it must be on the west side of the island."

Darien looked at her watch. "I'd say let's roar over there and take a look, but by the time we got to the car, the sun would be down."

"True. I can rage against the dying of the light just as effectively from here."

"Okay. I know that's a quote I'm supposed to recognize."

"You mean you don't?"

Darien shook her head.

"I have so many things to teach you, White Rabbit."

"So you're doubling-down now?"

"You don't know that one either?"

"Nope."

"How on earth can you write if you don't read?"

"I read."

V. Jay-Jay raised an eyebrow.

"Okay. Maybe I don't read all those musty, dead poets that you're so partial to. But I read plenty."

"The dead poets, as you call them, would have a fair amount of relevance for your particular brand of fiction."

"And you know this because?"

"I read two of them last night."

Darien was stunned. "*My* books?"

V. Jay-Jay nodded.

"You read *two* of my books?"

'Yes."

"In one night?"

"Yes. Why do you sound so surprised? It wasn't like tackling two volumes of later Wittgenstein."

Darien sighed. "I'm pretty sure that was an insult. Once I have confirmation, I'll be sure to act offended."

V. Jay-Jay smiled. "Why don't you pull up a rock and enjoy what's left of the view?"

Darien picked her way out onto the rocks and found a reasonably flat place to sit. The colors in the sky were fading in intensity now. It would be dark soon.

"It really is beautiful here. I see now why Barb picked this place."

"Me, too." V. Jay-Jay stared out across the water. "It's so unspoiled. So quiet. Like it's yet to be discovered."

"All except for those two hundred, hopped-up bass boats that'll soon be roaring around all over the place."

"True."

"I feel bad for Quinn."

"Why?"

Darien was surprised by her question. "Don't you? I mean—isn't Quinn one of your classic *antiheroes*?" She made air quotes around the word.

"Quinn is just a tragic figure, period. Fishing notwithstanding."

"Why do you say that?"

"You disagree?"

"I don't know that I agree or disagree. I never really thought about it."

V. Jay-Jay didn't reply.

Darien struggled with whether or not to follow-up on V. Jay-Jay's revelation that she'd read two of her books. She suspected that V. Jay-Jay was waiting for her to ask—no doubt so she could give her a blistering review. She knew it was in her best interest to keep silent.

She also knew that stuffing Pandora back into her tidy box of blissful ignorance was impossible.

"Can I ask you something?"

V. Jay-Jay looked at her. The light was fading fast now. Darien could hardly make out her features. "Of course."

"Did you like my books?"

Oh god. She regretted the words as soon as they left her mouth. She sounded like a pathetic teenager. But it was too late. Her weakness and vulnerability were all out there now—just like one of Quinn's bad casts. She knew as soon as she let her question fly that she'd overshot her mark by a mile.

V. Jay-Jay took her time replying. That didn't do much to ease Darien's discomfort.

"I liked them just fine."

"You did?" Darien wasn't sure she'd heard her right.

"Did you think I wouldn't?"

"I guess so." Darien shrugged. "I mean—they're not exactly Wiener-whosis."

"Wiener-whosis?"

"That guy you mentioned earlier."

"Wittgenstein?"

"Yeah. Him."

V. Jay-Jay shook her head.

"What?"

"You're too hard on yourself."

"I thought you wanted me to be hard on myself."

"I think you could push yourself more when it comes to your writing. That's not the same thing as beating yourself up."

"I don't beat myself up."

"Yes, you do."

"What happened earlier doesn't count."

"The fact that you think your reaction to seeing that man today doesn't 'count' is a perfect illustration of my point."

"Vee? Don't start this stuff again, okay?"

"Let's step back and reconnect the dots here. Didn't you ask me for my opinion?"

"Of my books." Darien held up a clarifying index finger. "Not my past."

"To be fair, it would be impossible for me to express an opinion about your past since I don't know any details about it."

That much was true. Well. *Mostly* true. Darien had certainly cracked open a door on all of that with her performance at Hero's Welcome deli earlier. She decided to turn the tables on V. Jay-Jay.

"Why do you wanna know?"

V. Jay-Jay looked confused. "Why do I want to know what?"

Darien spread her arms. "The world according to me. Why do you care? Nobody else does."

"I doubt that's true."

"Trust me. It's true."

"I disagree. What about your adoring fan base?"

"What about them? They don't know anything about me."

"They don't?"

"No. Like you, I don't write under my real name."

"Darien Black isn't your real name?"

Darien shook her head. "Black is my real last name, but 'Darien' is just a name I borrowed from a poem I liked in high school."

V. Jay-Jay was silent for a few moments. Darien could tell she was racking her brain to come up with the reference.

"Keats?"

Darien nodded.

V. Jay-Jay smiled. "You chose well."

"Yeah. I liked the irony of taking a name that was universally associated with one of the biggest literary blunders of all time."

"I think this is a nuance that will be lost on most of your readership."

"I didn't pick it for them."

"So, what is your real name?"

"Why do you wanna know?"

"Tit for tat, right? If memory serves, I told you mine."

Darien drummed her fingertips against the smooth surface of the rock.

"As I recall, that was part of an information exchange."

"And your point would be?"

"If I tell you, then I get to ask you another question, too."

V. Jay-Jay sighed. "Fine."

"Okay. It's Jimmie. Jimmie Dean."

"Really?" V. Jay-Jay's voice was tinged with suspicion.

Darien nodded.

"Your parents named you after an icon of social estrangement?"

"No." Darien rolled her eyes. "That's *James* Dean. My parents named me after a country singer who became a sausage magnate."

V. Jay-Jay started to chuckle. Then her chuckle turned into a laugh—and not just any kind of polite, garden-variety laugh, either. It was a full-throated, shiver-your-timbers kind of laugh that spread out, wrapped up, and shook every part of her glorious, compact frame. The sounds she made were bright and musical. The sweet, strong, happy noise swirled around their heads like a stray zephyr of mirth.

V. Jay-Jay's lapse of composure was stunning, but it was also infectious. Darien found herself beginning to smile. It was impossible not to. How had she never seen the humor in this before? It *was* ridiculous. And funny. Soon she was laughing just as hard as V. Jay-Jay, and the two of them were perilously close to losing their hold on the rocks and slipping into the water.

Darien reached out and took hold of her arms to steady her. To steady them both.

To steady us against what? Her head was spinning. *Against falling?*

Were they falling? If they were, it wasn't into a place Darien was unwilling to go. She knew that now.

They swayed and held on to each other as their bodies continued to shake—now with something different from laughter—something that inhabited the other side of laughter.

It was too much. Holding on to where they were was too much. It wasn't sustainable. Not any more.

They slid off the rock into the lake. The shock of it was incredible—a blinding contrast to the heat of V. Jay-Jay's body. Cold water washed over them and penetrated their clothing. Darien wanted to cry out—but she didn't. Her understanding of the differences between pain and pleasure, hot and cold, liquid and solid grew hazy. Uncertain. Everything around her dissolved into a crazy confluence of sensation.

It was night and the water was fathomless—dark but full of light—familiar but unknown. Realities melted away from them like forgotten punch lines from jokes that no longer mattered.

Old things had passed away, and all things were becoming new.

Essay 7

"Many are called, but few are chosen."

How many times had I heard that? How many times had I recited that in the quiet of my cell, over and over—like a talisman against failure? I clung to the words like a lifeline that would lead me off the path of perdition and back into the safe harbor of God's grace. Over and over I punished myself with the words. Like a flagellant wielding a slender bough of birch.

Countless times. Endless nights. Forever and ever, amen.

"The decision to follow God is not an easy one." That's what the Abbess told us as we all knelt before her in our short, white veils. "Many are called, but few are chosen. Some of you will persevere, but others will fall away. For this, we must all be prepared."

Prepared? Prepared for what? For failure? For mortification? For ostracism? For a lifetime of disappointed hopes?

What kind of affirmation was *that*? What twisted brand of encouragement was *that*?

We were young and scared. We were vulnerable and naïve. We had given up everything before we even understood what everything meant. We needed love and encouragement, not odds and prognostications about how many of us were headed toward certain failure.

Even then, I had issues with authority. That alone should have convinced me that this path I had chosen to walk would not be an easy one. A life in the church was all about subjugation—about bending your will to another's. And not just to one other—but to a sequence of others. All the way up the food chain to the man at the top. Because in the church, as in the rest of life, there was always a man at the top.

"Have many friends," they taught us. "Have many friends, but not one."

Not one.

She wasn't like me. She was smaller. Meeker. She didn't question authority. She didn't question anything. Coming here was never a choice: it was a destination. She belonged here and she knew it. Living a life by rule and method wasn't suffocating to her, it was liberating. Empowering. It was everything.

Have many friends, they said.

Many. Not one.

After morning prayers and breakfast, we worked together in the washhouse. We'd spend hours upon hours bleaching, washing, and ironing. Folded stacks of stiff, white cotton would rise around us like columns in a pagan temple. As we worked, we prayed. We prayed that God would open our hearts to love others as we were learning to love each other. We prayed that we might persevere and take our places among the chosen. Mostly we prayed that the heat and longing that closed in around us like the soft, moist air of the clothes press would dissipate if we remained true to our vows.

Many. Not one.

She held out longer than I did. She had a deeper faith. A less forgiving nature. A greater willingness to embrace the teachings and the strictures of our order. When I would try to talk with her about what was happening—about what I was feeling—she would ignore it. She would recite the Psalms of the Divine Office. Her chanting and humming would go on and on until I would surrender and concentrate on my work.

At night I would return to my cell awash in loneliness and misery. My insistent prayers for release from this torment went unanswered. Because I could not touch her, I began to touch myself. The ecstasy and release I experienced only served to increase my feelings of isolation and hopelessness. The hours until I was reunited with her inside the solitude of our white prison were torturous. My days and nights were now marked by the ticking order of a different Office.

It wasn't until I called her by her real name that she relented.

It was Friday, the day we took in laundry from our sister house in town. I had been running sheets through the clothes press for hours when the unit jammed. This wasn't uncommon. The thing was antiquated and badly in need of servicing. When I bent over it to try and dislodge a thick wad of twisted fabric, the rollers lurched forward and the sleeve of my tunic got caught. I couldn't pull it out and I couldn't reach the stop switch. I pulled back with all my might, but I was being dragged by my habit into the machine.

"Help. Help me," I cried. "Felice—you have to help me."

She was at my side in a flash. Without a second thought, she yanked the power cord from the wall and the unit rolled to a stop. My arm was only centimeters from being crushed.

"My god. My god." She was practically crying. "What happened?"

"It jammed," I explained. "I got caught trying to fix it."

She was staring down at the sleeve of my tunic. "We have to get you out of this."

"I know. Should we cut it?"

"No." Her voice was full of trepidation. "We can't ruin your habit. Sister Agnes would be furious about the waste." She met my eyes. "You have to take it off."

My heart began to race. "Take it off? How?" I waved my free arm. "I can't."

"I'll help you."

I didn't reply because I couldn't trust myself to speak. So I nodded.

When she unpinned my veil, I noticed that her hands were shaking. Then she moved behind me to reach the buttons on the back of my tunic.

"Lean forward." Her voice was low and husky. I felt warm, moist air move over my back as she separated the folds of the rough serge fabric. Her hands slid beneath the tunic and pushed it away from my shoulders.

"I need you to turn toward me so I can free your arm."

I was sweating. I could feel water dripping down my forehead from beneath my short hair. Moisture was running along my arms and pooling between my breasts. And those weren't the only places I was getting wet. All of my guilty fantasies about her were roaring to life. I closed my eyes tight to shut out the memories of all the things I'd imagined doing to her. With her. I was afraid she could sense it. I was terrified she would know what I was thinking and would recoil from me. That she would rebuke me and leave me there, half undressed, unmasked in my shame for Sister Agnes to find.

But she didn't.

When I turned to face her, she pulled my tunic away. I was wearing only my thin, white chemise and I should have been embarrassed to be so revealed before her, but I wasn't. I allowed myself to meet her gaze.

"You called me Felice," she said.

I nodded.

She took a step closer. I could see moisture gleaming on her nose and along her upper lip. "How did you know my name?"

"Because I know you."

"How can you know me? I don't even know me."

I wanted to move closer to her but I couldn't. I was still a prisoner of the machine. I was a one-armed creature, trapped in a web of my own making.

I raised my free hand and laid it against her chest. I could feel her heart beating beneath my palm.

"I know you." I said again. This time, the words were liquid, like the soft, sloshing sounds of water against the granite sides of the ancient washtub. "I know you."

She closed her eyes. Then she took hold of my hand and moved it down to cover her breast.

"Free me." I implored her. "Free us both."

I'd never been with a woman. I'd never been with anyone. But when she touched me, I knew that this was the absolution I'd always sought. She released me from the tangled confines of my habit, and allowed me to do the same for her. I unwrapped her slowly, like the great, mysterious gift she was. We didn't speak. Not with words. We didn't have to. Within the starched, white confines of our fabric prison, we discovered an explosive new world filled with sensation and color.

Somewhere along a twisted path of my subconscious, I understood that this loss of innocence came with a price. That my life as part of this enclosed community would never continue as it had been. But as we lay together atop our bed of broken vows, I didn't care.

When finally we disentangled ourselves, I dislodged my habit from the machine. We dressed in silence. I could sense the change in Felice. She was somber. Her eyes were dark. Lifeless. She wouldn't meet my gaze. When I reached out to help her with her veil, she shrank from my touch. I tried to conceal my hurt. My panic.

"It's all right," I said.

"No," she replied. "It isn't. It won't ever be."

She strode to the door to leave. I stood in stunned

silence and watched her go, surrounded by all the top-
pled columns of wash that had borne silent witness to
our loving misdeeds. But when Felice turned the knob,
the door wouldn't budge. She shook the knob and pulled
at it. Her attempts grew more frantic with each failed
attempt.

"It won't open!"

I hurried over to try and help her. Surely the door was
just stuck? It, like everything else at the abbey, was
ancient. Slow. Uncooperative.

I tried to turn the knob several times. It was hopeless.

"It's locked." I met her eyes. "From the outside."

Felice backed away and wilted to the floor. "It's her.
She *knows*. She *saw* us."

She meant Sister Agnes.

"You don't know that." I tried to reassure her, but it
was pointless. In my heart, I knew she was right. Sister
Agnes was the sacristan of our order. She, alone, held
all the keys.

Have many friends, they said.

Many. Not one.

We heard the sound of a key turning in the lock. The
door swung open.

Sister Agnes filled up the opening like the agent of
an angry god. She would not look at either of us. She
turned sideways and pointed a long, thin finger up the
rocky hill toward the main house.

"The Abbess is waiting for you both. Go. Now."

I followed Felice on that last, fateful climb. She never
looked back at me. I watched her small, straight back
disappear behind the large, paneled door that led to the
Abbess's office. I was instructed to wait outside. I never
saw Felice emerge. I never saw Felice again. Ever.

I had already made my decision. I knew my life in the
church was over. Many were called. I would not be
among the chosen. I had made certain of that.

I had no idea what Felice would decide. Or what the Abbess would decide for her.

The next morning, I packed my small, cardboard suitcase and walked the three and a half miles into town. I couldn't go home. I had no home to go to. I had only a heart full of pain, and the soft, sweet, tender memory of a timorous and ill-fated first love that would never fade.

8

Big Girls Don't Cry

Quinn got up early so she could get the boat over to Plattsburgh as soon as the Dock Street Marina opened. She wanted to be first in line to get her registration for the tournament handed in. She wasn't sure if the officials would bother looking her boat over, but she was prepared if they did. She had read over all of the watercraft requirements more than a dozen times, and her pontoon, while unorthodox, complied with every single rule. Junior made sure of that. Every time he threw up an obstacle, Quinn found a way to work around it. And, thanks to her friends at Astroglide, she had the cash for the entrance fee. Until last night, the only thing she'd been missing was a man's name on the form.

But that wasn't a problem any more. Not since Marvin showed up and offered to help her out.

Marvin. Boy, she never could've predicted that. Nobody else would, either. And he wasn't exactly happy to be offering to help out. He made that much clear.

"Why do you want to do this if it makes you so mad?" She asked him that question last night, while they stood on the pier beside the boat. He looked big and imposing in his baggy pants and oversized, yellow windbreaker. He was taller than Quinn, too. She'd never noticed that about him before.

"Let's get something straight," he said. "I *don't* want to do this."

Quinn felt like he was spitting the words at her. It didn't make any sense.

"I still don't get it."

"You don't need to *get* it. And if you don't want my help, that's fine with me."

Quinn reached out a hand to stop him. It looked like he was going to walk away. "No. Wait. I want your help."

"Fine. Show me where I sign the damn paper and let's get this over with."

"It's not that simple."

"What do you mean?"

"I mean you have to do more than sign the application. You have to go out with me. Every time."

He blew out a breath and looked back up toward the inn. She could see the muscles in his jaw working.

"It's only three days," she added.

"Three days?" He looked at her like he was trying to figure out if he could pick her up and toss her into the lake. "On that piece of shit?"

Quinn looked at her boat. She'd done a good job tricking it out. Everything was in place for the tournament. Twin engines with a cutoff switch. A live well made from a cooler with an outboard aerator. Junior's chair. A big fridge for her beer. Even her corporate sponsor logo was in place. It looked spiffy, too. The neon letters danced in the moonlight. The subtle rocking of the boat made them look like they were animated.

"It's not a piece of shit. It's perfect."

Marvin was unconvinced. "The only thing that's 'perfect' is your chance to end up on the bottom of this lake. I've watched you pilot this thing. You don't know your ass from a hole in the ground."

"Montana helps me. And it's not like I have to parallel park it or anything. I do okay."

He shook his head. "I don't know what I'm worried about. They'll never approve this thing for the competition."

"Does that mean you'll help me?"

He stared at her but didn't say anything.

"Well?" Quinn asked again.

He held out a hand. "Gimme the goddamn paper to sign. If you get in, we'll talk about it."

Well. She got in, all right.

As it turned out, the tournament administrator did walk out to look at her boat. Quinn thought his eyes were going to pop out of his head when he saw it, tied up between a Bass Tracker and an Allison XB that each looked like they could break world records for speed. Each time he cited an obstacle—and there were a lot of them—Quinn showed him how she had complied with the letter of the requirements. He really had no choice but to let her in. When he handed her the registration card, a set of numbered badges, and the schedule for weigh-in times, his gruffness waned a bit.

"Look, lady," he said. "Why don't you save yourself the fifteen hundred bucks and stay off the water? These boys," he gestured toward the sleek, hopped-up boats that clogged row after row of slips in the marina, "all play for keeps. They're pros with years of experience and the best tracking equipment money can buy. You won't have a prayer."

Quinn took the registration card and the ID badges from him. "Thanks. I'll take my chances."

He held up both hands. "Don't say I didn't warn you."

Quinn smiled at him and picked her way back through the latticework of wooden docks to climb back aboard her boat. Winning didn't really matter to her. She understood that now. She wanted to be part of something that nobody ever thought she could do. The more people tried to talk her out of it, the stronger her resolve to compete grew. And now, thanks to Marvin, she was going to get that chance.

She felt bad about Junior, though. Even though he'd started out acting like an old curmudgeon, she could tell that he was starting to loosen up. He'd been talking more. On their last couple of trips out he'd even pointed out some great spots to her—places he said the pros would never look at twice. Places Phoebe was known to frequent.

"You pay attention to her," he said. "She'll show you where the big'uns are. You drop your line in any of her favorite spots and you'll be likely to haul up a winner."

That seemed to make sense. But Quinn didn't know how to guess where Phoebe might be found. "How do I know where to look for her?"

He handed her a dog-eared map of the islands that he'd marked up with a red grease pencil.

"These are all the places I seen her over the years," he explained. "Ever time I fished in any of these spots, I bagged a keeper."

Quinn stayed up late that night poring over every detail of the map. She memorized the locations of all the places where Junior had made his fat, little tick marks. She took her own pencil and drew straight lines connecting all the spots, trying to plot routes that made sense. One thing she knew was that tournament fishing was all about speed. You had to get from one hole to the next fast—that's why the boats belonging to the pros were doped out like water rockets.

When Quinn showed her route map to Montana, Montana just stared at it with an odd expression on her face.

"What's wrong with it?" Quinn was afraid she'd done something stupid again.

"Don't you see it?"

Quinn looked down at the series of red marks and intersecting lines. It didn't look like anything to her but a small fortune in marine gas.

"No."

"Pisces."

"What?"

Montana pointed down at the map. "The pattern you've drawn here. It's Pisces. The fish. You know—the constellation?"

Quinn looked at the map again. *Holy shit.* How had she not seen that? Not only did it look like the outline of a giant fish, it looked exactly like Phoebe. At least, it was how Quinn remembered Phoebe looking in that weird-ass dream.

When she got back, she'd show the map to Marvin. He said he'd help her out if the boat got approved. He was on the hook now.

Quinn laughed at her own joke.

Yeah. They were all on the hook now.

Montana was waiting when Quinn cut her engines and drifted in toward the dock at the inn.

"Toss me a cleat line."

Quinn left the bridge and threw a rope to Montana. Montana caught it and pulled the bow of the boat in.

"You really need to remember to turn this thing around when you come in."

"I know." Quinn apologized. "I keep forgetting."

Montana tied up both ends of the pontoon. "How did it go?"

Quinn gave her a toothy grin. "We're in."

"What?" Montana's eyes were like saucers. "No shit?"

"No shit. Look." Quinn held up the badges.

"But I don't understand. How did you get them to waive the whole man requirement?"

"I didn't."

"Then how can we be in?"

"Because we got another man." Quinn hopped off the boat to join her on the dock.

"Who?"

"Marvin Pants."

Montana blinked. "Who the hell is Marvin Pants?"

"Smile when you say that name, little girl."

The voice from behind her made Montana jump about a foot into the air. Quinn caught hold of her arm to keep her from going off the edge of the dock into the water.

"Jesus, Mavis!" Montana groused. "Don't sneak up on people like that." Montana turned around to face her. "You scared the crap outta me." Montana did a double take when she saw the large man standing behind her. "Why are you dressed like—that?"

"Montana?" Quinn explained. "Meet Marvin."

Montana looked back and forth between Quinn and Mavis. "Marvin?"

"It's a long story, missy. And it's one I ain't telling. So just do us all a favor and don't ask."

Montana looked back at Quinn. "Mavis is a man?"

"No." Quinn corrected. "Marvin is a man. Mavis is Mavis." She looked at Mavis. "Right, Marvin?"

"Right. Now the two of you get out of my way. I want to check this piece of junk out to be sure it's seaworthy before I park my ass on it for three days."

Marvin pushed past Montana and climbed aboard the pontoon. Montana watched him with a dazed expression.

"I don't get it. She's a *man?*"

"I guess she is for about half the time."

"Which half?"

Quinn shrugged. "Right now, I guess it's just the for the half we need. So that's all I care about."

Montana watched Marvin moving around on the boat, checking the engines and everything else Quinn had rigged. She looked down at her feet.

"I sure never saw that one coming."

———

"Is this seat taken?"

Towanda smiled up at Cricket. "It is now."

"Thanks." Cricket pulled out the vacant chair and sat down. Hero's Welcome was hopping this morning and all of the tables were already taken. Cricket had been wandering around inside the store for fifteen minutes waiting for one to open up. She was relieved when she recognized Towanda. She set her cup of coffee and her blackberry scone down on top of the table. She had a folded copy of *The Island Times* tucked beneath her arm.

"I've seen those papers around." Towanda pointed at the tabloid. "Anything good in them?"

"There are some great deals if you're in the market for a used pickup that's been wrecked. But I prefer to read the personal ads."

"It has personal ads?"

"Hell, yes." Cricket picked it up and flipped it open to a page with a folded corner. "SWM seeks BBW-Dom. Must like B&D and water sports."

"Water sports? What the hell does that mean?"

Cricket lowered the paper. "You're kidding me, right?"

"No."

"Don't you write this stuff for a living?"

Towanda shrugged.

"Water sports equals golden showers. You've heard of those, right?"

"Of course I have."

"Let's see what else we have here." Cricket scanned the columns of type. "Ah. Here's a winner. MWM iso SF for ANR. NSA."

"Do I even want to know what all of that means?"

"Probably not, but I'll tell you anyway."

"You mean you know?"

Cricket peered at her over the tops of her glasses.

"Right. Okay." Towanda picked up her coffee mug. "I guess that's a yes."

"Let's break this down." Cricket held the paper up. "Married White Male in search of Single Female for Adult Nursing Relationship. No Strings Attached."

Towanda choked on her coffee.

"Are you okay?"

Towanda continued to sputter and hack.

"Raise your arms over your head."

"I'll be okay."

"Here." Cricket pushed a glass of water toward her. "Have some of this."

Towanda waved it off. "Why do people always try to get you to drink something when you're choking?"

"Beats me."

"Beats you? Aren't you a nurse?"

"Yes. But plainly that fact doesn't make me any more of an authority on choking than being an erotic author makes you on the unique language of personal ads."

"It's true. I don't have a lot of experience with them."

"Why do I find that hard to believe?"

"I don't know. Why do you?"

"Probably because you're supposed to be our reigning authority on deviant sex acts."

Towanda rolled her eyes. "You spend too much time listening to Viv."

"You mean she's wrong?"

"I don't write about 'deviant' sex acts. I write serious books about consensual, adult relationships—something Viv wouldn't know the first thing about."

"So *MILF Money* is a book about adult relationships?"

"In fact, it is. Have you read it?"

"No."

"Because?"

"Frankly, I found the title off-putting."

Towanda laughed. "And yet, you read personal ads."

"Touché."

"So you see?" Towanda picked up her coffee again. "Appearances can be deceiving."

"Okay." Cricket closed the paper and set it aside. "Let's talk about some appearances that aren't so deceiving."

"Such as?"

"Such as the thing between you and Viv."

"That's a long story."

"Lucky for us, the refills here are free."

Towanda smiled. "Maybe I don't care to discuss my relationship with Viv."

"Relationship? That's a new term for it."

"Really? What would you call it?"

"Well. The phrase 'cage fight' springs to mind."

Towanda shook her head. "It hasn't always been like this. There was a time when we were a lot—closer. But everything changed when I met Barry."

"Who is Barry?"

"Barry Faderman. My husband. Viv flipped out when we got married. I think she felt betrayed."

Cricket was surprised that Towanda was being so forthcoming. She wasn't sure how much more she could ask.

What the hell? In for a penny, in for a pound. She decided to go for it.

"Were you two involved?"

Towanda raised an eyebrow.

"Romantically, I mean."

"Hell, *no*." Towanda practically spat the words out. "Viv's issue with me relates to her belief that I'm sponging off the experiences of others."

"Others? What others?"

"You name it. In her view, I don't have the right to write any stories about 'authentic' lesbians."

"Why not?"

"Because I 'suck dick,' as she so charmingly puts it."

Cricket noticed that Towanda's colorful description turned more than a few heads in the tiny deli. It was clear that this wasn't typical breakfast conversation in Clifstock.

"You're straight?"

"Yes. But that has nothing to do with my ability to write good fiction."

"Why not write good fiction about other straight people? Why write about lesbians?"

"Let me ask you something." Towanda leaned forward. "Why do you write books about nursing?"

"Because it's what I know."

"The same thing is true for me."

"You know about lesbians?"

Towanda nodded.

It wasn't the most implausible thing she'd ever heard. After all, Kübler-Ross wrote what arguably was the definitive book about death and dying without the benefit of being dead.

"I guess that makes sense."

"But?"

"But I'm curious about how you learned so much about lesbians?"

"You'll have to take my word for it." Towanda broke off a corner of Cricket's scone and popped it into her mouth. "I've done my time."

⁓

Run.

That was always her instinct when things went south. Run as far and as fast as she could.

211

Running kept her safe. Running kept her focused on the future and not the past. Running made sure that anything she didn't want to look at too closely stayed behind her where it belonged. That was especially true for all of those broken, disconnected fragments that had no relationship to who she was now. They were the random pieces of her former life that didn't fit—like curly bits of celluloid on the cutting-room floor of her subconscious.

She didn't want to look at them, and she didn't want to add to them, either. And if she ran far enough and fast enough, she wouldn't have to.

Running made her good at her job, too. That's what asset recovery was all about: sleight of hand. Being smarter and faster than the people who were trying to outrun their obligations.

Darien knew all about the rules of that game. She'd spent a lifetime perfecting her own techniques.

But were they obligations? Had they ever been?

How could things you never chose obligate you?

If she could answer that one, she could give up spec fiction and make a fortune writing pop psychology books.

And maybe she wouldn't be sitting here alone in the dark, staring out the window at a blank landscape, second-guessing everything she thought she understood about the newest tangled mess in her life.

Her head was reeling from everything that had happened last night.

They were both pretty shell-shocked when they finally got untangled and climbed out of the water. It was odd, but Vee seemed calmer than she did. Less rattled by the sudden turn their surprising friendship had taken.

Maybe that was just because Vee was more composed, generally? Darien's demeanor wasn't anything like composed. She could barely make eye contact with Vee when they shook themselves off and started their squishy climb back toward their rooms at the inn. They trudged across the sloping lawn in silence and parted by the flower garden, just outside the entrance to the restaurant. Darien's room was in the garden house, located in the center of the property near the barns. Vee had a waterfront room at the extreme north end of the inn.

They didn't say anything to each other when they parted. Vee gave Darien a small smile, and Darien responded with a soggy, half-hearted wave.

She felt like a complete idiot. She blamed her lack of self-control on how rattled she'd been after running headlong into one of the worst roadblocks of her life. It completely knocked her off her footing. It made her feel vulnerable again—and she hated that. She hated that even more than the gut-punch of seeing *him* again.

And Vee had been right there to witness it all.

That meant she couldn't pretend it hadn't happened. Vee made it clear that she wasn't going to let Darien off the hook. And after everything that happened between them last night, she was certain of it.

Darien had been back in her room for about thirty minutes and had just emerged from the shower when she heard the soft knocking at her door.

"Hang on a minute!" She pulled on a t-shirt and a clean pair of sweat pants and walked over to open the door.

Vee was standing there. She had changed clothes, too, although her hair was still wet. For some reason, that made her look smaller. More youthful. She looked scared, too. Like she wasn't at all sure why she was there. Or maybe she was scared because she didn't know how Darien would react to seeing her there, outside her room, at nine o'clock at night?

"I have no idea why I'm here." Vee sounded like she meant it.

"I do."

Darien reached out and took Vee by the hand and pulled her forward into the room.

Within seconds, they were wrapped around each other and headed for the bed.

"Wait a minute." Vee tried to slow them down. "Shouldn't we talk about this?"

"What?" Darien was taking deep breaths. "What do you want to talk about?"

"What are we doing?"

They were sprawled across the bed. Their clothes were already halfway off. They'd knocked the alarm clock off the nightstand. Darien thought what they were doing was pretty clear.

"You don't wanna do this?"

"I didn't say that." Vee tried to sit up. Darien rolled to the side so she could. "I just haven't done—*this*—for a long time. A very long time."

Darien rested a hand on Vee's bare back. Her skin felt warm and smooth. "They say it's like riding a bicycle."

"They lie. It's nothing like riding a bicycle." She looked down at Darien. "At least not for me."

Darien sat up, too. "Here." She handed Vee her discarded shirt. "Put this back on. We can talk."

"You're okay with that?"

Darien nodded.

Vee took the shirt. "You don't think I'm a freak?"

"Why would I think you're a freak?"

Vee shook her head. "Let's see. I practically throw myself at you, and then I run scared. Isn't that the classic definition of a cock tease?"

"You'd have to ask Towanda that question."

"Towanda?"

"According to Viv, she's the only one in this crowd with a cock."

Vee looked confused. "Towanda has a cock?"

"Yeah. She just keeps it in another suit. It's called a husband."

Vee rolled her eyes. But she smiled, so Darien knew she'd managed to defuse some of her angst.

Darien bumped her shoulder. "So what else did you want to discuss?"

"Aren't you confused by this? We don't exactly fit."

"I don't know. I think we fit pretty well."

"I really wish you'd be serious."

"I *am* being serious."

"It doesn't feel like it."

"Well, what does it feel like?"

"The truth?"

Darien nodded.

Vee exhaled. "Wonderful. Exciting." She slowly shook her head. "Arousing."

"And that's a bad thing?"

"No. Not bad. Just…."

"Just?"

"Unexpected. Not something I planned on."

Darien dropped her chin to Vee's shoulder. "I didn't plan on it either. But then, I never plan on any of the great things that happen to me. They always take me by surprise."

"You think this is a great thing?"

"I think it has been so far."

Vee didn't reply.

"I guess you don't agree?"

"No." Vee shifted on the bed so she was facing Darien. "I think it's incredible. And terrifying."

Darien smiled at her. "It'll only be terrifying if we fuck it up."

"We have nothing in common."

Darien took hold of her hand. "We have everything in common."

"We want different things."

"The world is big enough to make allowances for that."

"You don't know anything about me."

"You don't know anything about me, either."

"That doesn't concern you?"

"Not if we're willing to teach each other what we don't know."

Vee closed her eyes and leaned her forehead against Darien's. "This is insane."

"It's okay." Darien wrapped both arms around her. "I think it's supposed to be."

They didn't say much after that. Not with words anyway.

When Darien woke up several hours later, Vee was gone. She sat up and looked around the dark room to be sure. Her clothes were gone. And the alarm clock was back in its spot on the nightstand. The red numbers on its display mocked her. Three-fourteen a.m.

Of course. *Pi.*

215

The circumference of a circle is equal to Pi times the diameter. She remembered that from math class.

Isn't that essentially what she'd been trying to explain to Vee? Yes. They were a different kind of equation. But they added up to the same result.

But Vee was gone. Vee was gone because, somehow, the math just didn't work for her.

And Darien was left alone—alone and fighting her own impulse to run.

Essay 8

I don't know why they asked me to write this story for their chick-lit art show. I'm not a writer. And I sure as hell ain't a woman.

When I told that to Barb, she said "But you play one on TV."

I guess she was talking about my job, and she thought that was funny. But my job is no joke. And even though some people might think so, my life ain't much of one, either.

I work the night shift at the San Diego Central Jail. That's how I first met up with all these crazy women. They all got busted after a riot broke out during that lesbo smut meeting they called CLIT-Con. All I can say is, they picked the wrong time to tango. Judge Carla Roberts was on the bench that night, and she don't take shit from nobody—especially from spoiled white women who ought to know better. She could've let 'em all go with just a warning, but when that short redhead started mouthing off about some Bible beater, Carla just banged her gavel and said it would do them all good to spend a night cooling their wingtips in the can. Carla's like that. She runs a hardcore bench.

That's where I came in. I'm the night matron at the women's detention facility. That means I got to babysit all these yammering broads until their high-priced lawyers could make bail. Half of them got sprung in the first forty-five minutes. The rest? Hell. If the boys upstairs hadn't needed a bottle opener, they'd probably all still be in there. Don't even ask what I mean by that. You wouldn't believe me, anyway.

Let me just tell you one thing about lesbians. No matter how butch they try to be, they still act just like bitchy, stupid sorority girls when you get them all together in a group. Happy, sad, or mad—they're like a bunch of yapping dogs fighting over the same squeaky toy. And most of them even look like those fat, candy-ass dogs that only roll out of bed to eat or hump your leg. So don't even try to tell me that I'm like them—cause I'm not. Not one bit.

My mama died when I turned fourteen. That meant that me and my two brothers had to figure something out. I knew enough to know that if anybody found out we were alone, we'd get split up and sent to different places—if we were lucky. We didn't have any relatives who could take us in. Our apartment was not real expensive, and nobody paid much attention to us—the place where we lived then was just too big for that. So I decided to quit school and look for a job. I didn't have to make a lot of money—just enough to get us by until the boys were out of school.

I didn't get very far. Because I was big, I didn't have a hard time passing for eighteen. But I guess my size made me look dangerous, because most people thought I was going to rob them or rape their daughters as soon as their backs were turned. My stutter didn't help, either. I've always had it—and it gets worse when I'm nervous. So I think that combination just made me look dangerous and stupid.

It wasn't really hard for me to quit school. I was a loner and I hated it. Besides, I already knew most of what I needed to know about how things worked. It turned out I was right, too. I found out really fast that nobody wanted to hire a big black boy who couldn't talk straight or look you in the eye—and we were getting desperate. The little bit of money my mama had stashed in an old envelope beneath her nightgowns was nearly gone. I knew that if I didn't find something soon, I'd either have to call social services, or go to work for one of the gangbangers on the corner.

That's when I met Mrs. Alvarez. She was a Guatemalan woman who lived in an apartment down the hall from us. She cleaned houses for some rich white people, and I'd see her nearly every day—standing out in front of our building in her gray and white uniform, waiting on the bus to take her across town. She was a lot older than mama, and didn't have any kids left at home. One morning, when I was walking past the bus stop, she stopped me and asked where mama was. I wanted to run away from her—I didn't want to tell her that mama was dead and that we were living there alone, and that I was on our last fifty bucks and had no way to pay the rent that month.

I tried to tell her something about mama being away, but my stammer was so bad I knew she couldn't understand me. I tried to walk on past her, but she grabbed my arm and stopped me. Nobody ever just touched me like that. I was shocked. Then she called me by my name. Marvin. She knew who I was. She asked me if we had food. Her English wasn't all that great, but I understood her just fine. I could feel myself starting to lose it. She just squeezed my arm and told me not to worry. Then her bus showed up and she was gone.

That night, when I got home and stood at the door trying to get my key to work, I heard my brothers inside talking to somebody. That scared me shitless. I knew it meant that somebody called social services on us. I thought about running, but I knew I couldn't leave the boys like that, so I opened the door and went on inside.

I was shocked when I saw Mrs. Alvarez in there,

standing at the stove in our kitchen. She was cooking something, and it smelled really good. And my brothers were sitting at the table eating like they hadn't seen food in a month. That part really embarrassed me, but I tried not to show it.

Mrs. Alvarez told me to sit down. She already had a plate out for me. It was loaded up with eggs and bacon—and there was a big plate of toast, too. She gave me a big glass of orange juice and told me to drink it. Pretty soon, we were all eating big piles of scrambled eggs and thick pieces of toast with some kind of red, homemade berry stuff smeared all over it. She told me there was more food in the fridge. When I told her we couldn't pay her for it, she just waved her hand in my face and ignored me.

I remember thinking that she was pretty damn bossy for somebody who had just walked in off the street. No matter how much she knew Mama, she didn't know us at all. So why was she doing this? I tried to ask her that—but I learned real fast that when she didn't want to answer a question, she just did that hand-wave thing and pretended she didn't understand what you were saying. She was a small woman, but there was something about her that made her seem big. I knew it wouldn't be a good idea to mess with her.

When we finished eating, she told my brothers to go do their homework. I didn't believe it when they just got up from the table and went off to obey her. I always had to strong-arm them and practically tie them into their chairs to get them to study. Then she handed me a towel and told me to help her do the dishes. She asked me if I needed a job. I was too embarrassed to look at her, so I just nodded. She asked me how old I was, and when I said fourteen, she shook her head. She told me that I needed to be in school, but I said I couldn't go back because I told my teachers we were moving away to keep them from looking for me. She asked where I had looked for work, and I told her pretty much everyplace. Then I explained that nobody would hire me because I was big and acted slow.

She looked around our small apartment and asked who kept it so clean. We never had all that much, but Mama made sure that we always took good care of things. I didn't let my brothers slide on that after she was gone. I told Mrs. Alvarez that we just kept things tidy because that's what we knew.

She looked me up and down, and said she had an idea about something that might work for me—but she wasn't sure if I would want to do it.

I was desperate, and I told her that. I didn't care what it was, as long as I could make enough money to pay our rent and keep the boys in food. When she smiled and asked if I was sure, I knew I was probably in for something awful.

Later that night when she showed me what she had in mind, I knew I was right. She came back after the boys were in bed, and she was carrying a big pile of folded up clothes. When I saw what they were, I told her she was crazy. It would never work, and there was no way I was putting on a dress. Ever. She reminded me of what I said to her before—that I would do anything. I told her that anything didn't mean that. I was already a freak—there was no way I was gonna be a queer, too. I told her I'd rather hook up with one of the gangs that ran things in our neighborhood.

She started folding up the gray and white dress and said that she'd just have to call social services, because I'd soon be dead or in jail. She was halfway out the door before I stopped her. What choice did I have? I knew she was right. I made her promise that she'd never tell anybody.

She handed me the pile of clothes. I held up the

dress—it looked big enough to fit me. I didn't understand that part. Mrs. Alvarez was a small woman, and this would've wrapped around her body twice. She could tell what I was thinking, because she said it belonged to her cousin, Esmeralda, who got deported last year. Esmeralda must've been pretty big all over, because there was a giant bra, too. I looked at Mrs. Alvarez and she just did that hand wave of hers and told me to put it on, too.

I still don't know what it was that made me give in to this pushy little woman I barely knew. I think it was something more than just being desperate. There was something weird about that dress. As soon as I saw it, I knew it was going to change me. And when I put it on, I just felt different. Maybe it was because I didn't look like me anymore. But I don't think that was all of it. I just felt better. Like I wasn't shy anymore—and I didn't have to take shit from anybody just because I was big and strong. Once I had those clothes on, being big and strong felt like a good thing. It felt right. And I didn't stutter anymore, either.

So that night, Marvin became Mavis—and pretty much stayed that way.

Don't get me wrong. That didn't make me a fag. I still liked girls. But I knew that I could do things dressed like a woman that I would never be able to do as a man. I did, too. Working with Mrs. Alvarez, I made enough money to help my brothers get through San Diego City College. After that, a judge I cleaned for helped me get my GED and a job as a bailiff at Central. I should say that she helped Mavis, because by then, I was pretty much Mavis all the time.

I still am. For me, being Mavis is just less complicated than being Marvin. That's it.

9

Following Signs

Quinn was dreaming. She knew it the way you just knew things. Like when you had those dreams about falling off a cliff or getting chased by a steamroller—you pretty much understood that it wasn't real. Even though it felt real and scared the piss out of you. You just went with it and knew that at some point you'd wake up and everything would be okay.

This dream was like that, too.

She was out on the boat with her fish map. The one Montana said looked like that zodiac symbol for Pisces. She was practicing the routes, driving from one spot to the next to find the fastest ways to get around. She needed to figure that out before the tournament started. She needed to know how to get from one location to the next so she'd have the best shot at catching the biggest fish. The weigh-ins were every afternoon at two o'clock at Dock Street Marina in Plattsburgh. That meant she'd have to be on her way to New York— or, at least, fishing that part of the lake—every day at lunchtime. She wanted to be sure to pull into the marina with plenty of time to spare.

In her dream, the lake was calm and smooth—more like ice than water. All of the tiny islands looked different, too. Long, drooping lengths of red garland connected them to each other. Quinn thought they all looked like they'd been strung together as part of a great, land flotilla. The garland reminded her of the grease pencil lines on her map. It made sense.

Dreams were like that. Ordinary things had a tendency to take on fantastic proportions—especially if you ate a lot of beef before bed. Just like that time she dreamed that her Harley turned into a black stallion with raven wings and a peacock tail. She knew it wasn't real, but she enjoyed flying across the heavens, anyway. It was only later that she found out this same thing happened to the prophet Mohammed.

She didn't know much about his religion, but she figured he must've eaten a lot of beef, too.

The boat was running well. She'd made fantastic time zipping from one spot on the map to the next. But the smooth, unbroken surface of the water made it impossible to get a line in. She'd cast, but her hooks and rigs just bounced and skidded across the surface. Nothing would penetrate. She even tried heavier weights on the line. No dice.

She decided to try a different lure. Junior's mantra was always "If nothing else works, try a worm."

Worms were pretty disgusting and she had a hard time imagining why a fish would want to eat one. Even Phoebe pointed that out during their conversation. So Quinn went shopping for fake ones. Junior was helpful there, too. He told her that the color of the worms mattered, but that Lake Champlain bass were picky and she shouldn't waste her money on any of those crazy, day-glow jobbers. Big fish like Phoebe had refined tastes. They were more likely to be attracted by the dust-covered classics found at the back of the rubber worm aisle: black grape, chartreuse, pumpkinseed, blue fleck, and scuppernong. Quinn made sure she had plenty of each on hand.

She was rooting around in her tackle box trying to decide which one she wanted to try when she heard the voice. It stopped her cold.

"Don't waste your time, Einstein. They're not biting today."

Phoebe.

Nobody else had a voice like that. It sounded like pea gravel in a blender. There was no mistaking who it belonged to.

Quinn wheeled around. Phoebe was watching her from the surface of the cooler. Somehow, the aerator was hooked up and humming. A small column of bubbles rose around her.

"How did you get in there?"

"You tell me." Phoebe flipped her fat tail. "It's your damn dream."

Quinn sighed and sat down on a folding chair. "I was gonna try one of these pumpkinseed worms." She held one up. "But I can't get anything to break through the surface. It's like the lake has a shell on it, and everything just bounces off."

"That sounds about right."

"You mean this has happened before?"

"To the lake? No. But I'm sure it happens to you all the time."

"What's that supposed to mean?"

"If I have to spell it out for you, you're going to have to give me something to eat."

Quinn didn't remember packing any food for this dream—but then, she didn't plan for any of the other things that were happening, either. She figured she might as well check.

"Let me see what's in the fridge."

She walked over to the battered Kelvinator and opened its dented door. The shelves inside were lined with tiny containers filled with tomato aspic. She remembered that Phoebe had liked that the last time. She pulled one out.

"I have more of this."

"That'll work. Dump it in here."

Quinn complied.

"Do you want some crackers with that?" Phoebe was already busy sucking up the red goo.

"That depends. You got any hard-boiled eggs in that thing?"

"No. Just a lot of this stuff."

"Next time, try to plan ahead." Phoebe continued with her lusty slurping. She had a big appetite. That was one thing they had in common.

"How do I plan ahead for what happens in a dream?"

Phoebe seemed to be taking a moment to consider her response. That was a first. Normally, she'd just roll out some snappy reply.

"Dreams are just extensions of what takes place in your real life. The things you do, the things you don't do. The things you fear or worry about. So you really have more control over the content of your dreams than you realize."

"I don't get it."

Phoebe sighed. "Let's try an object lesson. Look down there at the contents of your tackle box. It's full of all kinds of different things: lures, sinkers, flies, hooks, rubber worms. Every one of them is tucked neatly into its own compartment. But if you took them all out, dropped them together into a can, gave the can a good shake, then emptied it all out onto the deck, what you'd have is a big jumble of mess. All the parts would be the same, but the way they'd be mixed-up together would make no sense."

Quinn blinked. She sort of understood that. Mostly.

"So that's what dreams are? Mixed-up parts of other realities?"

"Quinn Glatfelter, come on down!" Phoebe flipped her tail.

"You mean I got it right?"

"It was bound to happen. But don't get cocky. Breakthroughs for you are few and far between."

Quinn sat back on her stool. "So why is the water like this?"

"Like what?"

"Hard. Solid." Quinn looked out across the glassy surface of the lake. "I can't get a line into it no matter how much weight I put on it."

"That's because it isn't the lake."

"It isn't?"

Phoebe shook her head.

"What is it, then?"

"It's *you*. It's your subconscious."

Quinn took a deep breath and slowly let it out.

"Lemme guess," Phoebe quipped. "You don't know what that means?"

"No."

"The Lord giveth, and the Lord taketh away."

"Hey? Could you at least pretend to be nice?"

"It's *your* dream. You tell me."

Quinn slapped herself on the hand.

"What the hell are you doing?"

Quinn slapped herself again. "I'm trying to wake myself up."

"It doesn't work that way." Phoebe tossed her head toward the fridge. "Go get yourself a beer."

"There isn't any beer in there. There's only more of the aspic."

"Do us both a favor and go check, anyway."

Quinn got up and went to the fridge. This time when she opened it, the shelves were lined with amber-colored bottles of Backcast Pale Ale.

"What the hell?" She pulled one out. "How did this get in there?"

"You wanted one, right?" Phoebe asked.

"Well. Yeah."

"Same thing goes for the lake. You want the hard surface to go away? Then you have to make it disappear."

"How do I do that?"

"You start by imagining a lake that isn't hard and solid. You allow yourself to think about a body of water that's open and fluid—that has depth and dimension. And as you begin to do that, other people in your life will be able to explore it with you. You won't continue to be confined to whatever skates across the surface." Phoebe tossed her head. "And maybe you'll learn to ditch the damn dog collar."

"How do you know all this stuff?"

"Duh? See these liver spots on my ass?"

"You mean you know all this because you're old?"

"They don't call you Einstein for nothin', do they?"

Quinn shrugged.

"Besides. I already told you: this is *your* dream. All of these pearls of wisdom I've been shoveling at you are really coming from your own subconscious."

"You mean I've already figured this out?"

"If you have to ask me that question, then probably not."

Quinn heard a faint beeping sound. She looked around the boat but didn't see anything wrong. *Maybe one of the 12-volt batteries was running out of juice?*

"It's not a battery."

Quinn looked at Phoebe.

"It's your alarm clock. Put my ass back in the water before you wake up. I don't wanna spend eternity in this damn tank."

Quinn put her beer down and approached the cooler.

"I can't put you in the water. The lake is solid. Remember?"

"Just do it."

Quinn hesitated. The beeping noise was getting louder.

"Take a leap of faith, here." Phoebe was getting impatient.

Quinn picked her up and carried her to the side of the boat. Phoebe flipped out of her hands and dove into the water. The splash she made was like a small tidal wave. The cold water flew up and hit Quinn in the face. She bolted into wakefulness. Her room was still dark but the first rays of sunlight were starting to creep in beneath the window shade.

Her alarm was still going off.

And her face was wet.

"Do you have a minute?"

Montana caught up with Barb on the lawn between the inn and the barn. Barb was heading for her workshop. She wanted to get a couple of hours in before the afternoon session kicked off.

"Sure." Barb stopped and faced her. "What's up?"

"I wanted to talk with you about Marvin."

Uh oh.

"Ah. So you met him?"

Montana nodded. "I was pretty blown away by that revelation."

"I can imagine."

"But you knew about it all along?"

"I did. Yes."

"Why didn't you tell anyone?"

"Because it wasn't for me to tell."

"I just don't get it."

Montana seemed pretty distressed. Barb thought her reaction to the news about Mavis was oddly disproportionate to the magnitude of the revelation.

"I can understand that it's a surprise. But it's not like her character changed or anything."

"No. That's true. Marvin is just as big an asshole as Mavis."

Barb laughed.

"Why is he—she—helping us with the tournament?"

Barb demurred. "Why don't you ask her that question?"

"She told me to mind my own business."

"That sounds like her."

Montana threw up her hands. "I'd just really like to know."

Barb sighed. "Come along with me."

"I don't wanna keep you from your work."

"You won't. I can spare a few minutes."

They walked on to the barn in silence. Once they were inside, Barb turned on the overhead light and hauled out an old wooden stool.

"Have a seat."

Montana sat down and looked over the small models that Barb had strewn across the workbench. They were an eclectic assortment of tiny, metal fish. Some were standing up like humans. Others had wings. Several of them were twisted up with hunks of glass or wire. One of them was partially submerged inside a piece of rock. Another one was trapped inside a bottle.

"These are incredible." Montana picked one up. It was a walking fish, and it had two heads. "Are these supposed to be us?"

"Not you," Barb corrected. "Your stories."

"God." Montana twisted the two-headed fish around. "Which one of us is this?"

Barb smiled. "Guess."

Montana blushed and put the tiny sculpture down. "I'd rather not."

"Aren't you happy that Quinn can now compete in the tournament?"

"Of course I am."

"Then what about Mavis's involvement is so unsettling to you?"

Montana didn't reply.

Barb didn't push it. She slowly started to assemble her tools. She wanted to get her prototypes designed for the next couple of essays. Eight of them were near enough to completion now that she felt like she could make serious headway on the forms. The whole concept was really starting to come together now. She liked the direction it was taking. And if she could just light a fire under the damn Outliners, they might have a ghost of a chance at getting this wrapped up before their time ran out on Sunday.

"How did you figure it out?"

Barb looked at her. "How did I figure what out?"

"That Mavis was a man."

"She told me."

"She did?" Montana seemed surprised by that. "Why?"

"Probably because we were getting ready to spend a week together, driving across the country in her truck."

"You didn't suspect anything before that?"

"No. Why would I?"

"I just wondered."

"To be frank, it never occurred to me. But then, I don't normally spend a lot of time speculating about anyone else's gender or sexual identity." She paused. "Do you?"

"Sometimes."

"Why?"

Montana shrugged. "It's just a thing with me."

"How does Quinn feel about it?"

"Are you kidding? Quinn wouldn't care if Mavis had cloven hooves and a forked tail as long as she qualified her to compete in that damn bass tournament."

Barb smiled. "Then I guess there's no problem."

Montana sighed. "I guess not."

Montana had picked up the two-headed fish again, and was slowly turning it over and over.

Barb watched her for a minute. "Why don't you keep that?"

"What?" Montana looked up at her. She seemed embarrassed. "No. I couldn't."

"Sure you could."

"Don't you need it?"

Barb shook her head. "I can make another one."

"I, um. I do kind of like it. It's—*quirky*."

"I do, too. It reminds me that all things are possible."

"Do you really believe that?"

"Mostly."

Montana sat quietly on her stool for another minute. Then she got to her feet. She was still holding the small fish in her hand.

"Thanks. I think I would like to keep this."

"Good."

"I guess I'll see you later at the cocktail hour?"

"Count on it."

Barb watched her head toward the door.

"Montana?" Montana stopped and turned back to face her. "I think you should try talking with Mavis again."

"Why?"

"Because she has a way of knowing when things really matter."

Barb was gratified when Montana didn't try to argue with her. She just nodded and went on her way.

After Montana left, Barb opened a drawer in her toolbox and pulled out another small, two-headed fish. She held it up and smiled. "I love it when a plan comes together."

─────

"You sure as hell look like something the cat drug in." Viv didn't wait for Darien to invite her to sit down. She just pulled out a chair and perched on it.

Great.

Darien had been hoping to finish her breakfast in solitude. Coming in early like this was usually a safe way to guarantee that. Half the time, she was the only one in here with Page Archer, who, by all accounts, never slept.

"I didn't sleep well last night." She hoped Viv would drop it.

"There must be a lot of that going around. I just passed V. Jay-Jay in the breezeway and she looked like death takes a holiday, too."

"You did?" Darien tried to make her question appear casual. "Where was she headed?"

"Who knows?" Viv took a sip of her coffee. "Probably the deli up the road. And who could blame her?" She held up a menu. "These prices are ridiculous."

"They're not that bad unless you order a la carte."

"What are you talking about? Everything on the damn menu is a la carte."

"Except the aspic."

Viv rolled her eyes. "Yeah. They throw that crap in for free."

"I hear that Quinn likes it. Apparently, she's been loading up on it every day when she goes out on the boat."

"It wouldn't surprise me. That woman doesn't have the sense god gave a lab rat."

"Why are you so hard on her?" Darien didn't really care. She just wanted to keep Viv talking so she could hide her panic about why Vee left the inn.

"I'm hard on everyone. Or haven't you noticed?"

"Yeah. I guess that's true."

"You think that's tough? Wait'll I get my hands on the numbskull who defaced the Town of Clifstock sign."

Darien hadn't heard about that. And Viv seemed pretty steamed about it. She was practically yelling. "What happened?"

Viv jerked a thumb toward the lobby. "Page Archer just told me that someone took black paint and changed the *f* in Clifstock to a *t*."

Darien thought about it. "Welcome to Clitstock?"

"Bingo."

Darien smiled at her. "It *is* kinda funny, Viv."

"No it isn't. Lawless behavior like this is precisely what's wrong with America."

Darien wondered why Viv continued to make her pronouncements in such a bombastic tone. Then she got an idea. She leaned to the side and peered past Viv to see Page Archer, working away at the front desk.

She bent forward and spoke in a whisper.

"Where'd you get the black paint?"

Viv leaned forward, too and cupped a hand beside her mouth. "In the barn, beneath Barb's workbench."

Darien chuckled and gave her a fist bump. "Nice work."

"Thanks. I do try."

Darien sat back against her chair. "You must've taken a ladder, too. That sign is pretty high."

Viv shook her red head. "Wanda was tall enough to reach it."

"Wanda?"

Viv nodded.

"Wait a minute. *She* helped you? I thought you two hated each other?"

"What are you talking about?"

Darien squinted at her. "Did we just fold space and end up in a new galaxy?"

"Of course not. Wanda and I have artistic disagreements. They have nothing to do with our close, personal friendship."

"*Artistic* disagreements?"

Viv nodded.

"With all due respect, Viv, I have to say that I've never ended up in a wrestling match because of an artistic disagreement."

"I'm very passionate about the things that matter to me. That includes my steadfast commitment to the integrity of our literature."

"I guess."

"Passion and good information are the most important aspects of my business career, too."

None of this was really holding water for Darien.

"Viv? You're an actuary."

Viv gave her an energetic nod. "So?"

"So, that's like being a white-collar bookie."

Viv took a moment to let that sink in.

"True. And now that you mention it, I need to get with Cricket about her payouts on that most recent fracas. I think her calculations were flawed. Those ratios were seriously skewed. She never even counted V. Jay-Jay's twenty. And in my view, a verbal bet is just as binding as cash in hand."

Viv's mention of V. Jay-Jay sent Darien into another silent tailspin. *Where had she gone? And what would happen when they ran into each other later on? That is, if Vee showed up at all. Right now, Darien wasn't sure about anything.*

Viv was still prattling on about actuarial science.

"You can never overestimate how much some unassuming event will end up costing. I told Page Archer the same thing yesterday after that group of Bible beaters came in here and wanted to rent the beach for a sunrise service. In my humble opinion, that is a catastrophe in the making. All it would take is for one of those octogenarian holy rollers to slip on the rocks and, bam—this entire inn ends up on the auction block."

Holy rollers?

"Who is renting the beach?"

Viv waved a hand. "Some born-again zealots who are up here *spreading the word*." She put air quotes around the last part of her statement.

Darien didn't have time to follow up with more questions because her heart leapt up into her throat and cut off her air supply.

V. Jay-Jay had just walked into the restaurant.

—⁓—

Quinn stopped in at the A&B supermarket and picked up a couple of party-sized bags of Cool Ranch Doritos and a fridge pack of grape Fanta. She knew it would probably be a while before Junior could return to his dietary staples, but she didn't really know what else he liked, and she wanted to take him something. He didn't seem like the cut flowers type, and she wouldn't have known where to get a bouquet, anyway. The German lady who did all the arrangements for the inn only came in twice a week, and she wasn't due back until next Tuesday, after they all would be gone.

She figured that Junior would get around to indulging in his favorite food groups soon enough, so why not make sure he had plenty of stash on hand?

When she got to the salvage yard, she knocked first on the door of the fieldstone and clapboard house that sat back from the water a ways. But there was no answer. She could see that the lights were on inside the big shed that served as their workshop and store. There was a hazy column of gray smoke belching up from the flue pipe that jutted out of its rusty metal roof. She decided to check it out.

She cinched up her hold on the grocery bags and picked her way down along the runoff ruts that served as a path from the house to the shop.

Sure enough, she could hear the TV blasting as soon as she stepped inside. She knew it was pretty early for game shows and soap operas, so she had no idea what the brothers might watch at this hour of the morning. It was barely eight o'clock.

She threaded her way back through the piles of musty-smelling, cast-off marine equipment until she reached the corner where the Ladd brothers kept their mismatched La-Z-Boy recliners. Junior's new model looked a bit sportier than his former chair, which still sat proudly on the bridge of Quinn's pontoon. She knew that, eventually, that chair would take its place back inside this hallowed monument to things that had outlived their usefulness.

Junior saw her approaching. He was dressed in plaid flannel pajamas and an old, pea green chenille robe that looked more like a kid's bedspread. It had some kind of elaborate western motif going on with its piping—big, lariat-shaped swirls and curlicues all over the place. Quinn thought she could even make out a cowboy hat on the sleeve.

"I brought you some treats," she said. She held up both bulging plastic bags.

He nodded and pointed at the top of the console TV. "Won't be eatin' none of them chips for a while."

It was clear that Junior recognized the telltale, blue and orange packaging of the Doritos.

Quinn set the bags down. "Where's Big Boy?"

"Right behind you."

Quinn turned around to see the older Ladd brother approaching. She had to stifle a laugh. He was wearing a fussy, yellow apron festooned with big tomato appliques. On his right hand, he wore an oversized oven mitt that was shaped like a giant fish. He was carrying a beat-up metal pot full of something steaming.

"Clear off one of them tables for me," he ordered Quinn. "I gotta set this down."

Quinn did as she was ordered and Big Boy set the pot down on a stack of old *Maclean's* magazines. Whatever was in the pot smelled great—even though it looked like a runny mass of caulk.

"What is that stuff?" Quinn asked.

"Maypo." Junior was reaching for his cereal bowl. "This'n chicken noodle soup are about the only things I can eat right now."

"What's Maypo?"

"It's oatmeal with maple in it." Big Boy eyed her. "You want some?"

"No. I already ate breakfast."

Big Boy claimed his own seat in the other recliner and lapsed into his customary radio silence. Quinn noticed that he didn't bother taking off his apron. He did leave the big fish-shaped oven mitt on the handle of the pot, however. Quinn thought it was comical hanging out in the air like that. It reminded her of how Phoebe looked every time she jumped out of her hands and dove for the water.

She wondered if she should tell Junior about her dreams?

No. He'd just think she was off her rocker. She had other business to take care of on this visit. It was best to keep things simple.

"So I came here to tell you that I found somebody to take your place on the boat."

Junior had been shoveling healthy spoonsful of oatmeal into his mouth. He stopped midstream and glared at her.

"Who?"

"It's another one of the guests at the inn. Name's Marvin Pants."

Quinn thought it was best to keep the details to a minimum.

"Marvin who?"

"Pants."

Junior shoved another big spoonful of the oatmeal into his mouth. "Never heard of him."

"He's not from the islands."

"He know how to fish?"

"I don't know about that. He knows how to drive a boat, though."

Junior looked down at his bowl of oatmeal. "I guess that's something."

"I thought you'd want to know. I went over yesterday and got registered."

"They passed that boat?" Big Boy sounded surprised.

Quinn nodded. "Yes sir, they sure did."

"Ain't no accounting for taste, I reckon." He turned his attention back to the TV. Quinn glanced at the screen. It was some old movie.

"What are you watching?"

Big Boy grunted.

"It's that one about falling," Junior explained. "With Jimmy Stewart and Miss Ellie."

Miss Ellie?

Quinn looked more closely at the screen. "You mean Barbara Bel Geddes?"

Junior nodded. "And that other blonde one. The Novak girl."

"*Vertigo?*"

"Yep. That'n. Big Boy likes watchin' these to look for Alfred Hitchcock." Junior ate another mouthful of hot cereal. "We haven't seen him yet."

"I think you already missed it. He shows up pretty early on."

"He does?" Junior looked over at his brother. Big Boy grunted. "Oh, well. There ain't nothin' else to watch until lunch and the stories come on."

"I wanted to tell you that I'll still fix the Panhead."

Junior took his time answering. "No call to do that. A deal's a deal, and I ain't holdin' up my end of the bargain."

"It's not your fault your gall bladder ruptured."

"We can't pay for it." Big Boy was staring at Quinn with his owl eyes.

"I don't expect you to pay for it. I said I'd fix it if Junior helped me, and Junior helped me."

Big Boy lapsed into silence again.

Quinn looked back at Junior. "You helped me."

"That young girl gonna ride along?"

"You mean Montana?"

Junior nodded.

"Yes sir."

"Well. I suppose you'll do okay, then. She knows her way around that boat."

"She does."

"I didn't have much else to show you, anyway."

Quinn doubted that was true. She figured she could spend the next twenty years on a boat with Junior and not scratch the surface of all he knew about life and what swam in the waters that surrounded these islands.

"I'll always be grateful to you for taking a chance on me."

"You just stick to that map I give you. And don't try none of them fancy rigs on your line. And remember to cut the engines and let the boat drift into them best spots. These fish are smarter'n you and they won't respect you if you roar up into their backyards with all your guns blazin'."

Guns blazing. That made her think about Mavis—*Marvin*. She'd have to tell him to leave his gun in the room.

"Yes, sir. I'll remember."

"And don't never be late for them weigh-ins. You miss one, and it's sayonara. Them Japanese anglers always have the fastest boats and they ain't never late for nothin'." He shook his head. "You really have to hand it to them people when it comes to following the rules."

"I won't be late. I already marked all the spots on the New York side of the lake. I'll make sure I finish up over there."

Junior held up a fat finger. "Don't plan on nothin'. You just finish up wherever you finish up. The fish'll let you know when you're done."

Quinn had no idea what that meant, so she just nodded.

Junior was still staring at her.

"Any other advice?"

He shook his head.

"Okay, then. I guess I'll head out."

"Hold up one more minute." Junior set his cereal bowl down and pointed at a small metal box that sat between a couple of faded photographs on the dusty shelf behind his recliner. "Hand me that old Lucky Strike box."

Quinn retrieved the dented cigarette box and gave it to him. Junior wiped off the top of it with his sleeve. He opened it up and showed its contents to her.

"These here are some flies my granddad tied. Ever time I won one of them tourneys, I was using one of these." He handed the box to Quinn.

The flies were spectacular. Intricate. Precise. Alive with color. They were like small works of art. Quinn couldn't imagine the hands that tied all those delicate little knots.

"These are really beautiful."

Junior nodded. "You take them and use them when the time is right."

Quinn was stunned. Nobody had ever given her anything this meaningful before—especially not anything with this much significance. She ran a fingertip across all the fussy, feathered surfaces. There were more than half a dozen flies in this old cigarette box. All of them tied by the legendary angler, Laddie Ladd—the man whose name was synonymous with fishing the Inland Sea.

"You want me to use your granddad's flies?"

"I figure you could use the help."

Quinn didn't know what to say. She looked up at Junior. "How do I know when the time is right?"

He sat back and pulled on the wooden handle of his recliner. The footrest flew up and came to a stop beneath his feet.

"Nobody else can tell you that. You just have to know."

Quinn stared down into the box again. She wasn't sure if she'd ever know. Not about flies. Not about fishing. And not about life. She closed the tiny box.

Tomorrow would be soon enough to start figuring things out.

She sat down on a low stool beside Junior's chair and watched the rest of the movie.

Essay 9

"And these signs shall follow them that believe; In my name shall they cast out devils; they shall speak with new tongues; They shall take up serpents; and if they drink any deadly thing, it shall not hurt them; they shall lay hands on the sick, and they shall recover."
—Mark 16:17-18

I guess you'd say I was afflicted with a kind of sickness that couldn't be healed by the laying on of hands. My parents were led to understand that some demons were like that. They were told that some demons required more time and focused attention. I don't think it ever occurred to them to wonder if the form the intervention took was a factor in its lack of success.

When the first few prayer sessions with our local preacher didn't succeed at giving me more than a pair of bruised knees, my parents grew desperate. That's when my grandma stepped in and said they should send me to a healer she'd seen work miracles one hot summer night beneath a big canvas revival tent. He was an evangelist, and his special ministry had blazed a trail of fear and repentance across five states. When his dog and pony show set up camp in our small county, my grandma had a front row seat. She went back to hear him every night. And every night, new and even more extraordinary happenings took place. She was a convert—one of many. And her peculiar brand of religious zealotry infected my young life like a tick-borne virus.

Understand that my parents weren't bad people. They were just simple and uninformed. They knew just one way to react when they discovered that their only daughter was a Sodomite. They prayed and asked for God to lead me out of sin, and to plant my feet firmly on the road to righteousness. When their prayers continued to be unanswered, they resorted to more extreme measures.

It isn't that I was opposed to traveling any road that led to a righteous life. I simply didn't think I should be expected to deny who I was to do it. That part didn't feel Christian to me. All of the stories I grew up hearing about Jesus talked about his love and forgiveness, not his judgment and wrath. The way I saw it, God made me the way I was for a reason. I never really *chose* to like other girls— I just *did*. And I especially liked Charlene.

Charlene—we all called her Charlie—was three years younger than me. We met at summer church camp, although I had seen her before at school. Being around her made me feel alive in ways I never thought possible. We spent every spare second together, even though we were in different age groups. It wasn't long before spare seconds weren't enough. We began to sneak out of our cabins after lights out to meet by the lake. It was there, beneath the hazy half-moon, that we began our sweet voyage of discovery. It felt so happy and innocent. So simple. At least, it did until we were discovered by one of the camp counselors.

Charlie and I were separated from one another until our parents could come and pick us up. We were told that our behavior was an abomination to God and that we would burn in hell if we continued along our destructive paths. I knew they were right about one thing: I was burning—but it was with a different kind of fire. And no amount of isolation, preaching, or prayer would be enough to extinguish it.

Charlie had a different experience from me. She didn't have a mother—at least, not a mother she knew. And her father was not a kind man. His response to the discovery of her transgression wasn't characterized by grief or despair—it pretty much involved trying to beat the demons out of her. Charlie ended up collapsing at school, and when the principal realized what was wrong with her, she called the sheriff. That was the good news. They took Charlie out of the home and put her into foster care, where she stayed until she was old enough to live on her own.

But I was never allowed to see her again. My parents made sure of that. And once my grandma became involved with the orchestration of a plan to ensure my salvation, I wasn't home all that much anymore. They pulled me out of school and shipped me off to Kentucky to "study" with a man who had experience turning young people away from the evils of homosexuality.

It would be an understatement to say that his methods were unorthodox. At first, the snakes terrified me. He kept dozens of them, stacked up in special little, glass-fronted boxes inside a boarded-up porch at the back of his house. They were mostly timber rattlers, but he had other kinds back there, too. It amazed me that his wife and three kids just breezed in and out of that dark, close space to retrieve things like jackets and canned goods. I stayed alone upstairs in another small room. I think it had been some kind of closet because it had no windows. It was at the back of the house, and I knew it was over the porch. Every night, when I'd be locked into my room, I'd imagine I could hear the white noise of the snakes moving around beneath the floor-boards. I knew they were awake, too. And I knew that it would only be a matter of time before they figured out a way to reach me.

I didn't have to wait very long.

It was on the sixth night that he finally showed up. I wasn't surprised. I knew he was coming. I could see it in the way he looked at me. I could feel it in the way he touched me—touches that were supposed to be casual, but were tainted with malicious intent. I knew the difference—just like all women everywhere know the difference. When I heard the sound of a key turning in the door lock, I knew my time had come. My education was about to take another path. When his shadow filled up the entrance to my dark asylum, I didn't bother to call for help. I knew it would be pointless. Who would help me? Not the shopworn woman he called his helpmeet. Not his daughters—they had matching sets of empty, unseeing eyes. I was on my own, and I knew it.

The first night, he came alone. But I managed to evade his attempts to turn me from my sinful ways. I didn't cry. I didn't make any sound at all. I hunched myself into a tight ball and withstood the weight of his advances and whispered entreaties. Eventually he grew weary of the struggle. I could feel his anger. His indignation. He got up from my bed and left as silently as he came. But I knew he'd be back. I knew this rite of passage was just beginning.

He made me wait. Many more nights passed—all of them sleepless for me. I grew weak and tired. I was half sick from fear. I could no longer trust my instincts. Night after night, I was forced to attend his revival services. I'd bounce along those backcountry roads on the rear seat of his truck, strapped in beside a stack of wooden crates. I began to hear the voices of the serpents. They'd whisper to me during those long rides through hot summer nights. *Surrender. Let us teach you. Let us show you the power of God's love.*

It was two weeks before I heard him at my door again. And this time, he didn't come alone. I saw the shadow of the box he carried right away, and I knew what it meant. I would be given a choice: I could serve God, or I could face his judgment. When he reached into the box and withdrew the serpent, I knew I was lost. I had watched the snakes writhe and coil their long bodies around his arms enough times to know what was happening. There was no light in the room, but I could sense every moving inch of the threat above me. I begged him to spare me—to show me another way—*any* way but this one.

He relented and showed me a path of mercy. He returned the snake to its box and led my shaking hand to the waistband of his pants, where another servant of God promised release from my torment. Without being told, I understood what to do. I didn't fight him that night—or any of the nights after that.

As the weeks passed, I silently took my place in line beside the others—all those women with the sallow faces and lifeless eyes. I knew I wouldn't last long. I began to fantasize about death, realizing that it offered the only true release available to me. I imagined how it would occur—gloriously—on the altar of one of his makeshift, backwoods churches at the height of their ecstatic celebrations. I believed that a merciful and loving God would take me—would welcome me home and free me from the prison of fear and shame that had become my world. But it didn't happen, and I grew tired of waiting for an intervention that might never come. I knew I didn't have the strength to last much longer. Death was clutching at my insides like a cold hand. It was now or never. I needed to flee while I still had the stamina to run.

In the end, I didn't choose my moment. My moment chose me. We were on our way to a revival service in Gastonia, North Carolina. I was riding alone with him— like always. He stopped for gas at a truck stop, then pulled over and parked so he could go inside for a rest-room break. I knew I only had a few seconds to decide. My heart was pounding so hard I thought it might burst through the thin wall of my chest. I opened the door and got out. But before I ran, I pulled out the boxes containing the snakes and kicked off their lids.

I heard the first screams and yells before I got around the back side of the building. I knew this commotion would flush him out—but I also knew the diversion would give me the time I needed to get away. I just prayed that nobody else would get hurt in the process.

I ran as far and as fast as I could. I had nothing but the clothes on my back. I couldn't go home and I couldn't go back to Kentucky. But I didn't care. I ran. And I kept on running until I was sure I was far enough away that he wouldn't find me. Eventually, I made my way to another rest stop. It didn't take me long to find an obliging trucker who was willing to give me a ride. One thing I was sure about was what it would take to earn my keep. Thanks to my mentor, I'd learned those lessons well. It was another couple of years before I had the wherewithal to take those lessons and weave them into a legitimate line of work that could sustain me. And if, along the way, I could help a few others avoid the same missteps? Well. That would be just fine, too.

I never found Charlie again, but I did find a succession of other Charlies. I learned to embrace the truth of who I was, and I never again subjugated myself to some-one else's idea of what I should be. You could say that everything in my life is different now, but two things remain unchanged: I don't look back, and I never stop running.

10

Heal Thyself

Shawn had a plan. And it wasn't a plan she was ready to share with Kate—at least not until she had her ducks in a row.

That's what today was about—getting her ducks in a row.

Kate's revelation that Linda had made her a job offer was a game changer. Shawn understood that. What wasn't clear to her was how well Kate understood it. Shawn knew Kate well enough to realize that trying to force any kind of decision would be a mistake. So the best she could do was go ahead with her own plans, and hope they might eventually intersect with whatever path Kate finally decided to follow.

The house was incredible. A Craftsman. It sat on three acres of land with two hundred feet of lake frontage. Everything about it was perfect—proximity to town, exquisite Green Mountain views, the warmth and simple beauty of the architecture, a big fenced yard for the dogs. This place had it all.

And it was here. Vermont.

She looked out across the lake. The ridges on the opposite side were clearer today. She could even make out the slow revolutions of the windmills that sat atop Georgia Mountain. Doug Archer was still pissed about how they spoiled the landscape whenever they drifted into view from the islands. "Calvary," he called it. Shawn laughed at his description, but it really was pretty apt. They did look like crosses. The only problem with his analogy was the math.

"What's the fourth one for?" she asked him.

"Me," he opined.

That seemed to work, too. Doug was a good man with a big heart, but he worried about things. He had what Ursula Le Guin called "French diseases of the soul."

Just like her.

Shawn never expected to fall in love with Vermont. That part of this trip had been a surprise. A revelation. Being here reminded her of all the happiest parts of her childhood. Being here reminded her that lives, like the months in a year, made more sense when they were measured in seasons. Living in a place where summers felt endless and winters never amounted to more than annoyances left her feeling incomplete. She remembered once reading a story about this phenomenon in a grad school writing class. It was something about a woman who read Wallace Stevens—and how she died a slow death from living in a place where the climate never changed.

Lately, her life had become a badly constructed sentence—a dangling participle that modified an unintended subject: *work*. Her work had overspread everything like the ubiquitous kudzu vines that filled up the hot, summer landscapes of North Carolina. And it had happened so gradually that she hadn't even noticed its creeping progress. She was being strangled by work. Death by kudzu was like death by a thousand cuts. Slow. Interminable. But steady. Certain.

It was time to change that.

She knew the physical part of the transition would be simple. Her Charlotte house was in the Dilworth neighborhood—an area proclaimed to be "highly desirable" by all the real estate magnates. She'd been approached more than a dozen times about selling it. And the truth was that she had no real ties to the area. She'd landed in Charlotte mostly by accident. It was the first place she got a job after grad school in Chapel Hill. Since then? Once she published her first book, *Bottle Rocket*, things had started happening so quickly that she never took the time to think about what came next.

Then she met Kate, and everything changed. Now thinking about what came next was practically an obsession.

She needed to change that, too.

Buying this house was her first step. She'd make the move, and then Kate could decide whether or not she wanted to join her. If Kate chose to keep her job in New York, then at least Shawn would be closer to her than she now was in North Carolina. And maybe she could even keep Patrick, so he wouldn't be consigned to life in a third-floor walkup apartment.

But the most important thing was that Shawn would be living her life intentionally. Not waiting around for something that might never happen.

She looked down at all the paperwork in her lap.

Yeah. She was going to do this.

"You look lost in thought."

It was Linda Evans. Shawn hadn't noticed her approach.

"Hey. What are you up to?"

"Not much." Linda smiled down at her. "Thought I'd avoid work a bit longer by taking a stroll before lunch."

"I thought you'd already finished your piece?"

"I have. That's not the work I was referring to."

"Oh. *Lily* stuff?"

Linda nodded.

Shawn indicated a vacant chair that sat several feet away from her spot on the lawn. "Why don't you join me?"

"Sure I won't be disturbing you?"

"Of course not."

"Okay." Linda held out her sweaty glass. "Hold this for me while I pull that thing closer?"

"Sure." Shawn took the glass from her. It contained some kind of straw-colored liquid and a few melting ice cubes. She had no idea what it was. Linda's morning beverage concoctions were becoming legendary.

"What are you drinking?"

Linda laughed. "Tonic and bitters."

"Really?" Shawn sniffed it. "Is that any good?"

"It's a digestive. Helps settle a queasy spirit."

"There's a drink for that?" Shawn handed the glass back to her. "Who knew?"

"Stick with me kid." Linda settled herself in the big, white chair. "I can teach you things."

"I don't doubt it."

They sat quietly and studied each other. Shawn understood that they were having a nonverbal conversation—and the topic was Kate.

Linda finally broke the silence. "So, how are things?"

"You tell me. You know her as well as I do."

Linda smiled. "I wouldn't go that far."

Shawn sighed. "I don't know, Linda. I love her, but figuring out what's going on inside that head of hers is like trying to read tea leaves."

"I can imagine."

"How did you manage it?"

"I guess I never tried to figure her out." Linda shrugged. "I just gave her space to get to wherever she'd eventually end up. It's not a very dramatic approach, but it saved a lot of rubber."

"Yeah. My tires are about worn to the rims."

"Maybe that means it's time to park the car."

"That's exactly what I'm thinking." Shawn held up the listing details for the house. "I'm moving."

"Moving?" Linda took the papers from her. "Moving where?"

"Here."

"Okaaayyy." Linda was scanning the information. "This is gorgeous." She looked up at Shawn. "But don't you think it's a tad dramatic?"

"I'm not doing it for dramatic effect. I'm doing it for me."

"Fair enough. Still. It seems—sudden."

"I suppose it is. But I love it up here. And I want to make a change."

Linda nodded. "Change can be good. But it also can be a lot easier if you approach it in smaller steps."

"I'm not looking for easier."

Linda didn't reply. Shawn felt bad about her brusque response.

"I'm sorry. I don't mean to sound so arrogant. I just know myself. It's going to take something—*dramatic*—for me to shock my system into getting off this gerbil wheel and moving forward with my life."

Linda handed the papers back to her. "Without Kate?"

"I hope not."

"I hope not, too. You're good together."

"I think so."

Shawn wanted to ask Linda if Kate had made a decision about the job at *Gilded Lily*. But she knew she couldn't. It wasn't right. Kate would tell her when she was ready.

"She hasn't made up her mind yet."

Shawn looked at Linda in surprise.

"I could tell you wanted to ask but weren't going to."

"I hate being so pathetic."

"You're not pathetic." Linda took a sip of her drink.

"Is it working?"

Linda lowered the glass. "Is what working?"

"Your drink. Is your spirit less queasy?"

Linda laughed. "Not yet. But it's getting there."

"Maybe I should give it a try?"

"No." Linda patted her on the forearm. "Stick with your plan. Buy your house. Different kinds of problems take different kinds of tonic. I have a feeling you may have just found yours."

—m—

"Are you going to tell me why you disappeared?"

Darien and V. Jay-Jay were walking along the cliffs that rose above the water on the north side of the property.

"I didn't disappear. I needed time to think."

"So you left without saying anything?" Darien waved a hand. "I call that disappearing."

"If you're going to use epic terminology like this, there's no point in trying to have a conversation."

"Okay. What would you call it?"

"What would I call what?"

"Come on, Vee." Darien was trying hard to muzzle her frustration, but it was getting harder to rein in. "I woke up and you were gone. No note. No nothing. What was I supposed to think?"

"Maybe you were supposed to think that I was confused, and I needed time to think?"

"Well, you sure didn't seem 'confused' when we were together."

V. Jay-Jay didn't reply right away.

"Well?" Darien prodded her.

"You're right. I wasn't confused. Not about that part."

"Thank god. A breakthrough."

V. Jay-Jay stopped and faced her. "I won't deny that our physical intimacy functioned fairly seamlessly."

Darien rolled her eyes. "Physical intimacy?"

V. Jay-Jay nodded.

"Why the hell do you sound like you're writing an article for the AMA?"

"Look. This isn't easy for me."

"Forgive me if I have trouble understanding how *that's* possible. You're the author of four of the most popular—and I might add, *erotic*—sex romps in our entire genre. Yet when you and I spend the night together, you primly brush it off as 'fairly seamless' physical intimacy."

"I'm not brushing anything off."

"No?"

"Of course not."

"Well, what the hell is the problem, then?"

V. Jay-Jay shook her head. "Let's go down to the beach and find a place to sit."

"Why? What's wrong with where we are?"

"Look. I don't particularly want to have this conversation standing on the edge of a precipice."

Darien laughed. "Too metaphorical for you?"

"You might say that."

"Are you afraid I might push you off?"

"Too late for that one. It already happened."

Darien felt herself begin to relax a little bit. She gestured toward a shady path that wound its way down to the water. "After you."

They picked their way down to the rocky beach and found a large, flat rock that could accommodate them both. This one was safely inland, so there'd be no possibility of falling into the water. Darien was sorry about that. She wouldn't have minded another waterlogged encounter. Not even a little bit.

Once they were settled, V. Jay-Jay pointed out a dotted line of boats moving across the water.

"I can't get over how much traffic there is out there today."

Darien followed her gaze. "It must be the tournament. It starts tomorrow. I suppose everyone is out scouting their spots."

"So I guess Quinn's big day is finally at hand?"

Darien nodded.

"It's hard to believe our time here is winding down. Two weeks seemed like an eternity to me when I first got here."

"Me, too. I don't normally stay in one place this long."

"I gathered that."

Darien picked up a smooth, flat stone and threw it at a low angle. It skipped across the surface of the water six or eight times before disappearing from sight.

"You're pretty good at that." V. Jay-Jay sounded impressed.

"I'm pretty good at a lot of things."

"So I noticed."

They smiled at each other.

"Tell me why you left my room?" Darien asked the question slowly. Quietly. She wanted Vee to know she was serious, and that she cared about her answer.

"I don't know. I woke up, and . . ."

"And?"

V. Jay-Jay shook her head.

"You can tell me."

V. Jay-Jay met her eyes. "That's just it. I *can't* tell you. I can't tell you because I don't know myself."

"You mean you don't know why you left?"

"No. I mean I don't *know* myself. I don't recognize who I am right now. And that scares the hell out of me."

Darien stared out across the water. As much as she wanted to argue the point with Vee, she knew she couldn't. Not with any kind of conviction. The truth was, she pretty much felt the same way.

"I'm sorry."

"Sorry?" Vee looked confused. "What about?"

"This." She waved a hand in frustration. "All of this."

"It isn't your fault. It isn't anyone's fault."

"I'm still sorry."

It was Vee's turn to pick up a small, black stone and hurl it at the water. It didn't skip, however. It landed with a loud plunk and disappeared immediately from sight. They watched as a concentric series of ripples spread out from the spot where it sunk.

"Well that was lame."

Darien looked at her. "It just takes practice."

V. Jay-Jay seemed to be considering her response.

"You think you can teach me?"

Darien was unsure about how to reply. She had a sense that her answer was important.

"I'm not sure. I think maybe if we're willing to work at it, we can both get better."

V. Jay-Jay looked back at the water. The circles were all but gone now.

"I guess that's a start."

―――

"Can I talk with you?"

Marvin gave Montana a good once-over before he answered. Usually it pissed her off when men did that. But something about the way Marvin was looking at her right now felt different. Not creepy. More like he was really seeing her—not just leering at her boobs or her ass.

"You can talk with me if you can explain how many cars that woman robbed to come up with all these damn twelve-volt batteries."

Marvin was standing beside the bank of batteries Quinn had daisy-chained together to run the ancient Kelvinator.

"She didn't steal them. She got them all from Junior."

Marvin pursed his lips and slowly shook his head.

"What about this piece of shit?" He kicked the base of the refrigerator with his foot.

"She got that from Junior, too."

"Why am I not surprised?" He bent down and checked the network of cables that all terminated at a small inverter. "How'd she figure out how many amp hours it would take to run this thing?"

"She asked Viv."

"Viv?"

"Yeah. Viv did all the load calculations."

Marvin rolled his eyes and stood up. He looked around the rest of the boat. "I don't know why they approved this hunk of debris for that damn tournament. It's like a floating junkyard."

"Maybe. But it meets all the requirements."

"Yeah. All of them but one."

Montana was confused. "Which one did we miss?"

"The one that says you need a functioning brain stem."

"Come on, Mavis—*Marvin*. She's not that bad. And she really believes she can do this."

"Oh, yeah? I once knew a guy who really believed he could fly. It all went pretty well for him until the day he jumped off the top of Symphony Towers."

"It's not gonna be like that."

"For your sake, I hope not."

"If you feel that strongly about it, why are you helping her out?"

"Why are *you* helping her out?"

"Me?"

"Yeah. *You.* I don't see anybody else lining up to help crew this thing."

Montana thought about it. Why was she helping Quinn? It had started out innocently enough. Just casting lessons. Then teaching her how to drive the boat. When Junior started going out with them on their morning excursions, the whole enterprise took on a different flavor. Now it was more like a quest. Something she felt a certain ownership of. Even though she agreed with Mavis ... *Marvin*. They didn't have a snowball's chance in hell at winning. Still ...

She looked at him—the tall man who chose to go through life

dressed like a woman. It was obvious that he was on some kind of quest, too. She was tempted to point that out to him, but she knew it would be a mistake. He'd probably just toss her overboard.

She decided to play it safe.

"I don't know why."

He stared at her.

The wind shifted and the scent of something wonderful drifted down to them from the inn. Marvin noticed it, too. She saw his nostrils flex and flare.

"Prime rib," she said. "It's on the menu tonight."

"What did you want to talk with me about?" he asked.

She shrugged. She didn't know where her shyness was coming from. It wasn't typical for her. He didn't wait for her to figure it out.

"Lemme save you some trouble. I'm not the first man in the world to put on a dress."

"I know that."

"And before you ask—*no.* I'm not a fag, and I'm not a drag queen."

"I didn't . . ."

"And I'm not a transvestite, transsexual, transgender, or fucking Trans Am. I'm not a trans *anything.* I'm just a man who wears a dress. Period."

"Then what about Mavis?"

"What?" He practically barked the question at her.

"What about Mavis? If you're just a man who puts on a dress, then why not be Marvin in a dress? Why invent Mavis?"

He glowered at her. "You got some balls, little girl."

Montana could feel her face getting hot. She hated it when she blushed.

"I didn't mean to offend you."

"Why the fuck do you care what my reasons are?" He was still staring at her, but he didn't look angry any more. He looked interested—almost normal. At least for him—*her.*

He looked like Mavis.

"I honestly don't know why," she said.

He sighed. "Tell you what." He slapped his massive hand against the side of the green and white Kelvinator with its purple Astroglide decal. "You buy me a hunk of that prime rib tonight, and maybe I'll tell you a story."

She considered his offer. Two could play at that game. She smiled at him.

"Deal."

—*ww*—

"Well, that was unremarkable."

Towanda rolled to her side and wiped her mouth on a towel.

"Fuck you. I told you I was out of practice."

Viv laughed. "At least we didn't wake up the Canadians next door."

Towanda tossed the towel aside. "Not this time, anyway."

Viv stretched and folded her arms behind her head. It lifted her breasts to a tantalizing height. Towanda found it hard to look away. Viv noticed.

"See something you like?"

"Maybe."

Viv laughed.

"I don't know how you always manage to do this."

Viv was slowly running the sole of her foot along the outside of Towanda's leg. "Do what?"

"Tie me up in knots this way."

"I thought you liked being tied up?"

Towanda pushed Viv's foot away. "Not this kind of tied up."

"Is there another kind?"

"You know there is." Towanda crawled up the bed to lie beside her. "I don't know why we keep letting this happen."

"Because it's terrific?"

"You just said it was unremarkable."

"Baby, where you're concerned, unremarkable is still terrific."

"You're so full of shit."

"I know."

Towanda looked at the clock on the nightstand. "I need to call Barry."

"Screw Barry."

"Been there, bought the t-shirt."

"Honey, by my calculation, you've bought about five of those t-shirts."

"You can't blame me for all of those. Barry already had three kids when we got married."

Viv was running her fingertips in tight little circles across the taut skin of Towanda's bare abdomen.

"Well you sure don't look any the worse for wear from the two you cranked out legitimately."

"Is that supposed to be a compliment?"

Viv kissed her shoulder. "You tell me."

Towanda snuggled in closer to her. "This feels weird. And wonderful."

"I keep telling you."

"I know, I know. I can't do anything about it. I'm in too deep."

Viv slapped her lightly on the derriere. "Would you knock it off? You're married—not undercover in the mob."

"It's clear you've never been to a Faderman family reunion."

Viv seemed to consider that. "Although Barry's mother does exude a certain Meyer Lansky quality—which I've always admired, by the way—I'd have to say that in the aggregate, the Fadermans are more like refugees from a freak show than members of the mob."

"True. But there's just no way I can get out from under it all. Not with the kids still so small."

"Someday you'll have to explain to me how a nice Catholic girl like you ended up married to a cantor with three kids."

Towanda shrugged. "It seemed like a good idea at the time."

"Famous last words spoken by every person who ever bought an Edsel."

"Barry's not an Edsel."

"Really? What would you call him?"

"I don't know. Edsels were at least *exotic*. Barry's just—dull. He's more like a K car."

Viv chuckled. "You don't think we could manage the kids?"

Towanda pushed back and stared at her.

"What?" Viv asked.

"You want to try and wrangle five kids?"

Viv shrugged. "Why not?"

Towanda snuggled back in. Viv was just being crazy. She'd never last a week with her brood. Most days, she didn't even think *she* could handle it—and she had Barry to help out. He was a total dweeb as a husband, but at least he was a good father.

"Things are just better the way they are," she said. "We don't need to change them."

"You're okay with sneaking around and cheating on him like this?"

Viv's hand was doing wonderful things—gliding in and out of the moist space between her thighs. She shifted her legs further apart to allow her greater access.

"I wouldn't call this *cheating*, necessarily."

The hand stopped. "Wanda?"

"What?"

"You just had your tongue halfway up my twat. If that's not cheating, I'd like to know what the hell it is."

Towanda took hold of Viv's hand and pushed it back between her legs.

"It's not cheating if your husband doesn't care what you do." Her voice was husky. She didn't want to have this conversation. Not right now, anyway. "Barry doesn't care what I do."

"I'm not so sure about that."

"Oh, for the love of god." Towanda rolled over and straddled Viv. "If you're not going to finish what you started, then I'll just take matters into my own hands." She began to bump and grind against Viv's trapped hand. Her movements grew more frenetic. *Come on, Viv.* She kept moving. Faster. Harder. Surely, Viv wouldn't be able to keep holding out? *Not when it felt this good.*

"Wait." Viv was in motion beneath her now. "Wait a goddamn minute."

God. The woman was strong. She was lifting them both off the bed with her bucking and thrusting. The headboard was slamming into the wall like a piston.

259

Towanda was on her back. *When had that happened?* Viv's hot face and fire red hair swayed crazily in the space above her before starting a slow descent down her writhing body. *My god.* It felt like the woman was everywhere all at once. She knew she was moaning. Crying out. She didn't care.

The last thing she heard before exploding into sweet oblivion was the muted sound of an angry Canadian, pounding on the wall of the room next door.

Essay 10

"I said to my soul, be still and wait without hope, for hope would be hope for the wrong thing." –T.S. Eliot

They taught us everything we needed to know about living.

All of our work was focused on life: how to sustain it, how to prolong it, how to extend it. When reasonable measures were exhausted, we resorted to extraordinary measures. We never quit. We never gave up. We never stopped looking for that magic bullet, that Holy Grail, that last, best hope. We never lost confidence or broke faith with our higher calling. To do so would mean failure—would mean defeat. And we were incapable of admitting defeat.

Arrogance. That was our real creed. Our pearl of great price. We were taught to believe in the infallibility of science. In the manifest destiny of research, clinical trials, emerging phyto-remedies and advancements in second-line therapies.

I was part of the medical oncology team at Memorial Sloan Kettering. I dealt with cases like hers every day. Everything about her cancer was textbook. It presented in all the usual ways. Pain during vaginal intercourse. Difficulty urinating. Abnormal discharge between menstrual periods. Unintentional weight loss. And, later, persistent pain in the pelvic region. But she didn't tell me about any of it—not in any of the ways that might have

261

made a difference for her—or for us. She said that was because she always understood how it would happen. It was how her mother died. And her grandmother before her. Her people were Persian. They understood inevitability. They knew how to wait. She said she'd been waiting her entire life. Now it was here—and she no longer had to wait. The advent had occurred. Her magi had come at last. But the gifts they bore were not happy ones.

"Truth is not happy or sad," she explained. "Truth is not right or wrong. Truth is just true. It has no value. It cannot be altered because you will a different outcome."

She said she knew me and she knew that I would never give up. She said it was her job to accept the outcome for both of us. She said that for me, enlightenment would come when I learned the virtue of acceptance.

Carcinoma sarcoma. That was her diagnosis. The cancer had already spread to her lymph nodes and invaded her bladder and bowel. The biopsies proved what we already knew. She was staged at IVA. Surgical cures were not possible. She would have refused them in any case. She also refused radiation and chemotherapies.

"I want to die with a full head of hair," she insisted. She knew how much I loved her hair. How I gloried in it. "I want to die as I lived. Whole. With all of my parts."

It didn't take long. Without treatment or remediation, the disease progressed quickly. I did everything I could to persuade her to relent. Reconsider. Change her mind. She refused.

I hid my frustration and rage from her. Each day at the hospital I met with an endless queue of other patients who begged for extreme or more aggressive treatments, who clung to hope in the absence of reason, who reached the outer limits of "all we could do," and commenced clawing at the walls of their disappointed hopes with weak and bloodied hands. They were the would-be survivors who willingly prostrated their burned and poisoned bodies on the altar of an unknowing and uncaring science that would always fall just short of salvation.

She grew weaker. Lighter and more translucent—like a memory of herself. I could carry her from room to room.

"I want to feel the sun," she'd whisper. "I'd rather spend five minutes in the sun than five years on death row."

Death row. That's what she called the promise of all I had to offer her. The accumulated wisdom of all my years of study at the best medical establishments in the world withered and died on the vine of her simple pronouncement. Work became impossible for me. I could no longer tolerate the lies. The false hopes. The infernal spin that fed the ageing and outmoded ghosts that inhabited the great machine we called healthcare.

She left me in the early hours of the first day of spring. I dozed in a chair beside her bed. There was so little of her left that I shouldn't have noticed her going. Her exit should have been small and quiet—as unremarkable as her short life. But it wasn't. I awoke to a sound like a rushing wind. It was so loud that I was certain I had failed to close the only window in the tiny room. I staggered to my feet and stumbled toward it. The first rays of light were just beginning to paint the modest backyard of our house. I could make out some faint wisps of pink along the shadowy branches of the cherry trees that stood in a twisted line against our back fence. I reached for the window but realized it was already shut tight. The rushing sound went on and on. Louder. Stronger. More insistent. I raised my hands to my ears to try and shut it out.

Then I recognized it. The sound was within me. It was the surge of my own blood, raging at the end of her life.

I never returned to work. I couldn't. I had nothing more to offer. I was alone and unenlightened. My truth could not be altered because I willed a different outcome.

They taught us everything we needed to know about living.

But only the poets can teach us how to die.

11

Sometimes a Great Notion

"What the hell are you waiting for?" Marvin dropped into Junior's recliner with all the grace of Jean Luc Picard preparing to take command of the Enterprise. "Cast off and get this floating piece of shit underway."

Montana gave him a three-fingered salute and untied the cleat lines. She pushed the big pontoon away from the dock and hopped aboard. Quinn started the engines. The rebuilt Evinrude Starflite 125-horsepower motors belched to life. When they both ran—which was infrequent—she had the maximum horsepower allowed for tournament competition. If she got lucky, both engines would cooperate and she'd be able to navigate from place to place with enough speed to guarantee that she'd have plenty of time to make the two o'clock weigh-ins in Plattsburgh.

She had her Pisces map taped to the bridge. As soon as they cleared the no-wake zone near the inn, she'd hit the throttles and make for the Dock Street Marina. The tournament started promptly at eight-thirty, and she wanted to be there in plenty of time for check-in. The officials had to inspect the boats at the start of each day of competition. Once they were cleared and allowed to head out, she'd make for the first spot Junior had marked on her map. It was one of Phoebe's favorite haunts. He noted that he'd seen her there, hanging around near the drop-off at the edge of a weed bed, at least half a dozen times.

Quinn hoped they'd see her today, but she wasn't counting on it. Even though most of their encounters had taken place while Quinn was dreaming, she thought she knew enough about the opinions of the cantankerous bass to understand that Phoebe didn't much care about the wishes of others.

The lake was choppy today. It had rained overnight and there was a steady wind blowing in from the south. That would churn things up. The fish wouldn't like it. They'd be antsy—cranky and harder to catch. That meant she'd have better luck today if she stuck to the weed beds and used a jig and pig. Junior said a black and blue jig was the best lure for this situation—especially when you coupled it with something gaudy like a crawfish trailer. He said that when you fished the outer perimeter of tall weeds you needed to make sure your line had a big profile with lots of vulgar color. Quinn thought that part made a lot of sense. It wasn't that different from the way things worked in biker bars—only her people used body art instead of fake crustaceans. Still. She had a couple of bright, rubber beauties all picked out. Her favorite had chartreuse claws with bright pink tips—perfect bait to tempt an unwilling fish out of hiding.

She looked out at the cavalcade of boats on the lake. The high-priced, tricked-out rigs were all over the place today. The ones that weren't stopped or gently drifting along were roaring past her at breakneck speeds, hurrying from one favored spot to the next.

The fish wouldn't like that, either.

One of her damn engines kept cutting in and out. That made the pontoon's progress across the lake halting and jerky, like a car stuck in rush hour traffic. She could hear Marvin muttering something about what a waste of effort this was. But she didn't care. She had only one destination in mind and she knew they had plenty of time to get there.

She drummed her fingers against her pant leg. The small Lucky Strike tin in her pocket amplified the staccato sound. She'd been halfway out of her room this morning before she remembered to grab the box containing Laddie Ladd's artfully tied flies. She doubted that she'd need them, but decided to heed Junior's advice anyway.

"You take them and use them when the time is right," he said.

Her boat continued its lurching progress across the lake. Its wake was like a dotted line in the water.

With luck, she guessed they'd make it to the sandbar by ten.

—————

Several of the writers stood together on the lawn to watch Quinn's departure. They were mostly silent. It was hard to comment when they were unsure about whether they were witnessing the prelude to a tragedy or the first act of a comedy of errors. Whichever way the tournament was fated to come out, none of them could deny that Quinn had given it her best shot. There was something laudable in that. They were all aware of it as they stood there, watching her boat grow smaller as it moved away from the shore.

In typical fashion, Viv was the first to break the silence—and to brook disagreement.

"That has to be the greatest exercise in futility since Sisyphus got the bright idea it might be fun to push a boulder uphill."

Cricket considered her comment. "I don't think Sisyphus thought it would be *fun* to push a boulder up hill—I think he was forced to do it as a punishment for misdeeds."

"What misdeeds?"

"Beats me." Cricket shrugged. "Something Greek and archetypal."

"Maybe he coveted his neighbor's wife?" Towanda suggested.

Viv shot her a withering look. "Of course, *that* idea would occur to *you*."

"Well?" Towanda spread her arms. "You got any better explanations?"

"Better explanations for what?" Gwen joined the group. She'd been out for her morning walk. She still had her binoculars looped around her neck and an Audubon field guide to the birds of New England tucked beneath her arm.

"Viv was comparing Quinn's quest to the myth of Sisyphus," Cricket explained. "And we were trying to remember why he was cursed."

Gwen nodded. "I think it had something to do with his ability to outwit death."

"Did you say outwit?" Viv clucked her tongue. "Then I definitely picked the wrong analogy for Quinn's little enterprise."

Gwen rolled her eyes. "Why are you so hard on her?"

"You're kidding me with this, right?"

"No."

"As an actuary, I can give you a list of any one of a dozen disastrous scenarios for how this ill-fated enterprise is certain to end."

Gwen looked unconvinced. "I don't agree."

Viv was amazed. "You think she's going to win?"

"I didn't say that. I just said I disagreed that it would end in disaster."

Viv stared back at Gwen, and then faced Cricket with a raised eyebrow.

Cricket took the hint.

"Holding." Her hand shot into the air. "Twenty on averting disaster."

"Bullshit." Towanda reached into the pocket of her jeans. "I'll take some of that action. Here's twenty on wholesale destruction."

"I'll double-down on that prediction." Viv waved a handful of bills at Cricket.

Cricket collected the cash and looked at Gwen. "Talk is cheap. You want in?"

"What on earth would lead you to suppose that I'd be willing to gamble on something so ridiculously sophomoric?"

Cricket smiled. "So, that's your way of saying you don't have any cash on you?"

"Right." Gwen nodded. "Will you accept my marker?"

"Of course."

"I do have one question," Gwen continued.

"What is it?"

"If Viv is the actuary, why do you always seem to be the one holding the bets?"

Cricket chuckled. "First of all, since Viv is usually at the center of any betting that's going on, it's useful to have someone else do the holding. Beyond that, you could say I just have an aptitude for guessing which outcome is likelier. It's a skill I learned the hard way."

Viv agreed. "She could make a killing in the insurance industry."

"No thank you." Cricket ordered the bills so they all faced the same way. "Thirty-five years of being an army nurse was enough for me. The only kind of killing that interests me these days involves a tumbler and a bottle of single malt Scotch."

"Missed opportunities." Viv shook her head.

"Take my word for it, Viv." Cricket stuffed the bills into a zippered pocket on her jacket. "Missed opportunities come in all shapes and sizes."

"No shit." Towanda pointed a finger toward the pontoon. It was like a tiny fleck of sliver on the horizon but you could still make out its canvas awning and the splotchy green color of the Kelvinator. "Ask 'Marvin Pants.'"

Cricket followed her gaze. "What's that remark supposed to mean?"

"Oh, come on," Viv chimed in. "I saw your face when *he* walked into the restaurant last night with Montana. You about pissed your pants. We all did."

Gwen smiled. "Ironic turn of phrase."

"What-*ever*." Viv waved a hand. "None of us saw *that* one coming."

Cricket shrugged. "I think what he's doing to help Quinn is pretty damn admirable."

"Yeah? It sure begs the question about why he is doing it?"

Towanda disagreed. "I think it's pretty clear he had Barb's foot up his ass."

Viv looked at her. "You think Barb knew Mavis was a man?"

"You don't?" Cricket asked. "It's hard to believe they drove across country together without that revelation taking place."

"She just fell off the turnip truck." Towanda snapped her fingers in front of Viv's face. "Hello? Anybody home in there?"

Viv swatted Towanda's hand away.

"Will you two knock it off?" Gwen had had enough. "Who cares what Barb knew or didn't know? And who cares what prompted Mavis to reveal herself as Marvin—or Marvin to present himself as Mavis? It's not like his 'transition' is any more or less twisted than the ones the rest of us are up here to explore."

No one could argue with that. Or at least, if they could, they chose not to.

So instead, they stood together quietly and watched the sunlight glinting off the pontoons of Quinn's little boat until it disappeared behind Ladd Point.

<hr />

"Look at this stuff." Shawn tipped her plate toward the window so the sunlight could illuminate the glob of aspic on her plate. "It looks like a blood clot."

"Shawn, why do you insist on letting them serve it to you? Why don't you simply tell them you don't want it?"

Shawn looked at Kate with wonder. "Why would I do that?"

"Because you hate it?"

"I don't know that I hate it." She tipped her plate into the light again. "I'm intrigued by it."

Kate sat back and folded her arms. "You're intrigued by it?"

"Yes." Shawn set her plate down. "I keep thinking that maybe I'll develop a taste for it."

"That's not very likely to happen."

"Why not?"

"Well, for one thing, you'd have to eat some of it to develop a taste for it."

Shawn wrinkled up her nose. "Gross."

"I rest my case."

"See?" Shawn pushed her plate away. "This is the basic difference between you and me."

Kate sighed. "I have no idea what you're talking about, but I'm certain you're going to enlighten me."

"I might if you're nice to me."

"I'm always nice to you."

"No you aren't."

Kate opened her mouth to reply, but seemed to think better of it. Shawn noticed. "What is it?"

Kate unfolded her arms. "I promise I'll be nice to you."

They smiled at each other.

"Okay," Shawn continued. "As I was saying. Our approaches to The Tomato Aspic Problem highlight the differences in our basic approaches to relationships."

Kate raised an eyebrow. "Do tell."

Shawn raised an index finger and began to tick off the differences.

"First, when confronted with a difficult situation, I take the time I need to fully study the scope of the problem."

She waited for Kate to make a response, but Kate just waved her on. "Please continue. This is fascinating."

"You sure?"

Kate leaned back against her chair. "Oh, yeah."

"Okay. Second, I don't rush to snap judgments or structure my interactions to avoid having to deal with whatever the problem is."

Kate chewed the inside of her cheek but remained silent.

"Third," Shawn continued, "I always allow for the possibility that my ideas about something may change—so I don't close the door on opportunities I've already cast aside."

Kate folded her arms again. "Is that your entire list?"

"No. I have one or two more."

"By all means, let's hear them."

Shawn looked at her with narrowed eyes. "Are you pissed?"

"Not yet."

"Good, because that's number four. I don't get mad when somebody confronts me with a problem I'd rather ignore."

Kate regarded the gelatinous, dark-red glop on Shawn's plate. "I had no idea that aspic was this complex."

"Which brings us to number five."

Kate rolled her eyes.

"Hey, you said you wanted to hear the entire list."

"You're right." Kate sighed. "Please continue."

"As I was saying. Number five. Every problem, no matter how simply it presents, is usually masking something deeper. I try to look beneath the surface and find out what the real issues are, rather than dismiss something irksome as a simple annoyance."

"And what mystical truth lurks beneath the surface of your uneaten aspic?"

Shawn looked down at her plate. "I don't know yet."

"You don't know yet?"

Shawn shook her head.

"I fail to see how that's possible. You've contemplated the stuff twice a day for nearly two weeks."

"Like I said. Inherent opportunities abound."

"Well, by these calculations, it would appear that your problem-solving skills are highly evolved."

"I'd like to think so."

"Mine, on the other hand, are sadly purported to be the antithesis of yours?"

"Sometimes they are."

"Care to give me an instance?"

Shawn leaned forward. "I'd rather give you an opportunity."

Kate looked suspicious. "What kind of opportunity?"

"It's kind of a test case."

"What are we testing?"

"Your ability to withhold judgment and make a snap decision that might be something we both end up regretting."

Kate sighed. "Are we talking about Linda's job offer again?"

"No." Shawn shook her head. "This time, we're talking about an opportunity for me."

"For you?" Kate seemed perplexed. "What kind of opportunity?"

Shawn reached over and picked up a notebook that sat on the vacant chair beside her. She withdrew a folded document and passed it across the table to Kate.

"What is this?" Kate unfolded the papers and studied them. Shawn watched the expression on her face change from curiosity to surprise to disbelief. She looked up at Shawn. "You bought a house?"

Shawn nodded.

Kate held up a photo of the Craftsman cottage. "You bought *this* house?"

Shawn nodded again.

"In Vermont?"

"Yes."

Kate dropped the papers to her lap. "Why?"

"I don't know." Shawn shrugged. "It felt right." She considered her words. "It *is* right. I like it here. A lot."

"I don't know what to say." Kate seemed genuinely dumbfounded. "I don't know what to think."

Shawn leaned toward her again. "Don't tell me what you think. Tell me how you feel."

Kate shook her head.

"No. Really." Shawn reached across the table and touched the top of Kate's hand. "Try."

Kate stared out the window. When she looked back at Shawn, her expression was unreadable.

"Confused. Afraid." She lowered her eyes. "Excited."

"Excited?" Shawn squeezed the top of her hand.

Kate slowly nodded. "But don't forget confused and afraid."

"I won't." Shawn took Kate's hand between both of hers. "I promise."

"Why didn't you *tell* me about this?" Kate picked up the papers with her free hand and gave them a gentle shake. "It's crazy."

Shawn chuckled. "So I guess you've now had enough time to figure out what you think?"

Kate finally smiled.

"Do you wanna go see it?"

Kate stared down at their pile of hands.

"Try and stop me."

───

Two and a half hours.

Two and a half hours they'd been drifting around in these goddamn weeds and nothing. Not a single nibble.

It was ridiculous. He didn't know a lot about fishing, but one thing he did know was that fishing was like gambling. And in gambling, you never stayed with a cold machine or a table that wasn't paying out. You kept moving until your luck changed.

He watched Quinn try another cast.

You'd think she'd realize that nothing was going to happen here. You'd think she'd notice that not another damn boat had shown any interest at all in this spot.

But, no. She kept tossing out her lines and reeling them back in. Over and over, like some kind of idiot savant. She'd probably done it a hundred times now. Montana wasn't much better. The two of them kept taking turns. Quinn would pull her line in and Montana would throw hers out. She was working the other side of the boat, trying her luck with different kinds of lures. They were both crazy.

He shifted on the recliner. It wasn't his job to point anything out.

He checked his watch again. *Twelve-thirty.*

Only another hour and a half to go, and this first day would be over. Then there would only be two more to go. The tournament would be over—and Barb's damn workshop would be over. They could all get out of here and get back to their normal lives.

He watched Quinn and Montana. *What a weird-ass couple.*

He scratched his leg. These damn trousers were bugging him. They felt foreign. The fabric itched. He didn't like having to wear them. He couldn't wait to get off this boat and change back into something normal.

Normal.

Right. None of them had anything remotely like normal lives to get back to. He understood that now. Barb had done a good job assembling her crew of wackos. Together they were a big, simmering pot of hot mess. This whole production should make one helluva show.

Of course, none of that crap made sense to him either. Why did the government fork out taxpayer money to erect these high-priced monuments that glorified everything fucked-up about society? Shit. If you wanted a good dose of reality, you didn't have to pay to go to a damn museum. All you had to do was watch the eleven o'clock news.

He tried asking Barb about that one night, but she just laughed at him and fired up another smoke. Barb was a piece of work. He'd never met anyone quite like her. She just took things at face value and didn't ask a lot of questions. She reminded him of Mrs. Alvarez.

"I think it's time for a lunch break." Montana secured her fishing pole against the deck railing. "Who else wants a hot dog?"

"I do." Quinn turned toward her. "Let me tie this thing down." She reached for some bungee cords.

"Are you gonna leave your line out?"

Quinn shrugged. "Why not?"

"Suit yourself." Montana walked over to the gas grill. "How about you, Mav—Marvin? You hungry?"

"I could eat." He watched her open the valve on the propane tank and light the burner. "What else you got on board this thing?"

She waved a hand toward the dry storage area located beneath one of the padded bench seats. "Chips. Cookies. Some beef jerky. There's water and sodas in the fridge."

Sodas?

"No beer?"

"Nope." Montana shook her blonde head. "It's against tournament rules to have alcohol on the boat."

Well shit.

Even with the steady wind blowing, it was getting hot out here on the water. He got up and walked toward the refrigerator.

"Anybody else want a soda?"

"I'll take one of Junior's grape Fantas." Quinn walked over to join them and flopped down on one of the long seats.

Marvin handed her one of the plastic bottles filled with purple liquid.

"How do you drink that shit?"

Quinn slowly twisted off the cap so the foamy drink wouldn't spew out. "It's not that bad once you get used to it."

"I'd still rather have a beer."

"Well you aren't gonna get one until after the weigh-in. We aren't allowed to leave the boat."

"Say what?" Marvin wasn't sure he'd heard her correctly.

Quinn nodded. "Tournament rules. We're not allowed off the boat until we check back in at the Marina at two."

"You have got to be fucking kidding me?" Marvin was dumbfounded. He couldn't even get off this damn barge for a piss break? That had to be against the Geneva Conventions.

"Hand me that pack of hot dogs, will you Mav—Marvin?"

Marvin rolled his eyes and snagged the pack of McKenzie franks off the center rack of the fridge. He tossed them to Montana.

"Look, little girl. Why don't you make it easy on yourself, and just call me Mavis?"

Montana looked embarrassed. She concentrated on opening the pack of hot dogs and placing them on the grill. They made soft hissing sounds when they connected with the hot grate.

"She could call you Marvis." Quinn suggested. "Or Mavin."

Marvin glared at her. Quinn didn't seem to notice. She warmed to her idea. "I kinda like Mavin." She took a big swig of her purple drink. "It fits."

Marvin was about to ask Quinn if she'd like to see how well his foot would fit up her ass when he noticed something strange happening in the background behind her. Quinn's fishing rod was vibrating. He pointed at it.

"What the hell is going on with your gear?"

Quinn swiveled around on her seat. The rod was now shaking from side to side.

"Jesus!" Montana yelled. "You've got a live one! Get over there!"

Quinn stumbled to her feet and lunged for the rod just as it broke free from the bungee cords. She managed to grab hold of it before it slid off the side of the boat. The reel was wide open and singing as line flew out across the water.

"Stop the spin! Set the hook!" Montana was scrambling around the grill to get to Quinn.

Quinn flipped the crank lever on the reel and stopped the line from feeding out. She yanked hard and away on the pole, then lowered the tip and slowly started to wind in the line.

Marvin was mesmerized. Whatever was fighting on the other

276

end of the line was plainly massive. Quinn's pole was bent at an impossible angle. She kept switching the direction of the pole from left to right as she fought to keep winding up her line.

"Oh, god." Montana was right at her elbow. "Don't let the line break."

Something flashed in the water.

"There it is!" Montana cried.

Marvin could see it too—something oblong and bright, undulating just below the surface. It was getting closer.

"I don't think my pole can hold." Quinn was really struggling now. Her fishing pole was nearly bent in half.

"Keep the head down, keep the head down." Montana grabbed the net. "Just get it in as close as you can to the boat."

Marvin could see it better now. It was huge—and—pink?

"What is that thing?" He moved over to stand beside Montana. "That's not a fish."

"No." Montana's shoulders sagged. She looked up at Quinn who was still fighting to bring it in. "It's an umbrella."

"It's a what?" Quinn looked at her.

Montana pointed out at it. "It's a pink umbrella."

"And it's *open*," Marvin added. "No wonder it was such a bitch to reel in."

Quinn's pole lurched and was nearly yanked out of her hands. The umbrella surged away from them.

"Hey!" Quinn took a tighter hold of her rod and commenced fighting it once again. "This damn thing's *alive*."

Montana was peering out at it. "Oh, my god. This *cannot* be happening."

"What are you talking about?" Marvin followed her gaze. "I don't see anything."

Something splashed inside the umbrella. The pink fabric flounced out and flattened in rapid succession.

"There's a *fish* inside it." Montana got on her knees and signaled to Marvin. "Get over here and help me pull it into the boat."

Marvin hesitated. He hated fish—unless they were deep fried and covered with tartar sauce.

277

"Goddamn it, Mavis—Marvin." Montana threw her net aside and reached into the water. "Now!"

Marvin squatted down and blindly shoved his hands into the water. He grabbed hold of the first thing he could reach. It felt like one of the metal ribs. Together, they hauled the fussy pink and white striped umbrella up over the side of the boat. The damn thing looked like an oversized snow cone. Its handle was broken off and it was rusted into a semi-open position. It crashed to the deck like a ten-gallon water balloon and drenched everything in sight. The panel facing them was emblazoned with a ridiculous caricature of a wide-eyed cat. *Hello Kitty*, it proclaimed.

Montana was screaming at him. "Rip it open, rip it open!"

"What do you want me to use?" Mavin yelled back at her. "My teeth?"

The damn umbrella was in motion, sliding all over the deck.

Quinn dropped her pole and crouched down beside them. "What the hell is in there?"

"Goddamn it." Montana reached into her cargo shorts and pulled out a pocketknife. In one swift motion, she flipped open the blade and sliced the fabric away from one of the wire ribs. Three fat large-mouth bass flopped out and writhed around between them on the soggy carpet.

"*That's* what's in there," Montana proclaimed. "Now let's get them into the cooler, fast."

"Holy shit." Quinn grabbed the fattest of the struggling fish and held it up. "This thing is huge." Her hook and chartreuse worm dangled from its upper lip. She backed the hook out and tossed the line over toward her discarded rod.

Montana had already wrangled the other ones. Marvin thought the two fish hanging from her hands made her look like that statue of Lady Justice.

"Mavis?" Lady Justice was yelling at him again. "Snap out of it and open the damn cooler."

Marvin was too stunned to do anything but obey.

When the three big fish were safely stowed in the massive, thirty-gallon cooler, Quinn connected the aerator and waited until the water started to bubble. Then she walked to the Kelvinator and opened its freezer compartment. She pulled out two frozen grape Fanta bottles and held them up for Montana.

"One or two?"

"Hell." Montana dropped back on her butt and waved a hand at Quinn. "Use 'em both."

Marvin watched Quinn drop the two bottles into the tank with the fish. Then she closed the lid on the cooler.

"You cannot be serious?" He looked from Quinn to Montana. "There is no way in hell that can be a legal catch."

Quinn looked crestfallen. "Is it?" she asked Montana.

"Wasn't that your jig I saw you pull out of the mouth of the big one?"

Quinn nodded.

"Then that's a fair catch. The other two must've hitched a ride while you were hauling her in. Nothing in the rules against that."

"Well I'll be damned." Marvin shook his head.

"So." Montana got to her feet. "I'd say our work here is through." She walked to her grill. A soggy trail of water spread out along the carpet behind her. "We've got about an hour to kill before the weigh-in. Who wants a hot dog?"

Essay 11

If you're reading this, it means you've decided to find me. They told me I wasn't allowed to know your name or attempt to make any kind of contact with you—that only you could ask for communication between us. I understand that. It's a right I surrendered when I gave you away. So the only thing available to me is writing this letter. They said they'd add it to your file, and that if you ever wanted to know about me or find me, you could read it and use the information I made available.

I don't know whether you'll ever want to meet me, but if you're reading this, it must mean you're at least curious about the woman who gave birth to you. I don't know, either, about when you might find yourself holding this letter. It could be next month or next year, or it could be decades from now. I'm writing to you now to tell you about what happened so many years ago in my life, and how you came into being.

For starters, I want you to know that you were made during an act of love. Even though what happened ended up being a big mistake, I'm not sorry about what I did. And I have never been sorry that you were born.

I was very young—only eighteen—and I met the man who would become your father through the part-time job I had after school. I worked afternoons at a local dry cleaning establishment, taking in piles of mismatched and soiled clothing, and returning bags of freshly pressed shirts and suits to people who were always in a hurry. It was a hot and humid environment, even on the coldest days of the year. I got to know the regulars and memorized all of their special requirements. No starch. Extra starch. Make certain there are no double creases on the sleeves. Replace buttons. Bleach the collars. Some of the regulars made small talk with me, but even that was on the fly. Most people used our drive-up window and never bothered to come inside the store.

But he always did.

I got to know him. He was many years older than me. He was a professional. I could tell that by his suits. They were expensive. His shirts were all monogrammed. And he wore French cuffs. We didn't see a lot of that in our small, Midwestern town. I never asked him what he did, and he never offered any details. He wore a wedding ring, but he never brought anything but his own clothing to us. And no one else ever picked his items up. I knew his name and address, but I never thought about trying to find out more about him. There was no Internet in those days. And no cell phones. So I learned about him in the only way I could—bit by bit.

Everything about our world was changing. President Kennedy had been assassinated in Dallas, and nothing about the lives we lived seemed safe anymore. The news I listened to on the TV or the AM radio was all about the war. Every night, Walter Cronkite told us the latest about what was happening in Vietnam. Every day we waited to hear about how many soldiers had been killed, and how many more were being sent over. It seemed like everyone I knew at school had a brother, father or cousin in the service.

I think his appeal to me was more than just the exotic nature of the mysterious life I imagined he lived. In my immature mind, he reminded me of my father. By that, I mean the father I never got to know. He died when I was just a toddler. He ran a full service gas station and one day, a car he was working on rolled off the lift and crushed him against the back wall of the service bay. My mother never remarried, and she raised my brother and me by herself.

But I always had fantasies about my father—great notions about what kind of man he was, what noble and good deeds he performed, how strong and upstanding a figure he was in our church. And even though I didn't realize it at the time, this handsome stranger was exactly like everything I'd been led to understand about my father. So I found myself drawn to him like a moth to a flame. And he liked me, too. I could tell by the way he always teased me and noticed whenever I wore something new or styled my hair a different way. It never occurred to me that there was anything wrong with his attentions to me, or in my responses to him. I was a very young eighteen. Still a virgin, and still very shy in the ways of the world. My mother was very strict, and I did next to no dating.

One day, near the end of my senior year in high school, he came into the store and told me it would be his last visit. He was relocating to another office, out of state. I was devastated and unable to conceal my disappointment—my panic at losing the most important man in my life again. He took pity on me. He offered to come back at the end of my shift and take me out for a soda—just to say goodbye properly. Even in my sadness, I knew that something about this felt wrong—that my mother would be furious with me if she found out. But I didn't care. I agreed to meet him.

I'm sure you can figure out the rest. It only happened that one time. Then he was gone and I was left alone to deal with my guilt and shame about what I had done. I never told anyone, and I never tried to find him. I never thought I'd have to. Everything changed about two months later when I began to suspect that I was

283

pregnant. I was terrified. I thought my life was over. I knew my mother would disown me, and I was too ashamed to tell any of my friends. But time was my enemy. I knew I'd be unable to conceal my condition for long—I was already starting to show. Understand that this was a different time. Abortions were illegal. Like most girls my age, I had been taught that they were scary and dangerous procedures, performed in back alleys by untrained criminals. And I was Catholic; so even thinking about finding someone to perform one was a mortal sin.

I had to tell my mother.

Her anger and disgust were worse than anything I could have imagined. She told me I was a disgrace to the family. That there was no way she could submit herself, my brother, or the rest of our relations to enduring the shame of what I had done.

She resolved to withdraw me from school and send me away, to a place where no one would know my name. I would stay there until the baby was born, and then the baby would be given up for adoption. I had an aunt who lived in Seattle, and she told my mother about a place where girls like me could go. Within days, I was on a train to Washington. I had only one suitcase containing the things I would need for my stay there. Anything else I required would be provided. I was not permitted to see any of my friends or to say goodbye. My mother would have no contact with me during my absence. She insisted it would be better that way.

I don't know what she told people. Probably some story about a mysterious illness, and that I had been sent to seek treatment on the West Coast. I'm sure that was code language for what most of our friends and relatives already understood. I had fallen from grace and I was paying the consequences for my loose morals and bad conduct. I understood that the shame of my actions would follow me throughout life like a grim shadow.

I spent several months living in a dormitory-like setting with a dozen or so other young women who were victims of poor judgment, failed methods of contraception, or nonconsensual sexual encounters. On my first day there, I was led by the administrators to sign a stack of papers without any advice or counsel. The girls in the home used first names only. We didn't know anything else about each other's backgrounds or family situations. Our mail was read and censored. We were only allowed visitors from an approved list. We had only one payphone in the building, and had to get coins from the front office to use it. We shared a common living area where we could watch television, play games, or read from donated books and magazines. We were only allowed out of the home for short walks—and always had to be in pairs. We were taught very little about what to expect when our delivery dates came. One by one, after their babies were born, the girls would return to their lives away from Flossie's—that's what we called the Florence Crittenton Home where we each waited out our pregnancies.

You came into the world during the early hours of a Thursday morning—on my father's birthday. I remember feeling panicked and terrified. We weren't told anything about what to expect when this event finally happened. But when I got to the hospital, I was taken immediately to a room where I was heavily sedated. I remember next to nothing about my labor and delivery—but I do remember hearing you cry. It's an experience I'll never forget. Even in my weak and hazy state, I recognized the sounds you made like I'd known them my entire life. I knew you were mine.

After you were born and declared healthy, we were taken back to the maternity home from the hospital. We stayed together in a special ward with several other mothers and newborns for most of a week. You were brought to me during the daytime for feeding, but I never saw you at night or at any other times.

Ten days after you were born, I was taken to a different room and permitted to spend a few minutes alone with you. I held you and marveled at how small and perfect you were. How alert. How vital. How fresh and sweet you smelled. How much your wispy red hair looked like mine. I held you close and prayed that what was happening was *right*—that the best of your life was all ahead of you—even though the best of mine was about to end. When they took you away from me, I understood that I would never see you again. The pain I felt at letting you go was unlike anything I'd ever felt before. I didn't have words to describe it then. I don't have words to describe it today. I don't think any language has words for something like that. At least, mine never has.

I left that place and moved on to try and remake the rest of my life. I returned home for a short time, but I knew that I would never be able to live there again. The war had finally come to our house. My brother was in the army and had been sent to Cambodia. Every day, my mother went to Mass and lighted candles for him. But I was still an outsider. There were no candles for me. My relationship with my mother was changed forever. We moved around each other in the cold house like strangers. I was an empty shell, and it was impossible for me to return to the same life I had lived there before. I knew that I had to leave and find my own way someplace else.

I left, but the emptiness I carried away with me has never abated. Believe me when I tell you that the purest and happiest experience of my life occurred during those few minutes when I was left alone with you inside that small, plain room. As I held you close for the first and only time in my life, I understood the power of what it meant to love profoundly.

I want you to know that I never married, and never gave birth to any other children. I worked hard, and I spent my life trying to help other people deal with their own lives of pain and suffering. I found ways to be content, but I've never lived a single day without wondering where you were, if you were well, and if you were happy. I pray that you are all of these things.

The only selfish hope I allow myself is to believe that one day you can find it in your heart to forgive me for not being with you in any of the ways I have spent a lifetime learning to understand—and to long for.

12

Ghost of a Chance

"I'm not making this shit up. That weigh bag was so heavy she had to use both hands to carry it from the boat to the judges."

Barb was staring at Mavis with an open mouth. "How many did she catch?"

"Three. That's the limit for each day."

"And she's in first place?"

Mavis huffed. "Damn skippy. They said her official total was twenty-six point two pounds." Mavis took a couple of long swallows from her beer before holding the frosty bottle up to the sky to catch some of the last rays of the setting sun. "I sure could've used a few of these out there."

Barb was still having a hard time taking in the news. "Quinn's in first place?"

Mavis looked at her. "Something wrong with your hearing, woman?"

"I'm just . . ." Barb shook her head. "I don't know what to say."

"I do." Mavis slid her empty bottle into the six-pack carrier that sat on the ground between their chairs and pulled out a fresh one. "There's some kind of weird-ass, woo-woo shit going on up here. Being out on that water with her is like sailing into the Bermuda Triangle." She pointed toward Barb's canvas bag. "Hand me that opener."

Barb picked up the metal opener. It was stamped with a Backcast Ale logo. She turned it sideways and ran her fingertip over the embossed outline of a jumping fish.

"Do they really look like this?"

"Does who look like what?"

Barb handed her the opener. "Bass. Do they look like the drawing on that thing?"

Mavis turned the opener over in her palm. "Yeah. Pretty much. Only a lot uglier."

"I wouldn't say they're ugly. Maybe noble?"

"Noble?" Mavis popped the cap off her beer. It made a sharp, whooshing sound. Barb loved the way the metal opener clattered against the side of the glass bottle. Simple juxtapositions like that were the mainstays of her work.

Mavis handed the opener back to her. "You need to see one of them up close and personal."

"What do you mean?"

"Let's just say none of them is ever gonna win any beauty contests."

"Beauty is subjective—Marvin."

Mavis glowered at her. "Don't start that shit with me."

Barb chuckled. "I still think they're noble creatures."

"Well, if being covered in slime makes you a candidate for nobility, I'd rather be common."

"Come on." Barb shifted in her chair to face Mavis. The movement made her wince. She was still sore from her tumble earlier in the day. "You can't deny that there's something epic about this entire enterprise."

"Yeah? Well there was something 'epic' about every episode of *The Twilight Zone*, too."

Barb shook her head and sipped from her bottle of beer.

She noticed that Mavis was staring down at her legs. *Shit*. Her pant leg had hitched up when she changed position in the chair. The bruise on her ankle was really starting to show.

"What the hell is that?" Mavis pointed at her feet.

"It's nothing."

"It doesn't look like nothing." Mavis leaned forward. "Your ankle is swollen."

"It's nothing. I tripped over a cord in the barn and banged it when I fell."

"You *fell?*"

"Will you relax? It's *nothing*. I'm fine."

"You need to get some ice on that."

Barb held up her leg and examined her ankle. "Probably."

"You want me to go get some from the kitchen?"

"No. I'll ice it later in the room."

"How much later?"

Barb shrugged. "Later. I have a little project I need to finish up after dinner."

"What kind of project?" Mavis sounded suspicious.

"Just something little. A favor. It's not a big deal."

"You're working too much. You need to take it easier."

"I will."

Mavis rolled her eyes. "I mean like tonight."

"No. Not tonight."

"You are one stubborn woman."

"Kind of you to notice."

"Here." Mavis grabbed a fresh beer from the six-pack. "At least lean this up against it."

Barb took the beer from her and propped it against the outside of her ankle. It felt pretty good. She looked at Mavis.

"Stop worrying. You're like an old mother hen."

"Somebody needs to worry about you. You don't take care of yourself."

"I disagree. I picked you to be my travelling companion."

"Is that what I am? I thought I was your driver?"

"You say tomato—"

"Whatever in the hell we are, we're one odd, damn couple."

"You know? I'm okay with that."

Mavis shook her head.

"What is it?" Barb asked.

Mavis waved a big hand to encompass the inn, the lawn, and the lake that spread out before them. "I just have to say that I never would've predicted how all of this would end up."

Barb smiled. "Is that your backhanded way of finally agreeing that I knew what I was doing when I got this whole group together?"

"No. I still think they're a bunch of wackos."

"But you admit that the work we've been doing here is starting to make sense?"

Mavis took her time answering. "I think your little fish statues work pretty well to represent the different stories they wrote."

"How about yours?"

"Mine?"

"Yes. You thought I wasn't putting yours in the show?"

"No. I didn't know I *had* one."

"Of course you have one. You wrote an essay, didn't you?"

Mavis scoffed. "I suppose my fish is wearing a dress?"

Barb smiled. "Not even close."

"Well, as long as it's better looking than one of those damn bass, I won't complain."

"I really appreciate what you're doing."

Mavis looked at her. "What are you talking about?"

"Riding along with Quinn on the boat—and going as Marvin. I know that wasn't something you relished doing."

"You got that part right."

"It's heroic."

Mavis squinted at her. "You're crazy."

"Not about this, I'm not."

"You'd be better off if you quit believing in heroes. There aren't any. There's just a world full of confused and disappointed people fumbling around in the dark, trying not to trip over shit."

"Well, I agree with you about that falling part."

"That isn't what I was talking about, and you know it."

She didn't reply. They lapsed into silence and drank their beer.

Barb never grew tired of watching the purple martins. They were fixtures at this place. In the late afternoons, they would glide out over the water on warm currents of air, searching for insects. Gwen told her that mature Martins would feed their nestlings up to sixty times a day. She found it incredible that any species could be that dedicated to parenting. She never ceased being amazed at how much humans could learn from animals if they just cared enough to pay attention.

"It wasn't as bad as I thought."

The voice startled Barb. She nearly dropped her bottle of beer. "What?"

"Being Marvin again. It wasn't as bad as I thought."

Barb was intrigued. "What did you expect it to be like?"

"Like it always is." She shrugged her broad shoulders. "Not right."

"But you didn't feel that way out on the boat?"

"No. I didn't feel any way about it."

"You mean it felt normal?"

"No. I mean it didn't feel any way."

Barb smiled at her. "I think that *is* the definition of normal."

"Maybe for you."

"No. Not lately. For me, the definition of normal is pretty much a moving target."

"Yeah? Well I don't much like this falling thing."

"Trust me. I don't much like it either."

Mavis sat watching her for a moment. "I'm glad this trip is nearly over."

"Why? So you can get off the boat?"

"Well. That, too."

"Why else?"

"I think we need to get your ass back to San Diego."

Barb sighed. "It's true. I don't want to run out of time on this project."

"Fuck the project."

Barb looked at her. "Mavis?"

"What?"

"Don't start that shit with me."

Mavis actually smiled. It was such a rarity that Barb felt oddly victorious—like she'd won some unspoken contest of wills.

They stayed out on the lawn, making small talk in their matching white chairs, until they ran out of beer and daylight.

—◆—

"Why do you keep staring at them? It's rude."

Viv gave Towanda a dismissive look. "The last person who needs to lecture me about rude behavior is *you*."

"Well, clearly, somebody needs to do it." Towanda looked across the table at Gwen and Linda. "Don't you think the way she keeps staring at them is rude?"

Linda glanced across the restaurant at the couple in question. Darien and V. Jay-Jay sat at a window table, and seemed engrossed in conversation. They were leaning toward each other over their plates and glasses. They did not look unhappy.

"They do seem awfully chummy."

"See?" Viv slapped Towanda on the arm.

"I agree." Gwen broke off a piece of ciabatta bread and dipped it into the plate of herbed olive oil that sat at the center of their table. "I saw them out walking along the shoreline earlier today. They were in intense conversation about something—and they were holding hands."

Viv leaned forward. "I have it on good authority that V. Jay-Jay hasn't slept in her room the last two nights."

Gwen was surprised. "How do you know that?"

"How else? I asked one of the White Tornadoes."

"The who?"

"Duh." Viv rolled her eyes. "The housekeepers."

Gwen was still confused. "They told you that V. Jay-Jay hadn't slept in her bed for two nights?"

Viv nodded energetically. "It's confirmed."

"Who cares if she hasn't slept in her room for two nights?" Towanda rolled her eyes. "You haven't either."

Linda choked on her water.

Gwen patted her between the shoulder blades. "Are you okay?"

Linda continued with her coughing and waved a finger back and forth between Viv and Towanda.

"You didn't know about them?" Gwen was still patting her back. Linda shook her head.

Gwen looked across the table at the two culprits. "She didn't know about you."

Viv seemed oblivious. "Maybe if she spent less time in the bar she'd have more of a clue about everything that's going on around here."

Towanda elbowed her in the side.

"Hey!" Viv recoiled from her.

"What's the matter with you?" Towanda hissed. "You're acting like an asshole."

"It's okay." Linda had recovered from her coughing jag. "Apparently, I *am* pretty clueless." She gave Towanda a half smile. "And Viv always acts like an asshole."

"It's true." Viv drained her glass of wine. "I see no reason to buy into all those petty norms of 'polite' social behavior that stymie authentic interaction."

Gwen laughed. "There is something refreshing about your point of view, Viv."

Towanda *tsk*ed and rolled her eyes. "I think she's possessed."

"Oh, yeah?" Viv gave Towanda a good once-over. "And just how many times have I heard you scream that you wanted to be possessed?"

Towanda flushed. "I never said that standing up and you know it."

Viv stuck out her tongue and wagged it from side to side.

"Oh, that's really mature." Towanda huffed. "I honestly don't know why I keep allowing myself to get drawn in by you. It's a classic example of repeat circumstance neurosis."

"Girls." Gwen bent forward and lowered her voice. "Dial it back a bit. Those people at the next table keep looking over here."

"Who?" Viv cast about the dining room. Her gaze landed on a pair of portly diners who quickly looked down at their plates when they realized she was staring at them. "Oh, good god." She nudged Towanda. "It's the damn *frogs*."

"The who?" Linda asked.

"She means the Canadians," Towanda explained. "They have the room next to mine." She tipped her head toward Viv. "We have a tendency to keep them awake at night."

Gwen chuckled.

Linda looked baffled. "I don't get it."

Viv looked at her with wonder. "Do you ever bother to *read* any of the articles you publish in that lesbo magazine?"

"Of course I do. I'm the editor."

"Well it might be time for you to get out of the office and garner a little practical experience."

Linda sighed. "I think you may just be right."

"So." Viv held up her empty wine glass to flag their server. "Is Kate Winston taking you up on your offer?"

Linda blinked. "How did you know about that?"

"Please. As we've already demonstrated, the walls up here have ears."

Linda looked over at Gwen. Gwen gave her a sheepish smile and shrugged.

"You knew about this, too?" Linda pushed her wine glass away. "I really *do* need to stay out of the bar."

"It's okay." Gwen patted her on the arm. "I only know because Shawn told me."

"Shawn told you?"

Gwen nodded. "I *am* still her agent."

"Right. Of course. Well." Linda sighed. "I guess it's pretty much common knowledge, then."

"The only knowledge that's *common* is that you made her the offer," Viv clarified. "Do you know what she's decided?"

Linda was quiet for a moment.

"Well?" Viv shot the word out like an accusation.

Linda smiled and reached for her water glass. "In fact, I do know."

Gwen smiled. "But you're not going to tell us."

"Correct."

"Well, that's just plain ridiculous." Viv sat back against her seat in disgust.

"Calm down, pookie." Towanda nudged her. "We'll find out soon enough."

Viv was still fuming.

"Look at the bright side." Gwen snagged another piece of bread. "It's binary. Either she did or she didn't." She looked at Linda. "Knowing Kate, I'd say it's a fifty-fifty proposition."

Viv tapped her fingers on the table in agitation. Then she expelled a deep breath, pushed back her chair, and got to her feet. "Where the hell is Cricket?"

Gwen was confused. "Cricket?"

Viv stormed away from the table.

Towanda nodded. "She needs someone to hold the bets."

―――

"You are aware that everyone is watching us, aren't you?"

Darien nodded. "Of course. You had to know they would."

"I suppose so." V. Jay-Jay scanned the restaurant. "Where did Viv go?"

"Who knows? Maybe she spotted some actuarial infraction and had to go intercede."

"That's probably about as likely as any explanation."

Darien smiled and shook her head. V. Jay-Jay noticed.

"What is it?"

"I was just thinking how funny it is that we ended up as the object of so much scrutiny."

"It was bound to happen."

"Why do you say that?"

"Oh, come on. Look at us. We don't exactly fit together very well."

"On the contrary." Darien raised an eyebrow. "I think we fit together just fine."

V. Jay-Jay looked down at the tablecloth.

"Are you blushing?"

V. Jay-Jay didn't reply.

"Oh, my god." Darien leaned forward. "You *are* blushing."

"Please don't advertise it."

"Why not?"

"It's *embarrassing*."

"It's not embarrassing. It's charming."

V. Jay-Jay sighed. "I don't know what to do with you."

"I have a few ideas."

"Can you be serious?"

"What makes you think I'm not being serious?"

"You have a tell."

Darien was confused. "I have a what?"

"A tell. Like a card player or some other kind of gambler."

Darien raised a hand to her face. "You mean like a facial tic or something?"

V. Jay-Jay looked amused. "Or something."

"What is it?"

"Your tell?"

Darien nodded.

"It's something you do with your eyes."

"My eyes?"

"Yes. I noticed it about you on the first day we were here."

"You noticed me on the first day we were here?"

"Of course."

Darien felt irrationally pleased by that. She scooted closer to the table. "What did I do?"

"It isn't what you did. It's something you said. It was during our first group meeting. Viv made a comment about how Barb's concept for the sculptures reminded her of the funhouse at Coney Island."

"I remember that."

"Do you remember what you said?"

Darien thought about it. "No."

V. Jay-Jay smiled. "You said that in your experience, funhouses were rarely fun."

"Oh, god. That sounds like something I'd say."

"That's what I thought, too. It told me something about you."

"What? That I have a sophomoric sense of humor?"

"No." V. Jay-Jay rolled her eyes. "That you're self-deprecating. Which, I might add, you just illustrated again."

"Is that a bad thing?"

V. Jay-Jay slowly shook her head.

Darien sat back. "I remembered noticing you, too."

"You did?"

"Uh huh."

V. Jay-Jay didn't reply. Their standoff lasted about five seconds. Darien folded first.

"Come on, Vee. Aren't you going to ask me what I noticed about you?"

"I don't have to. I already know what it was."

"What?"

"When Barb was splitting us up into teams, I caught you staring at my legs."

Darien opened her mouth to disagree, but V. Jay-Jay cut her off. "Twice."

Darien sighed. "I guess I have more than one kind of tell."

"I guess so."

"Did it annoy you?"

V. Jay-Jay considered her answer. "No. I found it oddly exciting."

"Really?"

"Really."

"You do have great legs."

"Thank you."

They lapsed into silence again. Darien couldn't remember the last time she felt so at ease—so comfortable with where she was and where she thought she might be headed. She hated for their time together to end. That was especially true now, since they'd finally agreed to see where their fledgling relationship might go. There were still a lot of things up in the air, however. When they might see one another again, for starters. The logistics of that one would be tricky. Vee lived in Boston, and Darien, when she wasn't on the road, made her home outside Philadelphia. Vee hadn't mentioned anything to Darien about any ideas she had for when and how they might meet—or if she thought about it at all. And Darien was nervous about asking. She didn't want to appear stalkerish or over-anxious. And part of her really just wanted Vee to be the one to make the first move.

She looked across the table at her. Vee was so beautiful with her dark hair and olive-toned complexion. She was fragile, too. But her fragility was well concealed by the brusqueness she wore like a second skin. It had been a revelation to Darien to discover what a shy and uncertain woman lurked behind the curtain of diffidence that Vee presented.

She supposed they were alike in that way. And in many other ways, too. Especially when it came to exercising any kind of confidence about relationships.

"Why are you staring at me?"

Darien blinked. Vee was looking back at her with an unreadable expression.

"I'm sorry. I didn't mean to stare."

"It's all right. You looked really lost in thought."

Darien fiddled with her table knife. "I guess I was."

"What about?"

"I was just thinking about how soon this trip will be over."

V. Jay-Jay nodded.

"You'll go home. And I'll go back to work."

"I know."

"And I was just wondering." Darien was now drawing patterns on the tablecloth with the tip of her knife. V. Jay-Jay reached across the table and stilled her hand.

"You were just wondering when we might see each other again?"

Darien nodded dumbly. She felt like a loser. And an idiot.

V. Jay-Jay squeezed the back of her hand. "I have some thoughts about that."

Darien met her eyes. They looked almost teal in the light reflecting off the window.

"You do?" She hoped she didn't sound as giddy as she felt.

"Yes. Being up here and witnessing all this tournament hoopla has inspired me. So I'm thinking that I'll go back to Boston and purchase some horribly overpriced watercraft. Then I'll promptly default on the payments. With luck, the loan company will quickly dispatch a tall and bewitching asset recovery agent to my door."

Darien smiled. "We don't normally come to your door. We normally head straight for wherever the asset is stored."

"What if I promise to keep my asset wherever I am?"

"Then I probably would show up at your door."

"See?" V. Jay-Jay smiled back at her. "My plan will work like a charm."

"It might. However most loan companies will wait until you've missed at least three consecutive payments before contacting us."

"Three payments?" V. Jay-Jay didn't look happy with that suggestion. "You mean, three months?"

"Yep."

"Well that's certainly disappointing."

"I agree."

V. Jay-Jay sighed. "I suppose we could consider a more expedited approach."

Darien was trying to hide her smile. "Such as?"

"I could just invite you to come and see me. I mean, if you would be willing to consider it."

Now Darien did smile.

V. Jay-Jay squeezed her hand again. "Is that a yes?"

Darien lifted her hand and laced their fingers together.

"Oh, yeah."

―――

On day two of the tournament, the winds roared in steadily from the south. The lake was so choppy that most of the anglers retreated closer to shore. Quinn was fishing some of the spots on the Pisces map that were nested in tight along the shoreline. But it was so blustery that even in the buffered areas, casting was next to impossible. She had to keep adding weight to her lines just to keep them from flying back and hitting her in the face.

Montana kept yelling at her to cast *with* the wind, but it was easy for her to forget. She only knew one way to do things and trying to introduce variables at this stage just confused her. Consequently, she'd ended up losing several of her best rigs because the lines got blown off course and tangled up in trees that stood close to the water.

Being in first place was weighing on her. She couldn't deny that. She had worried all last night that she'd be too preoccupied now with winning to concentrate on the work she still had to do. And fishing was all about work. You couldn't be distracted. At least, *she*

301

couldn't be distracted. She understood she'd been a lot better off when nobody thought she had a shot. That meant that her best would always be good enough, and no one would judge her performance—regardless of the outcome.

But not anymore.

As soon as she walked away from the weigh-in yesterday with that first place card, she knew she was in for it. Now every pair of eyes belonging to every angler in the tournament was focused solely on her. Now it was hers to lose. Now it was hers to screw up.

And screwing up was one thing she knew a lot about.

For the first time since she got the idea about entering this tournament, she regretted her decision.

They'd been at it for nearly three hours now, and Quinn hadn't had a single nibble.

Marvin was being quiet—for once. He sat there on his natty throne, reading one of the back issues of *Guns & Ammo* he'd borrowed from Page Archer. Quinn was pretty sure that was because he realized that all of this would soon be over. If they showed up at the marina this afternoon with nothing in their live well, they'd effectively be out of the tournament. There'd be no way they could catch three bass tomorrow that would be large enough to make up for not putting any points on the board today.

Montana was on the bridge, doing her best to keep the pontoon from drifting into the rocks along the shore. It wasn't easy. The waves were pitching and rolling and kept carrying them closer than it was safe to be.

Montana was pointing at something in the water—probably a spot she thought looked promising. She yelled something at Quinn, but the wind just carried her words away.

Quinn squinted her eyes to try and see what Montana was pointing at. But all she could make out was roiling, gray water.

She thought about Junior's advice. "When all else fails, try a worm."

Well. All else had pretty much failed today. She decided to give it a try.

302

She reached into her tackle box and pulled out a long, pumpkin-seed-colored worm. Junior said to attach these with a couple of glass beads on the line, just to give the thing some glitter. She set the hook the way he taught her, with the head and the tip hidden in the egg sac area along the bottom seam. He called this setup a Texas rig. She guessed that probably was because somebody in the Lone Star State first figured out this method for getting reluctant bass to come out of hiding.

Once she had her line set, she walked to the edge of the boat and prepared to cast.

Montana was yelling at her again. The only word Quinn could make out was "wind."

She let her line fly just as a big gust blew in and pushed the boat sideways. Quinn's line twisted in the air and doubled back. She closed her eyes when she realized that the whole rig was hurtling right back toward her.

"With the wind!" That had to be what Montana had yelled.

She realized it now, but it was too late.

Quinn stood there wincing and waiting for it, but the line never hit her. She opened her eyes and scanned the area around the boat.

Shit.

There it was. Her rig and all of her line were tangled up in the bare branches of a dead tree. The worm dangled in mid-air, about eighteen inches from the water. The line was impossibly snagged. Quinn tugged the rod in every possible direction, but it was clear that she'd never be able to dislodge it. She'd have to see if Montana could maneuver the boat close enough for her to try and cut her line. She really wanted to save the worm—it was one of her favorites.

Marvin seemed to take pity on her. He got up from the recliner and walked over to stand beside her at the edge of the boat.

"Looks like you're up shit creek without a paddle."

"Yeah." Quinn waved a hand at her worm. The wind was causing it to spin around maniacally. Sunlight glinted off the glass beads. "I have to figure out a way to cut it down, too. It's one of my best worms."

303

"I guess you'll have to wade out there to get it."

Quinn shook her head. "We're not allowed to leave the boat. Remember?"

Marvin grunted. "Stupid-ass rules."

Montana joined them. "I told you to cast *with* the wind."

Quinn shrugged.

"Well there's no way I can get the boat in there. There are just too many rocks."

"Can we at least try it? I don't want to lose my rig."

Montana sighed. "If we get in too close and another one of these big waves takes us, I won't be able to keep the pontoons off the rocks."

"What if I stayed starboard and used a couple of those awning poles to keep us pushed back from anything too high?"

Quinn looked at Montana in surprise. *Was that Marvin?*

"Well?" he asked impatiently. "It could work. We did the same thing on the ferry when we had to dock in choppy seas."

Quinn was still too stunned to speak.

Montana chuckled. "I'm game if you are."

Marvin nodded and headed back to retrieve the aluminum poles.

Montana returned to the bridge and started the motors. If both of them worked, the boat was a lot more maneuverable—she could reverse their direction to turn and back the boat as needed. She joked that in calm water, she could damn near parallel park the thing. Quinn didn't doubt it.

When Marvin came back with two of the long support poles, Quinn took her place at the front edge of the boat. The rig was still swinging around wildly in the wind. She'd have a time trying to grab hold of it.

"Use that boat hook to grab the line."

It was clear that Marvin was reading Quinn's mind.

Quinn walked back to retrieve the telescoping rod they sometimes used to pull the boat in closer to docks or to pick up things she'd dropped in the water—like cleat lines. She kept it clipped to the front of one of the bench seats.

It felt like maybe the wind was calming down a bit. That was lucky. It would help them get in and out quickly, and maybe avoid doing any damage to the boat. The bottoms and sides of the pontoons were pretty scratched and dented up, and not all of the damage was her fault. The thing was already in pretty poor shape when she got it from Junior—like most of the stuff the Ladd brothers had for resale at their salvage yard.

When Quinn knelt down to unsnap the boat hook, she heard a loud splash. It startled her. She thought at first that maybe Marvin had fallen off the boat—or had finally tossed something overboard. He kept threatening to do that—to get rid of her non-fishing related stuff. For someone who didn't care about the tournament, he sure had strong opinions about how the boat should be set up.

Marvin called out. "Holy motherfucking shit!"

Quinn bolted to her feet and wheeled around to see Marvin, still rooted to his spot, pointing at the tree where her rig was caught. The line was still there, but it took her a moment to realize that a huge bass was now dangling from its end. The fish was flopping and twisting, trying to break free. But it was well and truly caught. That line was going no place.

Montana had seen it, too. She was screaming at Quinn. "Get over there! Get over there! Get a net under it—*quick!*"

Quinn stumbled toward the front of the boat and Montana started moving them in closer.

Marvin dropped one of his poles and grabbed the boat hook from Quinn.

"I'll snag the line and haul it closer. You get a net under it before you cut it."

They had to work fast. The fish was furious. It was flailing like a dervish. Quinn was afraid it would break free before she could reach it.

But Marvin snagged the line on his first pass. "Almighty god! This thing must weigh ten pounds!"

Quinn was able to position the net beneath the monster fish and clip the line. It dropped into the net with the force of a falling cement block. Quinn was barely able to hang on to it. She used both hands to haul it to safety over the deck of the boat and set it down on the threadbare carpet. Montana quickly reversed the engines and pushed the pontoon back out into deeper water.

Once the boat was out of harm's way, Montana rushed over to join them.

"Is it her? Is it Phoebe?"

Quinn reached into the net and took hold of the writhing bass. She lifted it up and quickly removed the hook from its gaping mouth.

"No. It's not her."

Montana didn't seem persuaded. "How do you know?"

"I just do. This one isn't big enough." She held it up with both hands. "Or mad enough."

Marvin snorted. "Well it's about the biggest damn bass I've ever seen. Ugliest, too."

The fish jerked in Quinn's hands. A glob of slime hit Marvin in the face.

"Nice one, Mavis—Marvin." Montana was laughing. "You asked for that."

He grumbled and muttered something unintelligible.

"Let's get her into the tank." Quinn carried their big catch over to the aquarium and carefully placed it inside. Montana started the aerator.

Marvin was already walking to the Kelvinator.

"I suppose this one's gonna take two of those damn frozen grape drinks?"

"Yep." Quinn got to her feet. "We have to keep her nice and cool for the long ride to Plattsburgh."

Montana looked perplexed.

"You don't want to fish any more today?"

Quinn shook her head. "Nope."

"Why not? We still have most of another hour."

"It's okay."

She looked out over the lake. The water was really settling down. With less wind roaring, she could make out the dull purring noises of other boat motors. Things would really start hopping now. All the anglers would be tearing up the lake, trying to make up for lost time. The fish wouldn't like that. The sun was high and it was past lunchtime. They'd all want to find quiet spots to snooze until late afternoon, when they got hungry again and started moving around.

She didn't blame them. Right now, a hot dog and a cold one sounded pretty damn good.

She smiled at Montana.

"We got what we came for."

Kate liked the house. Shawn was sure about that. She could tell by the way she kept touching everything inside it. The painted wainscot on the walls. The woodwork. The heart pine floors. The enormous fieldstone fireplace that dominated the open living space that made up most of the first floor. The cabinets and the countertops in the big kitchen. Touch was important to Kate. Touch was her currency. And the more she touched, the more certain Shawn became that she'd managed to find the right place.

Kate especially liked the kitchen.

Shawn did, too. It was one of her favorite things about the house. The builder had paid attention to every detail. Soaring ceilings. Tastefully painted, prairie-style cabinetry. Quartz countertops. Viking gas range. Wine fridge. And windows. Windows *everyplace*. And outside the windows? An unobstructed, drop-dead gorgeous view of the lake.

It was breathtaking. Incredible. Perfect.

And it was hers. *Theirs*—if Kate chose to live there with her.

If not? Well. It could be theirs whenever Kate chose to visit.

When they finished touring the house, they walked out back to look at the spacious, fenced yard. Patrick and Allie were already out there, sniffing and zigzagging their way around the perimeter, stopping to investigate every scent and pee at the base of every tall maple tree. The lake was visible from here, too. In fact, the lake seemed to be within view from almost every vantage point.

They stood leaning against the deck railing. The winds had diminished, and now a light breeze was blowing in from the water.

It pushed Kate's soft hair around in crazy patterns. She finally gave up trying to straighten it and just let it go wherever it wanted. Shawn thought that was a good sign, too. Kate was normally pretty fastidious about her appearance.

There was something wonderful in the air—a scent that Shawn couldn't quite identify. It came and went as the wind currents shifted. It made her feel happy and at home.

"What is that smell?"

Kate lifted her nose. "That clove-like scent?"

"Yeah. Precisely. It's like—cookies."

Kate smiled. "It's Dianthus. Sweet William."

"It's great. I love it. It reminds me of Pennsylvania."

"Did your mother garden?"

"*My* mother? Hell no. But my grandmother did. She had flowers all year round."

Kate pointed to a spot along the fence. "See those bright purple and red flowers that look like small carnations? That's Sweet William."

"Well, I always want to have them."

"I think you will. They're pretty hearty up here."

"Good."

"If I'm not mistaken, they attract butterflies, too."

"An added bonus." Shawn grasped the deck railing with both hands and took in a big lungful of air. "What else might they attract?"

"That depends." Kate demurred. "What else do you want them to attract?"

"Well now that I know they have these magnetic properties, maybe they can help me lure a certain TV personality up here on the weekends."

"Hmmm." Kate seemed to consider the possibility. "I don't know that their reach extends quite that far."

"I could plant more of them. You know—like a strength in numbers thing?"

"True." Kate turned around and leaned her back against the deck railing so she was facing the house. "I want to ask you something— and it's not something we've ever really discussed before."

Shawn felt a slight prick of uneasiness. "What is it?"

"How on earth can you afford to do this? Even if you sell your house in Charlotte, it won't come close to covering the cost of this place."

"Oh, that." Shawn was relieved. "I also have my book royalties and the advance on the new one."

Kate raised an eyebrow.

"Okay, okay. You're right. That's not enough, either."

"Not by a long shot. And the taxes up here are outrageous."

"How do you know that?"

"Viv."

"Of *course*." Shawn rolled her eyes. "God. That woman has a better news network than CNN."

Kate nodded. "So?"

Shawn sighed. "Don't worry that I've made an insane financial decision, okay? I have the money for this."

"You do?" Kate still sounded dubious.

"Yeah. I have . . . other money."

"*Other* money?"

Shawn nodded.

"Who are you? Paris Hilton?"

"No. It's not *that* bad. But I have some inheritance money. My paternal grandmother was a Pew."

"A pew?" Kate looked genuinely perplexed. "What kind of pew?"

"Not 'pew' like church pew. Pew like Sun Oil Company Pew."

Kate's eyes grew wide. "You mean like Sunoco gas stations?"

"Yeah." Shawn smiled sheepishly. "They're my people."

"Good god."

Shawn took hold of Kate's elbow. "Are you okay?"

Kate sank down onto one of the built-in benches that lined the deck railing. "I just need a moment."

"Come on, Kate. It's not that big of a deal." Shawn sat down beside her. "You can't tell me that this never occurred to you. How do you think I afforded to live in Japan for a year?"

Kate gave her a blank look. "Loans?"

"Well. Okay. I guess that would've made sense."

"So." Kate spread her hands to take in the house. "You paid cash for this?"

Shawn shrugged.

Kate slowly shook her head. "I guess I don't have to worry about paying for Patrick's braces."

Shawn was confused. "Patrick needs braces?"

Kate looked at her like she had just taken complete leave of her senses.

"Oh. You're *joking*. I get it."

Kate was still staring at her with wonder. "I just can't believe this."

"Why? It doesn't change anything."

"It changes everything."

Shawn was crestfallen. "It doesn't have to."

"You're crazy."

"I know." Shawn bumped her shoulder. "But I've always been crazy."

Kate took in a deep breath and held it for a moment before letting it out. She shifted her position on the bench so she was facing Shawn. "I was going to tell you this later, but now seems like a good time."

"Tell me what?"

"I accepted Linda's offer."

"You did?"

Kate nodded.

Shawn was elated. She threw her arms around Kate and hugged her. "Oh, my god. That's *fabulous*."

She could feel Kate nod against her shoulder. "I know."

"I was afraid to ask."

Kate gave Shawn a quick squeeze and sat back so they could see each other.

Shawn kissed her on the forehead. "I'm so happy for you."

Kate smiled. "It was a no-brainer, really. I just needed a little time to sort things out."

"I guess. When will you go back to Atlanta?"

"That depends."

"On what?"

Kate reached into her jacket pocket and fished out a small,

tissue-wrapped package. It was tied up with a piece of string. "On what you think about this."

She handed it to Shawn.

"What is it?" Shawn turned the small package over in her hands.

Kate sighed. "It was supposed to be a down payment—but now you don't seem to need that."

Shawn untied the string and began to unroll the small wad of bright blue paper. "Down payment on what?"

"On us."

"Us?"

Shawn finished unrolling the tissue and was stunned to see that it contained a beautiful, hammered-copper ring.

"Kate."

"Please don't tell me you hate copper. My choices were limited. It was either this or an indifferent alloy."

"I love copper." Shawn was practically speechless. "It's beautiful."

Kate smiled. "Barb made it for me."

"I don't know what to say."

Kate took hold of her hands. "Yes would be good."

Yes? Shawn felt her insides lurch.

"I'm . . . Are you . . . ?"

Kate squeezed her hands. "I'm told there's no waiting period in Vermont."

Shawn's head was spinning. "You're asking me to marry you?"

Kate nodded. Shawn had never seen such an expression of vulnerability on her face. It made her look shy and adorable.

"Now?"

Kate sighed and nodded again. Shawn could sense that some of her normal resiliency was creeping back in. "Contrary to popular opinion, I *can* be nearly as impulsive as you are."

"You want to marry me?" Shawn was still having trouble letting it sink in. "I never saw this coming."

"Didn't you? I did. Of course, initially, I was going to offer to share the house. But since you've already taken care of that, I'll just offer to share your life." Kate tugged her closer. "I promise to make a good return on your investment."

311

Shawn closed her eyes and leaned forward until their foreheads were touching.

"I love you."

"I love you, too."

Kate kissed her. "So I'm guessing this is a yes?"

"Oh, it's a yes, all right."

Kate gave her a shy-looking smile. "I'm happy."

"Me, too."

"We sound like idiots."

Shawn kissed her again. "Who cares?"

"I suppose you're right."

Kate held up the ring. "Want to try it on?"

Shawn beamed at her and held out her hand. The ring fit perfectly. The metal felt warm and solid. Just like Kate always felt whenever Shawn held her close.

She wrapped an arm around her.

She couldn't remember ever feeling this content. Sunlight was glinting off the lake. Patrick and Allie were rolling in the tall, lush grass behind them. They were sitting together on the deck of their new house. And the air around them was thick with the sweet smell of cloves.

"We're getting married." She couldn't stop thinking it, so why not say it aloud?

"We are," Kate agreed.

Shawn hugged her closer. "When do you wanna do it?"

"Sunday?"

Sunday? Shawn drew back and looked at her. "You mean, the day after tomorrow?"

"Yes. I told you—there's no waiting in Vermont."

"But, how do we make that happen? Aren't there things we have to do?"

"Like what?"

"I don't know. Like get a license?"

"That's easy." Kate snuggled back in and rested her head on Shawn's shoulder. "We just need to stop in at the town hall on our way back to the inn and do the paperwork."

"Really?"

"Really."

Shawn couldn't believe it. They'd gone from what she thought was zero to Mach 1 in the blink of an eye. But that was life with Kate.

She held her tighter. She hoped it would always be that way.

But something else occurred to her.

"Won't we need someone to do the ceremony? A justice of the peace or somebody?"

"Oh." Kate chuckled. Shawn could feel the soft vibration of it against her collarbone. "I've already taken care of that."

"You have?"

"Um hmm."

"Who'd you get?"

"You'll never guess." Kate was playing with a button on the front of Shawn's shirt.

As happy as she was, Shawn knew enough to be suspicious.

"Oh, god. Who is it?"

"Have you ever heard of the Esoteric Theological Seminary?"

"No."

"Well. It turns out that Viv is a Teutonic Chaplain."

"What the hell is that?"

"Beats me. But all that matters is she's legally ordained."

"*Viv* is an ordained minister?"

"Teutonic Chaplain."

"Whatever."

Kate kissed her on the neck. Shawn felt it tingle all the way down to her toes.

"So whattaya say, Harris?" Her voice had taken on that low and sexy timbre it got when she really wanted something. Shawn called it her 'come hither' voice. "Got any plans for Sunday?"

Oh yeah. Kate really wanted this. And Shawn was not at all inclined to deny her.

She smiled and hugged her closer.

"You betcha."

Essay 12

The first time she appeared to me, I thought it was some kind of paranoid delusion. That's what they call it when you've grown so afraid of reality that you create another place to go where you can feel safe. I knew a lot about that. And I knew a lot about delusions, too. I had a lot of them growing up, and they only got worse after my sister died. *That* she died was hard enough to deal with—but *how* she died was the part that nearly pushed me over the edge.

It's like that when you're a twin. I know that people say things like this all the time, but unless you've been a twin, you can't really understand how true it is. You go through life with this weird feeling that you're half of something—that there's always some big part of you that's missing. I think that comes from the fact that you both came from one egg. Once that first split occurred, way down inside your mother's womb, you both just kept right on dividing into smaller and smaller pieces until there were so many millions of fragments that you stopped being able to tell what belonged to you and what belonged to her.

It was always that way for us—even though we led completely separate lives. Felice was the serious one— the one who was good in school, always did her home-work, always practiced her clarinet, never got in trouble, and won perfect attendance pins at catechism class.

I was the misfit. I played sports, cut class, got kicked

out of band, made D's in math, and frequently got caught smoking out behind the church when I was supposed to be inside—learning about sacramental preparations for my first confession.

People called us Frick and Frack. We looked exactly alike, but we weren't. She did everything right, and I did everything wrong. We were behavioral opposites on the outside—but on the inside, we were identical.

Of course, I never learned the truth of that until many years later—and by the time I found out, I had already been firmly established as the black sheep in our family. That was because the only pre-teen passion I enjoyed more than smoking was "experimenting" with other girls. I got pretty good at it, too. So good that when it was time for us to go off to college, my sister got a scholarship to Loyola and I got enrolled in tech classes at the local community college so I could learn a "trade." I guess my parents thought that being queer meant I was destined to have a career rebuilding transmissions or welding pipe.

My sister was always the quiet one, the thoughtful one—the one who kept to herself. She never shared much about her internal life, but it was plain that she spent a lot of time contemplating it. That became clear to us when she announced that she was leaving school to begin "a new life in the church." I wasn't exactly sure what all that entailed—like I said, I missed a lot of those catechism classes. But my parents were pretty distressed about it. I think they had high hopes that she would eventually serve them up with a big brood of grandchildren. It was pretty obvious that I wasn't ever going to deliver on that promise.

They ended up being wrong on both counts.

It was less than a year later that she showed up on our doorstep. I was shocked when I saw the change in her. She was thin and drawn—like the camp survivors I had seen in a TV documentary about Auschwitz. She wouldn't eat, she barely talked, and she kept herself isolated in her room. She never told any of us about whatever had happened or why she left the place she had been living. She was more withdrawn than I had ever seen her. My parents tried to get her to go to church with them, but she refused. I knew she was in trouble. I could feel it in my bones. But even I couldn't reach her. She just retreated further and further into herself. At night, I would hear her through the thin wall that separated our bedrooms—crying. Praying. Begging for forgiveness. I felt her weakness and pain like they were part of me. But I couldn't reach her. None of us could reach her. I knew that one day, she would just disappear from sight—like boiling water vaporizing from a pot on the back of the stove.

I was the one who found her, hanging from a rafter in our basement. I'd gone down there to get a jar of tomatoes for a casserole our mother was cooking for a church supper. The laundry room was down there, and when I first saw her, I thought she was a piece of hand washing my mother had left behind to line dry.

Then I saw her shoes—the shoes on those small, drooping feet that were the same size as mine. And I noticed the overturned chair.

I couldn't speak. I couldn't cry out. I couldn't make any sound at all. I dropped down and collapsed against the stairs with my hands pressed to my mouth. Then I vomited on the floor.

She didn't leave a note. She didn't leave anything. None of us ever knew what happened to cause her to inhabit such a dark and desolate place. But on the night after her wake and burial, she came to me and told me everything.

I was lying awake in my bed that night, as I had every night since finding her body. At first, when I heard her soft voice, my sick and tired mind told me it was just

317

the normal, nighttime sounds I had grown used to overhearing through the wall of my room. Then I remembered that she was gone—and that the room next to me was as empty as my spirit. I sat up in bed, anxious and terrified. What was happening? Was I losing my mind?

That's when I saw her, standing near the foot of my bed. When I recognized her shape, I felt my heart rate slow, my breathing settle. I knew her as well as I knew myself—and seeing her again, even in this strange, half-light, I felt whole. Complete. And unafraid.

She told me that she had died unredeemed. That she had committed a mortal sin and would never attain peace or salvation. That her purpose was to warn me—to save me from making the same misguided mistake that had ruined her life and condemned her to an eternity of regret.

I asked her what that meant. In a voice choked with whispered desperation, I begged her to tell me what I must do—how I should change. But she didn't. She blessed me and dissolved into the darkness.

Night after night, I waited for her to return. Days, weeks, months passed. But she never came back. Not until years later, on the eve of my marriage.

By then, I had heeded her advice. I had changed my life. Mended my ways. Turned away from my perverted and self-indulgent path. My parents were ecstatic that their prodigal daughter had returned to the fold. I was to be married in our hometown, and had returned there to spend my last night at home in my old room. It was as I lay awake, marveling at how far I had come, that I heard her voice—just as soft and strong as it had been on the night after her funeral.

I was thrilled that at last she had reappeared. That I would be able to share with her how far I had come, and how much I had taken her warnings to heart. That I could reveal to her how truly united we were at last—on the inside as well as the outside.

But she stopped me. She told me that I had misunderstood her charge. That the mortal sin she referred to was not the act of taking her life—but rather the choice she had made to ignore the love in her heart. She said that in her arrogance and piety she had turned away from the happiness that God had offered her, and exchanged it for a path of loneliness and misery. That she came to warn me against making the same mistaken choice—to reveal to me that the path to fulfillment came through love and self-acceptance—not sacrifice and self-flagellation.

When I railed against her claims and demanded that she explain what she meant, she simply blessed me, told me to follow my heart, and faded from my sight.

I knew I would never see her again.

I was sick and distraught. I didn't understand what any of it meant. And I knew that there would be no simple answers for me. I had to choose whether I would go forward with the new life I had carved out for myself, or return to the path I had rejected and left behind. The only thing I was certain about was that I had become a misfit once again. I was half a person, and I knew I would never be whole again.

I had a foot in each world, and I didn't believe I belonged in either of them.

Sadly, I still don't.

13

The Swashbuckler

A blanket finish.

That's what the judge declared when their single catch from the day before rang in at a record-breaking eleven point four pounds. They said it was the largest bass ever caught in a tournament on Lake Champlain.

It was enough to put them into an exact tie for second place. Quinn was okay with that. Second place was still really good. Second place meant she still had a chance to win—a good chance. And the best part about second place was that it wasn't *first* place.

That meant she had slept better last night, although she did dream about Phoebe again. She was getting used to that, and the dreams rattled her less. She almost looked forward to them now. She'd find herself rushing through dinner and not wanting to tarry long in the restaurant with the rest of the group. Most of them had developed a tendency to sit around in the evening hours and chew the fat about their writing, or gossip about whoever wasn't present. But Quinn had other things on her mind.

Phoebe didn't have anything to say to her last night—or the night before that. All Quinn could remember was the sensation of drifting out in the center of the lake beneath the full moon, watching Phoebe swim around in lazy circles. Sometimes she'd break the surface, and the rings that spread out in her wake made the black water look just like that vortex in *Vertigo*.

But that was pretty much all that happened.

She wondered what Phoebe thought about how she was doing

in the tournament. And whether that big fish that jumped out of the water and took her worm yesterday was a friend of hers. It was too bad all those tournament fish had to be put back into the water all the way over in Plattsburgh. But she guessed they'd all find their way back to their favorite spots soon enough. One thing she knew about Phoebe was that she liked to move around. Junior's Pisces map was proof of that.

So far, they'd visited nine of the thirteen spots that Junior had marked with red X's on the map. That left only four for today. She knew that her approach to fishing those locations wasn't typical. Most of the pros would hit a spot and quickly move on if the fish weren't biting. They reminded Quinn of all those old biddies who played the slots at Harrah's when she worked there as a repair technician. They'd plop down with their piles of tokens and try a few pulls. But if the machine was cold and not paying out, they'd quickly move on to another location. On bad days, they'd sometimes get so frustrated they'd practically yank the arms off the machines. But they had one thing in common: they always kept moving until their luck changed.

Quinn felt like their luck was holding out just fine—even though they only caught one fish yesterday.

Today, Montana was having them start out at the farthest point north, and work their way down the lake toward Plattsburgh. Unlike yesterday, the weather today was perfect—sunny and warm, with only a gentle breeze blowing. That meant the lake was calm and moving around from place to place was quick and easy.

Two of the locations they tried had already been duds. They'd had a few nibbles in the bay behind Holiday Point, and Quinn had even hauled in a decent-sized northern pike—but no bass. The rock bed on the north side of Dameas Island seemed promising at first, but ninety minutes later, when she lost her best chartreuse spinnerbait, they gave up and moved on to the next X on the map.

It wasn't too hard to locate the series of small humps that sat just a ways off shore south of Hibbard Point. They were an extension of the City Reef, and terminated in front of a beautiful country inn called Shore Acres. Junior said sometimes this was the most productive spot on the lake. And even when it wasn't, he didn't really mind. He said that was because the food at this place was the best in the islands, and the bartender never skimped on the drinks.

Montana cut the engines and let the pontoon drift in closer to the shore. Quinn had her lure ready. She was going to try her luck with a Carolina lizard.

Marvin was getting bored with the whole enterprise. His huffs and grunts were becoming more pronounced. He'd already worked his way through all the back issues of *Guns & Ammo* that Page Archer had on hand. Now he was leafing through old Restoration Hardware catalogs.

Lucky for them, Page Archer had eclectic tastes.

"Isn't it about time for a damn break?"

Quinn looked over her shoulder at him. "It's only just noon. Let's try our luck here and then find a cool spot to make lunch."

Quinn could tell that Marvin was growing pretty fond of hot dogs and grape Fanta. He didn't even complain about them anymore.

"Well I don't want to sit here for another damn hour."

"We won't." Quinn threw her first cast. "If they're not biting, we'll move on."

Montana joined Quinn on the front of the boat.

"I'd try a drop shot and aim for that trench." She pointed at a darker-looking spot on the water.

"Okay." Quinn was slowly jerking her line. Left. Then right. She brought it in and executed a near-perfect backcast into the dark line of water. After her first gentle tug, she felt something. *There it was again.* Resistance. A *lot* of it. She tugged again. The line grew taut.

"I've got something!"

"Reel it in, reel it in." Montana was beside her with the net. "Keep the rod down."

Quinn slowly worked the line. Whatever was on the other end was big—and it was clear it didn't want to be caught. It was crazy heavy, and it was fighting to stay on the bottom.

"Good god—this thing is like a *slug*."

"What do you mean?" Montana was on her knees at the edge of the boat, scanning the water.

"I mean it's like dead weight."

"It's not fighting you?"

"No." Quinn shook her head and kept winding in her line. "It's just heavy."

"Hang on. I think I see it. It's—what the hell *is* that?"

The creature Quinn had hooked was shimmying closer to the boat. She could tell that it was black, and fairly long.

"Is it an eel?"

Montana got to her feet. "If that's an eel, it ate an inner tube for breakfast."

Their excitement was enough to rouse Marvin from his home décor stupor. He put down his stack of catalogs and wandered over to join them.

"What'd you find this time? Jimmy Hoffa?" He laughed at his own joke.

"Okay, get the net ready." Quinn lifted up on her pole. "Here it comes."

Montana worked the net beneath it and lifted it out of the water. Her eyes grew wide. "Oh. My. God."

Quinn began to chuckle.

"What is it?" Marvin pushed his way between them and looked down into the net.

"Is that what I *think* it is?" Montana thrust the net at Marvin and backed away from it like it contained radioactive isotopes.

"Yep." Quinn reached into the net and withdrew the object. "I'd say that this right here is one of your more advanced models." She proceeded to remove her hook from the impressively proportioned dildo.

Montana was shaking her head. "That's just gross."

"Why?" Marvin glared at her. "Because it's black?"

"*No.*" Montana pointed an accusatory finger at the pleasure aid. "Not because it's *black*. Because it has to be at least *fifteen* inches long."

Quinn was still chuckling. "I have to admit, that is pretty unusual."

Marvin shrugged. "Not in my neighborhood."

"Oh, come on, Mavis—*Marvin*." Montana threw up her hands. "How come that's the *one* stereotype you guys never deny?"

"Wouldn't you like to know, little girl?" Marvin smirked at her, dropped the net, and sauntered back to reclaim his seat on the recliner. "Let me know when it's time for lunch."

———

Barb was having a hard time holding her tools today. When a dolly slipped out of her hand and she smashed her thumb with a finish hammer, she knew it was past time to take a break. She stepped outside the barn and sat down on a stool to have a smoke.

It was beautiful today. Across the field that spread out behind the barn, she could see the bright blue water of the lake, shimmering beneath the midday sun. She took a long drag on her cigarette and wondered how the tournament was going.

It was mind-blowing that an abject amateur like Quinn would end up holding her own in a contest choked with career professionals. Even Mavis was finding it difficult to be critical of what had started out as a fool's errand. Now, when Barb would query her for specifics, Mavis would just shake her head and say she couldn't explain it.

Her throbbing thumb hurt like hell. But at least it was taking her mind off how badly her hands were cramping. The pain had kept her awake most of the night. That was happening a lot more lately. Normally, she was able to persevere and push through it so she could work.

Not today.

She was glad she'd been able to finish making the rings for Kate. She completed the second one last night, and now had it shined up and ready. She'd give it to Kate tonight at the party—plenty of time before the ceremony tomorrow morning. Barb didn't normally work with copper and she had only modest experience making jewelry, but she thought the rings turned out pretty nicely. Kate seemed to think so, too.

Barb smiled when she remembered how shy and faltering the normally self-composed Kate Winston had been when she first approached her about making the rings. Barb had been moved by how self-revealing she was. How vulnerable. It pleased her to know that Kate and Shawn were headed toward a happy ending, and that she'd played a small role in orchestrating that outcome by inviting them to participate in this project.

She heard footsteps on the crushed gravel behind her and turned to see her cousin, Page, approaching. She was carrying a tall Styrofoam cup.

"I brought you a smoothie." She held it out to Barb. "It's strawberry. I tossed in a double shot of protein powder."

Barb took it from her. "How'd you know I was hungry?"

"You didn't finish your breakfast." Page retrieved an empty milk crate from a stack beside the dumpsters and sat down on it. "And I know your appetite."

"Yeah."

"Rough day?"

Barb nodded.

"Why didn't you tell me?"

"What were you gonna do about it? Chew my food for me?"

"No." Page gestured toward the smoothie. "Put it in the blender for you."

Barb smiled. "Thanks, cuz."

"Are you through working for the day?"

"Probably. I need to start packing my shit up."

"You don't have to leave tomorrow. Why don't you stay on a few more days—at least until you feel better."

Barb took a sip of the smoothie. It was delicious. Page must've used fresh strawberries and real ice cream. That figured. She was a hardliner. She didn't mess around with candy-ass stuff like Greek yogurt.

"When we leave is up to Mavis. She's the one who does all the driving."

"Does she have to get back to work?"

"Not right away. She's taking some time off to help me out."

"How much time?"

Barb shrugged. "As much as I need, I guess."

Page took a moment to respond. "You've got a good friend there."

"I know. Strange, isn't it?"

Page laughed. "With your track record, I'd say it's more than strange. It's surreal."

Barb sipped some more of her smoothie. It was cold and it went down nicely—a lot better than most things.

"Hey." She got to her feet. "Do you wanna come inside and see the model for the show?"

"I was hoping you'd offer."

"Come on, then. You can give me your unvarnished opinion."

"I always do."

"I know."

They walked into the area of the barn where Barb had her makeshift studio.

"Voila." She gestured toward the array of little sculptures arranged on a plank table. "Behold, the Birth of Pisces."

"Pisces?" Page ran a finger over one of the tiny fish figurines. "Is that what you're calling it?"

Barb nodded. "I think so. It fits." She smiled. "Especially with the backdrop of this bass tournament going on the entire time we've been here."

Page rolled her eyes. "Which one of them is this?"

The fish she indicated was tightly wrapped with a smooth, silver coil.

"You know I can't tell you that. Not yet, anyway."

"It's just as well. I'd rather not know."

"You say that, but you don't mean it."

"For your sake, I hope their essays are better than most of their books."

"You know what, Page? I've known the majority of these women for years. Read their stuff. Toured with them. Spent time with them at conferences." She chuckled. "And in jail."

Page rolled her eyes.

"But I have to tell you—I never would've been able to predict the breadth of raw insight, angst, and sheer honesty they've shown

327

me in the work they've produced up here." She shook her head. "It's downright humbling."

Page was studying her. "So when they finally dug beneath the surface, they uncovered some real depth?" She pointed at the figurines. "Like your little fish here?"

"Exactly. Just like any woman. Like *every* woman." Barb smiled at her. "Like you."

Page ignored her observation and continued to examine the tableaux of figurines.

"This is an odd configuration. What's the significance of it?"

"It's supposed to replicate the constellation, which has thirteen stars tied to planets."

Page thought about it. "Thirteen essays. Thirteen planets. That part certainly makes sense."

Barb nodded. "I like the symbolism of how it came into being, too. Aphrodite and Eros changed themselves into fish to escape being brutalized by a monster."

"Why are they all connected to each other with string?"

"Ah." Barb lifted a loose end of the string that linked all the fish together. "Aphrodite and Eros tied their tails together so they wouldn't get lost in the sea."

"Sounds like a plan. Someone should've suggested that idea to Quinn."

"Think it would've helped her out?"

"Probably not."

Barb laughed. Page never minced words. She'd always been that way. Ever since they were kids.

"Well? What do you think of it?"

"I think the entire NEA is a ridiculous waste of taxpayer money. But if it's money that's going to get spent anyway, I'm glad some of it came your way." Page looked at her. Her clear, blue eyes were full of approbation. "It's incredible work. I'm proud of you."

Barb knew it would be difficult to respond without stammering, so she didn't reply. And that was okay. Her cousin understood her better than most people, and she knew how much her approval would mean.

Page took hold of her arm.

"Come on. You've worked enough for today. Let's go back outside and sit in the sun."

———

"The Gut" was a bay-like area located west of the drawbridge over Route 2. It was reputed to be a good spot, even though it was a stretch of water that saw a lot of boat traffic. Bass were rumored to like hanging around near the bases of the concrete and stone support pillars. Quinn could imagine that on hot summer days, these shaded areas would be a lot cooler for the lazy fish. Plus the water was a lot deeper through here and the bass liked the safety that provided. She guessed the constant rumble of cars and trucks roaring by overhead didn't bother the fish too much. Probably because they knew they didn't need to fear them. The majority of their predators crept up in high-priced boats.

Ladd Point, on the other side of the bridge, had pretty much been a bust—at least for largemouth. This part of the upper Inland Sea had plenty of rock ledges and weed beds to explore, but Quinn thought all the marina traffic had probably churned things up too much. It was a beautiful day, and the gentle winds and calmer waters were luring recreational boaters out in droves. Quinn eventually gave up, and Montana moved them along to one of their last spots on Junior's map.

They were all feeling pretty somber. It was nearly one o'clock, and the final weigh-in of the tournament would commence in about an hour. Quinn knew she was running out of time. She feared that what was shaping up to be her biggest catch of the day would only win her points in certain "specialty" shops. But she did have to admit it was pretty funny when Marvin slipped the enormous dildo into the live well while Montana was distracted grilling their hot dogs.

Quinn was fishing around the bases of the big support pillars. She could tell that Marvin was antsy about spending too much time beneath the bridge. He'd flinch whenever a big rig would roll over the drawbridge above their heads. Quinn wanted to tell him to relax.

They were nearly finished. It wasn't going to happen today. Not today, and not any other day, either.

But she'd had a good run. She wasn't sorry about any of it. She gave it her best shot, and she learned a lot. Coming to this place had been one of the best things she'd ever done. She proved to herself that she was good enough to do something nobody else believed she could. And even though she wasn't going to be leaving Vermont as a winner, she understood that this experience had changed her life forever.

A lot of that was due to Phoebe—the cranky old fish who refused to play by anybody else's rules. Quinn had learned more from her in two weeks than she'd learned in all twelve years of school.

She knew that Phoebe thought she was thickheaded. A human lunker—big and slow. That much was certainly true. It took her a long time to figure things out. But during the last couple of days, she had started to gain some insight. The process was a lot like watching photos taken with old Polaroid cameras. Landscapes and images of people you knew would slowly materialize from nothing. The old anglers said that clarity like this was what you got when you spent a lot of time on the water, alone with your thoughts and your fishing pole. There were even spots on the lake that Junior called his church pews—the places where he felt the most peace and contentment.

She still couldn't find the words to describe what had changed for her, but she was aware of it just the same.

Another big truck rumbled overhead. She didn't need to see Marvin to know he was flinching. They needed to move on. Nothing was going to happen here.

She pulled in her line and signaled to Montana that she was ready to give up.

"Are you sure?" Montana pointed at the opposite side of the bridge. "We could try over there."

Quinn could tell by the tone of her voice that she didn't want to quit. Even though Montana started out this process thinking she was nuts, it hadn't taken long for her to be infected by the thrill of competing in the tournament. Quinn hated for her to be disappointed. But the sooner they got it over with, the sooner they all could get on with returning to their everyday lives. They were having a big party at the inn tonight, and they'd all be pulling out tomorrow right after Kate and Shawn tied the knot. Of course, when that happened depended on how long it would take to get those Bible beaters to clear out so they could use the beach for the ceremony.

Quinn was glad they had at least one happy ending to look forward to. She hoped it would take some of the sting out of losing today.

"We've got one more spot we could think about trying on our way to Plattsburgh." She stashed her rod. "But I think we might as well call it quits and head on in."

She didn't need to tell Montana that she had no faith that their luck would change once they got to the Middle Reef. From there, it was pretty much a straight shot down to the ferry crossing and the Dock Street Marina.

Quinn guessed that Montana probably wanted to argue with her, but she was relieved when she didn't. When the engines started, she could feel the soft rumble beneath her feet. The boat slowly pulled away from the shadows beneath the drawbridge and moved into the open water.

"Is that it?"

Quinn looked at Marvin. "Is what it?"

"Are you finished?"

She shrugged. "I guess so."

Marvin got up from his recliner and came over to stand beside her. They stood together and watched the water roll past the boat. Montana was picking up speed.

"I know I gave you a ration of shit, but I'm really sorry it didn't work out." He slowly raised a big hand and left it hovering in the air for a few seconds before allowing it to land on her shoulder.

Quinn nodded. Marvin was good people. He was a lot softer on the outside than Mavis. She understood that now. He needed Mavis. He wore her like a suit of armor.

Marvin dropped his hand and shoved it into his front pocket like he was embarrassed about what it had done, and wanted to hide it from sight.

"So what happens now?"

She looked at him. "You mean with the tournament?"

"Yeah."

"We go check in and report that we have no catch. That's pretty much it."

"You sure you don't want to try that last spot?"

Quinn nodded.

"Do we at least wait around to see who wins?"

"We can if you want to."

"Don't you want to? You're in second place. You might still finish near the top."

Quinn sighed and looked out over the blue water. They were moving into the channel now, heading south. In the distance, she could see sunlight glinting off cars on the ferries. All day, three hundred and sixty-five days a year, the big, slow boats carried people back and forth from Grand Isle to Cumberland Head. Rain. Wind. Snow. It didn't matter. In the worst of the winter months, the bows of the ferries were outfitted with icebreakers. They never stopped. They always kept moving.

They were like Phoebe.

Quinn stared down at the water ahead of them. Right now, their boat was dead center in the channel—probably straddling the line that divided Vermont from New York.

That figured. Quinn was always in the middle—never quite here and never quite there. It was the story of her life.

She drummed her fingers against the pocket that contained Laddie's box of flies. She hadn't used any of them yet.

"You take them and use them when the time is right." That's what Junior said.

Well. She was nearly out of time, so that had to mean now or never.

Bixby Island was off to the left—*port*, as Marvin kept correcting her. There were shoals there. The Sister Shoals, if she remembered right—near Bixby and another small island. That meant sheer drop-offs into deep water—perfect lounging places for bass.

"Hey." She turned around and waved at Montana. "Let's go over and give it one last shot by the shoals along those two islands."

Montana beamed at her and slowed the engines. Quinn thought she had never seen the girl look happier or more beautiful.

Marvin grunted and shook his head.

Quinn pulled the Lucky Strike tin out of her pocket and stared down at the flies. She had no instinct about which one might work, so she closed her eyes and allowed fate to chose. The winner was a beauty. A jointed yellow tail—intricately tied with deer hair that had been dyed black and bright yellow. She began to ready her line.

"You are one crazy woman." Marvin clucked his tongue.

Quinn smiled at him. "You gotta try, right?"

He shook his head. Quinn could tell he was trying not to smile. "Where's that net?"

"You think we'll need it?"

"Who knows? It's better to be prepared."

She pointed it out, and Marvin crossed the boat to retrieve it.

Quinn added weight to the line. She wanted the tip to sink to about mid-depth so she could work the fly along the edges of the shoal.

Montana cut the engines and allowed the boat to drift within a safe distance from the islands. She was becoming a master at maneuvering the thing into exactly the right spots. She walked back to join Quinn.

"Ready?"

Quinn nodded and yanked out a big length of leader.

"Okay." Montana took a deep breath. "Remember what we practiced. Ten. Two. Cast."

"Right."

Quinn gave the rod a couple of practice bobs before setting her feet and allowing the line to fly. It unfurled and came to a perfect, soft landing right at the edge of the shoal water on the Vermont side of the Middle Reef buoy marker. She began to jerk the fly by slowly moving the tip of her rod to the left, then to the right.

"*Good* job." Montana patted her on the back. "Now strip the line a little bit."

Quinn didn't get a chance to comply. Something hit the end of her line with a vengeance. She reflexively yanked back on the rod, as much to hang onto it as to try and set the hook.

"Strike!" Montana was yelling. "Bring it in, bring it in!"

Quinn was fighting the thing. It was running fast. And hard.

"I don't know if I can hold it—it's really pulling, and it's *strong*."

"Keep the tip of the rod down. Keep reeling it in. Let it play itself out."

Quinn's pole was bent at an impossible angle. She was struggling to wind up her line.

"Keep the damn tip down!" Montana waved Marvin over. "Get ready with that net."

"Jesus, Mary and Joseph!" Quinn was amazed that the fish had the stamina to keep resisting. "What is this damn thing? A whale?"

Montana was on her knees, scanning the water. "There it is!"

"Where?" Marvin was leaning over her. "I don't see it."

"*There!*" She pointed at something flashing near the surface of the water. "Rounding the buoy. Good god. It's *huge*."

"Hey." Quinn shook the handle on her reel. "Something's wrong!"

"What is it?" Montana scrambled to her feet.

"I don't know. It feels like it's *stuck*. I can barely reel it in."

"Is the line snagged on something?"

Quinn tried again. The handle turned, but slowly. At this rate, it would take her half an hour to bring the fish up, and that was if her line didn't break first.

"No. But I don't know what's wrong with it. The line keeps hitching when the fish changes direction."

"It sounds like a bad drag washer."

Quinn looked at Marvin with surprise.

He shrugged. "I borrowed some *Bass Angler* magazines from Page."

"I don't think it matters." Montana was pointing at the water. "It looks like we've got bigger problems—that thing is coming in on its own."

"Holy shit!" Marvin was leaning over the side of the pontoon. "What the hell is this—a remake of *Jaws*? That damn thing is charging the boat!"

"No, it isn't." Montana corrected Marvin. "It's going *under* the boat."

Quinn saw the flash of something familiar in the water. It was brown and silver. It moved with ease and determination. It was there, and not there—all at the same time.

The hitch in her breathing matched the action on her line. Her heart started thudding in her chest.

It wasn't possible.

"What am I supposed to do?" She began to panic. She didn't want to mess this up. *Not now.*

"Take up as much of the slack as you can." Montana took off for the bridge. "I need to turn the damn boat around."

Marvin was suspicious. "What the hell is this thing up to?"

Montana started one of the engines and slowly swung the back end of the boat around so Quinn was facing the right direction.

"That bitch is trying to lead us into the shoals!" Marvin glowered at Quinn. "Why didn't you let me bring my damn weapon?"

"We can't *shoot* the fish, Mavis—Marvin." Montana cut the motor. "Kill shots are against the rules. If we have to, we'll cut the line."

"We won't have to." Quinn's reel was working more easily now. "She's not fighting as hard. I think she's played out."

"I don't trust her." Marvin took up the net again. "Bitches like that never get enough."

"She's not a bitch." Quinn kept taking up the line.

"It's her, isn't it?"

Quinn nodded at him. "I think so."

"Her, who?" Montana rejoined them.

"Look!" Marvin pointed at the monstrous fish cutting through the water toward the boat.

"Oh, my *god*." Montana clutched Marvin's arm. "We're gonna need a bigger net."

"You think?" Marvin got down on his knees and shoved the net into the water. "Don't try to lift it with the pole. Let me see if I can get the net under it."

"She won't fight you." Quinn stopped turning the reel. The big fish was alongside the boat now.

"From your mouth to god's ear." Marvin pushed the net deeper into the water.

Quinn was right. Phoebe didn't fight. She calmly drifted into Marvin's net and waited for him to haul her up into the boat.

"Jeez Louise!" Marvin used both hands to raise the net. "This fucker has to weigh at least twenty-five pounds."

"I can't believe this, I can't believe this." Montana was practically in shock. "You got her. You actually *got* her. And she's *huge*."

Quinn dropped her rod to the deck and scrambled over to help Marvin.

"Help me lift her so I can get the hook out of her mouth."

Marvin looked at her like she'd taken complete leave of her senses. "I am *so* not touching this slimy thing."

"I'll do it." Montana knelt beside him and quickly plunged her hands into the water so they were good and wet. "Mavis—Marvin, go turn on the aerator."

Quinn knew she had to work fast. This wasn't like her dreams. Phoebe wouldn't last long out of the water. There was no time for chitchat or to kick back and ponder the enormity of the event. She needed to remove the hook, and transfer Phoebe to the tank, pronto.

After she wet her hands, she gingerly took hold of the giant fish and lifted her up—being careful to support her weight on both ends. Junior told her never to lift them up by the jaw. That approach never would've worked here, anyway. Phoebe was definitely a full-figure girl.

Montana took hold of her underside to lend support while Quinn took out the hook.

When she reached into Phoebe's mouth, something incredible happened. She heard a soft, popping noise—almost like a belch—and Laddie's fly shot out.

Quinn caught it in her hand and stared at it with disbelief.

Montana was stunned. "Tell me that did *not* just happen."

Quinn gaped at her.

"She wasn't hooked?"

"I guess not."

"She was just *holding* that thing in her mouth?" Montana was shaking her head. "This just can't get any weirder."

336

Quinn dropped the fly and took hold of the fish again. "Let's get her into the tank."

She carried Phoebe over to the giant cooler and carefully lowered her into the water. Marvin had the aerator running and was already at the fridge getting out the frozen bottles of water.

Phoebe sat calmly in the tank, just like she'd always planned on being there. Quinn watched her to be sure she was okay. It wasn't like she had a lot of room to maneuver, even if she'd wanted to. She was a big fish and she made the huge cooler look small.

Montana followed her over to the tank and knelt beside her. Quinn looked over at her with concern.

"Do you think she has enough room?"

"Oh, yeah." Montana nodded. "It's not like she's got anyplace to go."

Quinn wasn't sure about that. She knew that one thing Phoebe liked was moving around. For the better part of two centuries, she'd had her pick of about five hundred square miles of lake to call her own. The interior of this jury-rigged live well could hardly hold a candle to that.

At least she wouldn't be in there for long. After the weigh-in, she'd be released. Quinn was glad they weren't too far from Plattsburgh. At least Phoebe wouldn't have far to travel to get back to whatever she was doing in this part of the lake.

Marvin walked over and handed Montana two grape Fanta bottles filled with frozen water.

"Thanks." Montana leaned over the cooler to place the bottles at opposite ends, but recoiled before reaching into the tank. "What the hell is that thing doing in there?"

Marvin chuckled.

"You're a pervert." She thrust the bottles at Quinn and stood up. "I'm getting us out of here."

"Hey?" Marvin pointed at Phoebe. "Unlike you, she doesn't seem to mind it."

"What-ever." Montana stomped off to start the engines.

Quinn positioned the two bottles so they wouldn't be in Phoebe's way. She'd already added the right amount of noniodized salt to the tank when she refilled it with fresh water that morning.

"Here. I picked this up for you." Marvin handed Quinn Laddie's jointed yellow tail fly. "I have a feeling this one is going to be legendary."

"Thanks." Quinn pulled the Lucky Strike tin from her pocket and put the tiny rig away.

Marvin walked back to reclaim his seat on the recliner, and left her alone with Phoebe.

Quinn sat watching her and wondered what Junior would say when he found out that it was one of his granddad's flies that ended up hooking the most famous fish to ever swim these waters.

But that wasn't right. Phoebe *hadn't* been hooked. Phoebe had . . . *What had Phoebe done?*

Quinn still didn't know.

The only thing she was sure about was that she hadn't really caught her—not in any of the ways that counted.

Still. There she was, slowly swishing her tail in the cool water of Quinn's homemade live well.

Montana had them out in the channel now. They were gaining steam, roaring down that imaginary state line that would take them straight to Dock Street Marina. For once, both of the motors seemed to be working.

There was no longer any reason to tarry, and there was *every* reason to celebrate.

Quinn was aware of feeling many things—but celebratory wasn't one of them. Most of her emotions were tangled up together like the wad of fishing line she'd had to leave hanging in that tree yesterday. She wasn't sure she'd ever be able to sort them all out. And maybe she didn't need to.

For now, it was enough just to sit here and share this small bit of quiet space with the great fish that had spawned rumors, inspired myths, and defied anglers for generations.

True to form, and oddly like the stuff of all great legends, Phoebe kept her head down and held her peace.

Dock Street Marina was humming like a beehive. The final day of a big fishing tournament was a real media event in a lakefront community that made its living on tourism. A TV crew from the local station in Plattsburgh had set up near the judging area, and a cameraman was out shooting footage of all the high-dollar boats heading in for the final showdown.

The location of the slip you were assigned was based on your standing in the contest, so Quinn's spot was a primo one, not too far from all the action. It was a far cry from where she started out on the first day. But even her prestigious ranking wasn't enough to quell the eye-rolling and sarcastic remarks she overheard when they tied up and got ready to check in. That part didn't really bother her. She'd had a lifetime of getting used to it.

There was excitement in the air. People knew the point totals were close, and there was a lot of speculation about who was ultimately going to walk away with the big purse and the hopped-up Ranger bass boat. They had the dart-shaped, shiny black boat and its companion Evinrude E-Tech motor on display against a colorful backdrop inside a makeshift winner's circle.

There were people everyplace. Quinn could hear music playing. It didn't sound live, so she figured they must have loudspeakers set up out in the dock area.

Some of the teams had already checked in and were starting to line up. Anglers wearing snappy jumpsuits that were covered with corporate sponsor logos were making their way along the docks carrying their regulation, mesh weigh bags full of fat fish. This part of the process always went pretty fast. They couldn't really drag it out when they knew they needed to record the catches and get the bass back into the holding tanks that would take them back out to the center of the lake for release. Quinn knew the drill by now.

A tournament official checked them in. His eyes about popped out of his head when he looked into their live well. Quinn could tell he didn't quite believe what he was seeing. He stared into the tank with a stunned expression. His lips moved, but no sound came out. He could have been shocked by the size of the fish—or shocked by the size of the dildo. It was hard to tell. After about a full minute, he handed Quinn a mesh bag and a card with her weigh-in time stamped on it. He left the boat without saying anything.

Quinn checked her card. Since she was in second place, she'd be in the last group called up. That meant they still had a bit of time to wait on the boat before they took Phoebe out and carried her to one of the big, open cooling tanks in the judging area.

They kept hearing roars of cheering and applause as the weight totals were called out. She could tell by their reactions that Marvin and Montana wanted to go watch the show.

"You two go on ahead." She gestured toward the staging area. "I'll stay here with Phoebe until our group gets called up."

"Are you sure?" Montana seemed reluctant to leave. "I can wait here with you."

Quinn shook her head. "It's fine. I think I'd like to stay here."

"Come on, little girl." Marvin took Montana by the arm. "Let's give these women some privacy."

Quinn was happy when Montana didn't argue. The two of them hopped off the boat onto the dock.

"We'll come back and get you when it's our turn."

Quinn smiled at her. "We'll both be ready."

She watched them walk off until they disappeared into the crowd. Then she went over to check on Phoebe. They'd closed the cover on the cooler after the check-in. Too much unfiltered light was hard on Phoebe's eyes. Quinn had been amazed at how they looked up close—black, fathomless eyes that were like the inside of a well.

She inched back a corner of the cover so she could peek inside at her. She was shocked to see Phoebe's broad face, poking up out of the water, looking right back at her. Her mouth was working.

Quinn thought maybe she wanted something to eat. She remembered how hungry Phoebe had been in her dream.

She went to the Kelvinator and retrieved a small Ziploc bag.

Here goes nothing. She opened the end of the bag and held it over the cooler. She hesitated. Would it hurt Phoebe? *Probably not.* If she didn't eat it, it would just sink to the bottom of the water. It couldn't be any worse than most of the crap that floated around near the bottom of the lake.

She gave the bag a squeeze and a couple globs of the tomato aspic dropped into the water. She quickly replaced the cover and waited. She didn't want to push it with the sunlight. After a couple of minutes, she lifted the cover and took a quick look. The aspic was nowhere in sight. She smiled.

Dream my ass.

Another loud burst of cheering erupted from the crowd.

Phoebe didn't like it. Quinn could feel her agitation mounting. She was getting more active in the tank. Impatient. She wanted to get this over with.

Quinn checked her watch. They had at least twenty more minutes to wait.

To wait for what? So the tournament judges could hold the grandest and noblest fish that ever swam these waters up in front of cell phones and TV cameras? So they could post her picture on every news outlet and transform her from a legend into a sound bite?

That wasn't right. No one should do that. Not the judges—and certainly not her. She didn't catch Phoebe. Nobody could catch Phoebe.

Phoebe wasn't here so Quinn could win this stupid tournament. Phoebe was here for one reason, and one reason only.

"Things don't have meaning," Phoebe told her in the dream. "Once you understand that, you can relax and stop equating feeling with pain. And then you can learn how to let go."

Quinn covered the cooler before walking over to untie the cleat lines. As calmly as she could, she started the engines and slowly pulled out of the slip.

In a few minutes, they'd be out of the marina. Then she could make for the open water and head north for Bixby Island. If Phoebe had been hanging out there, she must've had a reason. So it would be there that Quinn would let her go.

"Tell me again what's in this?"

Cricket was downing her second Moby Dick. Doug Archer had created the signature cocktail to commemorate the last night of the retreat—and the somewhat esoteric catch Quinn and her crew had made earlier that day.

"It's cranberry juice, Blue Curacao, Grey Goose L'Orange, and simple syrup." Linda stirred hers with the stick of rock candy Doug had added as a garnish. "Pretty damn tasty, if you ask me."

"And appropriate. Did you get a load of that centerpiece?" Cricket pointed at the buffet table where the industrial-sized pleasure aid projected from an arrangement of red and purple Dianthus blossoms cut from Kate and Shawn's new backyard.

Linda shuddered. "I think Viv is selling raffle tickets to see who gets to keep it when the party's over."

Cricket rolled her eyes. "That wouldn't surprise me."

"I have to admit that, although that thing offends my traditional lesbian sensibilities, it *does* provoke one's curiosity."

"Trust me, if you tried it, it would provoke more than your curiosity. I look at it and see nothing but the certain risk of cervical puncture."

Linda choked on her drink.

"What are you two gabbing about?" Towanda joined them at the bar. She was carrying two empty Collins glasses.

"We were just admiring the flowers." Cricket patted Linda between the shoulder blades. "Weren't we, Linda?"

Linda nodded and cleared her throat.

"Yeah. *The flowers.*" Towanda made air quotes. "Right." She set her empties down on the bar. "So, do you think that if you sterilized that thing it would be safe to use?"

Cricket squinted at her. "You're asking me this question? Seriously?"

"Well. Yeah."

"Oh, god." Cricket scanned the bar area. "Where is Doug? I need a double."

"Come on. You're a nurse. What do you think?"

"I think you need a psychiatrist."

"Wanting a little variety in my sex life doesn't make me crazy."

"No." Cricket agreed. "Wanting that kind of 'variety' makes you suicidal."

Towanda threw up her hands in frustration. "I don't know why I keep hanging around with lesbians."

"Probably because you love eating coochie."

Towanda reeled around to face Viv. "Very funny. Where the hell have you been?"

"I was over there." Viv jerked a thumb toward the lobby. "Selling raffle tickets." She waved a handful of bills. "We're up to three hundred bucks." She lowered her voice. "Those two Canadians bought *six* of them."

Linda was confused. "Isn't this kind of thing against your religion?"

"What religion?" Viv was scanning the bar. "Anybody seen Doug? I want another one of those Moby Dicks."

"No pun intended." Cricket quipped.

"Your Esoteric Seminary thing." Linda pressed her point. "Aren't you some kind of minister?"

"Oh, no," Towanda clarified. "She's not a minister, she's a Teutonic Chaplain."

"What the hell does that mean?"

Cricket patted her hand. "It's an online church, Linda."

"How do you do a church online?"

"The same way you do your magazine online. Only this is a lot simpler. You log in, pay a hundred and fifty bucks, and voila." Towanda framed Viv's face with her hands. "You're ordained."

"It cost more than that." Viv groused.

"Oh, that's right. I forgot." Towanda draped an arm around Viv's shoulders. "She shelled out an extra fifty for the wallet ID."

Linda seemed suitably impressed. "And you're doing the ceremony for Kate and Shawn tomorrow?"

"As soon as those Bible beaters clear out." Viv sighed. "At first, I was concerned because I neglected to pack my vestments, but Page Archer said she had a sewing machine and could whip something up for me if I found the right fabric."

"Did you?"

"Oh, yeah." Viv tossed her head. "Wanda and I found a couple of great-looking tablecloths at TJ Maxx in St. Albans."

Towanda nodded. "They're dark blue with little cartoon fish all over them. Perfect for this wedding."

"Oh, my god." Cricket turned back toward the bar and was relieved when she saw Doug Archer reappear.

He sauntered over to where they all stood holding up his bar, and took in their row of empty glasses.

"Ladies?" He adjusted his bow tie. "It looks like we need another round."

"Here, here." Viv clapped her hands. "It's like they say: you can't walk on one leg."

"Don't worry, honey," Towanda cooed. "If one of us wins the raffle, you can always pole vault."

"I think it's simply genius."

Kate meant it, too. Barb's model for the exhibit had blown them all away.

Kate knew that Barb had been working to incorporate the fishing motif that had formed the backdrop of their two-week retreat into the show. She even had a preview of how it was all coming together the day she visited Barb in the studio to ask her about making the rings. At that time, the little sculptures weren't even arranged like the constellation or tied to each other—but getting a peek at them strewn across the big worktable had still been a jaw-dropping experience. They contained such simple and direct references to the life experiences they each had written about. Barb had managed to craft each one of them with some kind of unique twist that spoke to the author's individuality. Yet, taken together, they were all alike.

It was pretty incredible. No wonder Barb commanded the respect she had in the arts community. Works like this made it easy to understand why the NEA continued to fund her projects.

Mavis helped Barb move her model down to the inn for the party so the group could see it and react to the ways she had interpreted their essays. Shawn and Kate were standing near the table at the back of the restaurant where the exhibit was spread out. Darien and V. Jay-Jay were with them.

Shawn was bent over the table, examining the intricacies of the glass and metal work on the tiny fish.

"I can't believe the level of detail on these." She pointed at one. "Look how this one is riding a bicycle on a wave made of copper."

"I guess it's pointless for us to try and figure out who we are?"

V. Jay-Jay shook her head. "I don't think that's the point, Darien."

"It isn't?"

"No. These models are intended to be evocative of the stories we told—not the lives we lead today."

Kate was intrigued by V. Jay-Jay's observation. "You think there's a difference?"

"I hope so." V. Jay-Jay looked at Shawn. "Don't you?"

"I'm not really sure." Shawn seemed to consider V. Jay-Jay's observation. "I guess like all good art, this one hits us at about every level."

"That's sure true for me." Darien shook her head. "Besides, when this thing is finished and ready for display, isn't Barb going to tell viewers which fish go with what essays?"

"I think that's the plan." Shawn stood up. "It's hard to imagine the impact this will have when the fish are recreated at life size."

"Or the physical space the entire thing will command." Kate lifted up a bit of the string that connected the tiny statues. "Barb said she's going to use lengths of Manila boat dock rope to tie the fish together."

"Holy cow." Darien stared at the expanse of the display with wonder. "How long is it going to take her to recreate all of these?"

"She said about twelve to fourteen months." Kate shook her head. "Incredible. I had my doubts about this whole thing at first. But now, I'm honored to be a part of it. I think it's going to be a seminal installation—akin to Judy Chicago's masterpiece back in the 70s."

V. Jay-Jay was nodding enthusiastically. "You mean *The Dinner Party?*"

"Yes. Well, minus all the vulvas, of course."

V. Jay-Jay smiled. "A regrettable omission, to be sure."

"I don't know about that." Darien nudged V. Jay-Jay and pointed at one of the fish that appeared to be sporting a very red genital opening near its anal fin.

"Close, but no cigar. Fish lay eggs. They don't have vulvas."

"Well they don't drink alcohol either," Darien countered. "But that one is sure stuck inside a Jack Daniels bottle."

Shawn had to agree. "She's got a point there."

V. Jay-Jay capitulated. "I guess this is where that whole willing suspension of disbelief comes in."

"Well I, for one, am just eternally grateful that I was willing to suspend my personal disbelief long enough to make the trek down here." Kate linked arms with Shawn. "The outcome ended up changing my life in ways I never could have imagined."

Shawn tugged her closer. "Mine, too."

Kate noticed that Darien and V. Jay-Jay exchanged shy-looking smiles. She threw caution to the wind and decided to make a comment about it.

"It looks like you two might have drawn winning cards in the relationship lottery, too."

Shawn looked at Kate in amazement.

"What?" Kate defended her uncharacteristic observation. "You can't blame me for my candor. I've had *three* Moby Dicks."

Darien burst out laughing.

"It's true." The normally taciturn V. Jay-Jay seemed to take it all in stride. "We weren't looking for anything, but thank god we both had the sense not to run away when it showed up."

Shawn nodded. "That's the hardest part. Once you get over that hurdle, the rest is gravy."

"Gravy I can take." Darien reached for V. Jay-Jay's hand and smiled. "But that aspic has to go."

Shawn leaned closer to them and lowered her voice. "You didn't hear it from me, but I think there might be a plan afoot to raid the kitchen later tonight after the party."

V. Jay-Jay looked like a deer in the headlights. "Whatever for?"

Shawn chuckled. "Let's just say that some of the women have

decided to put feet to their prayers and take the inn's supply of aspic out for a midnight cruise."

"Oh, god." Kate rolled her eyes. "Does Viv know about this? It sounds like they might want to invest in some damage waivers."

"Oh, that part won't be a problem."

Kate gave Shawn a dubious look. "Do I want to know why?"

Shawn beamed at her. "She's the one driving the boat."

"So have you asked her?"

Barb didn't have the first idea what Page was talking about.

"Have I?" She cleared her throat. "Have I asked who about what?"

Page sighed and pointed at Mavis. "Have you asked Mavis about staying on an extra few days?"

"Say what?" Mavis lowered her Collins glass.

"Page thinks we should stay on a few extra days."

Page nodded. "So she can rest. She's been pushing too hard."

"You'll get no argument from me about that."

Mavis watched Doug Archer cross the room. He was carrying a pitcher of the blue-black cocktails. Apparently, mixing them one at a time was becoming impossible to keep up with. She drained her glass and gave the rock candy garnishes a shake.

"Will there be plenty more of these on hand if we stick around?"

"Of course." Page reached out for Mavis's empty glass. "Starting right now."

"Then I say why not?" Mavis looked at Barb. "The rest would do you good. You look like shit."

Barb sighed. "Thanks for the vote of confidence."

"For the record, Mavis was talking about your *appearance*—not your work." Page held up Mavis's glass. "I'll be right back with your refill. And Barb?" She gave her cousin a good once-over. "She's right. You *do* look like shit."

Page strode off to find Doug before he ran out of refills.

Barb watched her go. "Well, damn."

"Don't get your panties in a wad."

"Me?"

"You see anybody else standing here?"

Barb sighed. Then she noticed something that made her brighten up.

"What is it?" Mavis sounded suspicious. "You've got that look on your face."

"What look?"

"That one you always get when my luck is about to take a nose-dive."

Barb smiled at her. "Time to tend your own panties, *Marvin.* Your understudy is headed this way."

"What?" Mavis turned around just as Montana reached the spot where they were standing.

"Hi there. Is it okay if I join you two?"

"Of course." Barb grinned at the younger woman. "Mavis and I were just talking about you."

Mavis muttered something beneath her breath.

"I thought my ears were burning." Montana regarded Mavis. "Please tell me it wasn't anything about that centerpiece."

Mavis held up a hand. "I had *nothing* to do with that."

"I didn't even know that thing was still on the boat. I wonder why Quinn didn't liberate it at the same time she let Phoebe go?"

"Who knows why that woman does anything she does?"

Barb was looking back and forth between the two of them. "I think what Quinn did was profoundly unselfish and shows great depth of character."

"Saving the dildo? I think Viv would agree with you on that one."

Barb swatted Mavis on the arm. "You know what I mean."

"I guess I agree with you." Montana was taking her time picking her words. "At first, when I saw her leaving the marina on the boat, I was pretty steamed. We'd all worked so hard to get there—and I *know* we would've won—or come darn close. And I knew right away when I saw her leaving what she was going to do. I knew she was headed out to let her go." She slowly shook her head. "When she got back to pick us up, she didn't say anything. Not even to the guy who checked us in. He came running out to the boat to find out what happened. I think he knew what we had. I think he knew it was Phoebe."

Barb was interested in Montana's take on what had happened. She'd tried to get Mavis to talk about it earlier, after they returned from their final outing, but Mavis just shrugged it off like it wasn't an unexpected outcome.

"Why do you think she did it?"

Montana faced Barb. Her blue eyes were open and clear. Honest. "At first, I had no idea. But then I thought that probably she just didn't want to expose her."

"Expose who?"

"Phoebe." Mavis took up Montana's narrative. "She didn't want to hold her up in front of all those people who didn't give a shit about what she represented. To them, Phoebe was just another roadside attraction—like a bearded lady at the circus, or the asshole who climbs on a motorcycle and jumps thirty cars."

Montana agreed. "I think that's exactly right. I didn't realize at first that finding Phoebe was like a religious quest for Quinn—I thought she was just a big fish that nobody'd ever caught. You know—the ultimate prize. But when I saw the way Quinn picked her up—like she was some kind of holy relic—I knew that wasn't it."

"Well, that part is sure true. While you were driving us down to Plattsburgh for the final weigh-in, she sat on the floor of the boat beside that cooler like she was watching over the damn Ark of the Covenant."

"Maybe she was."

Mavis looked at Barb with narrowed eyes. "Don't start with that metaphorical bullshit."

"I don't have to." Barb smiled at her. "You've already taken care of it."

Mavis grunted.

"You know?" Montana gave Mavis a sad look. "I just wish we'd taken a picture of her."

"Why?" Mavis scoffed. "You think the world really needs another picture of a butt-ugly bass?"

"No. I mean—it would just be nice to have it. You know? So we could remember how it all happened, and what it was like to be a part of something so—I don't know. So magical."

"Magical?"

Barb elbowed Mavis in the side. "Be nice."

Mavis sighed. "Look, little girl. The only thing that makes any experience 'magical' is the way you remember it. If what happened out on that water today has real meaning for you, you'll always be able to see it—every time you close your eyes. You don't need a photograph for that. In fact, a picture would just make it—ordinary."

Barb was moved by how intently Montana was listening to Mavis. It was clear to her that, somehow, these two had formed a connection that was every bit as murky as the one Quinn had developed with the elusive fish.

"Besides," Mavis was still talking. "I'm just glad there isn't any documentary proof of my presence on that redneck barge."

Barb rolled her eyes. "You *had* to ruin it, didn't you?"

Mavis smirked at her.

Barb could tell that Montana was fascinated by the interaction between them. It was clear that she was trying to figure their relationship out.

That didn't make her unique. Barb figured that most of the women at this retreat were trying to do the same thing. Hell. It wouldn't have surprised her to find out that Viv was taking wagers.

She wondered if Cricket was holding?

She smiled at Montana. Part of her wanted to take the young woman aside and explain to her that sometimes the best relationships in your life were strange, quirky, and unexpected things that came at you out of nowhere. They were impossible to predict, and even more impossible to define. But in the end, you were a lot better off if you didn't ask questions, and simply gave yourself permission to enjoy the ride.

She understood that Montana was searching for connection—for belonging—in a world that had always treated her like a misfit. *They all were.* It was the biggest part of what drove them each to weave their fantastic tales about women and themes that were larger than life. The perversity of it all had been the revelation that their interior lives were deeper, richer, and more multifaceted than any of the stories they published under the various banners that defined traditional lesbian fiction.

Like most things in life, it was a paradox.

She looked over at Mavis.

One of many.

―――

Quinn was holding Junior's map up in the blue-white light of the full moon, scanning the night sky for any pattern of stars that matched the one created by the sequence of X's marking Phoebe's favorite spots.

So far, she wasn't seeing anything that came close. But it was really hard to tell. It was clear tonight, and there were stars out all over the place. Some of them were bright, white dots, rounded and clear. Others were more like tiny pinpricks. Whatever their shape, they were clustered together in great bands that spread out across the dark sky like currents in the water. But as hard as she tried, she couldn't see any combination that looked like the outline of a fish.

She was standing out at the very end of the dock, surrounded by the water on three sides. As was usual for this time of night, the lake was calm—almost glasslike in its stillness.

She wondered where Phoebe was right now? Whether she'd tarried in the waters near the shoals, or made off for some other special place? Quinn was pretty sure she was tired from the ordeal of hanging out in the cooler for so long. When she stopped the boat just off Bixby Island and carefully lowered her back into the lake, Phoebe didn't seem eager to leave. She just sort of hovered there near the surface of the water, slowly twitching her tail fin. At first, Quinn worried that maybe she was stunned or sick from being in the live well for too long. But when she reached into the water to check on her, Phoebe appeared to rouse from her stupor. She flipped her fin and took off like a shot. Quinn stood watching the water until her wake disappeared.

She knew she'd probably never see her again.

And in some ways, she understood that she didn't really need to.

Still. Standing around at the party and having everyone ask her over and over about what it had been like to catch her—to hold her—had been tough. She didn't really want to talk about it. She wasn't ready to. Not yet.

When Barb showed them the sculptures and Quinn realized that all those little fish replicas had been arranged just like the pattern on her Pisces map, she thought she'd sneak away and come out here to look for the constellation. The stars up here were brighter and more visible than she had ever seen them. Back home in Batavia, there was just too much ambient light from businesses and subdivisions to allow the night sky to reveal any of its mysteries. She'd be leaving Vermont tomorrow after Kate and Shawn's wedding, so she understood that tonight might be her last chance to get a good look at the cluster of stars that bore Phoebe's likeness. Maybe one day, after she fixed the Panhead for Big Boy and Junior, she'd have an excuse to come back. And maybe Junior would take her out on the water again—just the two of them this time—so Quinn could maybe catch another glimpse of her. If not? She always had her dreams.

Sounds of laughter kept drifting down from the restaurant. The party was still going strong. Quinn knew she needed to head back inside and spend a bit more time with the rest of the group. Already, the tournament and the days of preparation leading up to it had kept her from connecting very well with the other authors—except Montana. And Mavis.

Although Mavis would argue that she wasn't an author. But when Quinn counted up the tiny sculptures, she noted that there were thirteen of them. That meant that Barb had coerced her into participating.

Quinn wondered which one of the fish had been hers?

Her own had been pretty easy to pick out. At least she thought the fish outfitted with razor blades as fins was hers. But she knew she couldn't really ask. Not tonight. They'd all find out soon enough.

She scanned the sky again. No dice.

It was disappointing. She decided to give up on her stargazing for the evening and was halfway through folding up the map when she heard someone approaching. She was surprised to see Gwen coming toward her. She was wearing a loose, white shirt and it seemed to glow and float on the air as she drew closer.

"Here you are." Gwen joined her at the end of the dock. "I saw you leave the party and I wondered where you went."

Quinn gave her a shy smile. "I thought I'd come out here and see if I could find those fish stars."

"Fish stars?"

Quinn nodded and held out the folded paper. "Like the ones on Junior's map. They're the same shape as the one Barb used to arrange the little fish statues."

Gwen took the map from her and opened it.

"You mean Pisces?"

"Yeah. The fish stars."

"You won't be able to see it tonight."

"I know. I've been looking for about half an hour."

"No. I mean you'd *never* be able to see it tonight—not this time of year. It isn't visible in this hemisphere."

Quinn's face fell. "It isn't?"

Gwen shook her head. "You'll have to look for it at the end of winter. During the vernal equinox."

"The vernal equinox?"

Gwen nodded. "In March. One of the times during the year when day is as long as night." She smiled. "That's when Pisces comes into view."

"Okay." Quinn was disappointed, but in a strange way, she wasn't surprised. This all sounded about right. It sounded like a timetable that would work for Phoebe.

"Two fish moving in different directions." Gwen handed the map back to her. "Amazing."

"Why is it amazing?"

"Based on what I heard about what you did today, it sounds a lot like you and Phoebe."

Quinn shrugged. "I didn't move away from her."

"You didn't?"

"No. I just let her go."

"Isn't that the same thing?"

Quinn thought about it. Was she moving in a different direction? Maybe. But it wasn't away from Phoebe. If anything, the opposite was true.

"I don't think it is the same thing."

"Why not?"

"I don't know. Everything just feels—more connected. Like I passed some kind of big test, but I can't tell you what it is. I didn't even know I had so many empty places inside me until I came here and they got filled up." She gazed out over the dark water. It was full of light from a million stars. "I don't think that's different from Phoebe. Not at all." She looked back at Gwen. "I think it's just like her."

Gwen didn't say anything.

They stood together for a few moments and listened to the soft sound of the waves, rolling in and lapping against the rocky shore.

Then Gwen reached out and took hold of Quinn's arm.

"Walk me back?"

"Oh. Sure. You want to go back to the party?"

"Not right away. I think I'd like to walk along the lawn and look at the stars." She smiled at Quinn. "Keep me company?"

Quinn glanced out at the lake. Somewhere below the surface, Phoebe was moving through the dark, deep water, marking time and keeping her eternal vigil. Quinn knew she'd always be there, through a hundred lifetimes. And that all she had to do to see her again was watch the night sky, when winter turned into spring.

She tucked the map into her pocket and closed her arm around Gwen's hand.

"I'd really like that."

They moved along the gently rolling dock, floating on a swath of silver moonlight that carried them away from the water toward the safe haven of land.

Essay 13

I never really thought of myself as an immigrant. Not in the way my great-grandfather and his brothers were immigrants. When they grew sick and weary from lives that promised no more than growing old working the slate quarries that lined the Bristol Channel, they packed their few belongings and left Wales. It didn't matter to them that to afford the passage, they had to convert to Mormonism and promise service to the church when they arrived in *Zion*—what the church called its settlement in the new world. That part seemed easy. To them, anything seemed easier than long days spent hanging from ropes, pounding stakes into the hard shale and volcanic ash walls of pits that had taken eons to form.

When they got to America, two of the brothers quickly chose to disappear into the coal mining hills of Pennsylvania and West Virginia. They wanted to pursue their own dreams of happiness and prosperity, and they believed they knew more about how to find them than some crazy prophet who fled western New York with nothing but delusions and a bag of seer stones. One of them, however, remained true to his newfound faith. He took most of his meager savings, bought a handcart, and joined a small "company" of Mormon pioneers who pulled their wagons across an overland trail that led to the Salt Lake Valley in Utah. More than sixty thousand members of the Latter Day Saints made that arduous trek to their new promised land, and my great-grand-father was one of them.

His life in the new Zion was a simple one. He married, raised a dozen children, lived his faith, and made his living as a stonecutter. My grandfather followed in his footsteps, and became renowned for his skill as a master stone carver. Some of his greatest works adorn the east and west towers of the great Mormon temple in Salt Lake City.

My father chose a different path, but one that still harkened back to the family roots. He made his fortune managing a stone quarry that became the state's lead-ing purveyor of fine granite and quartz. In the summer months, my brothers and I would work in the company showrooms, leading homeowners and interior designers past great slabs of polished rock that were propped up on huge wooden easels in the warehouse. We grew up understanding that we were expected to take our rightful places running various aspects of the family business.

We were still a devout family, and remained very active in the life of the church. But all of that fell apart for me when I left home to attend college out of state. I had been awarded a very prestigious scholarship, and that led my parents to allow me to forestall my mission service until after I had completed my course of study in California. I had no idea when I left my home that September that I would never return there to live.

In my viscera, I always knew that I was different. That didn't really make me unique. I knew a lot of girls who were just like me. But in our huge community that felt small, we didn't dare to discuss it. Those aspects of human experience were so far removed from our culture that we possessed no vocabulary to talk about them, even if we had wanted to. So I did the things I was sup-posed to do: I kept silent, I ignored my yearnings, and I prayed for release from my unnatural impulses.

Everything changed for me the day I picked up a dog-eared novel one of my dorm mates had left on a book-shelf in the common area of our freshman hall. The cover displayed a black and white photograph of an androgynous-looking woman holding a lighted cigarette. Everything about her was compelling. Her clothes. Her haircut. Her tough-looking expression. I was captivated by the image. It haunted me. It was exotic. Alluring. Exciting. It was unlike anything I'd ever seen before. Later that night, alone in my room, I read the book. I stayed up all night reading it. I read and reread passages that confused and thrilled me in equal measure. In one night, this smart, savvy, sexy, and seminal book called *The Swashbuckler* had opened my eyes, my mind, and my heart to a culture and a way of life I had never imagined—but knew without a doubt I was destined to make my own.

I began to fantasize about the life I longed for. I wanted to reinvent myself—to be like Frenchy: strong, bold, and self-confident. Not ashamed of my sexuality. Willing to ask for what I wanted. Willing to embrace that I, too, could be twenty-one, good-looking, and go cruising for femmes in my best butch clothes.

Yes. I could be like Frenchy. *Just* like Frenchy. Because she also knew what it meant to lead a secret life. Our worlds were different, and not different. I was a woman who loved women, but I still had to hide who I was from my family.

As time went by, I concentrated on all aspects of my education. An important part of that was learning the language of my new identity. From the very beginning, I was addicted to the world of lesbian fiction. I read it all. And in those days, "all" wasn't anything like the many thousands of titles that are available to women today. The first gay bookstore I set foot in was located on a quiet backstreet in what everyone agreed was the wrong side of town. The lesbian "section" was a shelf in the back room that contained a couple dozen titles. But as a freshly minted, wide-eyed, baby dyke, I didn't care. Those books were like roadmaps to an undiscovered world. And I was a happy and voracious explorer.

Finally, I reached the place where it was impossible for me to deny or disguise my emerging identity. So I told my parents the truth. After innumerable tearful and angry encounters, they sadly were forced to admit that they couldn't shake or shame me out of my aberrant behavior. They retreated to the one course of action they believed was available to them: they disowned me. In short order, I was summarily excommunicated from the church. I was never permitted to see them, or my brothers, again—not even when my father fell ill, and died at age fifty-seven.

I was on my own, and I had to learn to make a life for myself. Thanks to my scholarship, I could remain in college and complete my education.

I had chosen my path, and it was up to me to make it work.

But it wasn't an easy time to come out. Being a lesbian was all about choosing the role you were going to play. And the culture was pretty unforgiving. The spectrum of options wasn't as broad or expansive as it is today. That part of my new life was oddly similar to what I had always experienced growing up as a Mormon. It seemed that I would forever be consigned to follow a path that would force me into some kind of mold. Some type of role. Some school of thought or mode of expression. Some way of being that could be pinpointed and classified and filed away for future generations to dissect and cite as a reference point for what it meant to be this way or that way in any time that was far enough removed from the present day to warrant study.

Three decades of fighting my way back from wrong

turns, mistaken identities, abortive career choices, and failed relationships led me to discover that the most important role in my life would end up being the one I never chose. It would be the one that chose me.

Two years ago, I was diagnosed with amyotrophic lateral sclerosis. ALS. You might know it better as Lou Gehrig's disease. But whatever you do or don't know about it, only two aspects of it are really relevant: It's rapidly progressive, and it's invariably fatal.

I didn't know much about it, myself—I never had any reason to. But after my diagnosis, I learned that familial ALS could sometimes occur when only one parent carried the gene responsible. In a case like mine, where that parent had already died from the disease, the likelihood that I or my brothers would contract the condition increased exponentially.

I guess you could say I drew the short straw.

We all know that we're going to die one day. We accept it and don't think much about it—at least not until it intrudes upon us and demands our time and attention. The fact that I find myself ahead of the curve here is more inconvenient than annoying. I worry that I won't have time to accomplish the work I've set out to do. Work that happily, finally feels important. That feels meaningful. That relates back to the place I started, so many years ago. Even at this vast and great remove, the tug of my connection to the prose of *The Swashbuckler* is like a lifeline.

"My father didn't die till he got where he wanted to be."

I didn't know how true that was for my own father—or for his father, or for any of the fathers who preceded us all—but I know how true it will be for me. I am closer now than I have ever been to where I always wanted to be. And wonderfully, mysteriously, unpredictably, I have managed, at the end of so much searching, to find the right companion for the remainder of my journey.

Frenchy said it just right. "If courage means being scared and going ahead and doing it anyway . . . if that's courage, then I'm courageous every day of my life . . ."

Epilogue

When Mavis turned her truck off Route 2 onto the road that led to the inn, she could see that the parking lot outside the office was crammed with cars from the county sheriff's department. They were parked at rakish angles, blocking access to the breezeway that led to the lake—and all of their light bars were ablaze with strobing blue lights.

Great.

She was pretty sure that whatever was going on had to have something to do with Barb's group of wackos. It had their twisted fingerprints all over it.

She unlocked the storage console that sat between her front seats and withdrew her badge and her automatic. Her instincts told her she'd probably end up needing them both.

One thing Mavis knew how to do was trust her instincts. Working as a bailiff in the San Diego County Jail had given her plenty of time to hone her skills.

She could hear the yelling and the fussing before she even cleared the breezeway. It looked like every guest at the inn was standing on the lawn, shading their eyes and watching whatever was happening on the beach at the base of the cliffs.

Page Archer was there, too, slowly shaking her head in disgust. Mavis approached her.

"What the hell is going on?"

Page waved a hand at the spectacle below. "You tell me. I was inside getting set up for breakfast when I heard the commotion. The next thing I knew, there were people screaming everyplace and that damn pontoon had run aground right in the middle of that sunrise service. I didn't even know those crazy women had taken the boat out. I thought they were all still in their rooms, sleeping it off."

"Who called the cops?"

Page pointed at two people standing off near the horseshoe pits. "I think they did."

Mavis recognized the two Canadians who were usually the biggest burrs under Viv's saddle. She could see the sheriff's deputies, standing in a solemn row in front of the stairs that led down to the water. She made an oblique gesture toward them.

"Why aren't they doing anything?"

"You mean the Keystone Cops?" Page rolled her eyes. "I think they're afraid of lesbians."

"In Vermont?" Mavis was doubtful.

"I know. Go figure."

Mavis took a deep breath. "Well. Guess I'd better get down there and see what's what."

"I'd appreciate it if you did. And Mavis?"

Mavis looked back at her.

"You have my permission to exercise extreme prejudice."

Mavis gave her a cocky smile. "I think we understand each other."

"That we do." Page waved her along. "Now, if you'll excuse me, I have a wedding breakfast to attend to."

She turned on her heel and marched back toward the restaurant.

Mavis approached the queue of police officers and did her best to appear casual. The melee raging below appeared to be gaining steam.

"You boys planning on doing anything about that?" She nodded her head toward the fracas.

One of the uniformed officers looked at her with owlish eyes. "No ma'am. We aren't checked out for this kind of thing."

"What the hell does that mean?"

Another one of the deputies spoke up. He had pale skin and an advanced case of acne. "We don't have riot gear."

"Not much call for that up here in the islands," another colleague chimed in.

Mavis watched the proceedings below. Six of the world's most esteemed lesbian authors appeared to be going mano-a-mano with an equal number of the white-robed, born-again nut jobs who had arranged to use the beach that morning for a sunrise service. Any sane person would say that what was going on was already out of hand—but Mavis could tell that it had the potential to get a lot worse if somebody didn't intervene—and soon.

She pulled out her San Diego PD badge and flipped it open.

"You boys mind if I take a crack at it?"

The apparent leader of their contingent looked her credentials over.

"No, ma'am."

"Great." She pulled out her service weapon. "Don't worry. I have my permit."

He nodded. "You let us know if you need backup."

"Yeah." Mavis racked the slide on her automatic. "Will do. You just concentrate on keeping these rubberneckers back."

She picked her way down the stairs that led to the dock and the beach. Quinn's pontoon was crashed up against the rocks—its motors were still running. Her La-Z-Boy had listed across the deck and was precariously close to sliding into the water.

What Mavis hadn't observed from her vantage point on the ledge above was that dozens of fish were jumping out of the water like crazy. She could see several of them writhing and flopping around on the deck of the boat. Others were swimming in determined circles and jumping toward the pontoon like they were caught up in some kind of frenzy.

Remnants and broken implements of articles being used in the sunrise service were strewn all over the rocks. There had to be two dozen people down there—most of them part of the disrupted religious celebration.

No one looked happy.

She took a deep breath and pushed her way through the circle of bystanders that surrounded the perimeter of the action.

"Knock it off!" she bellowed.

No one paid any attention to her.

"I said, knock it the *fuck* off!"

Still no response.

Okay. Fine by me.

She raised her service weapon and fired a sequence of three quick rounds over the open water.

The beach fell silent.

"Now that I have your attention, let me explain how this is going to go down."

Preacher-man immediately started to argue. Then V. Jay-Jay started up. Viv was next in line.

Mavis fired off another round.

"You," she pointed a finger at the preacher. "Shut up. You?" She pointed at V. Jay-Jay. "Siddown. You?" She pointed at Viv. "Get your hand off that woman's ass."

They all complied.

"Now I'm going to ask one person from each side of this goat fuck to explain to me what the hell is going on." She turned to Kate Winston, who was looking like she wanted to be anyplace but there. "Let's start with you."

Kate opened her mouth to speak, but Towanda cut her off.

"We didn't do anything wrong. Those damn fish started charging the boat!"

Mavis made rapid slashing movements across her throat. "I said I wanted to hear from her. *You* shut the fuck up."

Towanda fell silent and retreated behind Viv, who now had her hands in her pockets.

Kate cleared her throat and began her narrative.

"These women invited us to go out for a sunrise cruise—you know—to celebrate our wedding." She took hold of Shawn's hand. "We knew we weren't going to get much sleep—not after the party ran so late. So we agreed. We met everyone at the dock and we set out for a quick ride around the island. We didn't plan on being out for more than an hour. It was lovely. The sunrise was glorious. When we knew it was time to head back in, Darien started the boat and said she would drive us back to the hotel. That's when Viv spoke up and said there was something we needed to do before we went back."

Mavis took the bait. "What was that?"

"Well." Kate looked nervously at Viv. "Apparently, she and Towanda had raided the kitchen and stolen the big bowl of tomato aspic. They said they wanted to deep-six it in the lake as a wedding gift to us." She shrugged. "It seemed kind of sweet. So we waited while they dumped it all into the water."

Mavis thought that seemed pretty harmless. In fact, she was half-tempted to thank Viv for her thoughtfulness.

"Was that it?"

"No." Kate shook her head. "A minute or two after they dumped it, something strange happened. It was like the water started boiling. Fish started appearing out of nowhere. Bass. *Big ones.* They were going crazy eating the stuff. Then they started charging the boat—diving at the deck. It was terrifying. We screamed at Darien to get us out of there. She tried, but only one of the damn motors would start." She looked at Shawn. "It took us *forever* to get back across the lake—and all of those psycho fish were *following* us—like vigilantes. Finally, when we got closer to the inn the other engine kicked in."

Mavis was incredulous. "So you lost control of the boat and crashed into the sunrise service going on here?"

Kate dropped her eyes. "Not exactly."

"What do you mean by *not exactly?*" Mavis smelled a rat.

"Well. Darien thought she recognized one of the—*celebrants.* And it appeared to upset her. *A lot.*"

Mavis glowered at Darien. "You did this on purpose?"

Darien nodded.

"Jesus H. Christ." Mavis shook her head in disbelief.

"Young woman, you shall *not* take the name of the Lord in vain." Mavis glared at the tall, blond preacher.

"Right. I suppose it's *your* turn to talk. So—go right on ahead." He puffed out his white-robed chest.

"That unredeemed *Sodomite,*" he pointed an accusatory finger at Darien, "chose to embrace a path of unrighteousness and exercise her contempt for the Word of God by attacking me and this flock of faithful penitents. She has maliciously and willfully caused irreparable harm to my lawful mission to spread the truth of God's love and power among the masses of this liberal and pagan oasis of sin. I demand that you hold her accountable for damages to my ministry and my person."

Mavis regarded him impassively.

"What damages to your ministry and person did she cause other than disrupting your morning—whatever—service?"

He reached down and picked up an empty wooden box and held it aloft.

"One of my helpmeets was released when her infernal boat crashed into the middle of our celebration."

"Say what?" Mavis wasn't sure what he was talking about.

"Oh, for god's sake." Viv chimed in. "His damn snake got loose."

Mavis looked at her with incredulity. "Snake?"

"Yeah." She pointed an accusatory finger at the bank behind them. "*That* big motherfucker. Right *there*."

Mavis wheeled around to see what looked like some kind of water moccasin, coiled up against the base of a retaining wall made of stacked pink granite. It was gaping, and the interior of its huge mouth glowed as white as a naked light bulb.

As soon as the rest of the assembly realized what she was staring at, they all began to scream and duck for cover.

"Yeah. Not on *my* watch." Mavis took careful aim and capped the viper.

It was a classic kill shot.

When the preacher protested, she cut him off sharply. "You got a complaint? You feel free to file it with those gentlemen right up there." She jerked a thumb toward the line of deputies on the lawn above them. "I'm sure they'd be happy to take a statement from you—and hear all about your *lawful* explanation for why you brought an undisclosed, poisonous reptile into the middle of private property."

He fell silent, but it was clear he was still fuming. He fixed Darien with a murderous gaze.

V. Jay-Jay noticed it and took a step toward him.

Mavis held out a hand and stopped her.

"I got this, little girl. You just tend to your woman."

She stepped back and addressed the celebrants. "I think we're through here. Why don't you folks all mosey along and see about acquiring some better sense?"

She waited until they slowly picked up the salvageable pieces of their ceremony and headed for the steps to the lawn. The preacher was the last to leave. He looked back at all of them before he ascended the steps.

"The Lord won't forget what deeds you wrought here today."

Darien stepped forward. "That's true. And neither will he forget the deeds you wrought yesterday."

He glared at her, but she stood her ground. Finally he lowered his gaze and stormed off. Mavis was aware that they'd all witnessed some epic game of chicken—and that he'd blinked first.

She faced the group of six authors. They were the only people left on the beach.

"I suggest you all get your asses back to your rooms and get dressed." She checked her watch. "If memory serves, there's going to be some other kind of celebration going on down here in about two hours."

They all exchanged shy smiles.

Kate clutched Shawn's hand and led the group toward the steps. Mavis overheard her whispered comment as they passed.

"I gotta hand it to you, Harris. You sure know how to throw one hell of a bachelorette party."

Mavis rolled her eyes and stowed her weapon.

No wonder Barb calls this shit Herstory.

IN SEARCH OF PISCES
Lives in Transition

A Commemoration of Women's History Month

An Installation by
Barbara Davis
(1955-2016)

Presented by The Rolston-Devere Gallery
Major funding provided by a grant from
The National Endowment for the Arts

Figure 1
Rabbits
Essay by Quinn Glatfelter

Figure 2
Found Objects
Essay by Montana Jackson

Figure 3
An Obscure Object of Desire
Essay by Kate Winston

Figure 4
Bologna Sandwiches
Essay by Gwen Carlisle

Figure 5
First Blood
Essay by Shawn Harris

Acknowledgments

"Write what you know" is the mantra pounded into the head of every aspiring author.

Many of us take a circuitous route to get there.

Backcast is a book about the differences between perception and reality—and the ways we straddle the lines that divide truth from fiction. Bits and pieces of *Backcast* are drawn from my own life experiences. So, in a sense, this book is my closest attempt to date at writing about things I know—or have, at least, experienced. Knowledge stubbornly links arms with understanding, and these two can follow a meandering path to self-awareness. What I have attempted to do with the telling of these tales is shine a light on a few of the things I've come to know. The journey to understanding what is revealed will come, if it comes at all, in its own time. And that, if I have very great luck and live long enough to tell it, will be a story for another day.

I would be remiss if I didn't make mention of the comic fodder provided by my paternal grandmother, Lillian V. Stephens. She had, without exception, the sharpest sense of humor I've ever encountered. Inspiration for the wisecracking bass, Phoebe, derives entirely from her tales of an iconic carp by the same name. Rumor has it that my grandmother caught the legendary fish in one of the many streams that ran past her home in Indiana County, Pennsylvania. She is said to have kept the fish alive and given it a home in her rain barrel because "she had beautiful eyes."

Special thanks are due to my self-styled Vermont family. For the past fifteen summers, I have been blessed to spend the best days of my life with you on the shores of Lake Champlain. Shore Acres Inn will forever be known as the place where I felt the most welcomed, and the most at home. Susan and Mike Tranby deserve most of the credit for that. The rest of us—your staff, your neighbors, and your "regulars"—owe you debts of gratitude that can never be repaid.

Shirley Sibenhorn Page taught me to love the stories of the Inland Sea. I miss you, and I dearly wish you were here to read this book.

I am bound by love to make mention of my other family of choice. Father Frank and Flora? Thank you for your goodness and constancy. The heavens surely smiled upon me the day our paths crossed.

Great thanks are due to Dale Brown, the Dean of Bass Fishing on Lake Champlain. It would have been impossible for me to write this book without your insight and guidance. Thank you for all the time you spent, politely answering my ridiculous questions. And thanks, too, for authoring the book that became my primary resource, *Bass Fishing 101*.

As always, I am indebted to my beloved cast of usual suspects—Dee Dee, Cloudie, Skippy, Short Stack, Moran-Tek, and my dear Lodge Sister, Nurse Barrett. Thank you all for putting up with my epic rants and fits of ennui.

Thanks, too, to Louise and Christine, for your great gifts of friendship, support—and really rare steaks. Meeting you two has been better than finding out that the biggest box under the Christmas tree has my name on it.

I offer special thanks to the uncommonly talented voice actor, Christine Williams, for bringing my books to life in audio format. Bruno? You truly are The Voice That Launched a Thousand Subarus.

Thanks are due, too, to Susie and Aretha Bright—the dazzling wonder women at *audible.com* who were willing to take a chance on my little book about women and bass fishing. This decision surely will go down in the annals of literature as a true profile in courage.

What can I say about Lee Lynch? Just knowing she's out there makes me work harder to be a better writer, and a better steward of our literature. Thank you, dear friend. And thanks, too, for allowing me to quote from your seminal work, *The Swashbuckler*. You've touched so many lives with your impressive body of work, your personal integrity, and your great inner-goodness. I'm humbled and grateful to stand in your shadow.

Kelly Smith and Marianne K. Martin aren't just trail-blazers; they're about as close to royalty as we can get in this business. Believe me when I say that getting to work with the two of them at their little company on the Great Lake is more than a privilege—it's an honor. I love you both dearly.

And, Kells? I'll always remember your immortal question, "Do we need a verb here?"

At the beginning and end of everything, my greatest love and thanks are due to my beloved wife, Salem West. You are the best friend I've ever had. Every single day, I thank the mystical confluence of events that brought us together. Thank you for allowing me to share your life— even though it came packaged with a Siberian husky.

Ann McMan
Winston-Salem, NC

About the Author

ANN McMAN is the author of five novels, *Jericho, Dust, Aftermath, Hoosier Daddy,* and *June Magee, R.N., Festival Nurse,* and the short story collections *Sidecar* and *Three.* She is a recipient of the Alice B. Lavender Certificate for Outstanding Debut Novel, and a two-time winner of the Golden Crown Literary Award for short story collections. Her novel, *Hoosier Daddy,* was a 2014 Lambda Literary Award finalist. She resides in Winston-Salem, North Carolina with her wife, two dogs, two cats, and an exhaustive supply of vacuum cleaner bags.

Reading Group Discussion Guide

1   The differences between perception and reality are dueling themes in the central storyline and various subplots of this novel. How are these differences revealed or reconciled? Are any left unresolved at the end? Why? Why not? What is revealed about the characters that contradict what we thought we understood about them?

2   How does the lake function as a metaphor in the story? Do the characters behave or relate to each other differently on the water? How does Quinn's process of learning how to pilot the boat—and cast her fishing line—mirror her journey toward self-understanding?

3   What is the significance of the Pisces map Junior gives Quinn? How does it relate to the motif Barb Davis creates to represent the various tales of transition written by the 13 authors? Why does Barb choose to depict the women in the story as fish?

4   The great fish, Phoebe, is a creature of both myth and imagination. What role does she play in the central narrative of the book? Is she real, or is she a figment of Quinn's imagination? What does Quinn learn about her own motivations during her face-to-face encounters with Phoebe? Are these encounters real or imagined? Does it matter?

5   How does the Phoebe subplot function to tie the disparate storylines of the book together—much like the final series of sculptures are tied together with twine?

6   The 13 individual "transition" essays are presented without attribution. Why is that significant? What commonalities do the stories reveal? How do the essays the women write coalesce to create a unified picture at the end of the book? How are the themes they describe tied to each other and to Quinn's quest to catch the elusive fish?

7   How does the fishing tournament parallel the journeys the women make—individually and as a group—during their two-week retreat? How are their lives changed? How does the outcome of the fishing tournament change Quinn? Change others?

A FIELD GUIDE TO
DECEPTION

A NOVEL

WINNER OF THE LAMBDA LITERARY AWARD

"A Field Guide to Deception is beautiful, essential reading." *– Out in Print*

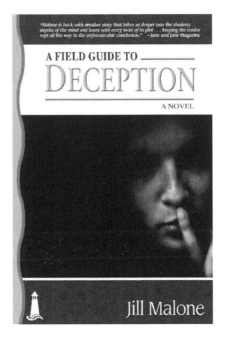

A Field Guide to Deception

Print 978-1-932859-70-6

Ebook 978-1-61294-003-8

www.bywaterbooks.com

the one that got away

"Every page of Carol Rosenfeld's novel delivers delectable dykedrama, replete with the quagmires of sexual obsession, high-stakes betrayal, and lesbian holiness. How can I laugh so hard at these characters and simultaneously feel tenderness for each and every one? Rosenfeld's fierce wit is addictive; I read the book in one go."

–LUCY JANE BLEDSOE, author of *The Big Bang Symphony*

The One That Got Away
Print 978-1-61294-060-1
Ebook 978-1-61294-618-8

Bywater BOOKS

www.bywaterbooks.com

Bywater
BOOKS

At Bywater Books we love good books about lesbians just like you do, and we're committed to bringing the best of contemporary lesbian writing to our avid readers. Our editorial team is dedicated to finding and developing outstanding writers who create books you won't want to put down.

We sponsor the Bywater Prize for Fiction to help with this quest. Each prize winner receives $1,000 and publication of their novel. We have already discovered amazing writers like Jill Malone, Sally Bellerose, and Hilary Sloin through the Bywater Prize. Which exciting new writer will we find next?

For more information about Bywater Books and the annual Bywater Prize for Fiction, please visit our website.

www.bywaterbooks.com